THE MALEFACTORS

Also by Caroline Gordon

PENHALLY
ALEX MAURY
NONE SHALL LOOK BACK
THE GARDEN OF ADONIS
GREEN CENTURIES
THE WOMEN ON THE PORCH
THE FOREST OF THE SOUTH
THE STRANGE CHILDREN

THE MALEFACTORS

By CAROLINE GORDON

Harcourt, Brace and Company
NEW YORK

PS
3513
O5765
m3

It is for Adam to interpret the voices that Eve hears.

—Jacques Maritain

PART

ONE

ONE

Claiborne had promised his wife to rise early on the morning of the *fête*, but he had not slept well the night before. He and his friend Max Shull were at breakfast on the east terrace when Vera came around the corner of the house, leading the bull. Claiborne had been reading the newspaper and until he looked up to see his wife and the bull standing at the end of the terrace had not known how bright the morning was. Through a gap in the trees on that side of the house the wide eastern sky was visible. He looked beyond the two figures to where the copper beech showed dark against saffron-colored light. The greensward ran as smooth as a carpet up to the ring which marked the tree's spread, after which the gardener saw to it that myrtle took over. Periwinkle he had called it when he was a boy. In his own country—at least when he was a boy—it grew mostly in graveyards. Hereabouts it was used to decorate lawns. Three-quarters of an acre was enclosed in this lawn. If one took hold of the turf, there where a dandelion stalk that the gardener had missed caught the light, this lawn might be rolled up, the way the ancients used to roll up sheepskins, and stowed away—but in what closet and what would be the ingredients of the dust that through the years collected on it, and where were the years bound? He reflected that impulses like this came to him often these days—very early in the morning or late at night, and sometimes during the day when he would look thoughtlessly at some object and it would take on a strange, even minatory aspect. A man who had been in the French Underground had told him that he had been much bothered by the same phenomenon during the Resistance. His own first cousin George Crenfew, who was a psychiatrist, said that it was partly nerves and partly due to a deficiency in his diet. Claiborne resolved that he would see his oculist.

He fixed his eyes now on his wife. She was already dressed for what she would have called her "morning's work," in a faded blouse and dungarees. Straws, glistening with moisture, adhered to the soles of her canvas sneakers. She had been working in the bull's stall long enough to get up a sweat. The sweat made the short, dark hairs about her forehead curl a little. The bull stood behind her on legs that might have been carved out of mahogany, moving his jaws from side to side, staring past them all out of eyes the color of old port. The hair on his brow, red as henna, broke into curls, too, and rippled even more deeply over his chest. That was Art. Joe Hess had come over last night and had showed Rodney, the stable boy, how to set it.

"Don't you want to come and see Bud in his tent?" Vera asked.

Max Shull rose, wrapping his plum-colored robe closer about his bulky body. "Woman, I've got work to do."

"But I'm going to take care of the Dunkards," Vera said. "Max, what is there to worry about except the Dunkards?"

"Oh, I've got a few odds and ends. Just as well to get them out of the way before the Queen of the Pambas shows up."

Max Shull always called Marcia Crenfew, George's wife, "the Queen of the Pambas." Marcia Crenfew had a degree in psychology and gave a course in marriage called "Eugamics" at Leonard, the great women's college nearby. She had also dabbled in anthropology and after graduating from college had spent six months at the headwaters of an African river engaging in research into the sexual habits of adolescent aborigines. The book in which she had embodied her findings was called *Puberty among the Pambas* and had gone into six editions. The handsome old stone farmhouse in which

4

she and George lived had been bought with its proceeds. Claiborne recalled with a start that George was writing a book too: a study of animism in the tales of Uncle Remus. George had given him some chapters of the book a few weeks ago and had asked for an opinion on them, but he hadn't got around to reading them yet.

Vera was shaking her head. "She won't be here for a long while. I went by there this morning and she was in a state."

"Was there something she couldn't cope with?" Max asked.

"She *said* it was the ice-cream freezer."

"You mean it got compulsive?"

"It broke down and she has ten people for lunch to-day. . . . But *I* think it was Catherine Pollard."

"*Catherine Pollard!*" Claiborne said.

"George's first wife," Vera said. "The one you all thought I was too young to meet, the one that had the wedding where you all got drunk for three days."

"George was at the wedding too," Max said. "You can't blame it all on Cat. I must say," he added dreamily, "that it seemed a good idea at the time. In the spring and all the chestnut trees in bloom. We took over that little restaurant on the Ile Saint Louis. Some people went down the Seine in a houseboat and didn't get back for a week."

"It must have been a good party—even if I wasn't there," Vera said. "Still, it was hard on George when she took the baby and left him."

"That was the *next* time the chestnuts bloomed," Max said. "How were we to know all that was to happen? . . . Vee, what's Cat like these days?"

"Awfully big and awfully calm. . . . Marcia can't do a thing with her."

Max put his hands over his face and groaned. "George never could either."

"What does Marcia want to do with her?" Claiborne asked.

"She wanted her to drive over here with me. To have her off her hands, I suppose, so she could put her great mind on other matters, but Catherine wouldn't budge."

5

"Did she refuse point-blank?" Max asked.

"Well, she was sitting out in the garden reading something —Marcia said it was her morning office, she's very religious now—and Marcia went out into the garden three times while I was there and asked Catherine if she didn't want to drive over here with me, 'to see the country,' and each time Catherine said, 'No, thank you,' she preferred to stay where she was. It made Marcia *wild!*"

Max suddenly put an arm about Vera's shoulder and drew her toward him. "God is so good to us," he said in a reverential tone. "God really is so good to us. That I should have lived to see this!" He held one hand up as if on a lecture platform. "But you needn't think, children, that any one of us could have moved this wonder to perform. It takes an outsider to give Her Majesty pause."

Vera reached a hand up to pat Max's flabby jowl. "Max, I don't see how I could live without you."

"You don't have to," Max said cheerfully.

Claiborne, watching him as he bustled off to his own cottage, reflected that he had often heard the Queen of the Pambas say the same thing: that she could not live without Max. Max gossiped about all of them but they never gossiped about Max, or if they did it was with an indulgence they did not accord any of their other friends. What made these women esteem Max so? What made *all* of them esteem him so? What did he have that made him more tolerable to them than they were to themselves? Or was it what he didn't have? Men like Max always get along well with middle-aged women. Was it because he was the way he was? Or was it, rather, that the wry good humor with which he accepted his condition disarmed criticism? Years ago, Claiborne recalled, Vera had decided that Max ought to go to a psychiatrist, and with characteristic frankness had asked him why he did not avail himself of George Crenfew's services. Max had come back with a paraphrase of the Marquis de Montespan's answer to Louis XIV's offer to make him a duke in compensation for having cuckolded him: "I thank you,

Sire, but I was born a marquis and prefer to die a marquis."
"I was born a queen," Max said, "and I guess I'll die a queen." There was not much she could say to that.

I don't blame him, Claiborne thought. He's lit on his feet. This is the place for him, all right. One of the best little *far nientes* in the country. Everybody busy all day long doing nothing. But when Max talks about it, it sounds as if we were all doing something very important. No wonder we all love him.

He looked off over the lawn. The grass—the only thing about the place which he could bring himself to take any interest in—which in a few hours would lie prostrate and brown under trampling feet was soft and springy under his feet now, every blade still sparkling with dew. He was suddenly overcome by the autumnal quality of the scene. Under a cloudless blue sky the motionless trees, the heaped, vari-colored fruits of the earth, the dusky boughs of the great copper beech whose leaves never showed green even in summer, were all bathed in a light which seemed to tremble on the verge of growing even brighter.

A yellow leaf had drifted down onto Vera's shoulder. He lifted it and holding it in his hand looked about him vaguely, hardly able to pay attention to what was going on around him for a preoccupation that had come upon him. It seemed to him that something of enormous importance was about to happen, or rather, as he put it, in the dialogue which he held intermittently with himself, that something that would change everything was about to be said, was being said now—*if one could only hear it!*

But what could happen? What could be said on this well-kept lawn, in sight of his own expensively restored Pennsylvania Dutch farmhouse? He raised his head and stared at the copper beech tree as if he could find the answer there. He had always loved this tree for its bronze-colored leaves. It had for him associations that no other tree on the place had. When he had first come to live here, there had been a hammock slung between that tree and a young maple.

7

It was that summer that he gave up the editorship of *Spectra,* the magazine that he and Bob Waite had got out for five years from a rat-infested basement on the Ile Saint Louis, the magazine that had published his sensational poem which brought about a revolution in English poetry, the magazine that had published Halloway's first stories. There was hardly any French or British or American writer who later came to fame who had not appeared first in the pages of *Spectra.* Even the hard-boiled French men of letters had been impressed. "You have inherited the mantle of Edgar Poe," Jean Siriol said, "and the financial genius of Jean D. Rockefeller." He himself hardly knew now how they had kept the magazine going. He had invested in the magazine every nickel of his modest inheritance beyond what was necessary for a bare living, and when that money was gone he and Bob had begged, borrowed, and all but stolen to keep the magazine going.

The moods that sway expatriates are as mysterious in their origin as the currents upon which migratory birds travel: he and Bob had realized at the same time that they wanted to return to the United States to live. But it had been understood that they were merely transferring the magazine from Paris to New York, and then one day (he hardly knew now how it had happened) he had found himself telling Bob that he was no longer interested in editing the magazine. Bob had taken the news hard; his wife, Alma, had taken it even harder —as well they might. It was he, not Bob, who had discovered most of the writers they had published. It had seemed to him then that he had earned a rest. It had seemed to him too that he was entering upon a new phase of his life. He did not know what it would be like but the feeling had been so strong that he had found himself anticipating the future with something like reverence. That summer he often lay on his back in the hammock under the beech—for as far back as he could remember it had fascinated him to lie on his back and look up into depth on depth of leaves. Vergil tells us that a mighty elm tree stands at the entrance to Orcus, its branches

8

hung full of dreams. In those days he had felt that those dusky boughs harbored Presences. Sometimes they had seemed to suffuse the whole garden with light. He had only been waiting for them to speak. And even when there were no signs, no tokens, he had not neglected to do them reverence, but had prayed—in his fashion—to Aeschylus, to Sophocles, to the Florentine, to Baudelaire, who had prayed—to Poe! But something had gone wrong. They had not spoken now in a long time. God have mercy on my poor soul! he thought, then realized that he and his wife were alone and that she was slowly inclining her head in his direction.

As often, when he sustained her direct gaze, he was startled to realize how blue her eyes were, so blue that sometimes when she looked at you you felt as if she were offering you a present that was perhaps out of proportion to the occasion. She smiled suddenly and, standing on tiptoe, stretched her arms over her head, so high that the bull's muzzle was jerked sharply upward.

Claiborne jumped. "For *God's* sake, Vera!"

She jumped, too. "I *wish* you wouldn't do that!" she said. "You make me nervous."

"What do you think you make me?" Claiborne asked.

"Oh!" she said. "I'm sorry," then smiled disarmingly. "Don't you want to come see the exhibits?"

Claiborne turned and looked over the west lawn. The stretch of greensward that they had agreed to call the "midway" shone scarlet and gold and purple. Carpenters had been working there for over a week, building the stands and racks that would hold the exhibits. Everybody in the valley had been invited to display the choicest products of his farm or garden, and many of the stands were already heaped with pumpkins and squash and eggplants and onions and potatoes and other fruits of the earth.

He said: "If you'll put that bull in his stall."

"But I wanted you to see him in his *tent*."

Claiborne, looking at her, thought how, if a man took her into his arms, she would smell not only of the powders and

9

perfumes she put on her body every morning before she went down to work in the barn but of cow manure.

She was president of the Red Poll Breeders' Association of the Atlantic Seaboard States, having been elected to that office when the former president, Jim Terry, died. She was, when you came down to it, the leading Red Poll woman, or, as we say nowadays, "queen," of the Atlantic seaboard states. (It's a good thing to have these offices filled by rich men but if you can't get hold of a man a rich woman will do.) It was Jim Terry who had got her started on Red Polls. Jim had experimented with other breeds and had come to the conclusion that the Red Poll was the finest of all "dual purpose" breeds, and Vera followed, as best she could, in Jim's footsteps. He himself had known the breed before Vera or Jim had ever heard of it. "Muley cows" they had been called in his youth, on the farm in Tennessee. If his wife had taken the trouble to consult him when she began raising cattle he would have suggested another breed. He had always hankered to raise Black Angus, or White Face or even Brahmas. But who wanted a muley cow? Still, she *had* got into the breeding of them by accident—Jim Terry's fault. Soon after the Claibornes had settled at Blencker's Brook he had given Vera a muley cow. Vera had bred the cow to Terry's prize bull, Marengo, who, until his death two years ago (he and Jim had died in the same month), had been the best Red Poll sire in the East. Blencker's Brook's Best Man, or, as they called him around the barn, "Bud," was the result of that breeding.

She was waiting to see what he would say. He said, "All right," and followed her around the house to the place where the tents were being set up.

The Wildwood Hospitality House had sent a man down from New York to superintend their erection. He and his half a dozen helpers had just finished setting up the big marquee under whose shelter Jack the Bear and his band would play. Near the fence stood two smaller tents, of yellow canvas. The flaps of these tents were fastened back. In the

10

middle of each lay a cement block in which a stanchion had been fixed. The bull would be displayed in one tent, the cow and her calf in the other.

Claiborne stood by silently while his wife backed the bull into the tent, fastened the chain to the stanchion and gave the bull a lump of sugar. It was only then that he noticed the several lengths of bright-colored leather that she had trailing over her arm. She wound one of them about the chain of braided copper that depended from a ring in the bull's nose, then looked up at him. "I borrowed these from the Archers' great Danes. Do you think green . . . or yellow?"

"Blue," he said. "Blue is for bulls. The cow and the heifer ought to wear pink."

She looked at him a second before she turned around. Max Shull had come up, now in clean suntans and a white sport shirt. "What do you think, Max?" she asked.

"Green," Max said decidedly. "After all, you want some contrast."

She frowned. "But it makes the chain look so bulky."

"You could twist a green ribbon around the chain," Max said.

She eyed him doubtfully. "Do you suppose that's done, Max?"

"Who's running this show?" Max asked. "Who's president of the Red Poll Breeders' Association? Be different if this bull was a Dunkard, but he don't want to turn plain. Do you, Bud?"

Vera laughed, then looked at her husband, sighing. "*Would* you meet Cynthia's train, darling?"

He said: "*Cynthia?*"

She smiled at him resolutely. "Darling, I *told* you she was coming today."

"What for?"

"A visit." Her lips tightened. She tilted her chin slightly. "After all, she's my own third cousin. *I* think it's wonderful she's coming the day we're having the party."

Involuntarily, he smiled. It was being married to him that

11

had taught her that trick. She had been brought up in France, mostly on the Côte d'Azur, with no relations nearer than Massillon, Ohio, the home town of her father and mother, which, as Max Shull put it, they had got out of as soon as they reached the age of consent.

He said: "Why can't Robin meet her? She's his kinfolks too."

Her face became devoid of expression, as it so often did when her younger brother's name was mentioned. "Rodney couldn't get him up," she said, and laid her hand on the bull's neck. *"Est-ce que tu seras un brave garçon aujourd'hui?"* she inquired tenderly. She spoke English with a British accent which Claiborne found irritating at times, but she always addressed animals and children in French. Her French he found as irritating as her English. The old nurse who had stayed with her till she was sixteen had come from the Auvergne. Consequently Vera spoke French as if she had mush in her mouth.

The bull withdrew his gaze from the horizon and, ducking his head, thrust his yellowish-pink nose into her ribs. Absent-mindedly, she took another lump of sugar out of her pocket and gave it to him. Her eyes sought her husband's. "I thought I'd just spoil him a little today. Two lumps of sugar couldn't possibly upset his stomach, do you think?"

Claiborne eyed the bull's body, barrel-shaped, weighing a little less than a ton. "I'd risk it," he said.

Vera gave the bull a pat on the neck and turned and looked back at her husband. "You couldn't go up to see Aunt Virginia a few minutes, could you, darling?"

Claiborne glanced up at a vine-clad window on this side of the house. It had been his own bedroom until his aunt, Virginia Claiborne, had come up from Tennessee, with Cousin Amy Allard, for what Max Shull called "one of them long Suth'en visits." They had got rid of Cousin Amy in a couple of months but Aunt Virginia had taken to her bed three weeks after she arrived and was still there—in the best bedroom in the house. Vera had felt that it was im-

12

portant that she should have the sunniest room, "since she's in bed all day long, darling." His mother had had the same notion. One of the rows between his father and mother that he remembered best was his father's declining to shift his quarters so that his sister might have a "sunny exposure." "I will be good God damned," his father had said, pushing his chair back and banging his fist on the table, and then, realizing that he was addressing a woman, changing his tune: "What I mean, Annie, is that I will not lift a finger to expose Virginia to anything. The good Lord h'ists the sun up there in the sky every morning. If she wants sun let her go out and expose herself to it."

The son said now: "Vera, I'm not going to fool with Aunt Virginia this morning. We got enough on our hands."

She gave his arm a quick pressure. "I know it," she said. "I'm sorry, darling. I just thought . . ."

"There comes George now," Max said, and set off at a lope over the lawn.

Vera took a few steps after him, then waited until her husband came up beside her. "Don't you think George looks better than he did this spring?" she asked.

"Sure," Claiborne said, and looked at his cousin with closer attention than he had accorded him for some months. George Crenfew was as tall as Claiborne himself and his shoulders were even broader, but from the shoulders downward his frame seemed to undergo an attenuation. His legs were so long and so thin that they seemed in danger of breaking at any moment under his weight. He carried his long, bony head so that his clever, sickly, sallow face was presented to you sidewise, as if in self-depreciation. His height, his excessive thinness, and his odd posture gave him the look of a long-legged bird that, having dived into an element which had proved foreign to it, was now rising up, head cocked on one side, to take the measure of its predicament.

George would need to keep his wits about him today, Claiborne thought. He had before him an ordeal that might daunt even a man whose profession was dealing with human

13

aberrations. How many women did the fellow have on his hands today? He enumerated them to himself. George's first wife, in his home as a visitor; *their* daughter, the twenty-year-old Katie; his second wife, Marcia, playing hostess to his first wife; Désirée, *her* daughter by her first marriage; Ellen, the ten-year-old offspring of Marcia and George—hanging around the stables, no doubt. (Frank Robinson, Marcia's first husband, had been burned to death in his bed as the result of lighting a cigarette while he was drunk, or he doubtless would have been with them today too.) *Women!* It is their callousness that makes them invincible. Queer to think of Catherine Pollard's being here today. He had not seen her since she walked out on George, one night in Paris. How many years ago? She had not been exactly callous, but certainly she had been difficult. A tall, handsome girl, with remarkable eyes, who drank too much and had a habit at parties of backing you into a corner and asking you questions that, as he had once told her, "only God can answer."

George Crenfew stood before them, raising his hand in his characteristic gesture of a peasant pulling his foretop. "How you, Sis Cow?" he inquired. "How you, Bre'r Bull? . . . Bre'r Wolf?"

George affected to live in the world of Uncle Remus. He had called Vera "Sis Cow" ever since she started breeding Red Polls. Tom Claiborne had automatically become "Bre'r Bull," and the nomenclature had been extended to the circle of their intimate friends. Molly and Ed Archer were "Sis Fox" and "Bre'r Fox." Max Shull was "Bre'r Wolf." George referred to himself as "Bre'r Turkey Buzzard," in reference to an ancient joke: Claiborne's advice to him to "flap North where the pickings are good," when he started the practice of his profession.

George said now, evidently continuing an old argument he had had with Max: "It's a mighty pretty little bower, Max. Don't know that I ever saw a prettier one. But I don't know that it suits Malthy."

Max composed his features into an expression of resigna-

14

tion. "Just what is it about it that doesn't suit you, George?"

"Oh, it'd suit *me*, all right," George said. "I could lay down in there right now and curl up and feel fine. But Malthy, well, it don't seem to me that that bower brings her *out!*"

"If you'd tell us which side of Malthy's personality you want brought out we might arrange to do it, George," Max said.

George shook his head as if baffled by the problem. Then his eyes met his cousin's. "You seen Malthy's bower, Tom?" he inquired.

"Not since it was finished," Claiborne said.

"Let's step over there now," George said.

George had started raising Nubian goats the same year Vera had started raising Red Polls—Marcia's idea of the way to cure his insomnia. It had been her idea, too, that they should settle in the country at a point equidistant between George's Park Avenue office and the women's college in which she taught—God love us!—her courses in eugamics. George had told his cousin that "the system works fine. Commute every day and you won't have no trouble sleeping at night. No trouble a-tall!" (George usually addressed his cousin in the vernacular. One of the Kennedy girls had reported that she had listened to Dr. Crenfew and Mr. Claiborne talking for half an hour and had hardly understood a word they were saying.)

They had arrived at the "bower" in which the Nubian doe would be exhibited: a long cage, woven of willow withes and twined with honeysuckle vines. Claiborne had forgotten until now that it was Vera who had woven it, in imitation of the huts which peasants in southern France and in Italy weave out of bamboo as shelters for fowl and beasts.

She stood contemplating it soberly, then looked up at her husband. "It doesn't look like the ones old Jacques used to make. Maybe I ought to have woven it tighter."

"It's not the shape," George said, "it's those vines."

"But, George, it would look so bare without any vines."

"They ain't the right kind of vines."

15

"You want a darker leaf," Claiborne said suddenly. "After all, Amalthea was a goat of consequence. Wet nurse to Jove."

"See what it is to have a classical education," George said. "That's what I been trying to tell you all along but you couldn't seem to get it."

"Ivy?" Max said suddenly. "Would ivy leaves do, George?"

"I kind of wanted Malthy wreathed in laurel," George said. "After all, she's a champion."

"We haven't *got* any laurel," Vera said. "And, anyhow, ivy leaves look much more classical, George."

"Well, since we can't get no laurel . . ." George said.

She said: "George, Max has got his hands full, and I've got those Dunkards, and Tom . . ."

"What have I got?" her husband interrupted.

She would not look at him.

"If you could just decorate the bower yourself, George."

"Where'll I get the ivy?"

"Anywhere . . . just anywhere. The clippers are lying on the front steps."

"You promised you'd meet Cynthia's train, darling," Vera said.

"Sure," he said wearily, "sure," and started for the gate.

She walked beside him. "Of course, I still have to dress," she said, "but it's not that. It's the Dunkards. If it weren't for those Dunkards . . ."

He grinned. "You win. . . . You take the Dunkards. I'll take Cynthia."

The Dunkards (Vera had told him that two carloads of them were coming from Echo Valley) had been the only people in this community to raise Red Poll cattle until Jim Terry and Vera started breeding them. The Dunkards would bring with them the blue ribbons and other badges of merit that their Red Polls had won at county and state fairs in former years. Max had made a glass case for the ribbons. He wondered how old Ed Appelkeller was going to take this celebration. Appelkeller had bred a champion bull but it would never have occurred to him to have a party in its honor. That was the sort of thing you got when women took to farming.

"It's ten minutes to one," Vera said.

"Oh, all *right!*" he said, and went through the gate and got into his car. She followed him. "Don't tell her about Bud," she said. "I want him to be a surprise."

"I'll tell her the party is for her," he said. "Then when she gets here and finds out it's for a bull . . ."

She had not thought of that and she ran a little way along the fence to keep up with the car, which was already moving. "*Tom!*" she called, and the intensity of her tone made him turn his head to look at her. "Tell her I'm *dying* to see her."

Claiborne pressed his foot harder on the accelerator. "I'll do that," he called.

The top was down. Dust, swirling upward, smote his cheek. A few grains were still gritty on his tongue when he left the drive and turned into the highway. He wondered how much rubber he had taken off his tires with that start. Well, the war was over. As soon as these tires wore out he could buy another set. . . . The twenty-second of September. Unusually dry for this time of year. But you could never raise a real dust in this lush, well-watered country. He glanced at the honeysuckle vines matted thick on the stone walls. In his own country, at this time of year, the honeysuckle and all the roadside weeds were white with dust and you could taste the dust even if you were driving on a black-topped highway. He came to the bridge over Blencker's Brook, slowed down and let his engine idle while he gazed into the water. The stream rose in those hills over there and, flowing south, made the great bend that almost encircled his farm—three hundred fertile acres, well watered, a stone manor house, a barn the size of Durham Cathedral, and a dozen other outbuildings. What more could a man want?

He turned his head to look back at the house, just visible through the trees. It was a typical Pennsylvania Dutch farmhouse—stone, white-stuccoed, shaped like the houses Cézanne

17

had painted in the south of France. "But they *owe* me a brick house!" he thought.

The house had been built in 1761 by a man named Blencker. His own great-great-grandfather's house in Virginia had been burned to the ground by "Blencker's Pennsylvania Dutch." ("They didn't even speak English while they plied the torch!" was the way his grandmother told it.) When he first came here to live he had intended to consult local records to find out whether the Colonel Blencker who had commanded the regiment was of the same family that had settled here, but he had never got around to it.

He and Vera had been living here twelve years. Before that they had gone back and forth between Paris and the Vincents' villa at Hyères. It was twenty-one years ago that he had married Carlo Vincent's daughter. The first winter they were married they had spent in Paris. Horne Watts was alive then, living with Max. George Crenfew, who in those days thought that he was going to be a painter and had abandoned his medical studies, was trying to live on his army bonus with that wild first wife of his—only they said she wasn't wild any more—in an attic on Notre Dame des Champs that was so cold that he worked in fur-lined boots and a ski cap that he sometimes forgot to take off at parties. The tall, golden-haired girl who shared his poverty had continued to call herself by her maiden name after they were married. ("Kept her own name but never could figure out who she was," Horne Watts used to say.) Hadn't she some pretensions to being a writer?

He started, looked at his watch, and resumed speed. He had not heard the train whistle but it was due now. Cynthia Vail would have to simmer in her own juices till he got there. A savorless broth she would make—unless she had changed since the last time he saw her, at Mio Sogno, the Vincents' villa. He tried to remember what she had looked like then but succeeded only in conjuring up an impression of a child, slight and sallow, always on the point of slipping into or out of a room. She had been one of the bridesmaids at his and Vera's wedding. There had been a to-do over that.

18

Max, who had made himself master of ceremonies, had argued that "the young person from Massillon" was too immature to be a bridesmaid, but Vera's mother had insisted that the girl be in the wedding. Margot and the girl's mother (they were cousins and closer than sisters) had been together in some Middle-Western convent. Margot had the girl over for visits and had even, he seemed to remember, provided her with a modest *dot* when she married a young instructor in Greek at the coeducational college she had chosen to attend.

After all those years on the Riviera, Pearl Clancy still had a goodhearted *American* streak in her. Vera's mother (Pearl Clancy she had been till she got to Paris and turned into Margot) was the granddaughter of the old ironmonger Arthur Clancy, and had eloped with a young worker in one of her grandfather's mills in Massillon, Ohio, when she was eighteen and he nineteen. Carlo Vincent, as he called himself after he became famous (what fools Americans can make of themselves if they live abroad long enough!) had been born Carlo Vincenzi, the son of an Italian marble-cutter, and as far as anybody knew had never had a paintbrush in his hand until he and Margot landed in Paris. His "Fountain in the Desert" had been exhibited when he was twenty-five, the same year that Malevitch showed his picture of a black square on a white ground in Moscow. An "Essentist" Carlo called himself, and was for the circle, whereas with Malevitch the rectangle was the "neutral form, which, when composed, would annihilate itself for lack of contrasting forms." How old hat all that sounded now! As old hat as Poe's "In the original unity of the first thing lies the secondary cause of all things, with the germ of their inevitable annihilation." He had read *that* when he was fourteen years old, lying on his stomach in the bay window of the upstairs hall at Eupedon, and had never been the same since. But in all probability neither Malevitch nor Carlo had ever read Poe. Painters never read anything; they figured they didn't have to. Maybe they didn't. Did the fact that Vera's father had been a famous painter account for

19

her persistent love for the kind of show they were putting on today? For it was her doing, not his. And she had Max to egg her on. Now that Max no longer took his painting seriously he wanted a party every day. That was what their lives were: a party every day.

He was at the station, with time on his hands. He should have remembered that the train was nearly always late. It was hot in the waiting room and he was out of cigarettes. He crossed the tracks to Joe White's Billiard Parlor, bought a package of cigarettes, then ordered a beer and drank it, standing with his back turned to the bar, gazing out on the street. The sycamores that shaded the sidewalk in front of Joe's place were more advanced than the sycamores out at the Brook; the sidewalk was spattered with yellow leaves. He and Vera had been driving past here the other day and she had laid her hand on his arm, as she had laid her hand on his arm a few minutes ago, and said: "Tom, what does that make you think of?"

"What?"

"The leaves . . . those yellow leaves there on the ground."

"Why, the leaves are all falling early this year. We need rain."

He had lied. He never passed this row of trees along here without thinking of Mio Sogno. He had come to it first down an *allée* bordered by sycamores, that summer he and Horne Watts and Max Shull took the bicycle trip. Five years before he died Carlo Vincent repudiated "Essentism" and repaired to Hyères to live the year around. He was reported to be painting steadily up to the time of his death but nobody had seen any of the pictures. When they rode into Hyères that evening in late September Max had announced that he was going to see those pictures. Horne fell in at once with the idea and said that as soon as they had finished dinner they would go up to Mio Sogno and call upon the famous painter, who would naturally be delighted to receive them! They kept their spirits up with that kind of talk all the way up the long ascent to the villa. But nobody came when they rang

20

the bell set in the tall iron gate. Max and Horne set off to find another gate. Some impulse took him another way. It was he who found the place where the wall was crumbling. . . .

"Was it the one-eleven you was meeting, Mister Claiborne?"

"That's right."

"She's already blown."

He said, "Much obliged, Joe," and set his glass down and crossed the street and stood on the platform, waiting, while the fast train thundered toward him through the blazing September sunshine.

TWO

Not many people got off. Cynthia Vail saw him at once and came toward him. He was not sure that he would have recognized her. She was not more highly colored than he remembered, but she was somehow more visible. No doubt it was her clothes: a brown suit and something on her small, cap-shaped hat that glittered like a gamecock's feathers. If this had been the South he would have kissed her—would have been expected to kiss her because she was his wife's third cousin—but he had turned Yankee, so he only grasped her thin, hard hand.

"How is Bob?" he asked when they were in the car.

"Quite well," she said, and smiled faintly. "At least he was when I last heard from him. . . . His name is Lester."

"I'm getting to be an old man," he said. "Can't remember all you young people's first names."

She turned her head and looked at him. Her eyes were not the indeterminate gray he had remembered, but green, or at least flecked with green. "You're forty-seven, aren't you? And Vera's forty."

"And you?" he asked.

"Thirty-four," she said composedly. "Not much time to lose, is there?"

"It all depends on what you've got in mind."

She laughed and was silent, looking straight before her, seemingly absorbed in some train of thought of her own. They were on the edge of town now. A sycamore, larger than the ones in front of Joe's place, stood in the bend of the road. A bronze plaque saying that George Washington had executed some maneuver in the vicinity had been inserted into its stout, writhen trunk. You could not see the grass for the yellow leaves fallen all around it.

She was asking a question: Was the sycamore the same as the French *platane?*

No, no, it is not the same. Nothing is the same! "I really don't know," he said aloud. "Always intended to look that up but never got around to it."

Nobody had answered that day at the villa when they rang the bell, but there was one place where the wall was crumbling. He went through the gap and was walking on thick-fallen leaves down an *allée* bordered with *platanes* when he saw the brown-legged girl walking on ahead. A basset hound ran behind her. The dog caught his scent and turned his noble, domed head, then padded on. The girl turned too, and looked at him over her shoulder before she walked on.

When he hurried and caught up with her, she said: "Are you one of the strange people?"

"I am a stranger."

". . . that the gardener was talking about? He said there were three."

The first thing he had ever noticed about Vera was her eyes, so blue under that smooth brow! All he wanted was for her not to turn her head away again! He said: "It's Horne Watts and Max Shull."

22

"Horne Watts. He's a poet, isn't he?"

"Yes. He's very good. But he drinks too much."

"And are you a poet too?"

"Yes. I'm very good too."

"Don't you drink too?"

"Yes, but not as much as Horne and Max."

It *had* been extraordinary, the way they had started talking together, as if they had known each other all their lives! They were walking side by side up the avenue when the other girl —this same girl, woman, who was sitting beside him now— came toward them, saying that there were two men sitting on the terrace. What should she do?

"Give them some tea," Vera said, and burst out laughing; she had just realized that she did not know his name and so could not introduce him to her cousin.

He tried again to remember what this girl had looked like in those days, but saw her only as small, not highly colored, following Vera down some garden path, or coming softly up to her aunt to say something in a low voice. And Vera? A thin girl, with really remarkable eyes, but no beauty then or since. Why was it that when she turned her head and gave him a fleeting glance over her shoulder lights seemed to blaze suddenly in a room where he had sat alone in the dark?

Life is a putting forth of the hand; a rocky path up from the beach to where the car is waiting; a girl on ahead, climbing so swiftly that the skirt she has slipped on over her bathing suit stretches taut every time one of the firm, brown legs thrusts her body upward. How could a man not put his hand out to clasp the warm flesh? One second I was down below her, the next we were standing on the ledge, side by side, the next we had left the path and were coming into that place where lavender grows wild among the rocks. She was shaking all over. That was how I knew what I was going to do. But you cannot turn back. There was another place on that same path where we used to go at night. A waste place behind the *pinède* where the gardeners piled the branches they clipped from the hedges—in the days when the hedges were clipped.

Toward the end Margot dismissed all the gardeners but one and the hedges went unclipped. That country is used to being ordered by human hands. You cannot let vegetation go its own way. All that part of the grounds was rankly overgrown and had a queer, lush odor, particularly at night. She came to me late at night after the others had gone to bed, so late sometimes that the sky would be showing the color of dawn. But she never came on Tuesday or Thursday nights; she had to drive in to Hyères Wednesdays and Fridays to see the psychiatrist. ("And I don't want him to find out about you." "How can you keep him from finding out about me?" "Oh, I have ways!") She had been going to a psychiatrist for her "bad father complex." ("Did that fool psychiatrist tell you that you had a bad father complex?" "Oh, I've always had it. Everybody knows that. Mummy says it's one of the worst she's ever known.")

At forty-five Margot Vincent's figure was still youthful, her hair determinedly golden, but her dazed blue eyes were already veined with red and she had a way of starting to say something and trailing off into a guttural murmur. Her young sculptor had gone to England, ostensibly to visit his grandfather—really for a much-needed period of recuperation, some of her friends said. At any rate, Margot was glad to have somebody to amuse her. She and Horne got on from the first. The three of them were up at the villa almost every day.

Carlo Vincent had died that spring of a heart attack, alone in his studio. The servant who was supposed to look after him had gone to Cannes to attend his own dying mother, without notifying anybody. It was Vera who found her father, fallen upon his easel, after two days. It was Vera, too, who got the job of destroying his pictures, according to a promise she had made him a few days before his death. She would never tell Tom how she had gone about her work of destruction, though he had often asked her. When she began having bad dreams they sent her to a psychiatrist. Would he have become Vera's lover so quickly if her father had been alive? Or if

24

her mother had not been the kind of woman she was? Or if her father had not been a painter and he himself a poet, and she committed to take only an artist for lover? He had tried once to talk to her about all that.

"I wish I'd come into your life some other way."

"You mean in Paris, perhaps?"

"No, without Horne and Max."

"But I *love* Horne and Max. You do too."

"I don't care whether Max lives or dies. I love Horne the way you love a man you share a raft with in the middle of the ocean."

"I don't know what you mean."

"Well, he's one of the best poets living, but nobody knows it, except me and two or three other people."

"Does *he* know what a good poet *you* are?"

"That's what holds us on the raft."

"And poor Max? He just climbed up on the raft and nobody's pushed him off yet?"

"Oh, he's all right—in his way. But *you* ought not to know he exists."

"Mario Duchesne stayed here one whole summer. He used to take the cook's grandson out driving. Mummy would never ask him back. . . . Do you think all those people are crazy?"

"A little."

"I'm crazy too. That's why I have to go to Dr. Mangrove."

"You're not crazy," he said, shaking her thin arm. "Don't let them tell you you're crazy. Do you hear? You're *not* crazy!"

"*No!* Not now! Not *now!*"

Even then it frightened me, the way she thought I could change the whole world. . . .

The woman beside him in the car was asking him in a voice so low, so discreetly pitched that he had the illusion that she had read his thoughts and judged it best to interrupt them, how and when he had first met Horne Watts.

"Horne?" he said vaguely. "I corresponded with him for years before I met him. Herbert, he signed himself in those

25

days. Herbert Horne Watts. Then he cut the Herbert out. Thought Horne sounded more virile." They both laughed. Why was it that people were always amused at the thought of a man's lacking virility?

Horne's name, as far as his private life went, had become a byword, and, indeed, his conduct toward the end of his life had been outrageous. But he had been a good poet, a master of a craft not easily mastered, for all that. He wondered suddenly what his own life would have been if Horne had not stretched out a hand to him? For Horne had been his first "literary" friend. He had just begun to publish his poetry in the *Little Review*—the very name had magic in those days—when Horne wrote him, hailing him as the "new Laforgue." Claiborne, at that time, had not read Laforgue, but he made a point of reading all his poems before he answered Horne's letter. They had corresponded all that winter (Vera was preserving Horne's letters for him somewhere in a long green box), fifteen- and twenty-page letters in which they had exchanged opinions on Dadaism, Cubism, Vorticism, the Symbolist movement, T. S. Eliot's *The Waste Land,* which had just come out, John Donne's poetry, John Webster's plays—Horne was in the process of supplementing his lack of formal education by a prodigious amount of reading. His father, who was a rich manufacturer, would not give him an allowance and he was living in Paris partly on the bounty of his maternal grandmother and partly on one of those fellowships which were just then beginning to be offered to indigent artists, with a painter friend, who, he wrote Claiborne, was not "constricted" by Cubism or any of those other isms but was "doing some damn good stuff." If Claiborne came to Paris he must stay with them. Claiborne had been too ignorant and inexperienced to recognize that in certain phrases in those letters Horne was trying to find out whether or not he were "one of them." And in those days he had had as much notion of journeying to Paris as of journeying to the moon. Then had come the sudden death of his uncle and of that uncle's only son, within two months of each other. There had not been as much money as people thought there was but there had been enough to put the idea of studying law out of his head forever. He had taken passage as soon as the funerals were over. Horne, who was living in a tiny atelier in the garden of an old house on L'Impasse des Deux Anges, had given him a boisterous welcome and had introduced him to his circle of friends. And a rum lot they were, Claiborne reflected. Well, they were all scattered now, and Horne himself, in a panic, Claiborne had always thought, because his creative energies were failing, had leaped to his death from the deck of an Atlantic steamer. . . .

She was asking him about George Crenfew and Catherine Pollard. Was it true that she used to lie in bed all day long when George was not using her as a model, partly because she liked to read, partly to keep warm, rising only in time to attend whatever party she was invited to, wearing sometimes for a frock the faded tapestry George had been painting her against?

He said: "You make it sound mighty romantic. I don't know about her lying in bed but she sure never wanted to go to bed once she was up. . . . I believe the drunkest I ever got was at their wedding."

He stared at her. *Drunker than you were at your own?* That was what she had said. He was taken aback by her brusqueness but there was something else more disconcerting: she was referring to some event they two had participated in, some memory they shared with nobody else. For a second he had been on the point of recalling it, but it was gone now.

He said uneasily: "It *was* rather a rowdy affair. . . . But *you* weren't drunk surely."

"No."

"Probably the only person there who wasn't. Remember when Horne went through the wall of the *orangerie?* Anybody else would have been cut to ribbons, but he was only nicked a bit here and there."

She said only: "Yes."

He was silent too, seeing the great white villa sprawled on the cliff, with its *allées* of *platanes* and cypresses and its flights of terraces that in midsummer blazed with flowers.

They had been married in September when there were not so many flowers in bloom. Carlo had been dead less than two years, and Margot, only three months before, had married her young sculptor. Everybody had agreed with Vera when she said that she did not want a big wedding; then everybody had invited everybody he or she happened to think of—many cables had gone off, many long-distance calls had been put through in the early hours of the morning. When the day came the house and the grounds were full of people. Max had rounded up a gypsy orchestra. There was dancing under a marquee on one of the lower terraces.

He and Vera had planned to drive to Antibes that day. They were going on a cruise with the Mortons. But they stayed after the ceremony to dance a few dances and drink a few healths, and then had had to stay on longer to see whether Horne would survive his plunge through that glass wall. . . . He knew now what it was he had been trying to remember. In that country you stand one moment in blazing sunshine and the next moment step into a shadow that chills your marrow. At some time during the afternoon he must have wandered off alone down a neglected garden path; he remembered greenery pressing him on both sides before, descending a shallow flight of steps, he stumbled and fell headlong at the foot of an ancient, moss-grown statue. When he sat up he had had for a second the illusion that he was confronting a living creature; something besides light trembled along the wreath that circled the satyr's head. And then he saw the girl—this girl—standing motionless in the black shadow cast by the herm. She had not made any move to help him up, to console him for his fall. She had merely stood there, watching him. But when he got up and limped over and sat down on the step she had come and sat beside him. She had something white in her hand and she asked him a question—some question he could not answer—in a low voice. He was intoxicated and dizzied too, by the fall, but he still remembered how pale her face had been under the broad, transparent hat, how watchful her eyes.

He said now: "What was it we talked about that day?"

"In the garden?"

"When we sat on the steps and you asked me something. What was it you asked me?"

"I showed you a poem I had written."

"So that's what it was about you."

"About me. . . . ?"

"That made you different from the others. . . . You had a poem tucked in the bodice of your bridesmaid's dress."

"I had carried it around for days—on the chance that I might find you alone."

He laughed. "And when you did find me I was *non compos.* . . . What did I say?"

"You said, 'Good God, girl, can't you see I'm drunk?' "

"Well, I'll have to make it up to you. . . . I suppose you've still got a few poems on hand?"

She nodded composedly and the next instant was asking him if he had ever heard that Horne and Max and Catherine Pollard used to try their hands at alchemy in the studio on L'Impasse des Deux Anges.

He said: "That's the kind of thing Catherine *would* think up. Queerest girl I ever knew. In some ways."

"How was she queer?"

"I don't know," he said absently. "Something about her eyes. We used to think that George might have got somewhere with his painting if she had ever let him sober up."

"He never got anywhere with his painting?"

"He gave it up years ago. He's a psychiatrist now. Does damn well. His new wife's a psychologist, too. She can tell you what ails you quicker than George can. Why are you so interested in all these people? They're all much older than

29

you. . . . And Horne . . . why, Horne's been dead for years."

"I've been dead, myself, for seven years."

She did not look at him as she spoke but down at her gloved hands, which were clasped in her lap.

He was silent a moment, then said: "Where? Massillon?"

The gloved hands flew apart in a rapid gesture. She looked up at him, smiling faintly. "Massillon made me. Rapulgee undid me. Rapulgee, Wisconsin. Or, as they say, Wizconzin."

He supposed that she was referring to her life with Lester Vail. He had seen the fellow's picture somewhere. He looked like an oaf. He had wondered why he had gone in for classics. Seven years' intimate association with such a fellow might undo any woman. Did she, like Francesca, have another man on the string, or was it enough for her to get out of Rapulgee and away from Lester Vail?

They were at the gate. He said as he handed her out of the car: "I don't believe you're a good influence on me. You make me think too much about the past."

She gave him another of her looks. "When you ought to be thinking about your future?"

"Well, here it is," he said, and escorted her through the gate and onto the crowded lawn.

THREE

The long stretcher tables were still laden with food but deserted except for a few people who stood beside them, holding plates of ice cream and cake. The crowds seemed to be moving in two directions, toward the big marquee, from which music blared, or up the midway.

Claiborne did not see his wife anywhere. He told Cynthia that they would probably find her near the bull's tent and they began to thread their way through the crowd. It was larger than Claiborne had expected it to be. There were people there whom he had never seen before, others with whom he had only a nodding acquaintance.

In the center of the midway, his next-door neighbors, Molly and Ed Archer, stood with Max Shull, their arms about each other's shoulders, competing, it seemed, with the rhythms of Jack the Bear. Claiborne caught the refrain which they were trying to harmonize: *"Ci-gît la seule en France qui était morte de ça!"*

Max saw him and broke away from the other two to embrace the newcomer. "Cynthia! My little chickabiddy!"

He released the smiling woman but kept his arm about her shoulders as if one embrace had not sufficed to show his affection. Molly Archer ignored Claiborne's attempt to present his cousin-in-law to her, smiling and still swaying in the rhythm of the song. She was a stout woman whose sapphire blue eyes and short gilt-colored hair contrasted dramatically with her darkly sunburned skin. "Have you heard about Marengo?" she asked.

Claiborne shook his head. "Have you had him dug up for the day?"

The color deepened in Molly's coppery cheeks. She stood up straighter. "You think you ought to joke about thish, Tom? Strikesh me as the crown of Jim's lifework."

"Strike me dead," Claiborne said. "What are you talking about, Molly?"

Her husband looked at Claiborne, a faint smile on his lips. "The crown of Jim's lifework," he said. "Shall we drink to that one?" and he offered his wife his arm while, still keeping his eyes fixed on Claiborne, he gestured toward a glass-laden table that had been set up between two mighty oaks.

Claiborne shook his head. "I've got to find Vera."

He watched the Archers move off, thinking that there was no accounting for the marriages women made. When he and Vera first came to live at Blencker's Brook, Molly's first husband, Jim Terry, had been alive—a burly, red-faced fellow

(Vera often commented on the fact that he and Molly were the same color and almost the same shape) with a passion for country life. He was the only rich Yankee he had ever known, Claiborne thought, who really seemed at home on the land—up at daybreak every morning and out in the fields or around the stables the rest of the day. He and Molly had never even gone away in the summer; there was too much going on at Blue Spring, they said. Jim's chief interest had been the breeding of Red Polls but he had been born in the Finger Lake section of New York State and grapes, as he said, were in his blood. He had experimented for years, and shortly before he died had succeeded in growing a grape from which a highly tolerable sparkling white wine was made. The vineyards were still kept up but you didn't hear much about "Blue Spring" these days. Ed Archer, Claiborne thought, still watching the thin, white-clad figure moving away across the lawn, probably had a file on them somewhere and if you asked him could probably tell you as much about them as Jim would have been able to tell you when he was alive.

It was Ed's business to know things or to know where the knowledge could be got. He was executive editor of the news magazine *Parade* and hired—and doubtless fired—experts on every subject that contemporary American readers might be supposed to be interested in. Everybody had wondered what Molly would do when Jim died. They had not had long to wonder. Barely a year after Jim's death she had married Ed Archer. Standing there, or watching quietly, taking so little interest in what was going on that he did not even need to look away from it, Ed Archer always looked as if no matter what came up he would be equal to it. God knows he was. As an editor he dealt with the world or whatever sections of it were habitable.

I never could stand the fellow, Claiborne thought now. Is it because he's so lucky? For Ed Archer had always been lucky. He and Tom Claiborne had graduated from the University the same year. Ed had not been able to get into the army on account of a football injury (he still limped slightly) but while Tom was being booted from one training camp to another Ed was at the front as a war correspondent. His book, written in three weeks, while recovering from the mumps, he always maintained, had gone through eleven printings. On the strength of it he had written a widely syndicated column —until he got the job of managing editor of *Parade*—and now he was married to Molly, which most people would consider a stroke of luck, since Molly had more money than she knew what to do with.

The Archers were slowing their pace as two women approached them from the opposite direction. One of the women was young and one was old, but both wore the flowing, full-skirted dress and deep sunbonnet of the Dunkard sect. Molly Archer was turning to stare curiously after them out of eyes that were already a little bloodshot. The Dunkards, as if unaware of her scrutiny, walked on at an even pace, their eyes on the ground.

"How did Molly get organized so quickly?" Claiborne asked.

"It was the shock," Max said. "You'd have thought it was Jim come back and not Marengo."

"Marengo?"

"Well, he's not here in the spirit."

"What in the devil is all this about Marengo?"

Max laid his hand on his friend's arm. "Have to brief you, my boy. Water has been flowing fast under Blencker's Bridge. We are now split into two armed camps. . . . Didn't you see how those Dunkard women refused to speak to the Archers?"

"I *told* Vera not to set those bars up!" Claiborne said. "Anybody who wanted a drink could go in the house and get it."

"It's not the drinking the Dunkards are sore about. It's that refrigerator . . . and the heifer."

"The one of Bud's get?"

Max's black eyes twinkled. "Marengo's get."

33

"She can't be much of a heifer. Marengo's been dead over a year."

Max's eyes shone even brighter. "Marengo sired this little twidget last spring."

"From the spirit world?"

Max shook his head. "Jim gave Laird and Laird some of the last semen they took. They froze it. It *works!*" He suddenly bent almost double and, rising, showed a quivering face and eyes full of tears. "Oh, Mister Discobolus, oh, Montreal! . . . *Country life!*"

"I wish it amused me as much as it does you," Claiborne said coldly. "Where in the hell is Vera?"

"Up with Aunt Virginia. Made a little exhibit and took it all up to Aunt Virginia's room. Pomona raped the orchard and took it all up to Aunt Virginia's room."

"How'd you like to take Cynthia up there now after you get her some lunch?" Claiborne said. "If you can keep your language clean enough for Aunt Virginia."

Max seized Cynthia's arm. "No trouble," he said. "Aunt Virginia'll calm me down. She'd calm *you* down. She'd calm anybody down! . . . Cynthia, I used to think your nose was too long. Now I think it's Sienese."

Cynthia said: "I think that's wonderful of you!" and looked at Claiborne.

"I'll be up there in a minute," he said. "Have to take a look at the exhibits."

A waiter came toward him, carrying a tray of drinks. He took one and sat down on a bench that was built around the big oak tree. The drink was weak. He set it down on the bench. Max and Cynthia had reached the terrace. There they paused. Max was making a gesture. She took a step backward, like a painter stepping back from his easel, to admire the wide-paneled door and its surmounting arch. They disappeared through the doorway. The waiter stood, looking at him vaguely as if he did not know where to carry his tray next. Claiborne summoned him with a gesture. "Throw that

34

stuff away," he said, "and bring me a triple bourbon. On the rocks."

The boy had scurried off. "Now why did I do that?" Claiborne asked himself, and leaned back against the tree trunk. In a few minutes he would have to go up to his aunt's room, but not until the whisky had taken its effect. He raised his eyes to the window immediately above him. His aunt had been lying in bed in that room for six years now. Doctors she had consulted in several Southern cities, as well as specialists whom the Claibornes had brought out from New York, had found nothing organically wrong with her beyond a mild anemia and atrophy of the muscles induced by lack of exercise. Nevertheless, she had not risen from her bed for six years. Vera was in and out of her room a dozen times a day. Having been brought up abroad and separated from all of her family except the immediate members (and a good thing, Claiborne thought, if she could have been separated from *them!*) she felt her own importance augmented by having any relation, even an invalid relation, living in the house. He himself never went into his aunt's room except when impelled by Vera's hints or his own sense of duty. And yet he was never without the consciousness of her presence.

The boy had brought his bourbon. He drank it in two gulps, then leaning back against the tree trunk half closed his eyes but kept his gaze fixed on the window. The small panes shone rosily in the afternoon light. The windows on the west side at Eupedon had showed the same glitter at this time of day. He and George Crenfew, when they were small boys, had hidden behind a lilac bush on the west lawn once, thinking that if they stayed there long enough they might catch a glimpse of Aunt Virginia taking a bath, but all they had seen was the western light striking on glass.

Except for his years in college and the army and in Paris he had always lived in a house in which his aunt occupied a room. Perhaps it was the same room—an emanation, like the medium's ectoplasm, which formed itself into a perceptible shape and then when he left a place, dissolved, to transport

35

itself through the air and reassemble its counterfeit form as soon as he had settled in another place.

What a nut *you* are! he told himself, and recalled his uncle's heavy, red-brick, turreted house on a quiet, tree-shaded street in Nashville. He had been living there when he got his first letter from Horne, hailing him as the "new Laforgue." He was just out of the army, going to law school by day and writing poetry by night in a lonely room on the third floor of his uncle's Victorian mansion. Judge Claiborne, newly widowed, and lonely too, his nephew realized now, though it had not occurred to him at the time, had wanted Tom to occupy a large bedroom with a southern exposure and a bay window that he said was "just right to study in." But it adjoined Aunt Virginia's bedroom. After they had sold Eupedon she had come to Nashville and for one winter had gone through the motions of keeping house for Uncle Robert. It was that winter that she had got the notion of going to law school—only she had insisted on attending night classes, it being her belief that her time was occupied by day, though Elzie, the fat, faithful cook, ran the house singlehanded under Aunt Virginia's supervision exactly the way she ran it without it.

It was Aunt Virginia, not Tom, who, after several years in night school, had got a degree in law and after that, at the age of forty-two, a job as legal adviser to some veterans' agency that paid her a whacking good salary and "launched her," as Cousin Amy Allard put it, "on her meteoric career."

It had been an extraordinary achievement, when you came to think of it, for a woman brought up in the kind of provincial seclusion in which Aunt Virginia had been brought up, but she had kept the job only ten years, long enough to amass a modest competence which even now sufficed for her material needs. On the tenth anniversary of her graduation from law school she had astonished the family by resigning from her job and buying a trailer in which she and Cousin Amy spent a number of summers. Neither of them could drive but they hired a boy to drive the trailer from one house to another in the neighborhood. The plan was for them to spend a month with the trailer parked, say, at Grassdale, another at Sycamore, and then, perhaps, a month with the trailer parked on the lawn of some of the Gloversville kin. But on one of the Grassdale visits, Cousin Amy imagined that the Grassdale people didn't like her drawing water from the well in the daytime and she took to stealing forth in the dead of night to draw the buckets full for the next day. Cousin Sidney Grassdale, who was a restless sleeper and always kept a loaded revolver under his pillow, had got up in the night and, mistaking the laden buckets in her hands for chickens hanging with their heads down, had taken a crack at her. She was saved from sudden death, as she reported the next morning, only by stumbling "in the nick of time over a God-given root."

The two of them had set out for Blencker's Brook the next morning, Sam Davenport towing the trailer with his Chevrolet. Claiborne had not been able to endure Cousin Amy's chatter—after all, she was no blood kin, merely a connection—and over Vera's protest had sent her back to a Seventh Day Adventist rest home in Tennessee. But Aunt Virginia had been lying here in this bed ever since. . . .

He started. A hand had been laid on his arm. Marcia Crenfew stood beside him. She said: "Tom! Where *have* you been? Do you have *any* idea where George is? Vera said she wanted a crowd, but this is a little too much, don't you think?"

Claiborne said: "In town. Meeting Cynthia. Have you looked among the goats? No, I think it's better to have a hell of a lot of people instead of just a few."

As often happened, when she engaged him in conversation, she stopped short, as if brought up against an invisible barrier. Then she said: "*I've* been up since dawn. We had ten people to lunch, Tom. They lost a disk out of the freezer and we had to *buy* ice cream. And Molly Archer kept asking Catherine Pollard if she wasn't afraid of germs. . . ."

"And is she?"

"Good heavens, Tom! How *could* she be? She lives in a perfect welter of them down on the Bowery."

"Good for her!" Claiborne said. "There's far too much talk about germs. I had a great aunt said she wouldn't believe in one till she saw one. How do we know there are any?"

She was silent. He knew without looking at her the expression her face wore: one of brightly veiled patience. Max had once described her as a "walking *arrière pensée.*" With her the thought behind everything was Freud's theory of infantile sexual repressions. A small woman, with prematurely white hair, a slightly receding chin, and lively blue eyes, she looked younger than her forty-four years. We become what we look on longest and most passionately. Did her preoccupation with infantile sexual frustrations give her that youthful appearance or was it merely that her curly white hair emphasized the even pink of cheeks as prettily rounded as those of an infant?

He said: "Marce, what made you ask Cat Pollard down here this week end?"

She looked up, surprised. "Why, I thought it was a particularly good week end to have her. They're awfully interested in agriculture, you know."

"Who's they?"

"Those people she has around her. That old Frenchman, Joseph Tardieu, started it. You know, that man Catherine took up with after she left George."

"I didn't know that she took up with any man."

"Oh, the relationship was perfectly Platonic, Tom. I mean she took up his ideas."

"And what were his ideas?"

"Oh, some of them are rather like yours. He thinks that agriculture is absolutely basic."

"He's damn right," Claiborne said.

"Of course, Tom, but I don't see that they need to go to such lengths."

"What lengths do they go to?"

"Well, this old Joseph Tardieu—he's a French peasant from

the Auvergne—thinks that people ought to live in communal villages and go out and work the land. He calls it the 'Green Revolution' and he says we'll never get anywhere without that. And Catherine abets him. They have farms scattered around all over the country where people live like that. They have that place in town too, on the Bowery. A flophouse, with a soup kitchen. I believe it's the longest bread line in New York."

"Yes . . . yes," he said impatiently, "but why did you ask her down here?"

"Why, Tom, Katie and Desirée have been spending week ends there all year."

"What for?"

"Their *social* work. They have to do some social work to get their credits in sociology. It struck me as an ideal setup. . . ."

"Till you found they meant business?"

She drew a long breath. "Tom, you know as well as I do that Catherine has always been—unrestrained. Always going off after some odd religion. They say she was walking across Union Square one day and heard this creature holding forth from a soapbox about the 'Green Revolution' and she stepped up and told him she was all for it and took him home with her and they've been together ever since."

"What's wrong with a 'Green Revolution'? Chesterton and Belloc and those boys have the same idea only they call it 'Distributism.' It's perfectly respectable—in England, at least."

"I don't mind their 'Green Revolution,' " she said. "I don't mind it at all. Pitching hay is *wonderful* exercise! But I can't think that Catherine exerts a wholesome influence over those girls. And then those people!"

"What people?"

"Anybody, Tom! *Anybody* who wants to can go there and stay as long as they want to. Bowery bums, alcoholics, ex-prostitutes . . . And of course young girls are fascinated by prostitution. I know when Louise Ashley came to Leonard

39

from Lady Margaret College she asked the class what they wanted to study. . . ."

"She *asked* them what they wanted to study?"

"Yes, Tom. That's the system there. They said prostitution, which was right down her alley of course."

"You mean Louise Ashley's been a prostitute?"

"*No,* Tom! She's a very well-known and able economist, but prostitution naturally has an economic basis, so she told me she just went ahead and gave the same course she gave at Lady Margaret."

"Well," Claiborne said, "it's a strange world. I began saying so as soon as I could talk and I'll go on saying so till my dying day."

"It may not be as strange as you think it is, Tom."

"Is that so? Now, you know I fancy it's even stranger."

She was silent a moment, then she said, "Tom, I don't think you'd find it quite so strange if you'd . . ."

"If I'd what?" Claiborne asked belligerently.

"Oh, be less introspective. Get out of yourself more."

"Into what?" Claiborne asked. "Into this?"

They had been moving up the midway, propelled, it seemed to him, by the hand she still kept on his arm, past stands which held glass jars filled with tomatoes, peaches, pickles, beans, and even small ears of corn, and now they paused before a long glass case in which were displayed clusters of rusty bolts, buckles, iron pins, rings, scraps of leather, arranged in various patterns.

"What in the name of God is that?" he asked.

"Oh, that's Robin's sculpture. Didn't Max tell you? I suppose he wanted to keep it a surprise."

She moved nearer to the case and laid her fingers on the glass above one of the designs: a buckle with part of a strap adhering to it, fixed upon a T-shaped hinge. The strap, split in two by age, gave the impression of taut, spread legs, the buckle had been polished till it glowed. The hole that pierced it might have been the dark well of a single eye.

"All stuff he got out of the old carriage house," she said.

"He had it all hauled into that little back room of Max's and he hasn't used anything else. Interesting, isn't it, that he put such a limitation upon himself? Makes the phallic concentration seem even more exaggerated. This one here, for instance. You get the impression that the phallus is there but that the subject isn't as yet prepared to make use of it."

"It might just as well be a crucifixion," Claiborne said, "the crucifixion of a Cyclops."

She gave him what Max called her "phallic smile" and pointed to an iron chain, several spikes, and an old hook, mounted on gilded wood. "What do you make of that?"

"I'm damned if I know," Claiborne said. "How long has he been working at this?"

"He's been working at it, off and on, all summer, Max tells me."

"Odd way to approach sculpture," Claiborne said. "Well, anything to get him up in the morning."

"What do you make of this?" Marcia said, and stopped before a painting that was displayed on a light wicker easel of the kind that used sometimes to appear in Victorian country parlors.

"That?" Claiborne said. "Why, that's the 'Original Oil Painting.' Max says you can't have a country fair without an original oil painting."

"Poor Max," she said, and slowly shook her head.

"Why poor Max? Max is one of the happiest fellows I know."

"Oh, *Tom!* It's all there in the picture—and it *is* sad!"

Claiborne regarded the canvas. The foreground was dominated by a dark oblong which showed violent contrasts of light and shade. The olive-green background was streaked with crumpled yellow. "I see the skull of some beast—presumably of the species *bos*—left to rot in a desert. What's so sad about that? We all have to come to it some time."

She indicated with her forefinger a spot on the canvas where all the colors, olive-greens, browns, yellows, even pinks,

41

seemed to swirl and fuse in iridescence. Her smile grew broader. "What do you make of that?"

"I was raised in the country by plain, sex-fearing people," Claiborne said, "and I don't make of it what you make."

"What *do* you make of it?"

"I have the advantage of you. I saw the sketches. That's one of Max's religious pictures," he said.

"Religious . . . ? Oh, *Tom!*"

"That picture was painted in Paris thirteen years ago—under the influence of Joe Paster."

"I never heard of *him.*"

"A rather shady character, one of these aesthetic Catholics, hipped on the beauties of the liturgy. Some people didn't like to be seen on the street with him. Had a nasty habit of falling on his knees and praying whenever the notion struck him."

"I wonder why Max chose this particular picture to exhibit."

"Because it's got a bull in it. It's called 'The Vision of St. Eustace,' and the erection between the horns, Madam, is a cross, not a phallus. St. Eustace was a Roman general who was converted when the stag he was hunting turned at bay and he saw Christ hanging on the cross between its horns."

She gave him another of her smiles. "Can't the cross be a phallic symbol?"

He seemed suddenly to lose control of himself. *"No!"* he cried. *"No! No!"* And he raised his hand to his forehead with the gesture of a man brushing away gnats. "She's got it upside down!" he cried. "They stood her on her head twenty years ago and she's never got right side up. It wouldn't be so bad if she was the only one, but we've got factories turning her out by the hundreds. Costs good money. . . ."

"Tom, you're tight!" Marcia said.

"Of course I'm tight!" he cried in the same hoarse, loud voice. "I've *got* to stay tight. Suppose I woke up? What'd I do to *you* if I ever woke up?"

Marcia looked frightened. She murmured, "Tom, *please!* People are looking at us." His head twitched as if he had

42

been a horse shaking off flies. He stood staring straight ahead, breathing heavily. Marcia took her hand from his arm as she saw a lean figure shambling toward them. "Oh," she said, "there's George. . . . George, where *have* you been?"

George Crenfew hastened his pace. "Nowhere much," he said, looking first at his wife and then at his cousin. "Moseying around . . . What you all been doing?"

"Gabbing," Marcia said hurriedly. "Just gabbing. But I've got to go. . . . George, do you know where Catherine is?"

"In Aunt Virginia's room," George said. "At least that's where I left her."

"Oh, she did come!" Claiborne said. "Hell of a way to entertain a guest!" he added in a harsh voice.

"She isn't like us," Marcia said. "Doing good is her métier. Isn't it, George?"

"Sure," George said. "Tom, you seen Malthy?"

The tall man drew a long breath. "I saw her a while ago. . . . She looked in good order."

"That was before they showed me how to put that sheen on her," George said. "Nothing illegal. Just a little rubbing oil. Made a world of difference in her coat."

"If you're going to look at the goat I'm going back to the house," Marcia said. "Tom, I forgot. Vera wanted to know if you'd show Catherine the garden. She wants to see that old wooden statue."

"Which one?" Claiborne asked.

"The one you got in Brittany."

"Oh," Claiborne said. "St. Ciannic. . . . Do I have to go in now?"

"Fifteen minutes," Marcia said. "Isn't that enough goat talk?"

"Plenty, plenty," George said before Claiborne could answer. Marcia had already started for the house. The cousins walked over to where the Nubian doe lay.

The wicker cage was twined so thick with ivy that the doe appeared to be lying on a bed of the dark green leaves. She

43

lay with her forelegs tucked under her. Her coat was an even cream color all over, except for the few dark hairs on her chest and her ears. Each separate hair seemed to have been brushed until it showed the softness of silk. At the sound of their approach she slowly lifted her muzzle. Claiborne fancied that a pinpoint of light glowed in the depths of her black-and-amber eye although she continued to stare straight ahead of her.

"Don't she look a lot better?" George asked. "Don't that ivy set her off now?"

Claiborne agreed that the effect was indeed admirable. George had sat down on the grass. Claiborne dropped down beside him. They were silent a few minutes, then George said dreamily: "Ever notice how much more interesting a goat's eye is than a horse's or a mule's? I like horses and mules too, but there's something about a goat's eye. . . . I don't know whether it's the shape or the way a goat can look straight through you and never see you. . . . They just don't give a damn, goats don't. There's not any animal that gives less of a damn than a goat. . . . Day in and day out, I mean. . . ."

Claiborne did not answer.

The doe's pen was a little removed from the main path. They had had to step around the low, spreading boughs of an apple tree to reach it and now a curtain of green leaves intervened between them and the people who moved up and down the path. Claiborne fancied that the leafy screen subdued a little the hum of voices. For the first time that day he felt relaxed. George had got out his pipe. The cousins smoked in silence.

Presently George said: "Remember Uncle Dod Widney?"

Claiborne nodded.

"I always thought it was sheep," George said, "but now I know there was some goat in it."

"In what?"

"His smell. Don't you remember the way Uncle Dod smelled?"

"The body odor was the strongest smell. Quite pungent.

44

Then there was smoke from the fireplace, then tobacco . . ."

"Dark-fired. The pure leaf. And on top of that a dram—when he could get it. And to bind it all together that muttony smell," George said dreamily. "I never realized what it was till the other day when I had a few minutes to kill before my train and I went down to see the goats, and old Ben got his horn caught on a nail and I stepped into the pen and they all pushed up against me, of course." He looked over at Claiborne and laughed. "Didn't notice it on the train, but Miss Andrews keeps my inner office too hot. I hadn't been in there no time before I smelled Uncle Dod—just as plain. I says to Miss Andrews: 'Who you got out there?' " He laughed again. "Been funny if Uncle Dod had stepped in."

Claiborne laughed too. "I can't imagine Uncle Dod needing *your* attentions," he said.

"Naw, he was a right self-sufficient old cuss. . . . How long's he been dead?"

"He was bedridden the last time I was at Eupedon," Claiborne said. "We had a hell of a time getting him off the place."

"What became of him?"

"Oh, he and Maria had a girl up the road. They moved in with her and her husband. Uncle Dod didn't last long after we sold the place."

"It was in the fall, wasn't it?"

"No," Claiborne said, "February."

It had been a raw day, with the sun struggling behind gusty clouds when he had gone to sign the deed. Holmes Jackson, who had handled the sale of the place, had offered to drive him out there. There were a few things he wanted to get: some pictures, some old knives and forks that had come down from the Reades, the Claiborne family Bible, his father's pistol, which he had reserved from the sale of the effects. The objects were piled on the floor in the front hall. He could have had them all loaded into the car within ten minutes after they stepped through the front door, and he and Holmes could have turned around and driven right back to town, but Holmes took it for granted that he wanted to go over the house and, picking up an ancient magazine from the table and lighting his pipe, turned off into the parlor, telling Tom to go ahead and take as much time as he wanted.

As Holmes turned into the parlor, Tom saw that it was three o'clock. A few weak rays of sun fell through a window on a landing to the bare, stained floor. He had stood there while all about him the long-prisoned air uncoiled itself slowly and rose, heavy with the odors of dust and damp and wood ashes and stale kitchen leavings and the urine of rats. He told himself that he could not stay there, and would have gone outside but from the parlor came the implacable rustle of the leaves of Holmes's magazine, and he went up the stairs and through the upper hall and into each of the bedrooms.

There were few objects left in any of the rooms. In his own room there was nothing except a chair with broken rungs and a pine washstand which had one of its doors smashed in. The bed and all the chairs were gone from his mother's room. There was not a rag in there that had ever belonged to her, nothing except the little cherry table that ever since he could remember had stood beside her bed and had held, besides her workbasket, her Bible and the flashlight which she took with her when she had to get up in the night to attend to anything. (The revolver that she also took with her when she went to investigate any unaccounted-for noises in the night always reposed between the two mattresses of her bed, just beneath her pillow.)

He stood beside the little table and looked out over the east field. In the year after his father's death he had often gone there with his mother. They would start immediately after breakfast. The weeds along the path would be pearled with dew. If he had a cut on his leg his mother would be sure to tell him not to get dew-poison—impetigo they called it nowadays. The east field tilted at its farther end to meet the sky. It had been in alfalfa that year after his father's death and so he always remembered it as being in alfalfa, each leaf

46

sparkling white, as if touched by frost. His mother's narrow bare feet would be thrust into down-at-the-heel black oxfords. There would be places in the fence where the tow sacking had worn through so that the barbs showed. He would go first and hold the wires apart. Her skirt sometimes caught on a barb. Standing, while she bent and carefully lifted the cloth from the barb, he was always aware of the men waiting on the edge of the field: Uncle Dod, Mr. Potter, and his two grown sons, Bob and Tilman. Once, her blue skirt, impaled on two barbs, had been raised half the length of her petticoat. As she bent to disentangle it, her leg showed white and he had marked the glint in Bob Potter's eye before he turned his head away and saw stretching before him, as far as the eye could reach, green leaf on green leaf, cold and heavy with dew.

It was a picture, or rather a sensation, that often came to him: a boy—it did not always seem to be himself—standing beside a woman on the shore of a sea that was now green, now some shade of purple, or even shot with sapphire. Had the dream been premonitory? He had got a good price for the place. A few years later the buyer had been forced to sell it to the government. A river had been turned out of its course and thousands of acres flooded to make one of the enormous lakes which now provided that section with electricity.

When he had sold the land he had had it in the back of his mind that he might be able to buy it back some day. Would he have sold the place if he had realized that in a few years it would lie fathoms deep under water?

"Too bad!" George said.

"What's too bad?"

"That you had to sell the place."

Claiborne glanced at George curiously. A first cousin was a relationship that in the South and in his own family connection was regarded as almost as close as that of a brother. Both of their fathers had gone to the University—to certain

47

Southerners that meant the University of Virginia—together. George's father had hung his shingle out in Gloversville, the Claibornes' market town, and when he died, at the age of forty-four, had a thriving law practice. Claiborne's father, Quintus Claiborne, had also taken his degree in law and had even been admitted to the bar, but, as in those days was often the case with young Southerners who had inherited a considerable amount of land, he had never seen any necessity to practice his profession.

He reflected now that it was strange how things turned out in this world. George's father, Ralph Crenfew, had been a competent lawyer and a model husband and father, but his untimely death had left his son unfathered except for the careless offices of Claiborne's own father, who had been too lazy or too indifferent to practice any profession—"except whoring and gambling," Claiborne thought, and had an instant vision of his father's dark, histrionic face.

George, as a boy, had spent all his summer vacations at Eupedon. No doubt he had looked upon Quintus Claiborne as standing to him in the relation of a father. Quintus Claiborne, idle, dissolute, and, toward the end of his life, his son thought, actually depraved, had yet been a fine figure of a man. Claiborne remembered long summer days he and George had spent wading White River. When they turned in at the front gate in the gloaming a dim figure would be discernible on the porch. His father would rise and come to the steps while they showed him what they had in their creels, or sometimes he would follow them around the house and bring a chair out of the kitchen and sit with them under the trees while they cleaned their fish, talking, perhaps, of a day when he and George's father had taken even more bass out of White River. And he had been like a boy every fall, counting the days before the quail season opened.

It was strange, Claiborne thought. He liked to think of his father as a figure moving through the woods, beside a stream, mingling with other men on the streets or at a country fair, but he could not ever remember looking his father in the face without feeling the necessity to look away. And yet his father's face often came before him, particularly of late years. It was only of late years that he had found himself able, so to speak, to confront it. Fixing an attention on the visionary lineaments of the dead which he had never been able to give the features of the living man, he had discovered what he had not known when his father was alive: that his father's habitual expression was one of unhappiness, almost of despair. He had concluded that for children unhappiness is the cardinal sin. It was not because his father had looked unkind or arrogant that he had found it necessary to avert his gaze from his face, but because he looked unhappy.

He turned suddenly to George. "What was the matter with them?"

"Who?"

"My father and mother. Why did it all come to nothing? . . . Or worse than nothing."

"Your father drank too much," George said slowly, "and gambled too, I reckon, but he was one of the most entertaining men I ever knew. And a damn fine shot . . . As for Aunt Annie—they don't make 'em like her any more."

Claiborne said: "You know very well that my father never did an honest day's work in his life."

"Maybe he felt he didn't have to. After all, that was before the bottom dropped out of things. A man who inherited a thousand acres of good land was thought to be fixed for life."

"The first thing he did after he was married was to sell off most of the timber," Claiborne said.

"He wasn't one to look ahead," George agreed.

There was a silence, then Claiborne said: "After he got too broke to pay the town whores' prices he took up with the girls on the place."

George whistled. "I never knew that."

"You don't believe it!" Claiborne said savagely. "You always looked up to him. You don't believe it!"

"Sure, I believe it—if you say so," George said. He looked at Claiborne and looked away, but not before Claiborne had

seen that his eyes were bright with pity. "Shall we move on?"
George asked.

Claiborne fell into step beside him, relieved that they were
no longer confronting each other. He felt sore all over, as if
the bright glance that had just been bent upon him had been
a whip laid across his shoulders. This man whom he walked
beside was his nearest kinsman, his all-but brother, and yet
he had never until today confided any of his inmost thoughts
to him. He was two years younger than George but it had
always been understood that he was the leader. Perhaps it
was the early development of his talent that had assured him
that leadership. He wondered now how much he owed to the
father whom he could not think of without shame. Or was
it that the early bent of his mind had been determined by
the accident of his living in the depths of the country the
year around? Eupedon was twelve miles from Gloversville. It
had not occurred to his parents to send him to Gloversville to
school when he was a small child, but his mother had wanted
to get Miss Bessie Rogers to live at Eupedon as governess.
His father had scouted the idea. "What could a Rogers teach
anybody?" he had ejaculated. "The boy don't need anybody
to teach him to read. Just let him read. Reading maketh a
full man," and he got on his horse and rode off somewhere.
Tom could not remember learning to read but he could not
remember a time when he had not read omnivorously, even
when he was thirteen or fourteen years old and keenly interested in outdoor sports. George, on the other hand, had
seemed to have no intellectual interests. But he was always
respectful toward his cousin's. Early in life Tom Claiborne
had realized that he must fend for himself. In the course of
writing his first verses he had experienced a kind of inner
illumination. The illumination had vanished, to reappear
only sporadically. In its place had come a cold determination
to write more verses. He had never mentioned his ambition
to George, but he fancied that George had divined it. "I wish
I knew what *I* was going to do," George had said once; and
Claiborne, walking beside him now, realized that he had al-

ways thought of George's life as, in some sort, a makeshift compared to his own. George's attempts to turn painter (it had soon become obvious that he had no real talent) had doubtless been in imitation of his cousin. In college George had even written some verses, which were best forgotten. His career, up to the time he became a psychiatrist, had been a series of fumblings about. But a moment ago he had looked at his cousin with eyes full of pity. It did not use to be like that, Claiborne told himself bitterly. Now anybody—everybody if they only knew it—can pity me!

They were approaching the big marquee. The sawdust-covered floor was crowded with dancers and the benches around its rim were full of spectators, while behind the benches many people who had been unable to find seats were standing to watch the dancers.

On the west side of the tent a platform had been erected to accommodate the eight musicians who made up Jack the Bear's orchestra. The middle-aged mulatto at the piano was evidently Jack the Bear himself. He wore a cream-colored suit and horn-rimmed spectacles. Everything about him was round except the goatee that ornamented his chin.

Claiborne saw his brother-in-law, Robin Vincent, among the young men and boys who surrounded the platform. Robin's fair head topped all the others. His handsome face was, as usual, impassive; he stood, drawn up to his full height, arms folded across his chest. A fine figure of a man until he moved and you realized that one leg was considerably shorter than the other. He had broken his hip, landing with a parachute in the Battle of the Bulge. Claiborne had always felt cheated because he had not seen more of World War I. When Robin got back from World War II he had questioned him about his experiences, but Robin could not describe the jump in which his hip had been broken except to say that he had "made a mistake and looked at the ground." Claiborne sometimes tried to visualize him as he must have looked when he fell. He could see the long body, prone and still convulsed by the impact of the fall, but he could never imagine the expression on Robin's face.

"The fellow's rich, too," Claiborne thought. "Why, he's got enough money to do any damn thing that comes into his head." But apparently no idea that seemed worthy of execution ever came into that handsome head. Claiborne—and Vera too—had expected that Robin would marry when he got out of the army, or that if he didn't marry he would, at least, set up a bachelor apartment in New York, but he seemed perfectly content to live at Blencker's Brook and squire first this and then that girl around.

"Let's get up close to the music," George said, and they made their way through the crowd toward the platform. Among the young men and boys Claiborne recognized several frequenters of his swimming pool. One lanky, blond youth kept his eyes closed, his thin shoulders hunched, and his hands upraised, occasionally snapping his fingers in time with the music. Another boy sat in the sawdust, leaning his back against the platform, his hands lying limp on each side of him, his head bent as if in extreme dejection.

A young girl who was sitting on a bench with some other girls looked up as they approached and after a slight hesitation rose and began treading her way toward them. It was Désirée. Claiborne watched her as she made her roundabout way, slipping past one group, then another, or standing sometimes for a few seconds with lowered head and eyes bent on the ground rather than interrupt some conversation. It occurred to him that Marcia was perhaps exercising maternal concern in the wrong quarter. Marcia and that poor fellow who had burned up in his bed had named the child Désirée but so far as he knew no man had ever given her a second look, while Katie, George's blonde, flyaway daughter by Catherine Pollard, had been turning the boys' heads ever since she was fifteen. She was out there now, dancing with the Hawthorn boy, while Désirée had probably been sitting here all afternoon with nobody asking her to dance. Katie certainly cut a better figure on the dance floor. Poor Désirée was already a little overweight and her olive-toned skin was slightly pitted with acne. He had heard Vera say once that she thought that one of the worst fates that could befall a mother was to have a daughter who was homelier than she was. If he and Vera had had a daughter would she have had beauty? No use worrying about that now. When Vera took that fall from her horse her pelvis had been broken. The doctor said it would be dangerous for her to have a child after that. But they had been married for twenty-one years. They could have had a child any time up to a few years ago. Too bad they hadn't got in under the wire . . . or was it too bad?

Désirée gave him a subdued "Hello," and took her stand beside her stepfather.

"Having a good time?" George asked, pinching her elbow.

"Oh yes," she said. "The music is wonderful, isn't it?"

"What's that they're playing now?" Claiborne asked.

" 'The Pearls,' " she said.

"Could you Charleston to that?"

She shook her head and looked away quickly but not before he had seen her expression. A muscle in her cheek had twitched in response to his seemingly innocent question. For a second, panic had looked out of her eyes. She was afraid that he would take her out on the dance floor and make a spectacle of them both with some antiquated steps.

"Well, what *do* you do to it?" he said, to break the silence.

The youth who was sitting in the sawdust looked up, showing heavily braced front teeth and wild blue eyes. "Bury it for a bunch of moldy figs!" he said.

Claiborne thought that he must be Charley Porter's youngest son, the one they had had to send off to a tutoring school; he couldn't remember having seen him around in a long time. "What's wrong with it?" he asked, leaning over a little so as to get the boy's attention.

The boy, staring straight in front of him, shook his head as if tried beyond his endurance. "They might as well have got Bunk Johnson," he said. "This guy . . . y . . . y . . ."— his voice quavered and broke—"this guy was old when they got Bunk a set of teeth so he could blow his horn. This guy! Why, this guy . . . y . . . y ought not to ever left New Orleans!"

"What's wrong with New Orleans?" Claiborne asked.

"It's all right if you like that sort of thing."

"What's wrong with it?" Claiborne persisted.

A red-haired boy turned around. "It hasn't got the new sound," he said.

"What's the new sound?"

The boy, even while he smiled good-naturedly, put his hand up as if fanning away invisible gnats. "Aw, drop in at the Royal Roost some time," he said, "or the Famous Door."

The music had stopped. The musicians stood up. The boys hastily fell back, forming a row on each side of the platform. Jack the Bear stepped heavily down off the platform and walked slowly between the rows of his admirers. He had taken his glasses off and held them in his left hand. Over his other arm, brought stiffly up against his chest, an embroidered cloth of sleazy silk was suspended. The saxophonist walked immediately behind him. The other musicians lingered on the platform a few minutes, laughing and talking, then they too left the platform.

There was a dead silence among the youths until the musicians had disappeared in the crowd, then the lanky youth said: "You see his rug?"

"Was that a rug?" Claiborne asked.

"Yep. His prayer rug."

"He a Mohammedan?"

"He turned Moslem when he was a bebop man."

"What made him quit bebop?"

"He was so moldy he couldn't dig it," the seated youth said.

"Oh, I don't know, Bill," the lanky youth said. "Some of 'em just aren't cut out for bebop."

"But he's cut out for being a Moslem?" Claiborne said.

"Well, he still wears a goatee," the lanky boy said, "and he turns toward Mecca five times a day."

54

"He can *stay* turned toward Mecca and it won't keep him from making those moldy breaks," his friend said.

The musicians had returned. The youths stood aside respectfully while they mounted the platform. Jack the Bear held his hands suspended in the air for several seconds after he took his place at the piano, then suddenly inclining his plump body to the right and opening his mouth so wide that his gold molars flashed, as if in delight, he crashed into heavy chords.

"Why, it's Black Bottom!" George said. "Tom, ain't that old Black Bottom?"

Claiborne did not answer. He was watching a couple on the dance floor: Cynthia Vail and Hob Dawson, doing a rumba. Her eyes met his. She smiled at him faintly over the man's shoulder before she was whirled away in the dance.

"You remember that cousin of Vera's?" he asked George.

George shook his head.

"Cynthia," Claiborne persisted.

"Seems like I remember the name," George said. "Tom, you remember Virgie Anderson?"

"Sure."

George sighed. "When I was dancing with that little old girl I used to think I was good. But I reckon I wasn't as good as I thought I was, or I'd a kept it up. . . . What's that they're playing now?"

"The 'Shreveport Stomp,' " the lanky boy said.

He was looking at George with more interest than he had hitherto showed in him. "Dr. Crenfew, didn't the Black Bottom originate in Nashville?"

"Sure. First time I heard it was at Pop Haw's. Tom, you remember Pop Haw's?"

Claiborne nodded. He was looking at the other boy, who, once the musicians were back on the platform, had resumed his seat in the sawdust. Claiborne's long arm suddenly shot out and propelled him to his feet and in almost the same movement whirled him about so that he stood facing Désirée.

55

"You know each other, don't you?" Claiborne said. "Now get out there and stomp."

The youth, his face impassive, slowly raised a bony hand and clapped it against Désirée's back. She flushed red and looked over his shoulder at her stepfather, but he did not make any move and she let the youth lead her out onto the floor and, with eyes cast down and face still suffused with red, followed his languid steps.

"She dances all right," Claiborne said after they had watched them a few minutes. "And it'll do him good to get some exercise."

"Oh, sure," George said, then added: "But I don't know whether you ought to have done that."

"Why?"

"Dessy's kind of shy."

"That's the best way to get her over it."

George shook his head. "I don't know. . . . She's kind of different from the others."

Claiborne laughed. "I wouldn't know. I never had any children."

"Well, I got plenty," George said. "Plenty," he repeated softly. "What say we go get a drink?"

They stopped at the nearest refreshment booth. The glasses had given out. Drinks were being served in paper cups. "Make 'em double, then," George said.

Claiborne was looking at a truck drawn up under a tree nearby. It was shaped like one of the vans in which horses were hauled about the country, but it was painted white. One side had been let down to make a sort of counter behind which two figures were visible: a curly-haired young man who wore a white suit a little resembling a milkman's, a white cap, and white gloves, and beside him a Red Poll heifer.

"I suppose that's the famous refrigerator," Claiborne said.

George turned with alacrity. "I been waiting to see that."

There was a small crowd gathered in front of the truck. There was only one woman in the crowd, Minta Hess, who,

56

with her brother, Joe, lived on the dairy farm next to the Claibornes'. Their herd, like that of most dairy farmers in the vicinity, was Holstein-Friesian, but Max Shull maintained that they had mistaken their true vocation and were, by nature, Red Polls, pointing out that Minta, in particular, had the ideal Red Poll conformation, even to the "square barrel" and "wooden" legs. On this occasion she wore dark glasses, as if to disguise her identity, if not her sex. In response to her welcoming gesture George sat down on the bench beside her. Claiborne went to stand behind the bench, with Joe.

The eyes of all were fixed on the curly-haired young man. He had laid aside his white gloves and now held a light aluminum case in his hand. He opened it, disclosing plastic ranks of varicolored tubes. "The refrigerated case," he said, "containing, as you see, plastic tubes of bull sperm, dyed various colors for identification. The inseminator also carries his packet of inseminating tubes, his rubber gloves, and other equipment. The prepared semen which he brings to your barn has been rushed to him only a few hours ago, by plane or parachute. . . ."

A lean farmer raised a weathered, bitter face. "Does getting it to 'em by parachute bring more calves than when the bull takes it?"

The young speaker (he looked more like an athlete than a dairyman) thrust his hands deep into his pockets and, balancing his heavy body on the balls of his feet, leaned toward his audience, lowering his voice confidingly: *"Timing!* You all know what a job that is, with a hard-breeding cow." He paused while his eyes roved over the faces. His smile became wider. He leaned forward. "Mr. Schofield!" he said. "Mr. Schofield, would you be so kind as to step up here beside me a moment?"

There was a stir in the crowd. A middle-aged man in a dark, ill-fitting suit climbed over the endgate to stand beside the speaker.

"Mr. Schofield," the inseminator said, "would you tell

these dairymen here the experience you related to me the last time I saw you—with that hard-breeding cow of yours?"

The dairyman laid his straw hat down, then, as if he were afraid it was out of place, quickly raised it and held it below the counter. His eyes raced from face to face. He spoke in a rapid singsong: "She was a hard breeder. I couldn't never tell when she was in. The other cows, you throw a strap over 'em in the barn and if they act skittish, you know they're in or'll be in in a couple of days, but her, you couldn't never tell. I had her with the bull six times once, but she never caught. . . ."

"Was that in the summer or in the winter, Mr. Schofield?"

"Started in November."

"And took her to the bull in December, January, and February, and once in March, as I recall," the inseminator said sadly. "Four months that cow was out of production! And a good cow, too, wasn't she, Mr. Schofield?"

"I've knowed her to be giving thirteen gallons of milk after she's been fresh three months," Schofield said.

"How'd she test?"

"I never kep' records but one year. She made thirty-five thousand pounds testing over four per cent butterfat that year. Next year, looked to me like she fell off a little, but like I say I never kep' records but that one year, but looked to me . . ."

"A *valuable* cow!" the young man said. "Any cow that tests that high, a man wants to keep her in his herd. And yet this fine producer was as good as lost to Mr. Schofield's herd for four or five months of the year! For this happened several years running, did it not, Mr. Schofield?"

"That's right."

The young man nodded his curly head. "Thank you. *Thank* you! I know *you* don't need any help getting down off this truck. Any man that milks thirty head of cows a day . . . thirty is right, is it not, Mr. Schofield?"

Schofield was silent a moment, staring at him, then he said, "That's right."

"Git down off that platform, Dave!" a voice called. "Can't you see he's through with you?"

The inseminator smiled deprecatingly but kept his eyes trained on the crowd until Schofield had clambered out of the truck, then he said: *"Now!"* and struck his open palms sharply together. *"Suppose* Mr. Schofield had been a member of the Blencker County Society for Artificial Insemination! What would he have done in that case—with that hard-breeding cow?" His voice sank to its confidential tone. *"He wouldn't have done a thing.* Not a blamed thing! If he was a member of the Society that cow would have been listed along with all his other cows and her record would be studied each and every morning by an expert and if there was any chance of her coming in heat that day the inseminator would check her when he made his morning rounds. If she came in heat that morning he'd plan to breed her that very day. If she came in in the afternoon he'd try to breed her by noon of the next day."

There was a silence. The young man smiled, then said: "But suppose Mr. Schofield isn't a member of the Society. . . . Well, whether he is or he isn't, he's a busy man. A very busy man! Say this cow acts skittish one morning when he throws the strap over her and he thinks she may be coming in but isn't sure. He may be just too busy to fool with her that day. But he's not going to feel right about that. No sense in feeding a cow who isn't producing. Suppose that after he finished milking all his other cows and getting his cans out to the cooler and then forking out the manure and hosing out the stalls and a few other chores like that, he puts off sowing that winter rye he intended sowing and trucks that cow over to the bull. Trucks her ten or fifteen miles, maybe, and she doesn't catch. He's got to do it all over again—no telling how many times either. And even if she does catch the first time, why, a man has got something better to do than joy riding cows all over the county." He shook his head. "You all know my old daddy? An A-One dairyman, if I do say it myself. But he had his notions about how to raise us four

59

boys. Happened we lived two miles from one of the best Holstein bulls in the country. No trucking for us. Had to drive the cow over. The times I've walked along that dusty road behind Old Bess or Old Daisy, praying I wouldn't meet anybody I knew! Man feels like a fool, tied to a cow's tail. . . . Well, that's all over. That's the inseminator's job: to get the bull sperm to your cow. You don't have to get her to it."

A man in the back of the crowd said: "I've got a neighbor was a member of the Society. He quit after he got a run of six bull calves."

The inseminator smiled pityingly. "How does a cow conceive?" he asked in ringing tones. "I do not need to ask *you* gentlemen that! If she has been bred, one of the millions of spermatozoa finds the egg that has matured in her ovary and unites with it in the oviduct and, after a journey through the oviduct into the uterus, begins the formation of the calf. Neither the inseminator nor the individual breeder can control the sex of the calf. It is a matter of chance. There are some things we still have to leave to the Lord."

"Amen, brother!" Crenfew whispered to Claiborne.

The inseminator took his handkerchief out and wiped the sweat from his forehead. "There is another question," he said. "It has not been asked yet, but I know that it is in the mind of each and every one of you. *Is* artificial insemination, on the whole, superior to natural mating? In other words will you get more and better calves if you join the Society and simply telephone the inseminator instead of taking your cow to the bull? The answer is *yes!*

"Why? First, because the rate of conception has been raised. *How?* By means of various advances in science." He took one of the colored tubes from the rack and held it up before them. "An antibiotic has been added to the semen. Second, the semen has been diluted with egg yolks and citrates. Third, a photoelectric cell is used to help determine the concentration of sperm. But all these advances, revolutionary as they are, are old stories to you progressive, forward-looking dairymen. You are already convinced that

artificial insemination produces *more* calves than natural mating. The next question is: Will they be *better* calves. Again, the answer is *yes!*

"*Why?* Farmers will now be able to plan breeding programs that they were never able to plan before. They don't need to breed their cow to the best bull in the neighborhood, or county, or even in the state. If they see a bull on television or read about one in a breeder's journal that they'd like to have their cow bred to they can have the semen shipped to them. They can plan line breeding and outcrosses that are not subject to the accidents of natural mating. And they can fit the hardest-breeding cow into such a program. No matter when she comes in heat, the semen will be there, waiting for her.

"That is all I have to say to you today, but I have something I want to show you. You all knew Marengo, the great Red Poll sire, bred right here in this community, on Blue Spring Farm, by the late Mr. James Terry." He replaced the tube he had been holding in its rack and, turning, laid his hand on the heifer's red brow. "You see this little lady here? Marengo's Sweet Girl out of Clover's Daisy, of Sweet Clover Farms. Marengo himself was out of Red Lady by Red Argonaut. One of the greatest Red Poll bulls that ever stood. How many of you here had service from Marengo?"

The dark-faced man who had asked whether transportation in a parachute improved the viability of bull sperm said: "I used to haul gravel for Mr. Jim Terry. He always give me my service when Marengo was alive. But him and Marengo died about the same time and looked like Mrs. Terry kind of lost heart."

The speaker smiled triumphantly and, shifting his hand to the heifer's neck, inclined her gentle head so that she seemed to be bowing to the crowd. "*Exactly!*" he said. "Most of you around here knew Marengo. Does this look like one of his daughters?"

Joe Hess said: "Her nose is off color. I never had nothing

61

to do with Red Polls myself but I know a good one when I see one."

"You can't see this little lady as well as I'd like to have you see her," the inseminator said. "In a minute I want to let this endgate down and get her out there in the crowd where each and every one of you can go up and look at her. I think you'll see that there's nothing cloudy about that nose. It's a true lemon color. Just like her daddy's before her. They say a nose gives no milk, but as you gentlemen know, a cloudy nose is often a warning of an outcross in a strain that ought not to be there. But there's nothing wrong with this little lady's breeding." He stood on tiptoe and struck his fist into his cupped palm. "Gentlemen, this heifer that you see before you is the realization of a long-sought dream. Men in white have been working each and every day since the last semen was taken from Marengo—one week before he died—to bring this little lady before you."

Crenfew made a gurgling sound. "Oh Death, where is thy sting?" he ejaculated.

"Shut up!" Claiborne said, and fixed his attention on the speaker, who suddenly clasped his hands in front of him and rising on his toes said in a hushed voice: "The long-sought dream of preserving spermatozoa indefinitely by freezing it at temperatures below zero has at last been realized! Calves *can* be produced from frozen semen. This little lady is here to prove it. Walk around her. Pinch her if you don't believe it. What has been done can be done again. It is only a question of time before the use of semen banks will be routine. Then when you get a good bull you don't have to worry about him laying down and dying on you, or even getting sick. You can breed to him when he's sick, for you will already have taken the semen from him when he was in health. You can breed to him after he's dead, as Marengo was bred to exactly one year and fourteen days after his death, to produce this little lady here."

The endgate had been let down by two white-coated attendants. The heifer was being made to descend to the ground. The dairymen were crowding around her.

"Want to have a look at her?" Crenfew asked.

"God, no!" Claiborne said.

"Oh, all right," Crenfew said. The cousins turned away. Crenfew was whistling softly. "Seems to be all up with natural mating. Glad I came along when I did. . . . Hello, there's Max."

Max, his features fixed in a wide, almost electric grin, was waiting for them on the edge of the crowd. He said: "Tom, Vera wants you."

"I know it," Claiborne said.

"Less go take a look at Bud," George said. "Poor old boy! Soon be like the bison of the plains."

Max fell into step beside them. His dark face still sparkled with mirth. He spoke in a hushed voice. "I almost missed it. Good God! Think if I'd missed it!"

"Where did you come in?" George said.

"When the antibiotic was added to the semen," Max said in a reverent tone. "Was each and every moment as good as that?"

"That was a high point," George said. "But it was all good."

"Who is that fellow?" Max asked.

"Old Man Tracy's youngest son. Didn't you ever see him play? Best tackle the high school ever had. Flunked out his first year at Rutgers, then got in the Ag College and struck his stride."

"He'll be in politics before he's through," Max said.

Claiborne was silent, listening to a conversation that was going on between two men who were walking behind them: Joe Hess and Dave Schofield.

"Why, Dave," Hess said earnestly, "you ever see him work? He's just like a doctor. Puts on a pair of rubber boots when he gets out of the car and uses a glove that's been sterilized and a new tube for every breeding. And when he's through he breaks it so it can't be used again and scrubs his glove and all his other stuff in a solution."

63

"You can have them rubber gloves," Schofield said. "I got six children. Old Doc Mayhew brought every one of 'em and every one is alive today, except one that was killed in the war. My daughter had her baby last year. In a hospital, like they said for her to do. And it was born all right and was all right for a week till it caught mumps from some of them rubber gloves and died."

"We sure were sorry to hear about that little lady," Hess said.

"It warn't a girl. It was a boy."

"I mean that little baby," Hess said. "But, Dave, that's folks. He ain't talking about folks. He's talking about cows."

"They ain't as different as he makes out," Schofield said.

Max leaned toward Claiborne. "Joe's still under the spell!" he whispered.

Claiborne did not answer. They had arrived at the tent. The young bull was chained to the stanchion fixed into a cement block. In the shadow of the canvas top his eyes glowed like garnets. His chain was wound with green ribbon. He stood breathing placidly, staring straight ahead of him, his jaws moving from side to side occasionally. Rodney, the stable boy, sat a little way off on an upturned box. At the side of the tent four men were ranged in garden chairs. All of the men were bearded and wore the black suit and black, broad-brimmed hat of the Dunkard sect. Three of them were whittling while they talked in low tones. A third, an old man whose beard and hair were touched with gray, sat a little apart from the others, his arms folded, his head tilted a little to one side, eying the bull.

Crenfew recognized in one of the men a breeder from whom he had once bought some goats and sat down beside him. Claiborne, after a moment's hesitation, took a vacant chair beside the old man and then wished that he had not sat down. These Pennsylvania Dutch farmers were different from farmers he had known in the South; he never felt quite at ease with them. And old Ed Appelkeller was not a man to

64

be approached lightly. Acknowledged as the most expert judge of livestock in his community, he also enjoyed widespread fame as one of the foremost Red Poll breeders in the East. But the grizzled head, looking strangely medieval with the roll of hair falling to the man's shoulders from under the broad hat brim, was already turning in his direction.

Claiborne said: "Well, Mr. Appelkeller, how does he look to you?"

The old man (he was in his seventies, though still hale) brought his mild gaze to bear upon the bull. "He fills the eye, Mr. Claiborne," he said in a deep voice.

In deference to his host, he had shifted his position and now sat leaning a little forward, a hand resting on each knee. The hands were so roughened and discolored by labor that they appeared to be composed of some material other than flesh. They seemed large too, in proportion to the thin arms and meager body, or rather they seemed to have grown larger in the course of their labors. It was as if all the strength the man could muster had come to reside in these overlarge hands resting now on his knees. A man would not be afraid to confront his Maker with hands like that, Claiborne thought.

Joe Hess and Dave Schofield had slowly circled the bull twice and now came to stand near the garden chairs on which Claiborne and Appelkeller were sitting. Hess looked at the old Dunkard. A gleam came into his light-colored eyes. A smile twitched the corners of his lips. "Well, Mr. Appelkeller, you going to sign up with the Society?" he asked.

The old man shook his head. "I'll have nothing to do with it," he said.

"Me neither," Dave Schofield said. "I ain't going to have that fellow tromping into my barn. Bring Bangs, like as not."

Hess compressed his lips. "Dave, it's like I told you," he said impatiently. "Everything he puts on has gone through a solution. He ain't half as likely to bring Bangs into a herd as you are, clomping around with manure on your boots."

"Good, clean manure never hurt nobody," Schofield said. "If a man has got Bangs in his herd he can carry it around in one of them tubes a heap easier than on his boots."

The old Dunkard, after Hess's question, and his answer, had resumed his contemplation of the bull, but now he turned to look first at one man and then at the other. "It ain't a question of disease," he said. "It's what's right."

"You mean artificial insemination ain't right?" Hess asked.

Appelkeller nodded. "A bull was made for breeding. A man ain't got a right to keep him from it."

Hess laughed. "You cull your cows as sharp as any man in this county. I heard a fellow say once a cow had to produce nine gallons a day of high-test milk to even stay in your herd."

"That's nature," Appelkeller said. "The first man was given dominion over all the beasts of the field."

"Well, we drive 'em hither and yon and butcher them. Is that right?"

The old man said slowly: *As a beast of the field I am with Thee all the day*. The cattle was put here for a picture of ourselves. It's up to us to guide 'em and use 'em, the way the Lord does us, but only according to what's right."

"Well, what's wrong with inseminating a cow artificially?"

"It's against Nature. Cattle have got their nature, same as a man's got his nature. It's up to a man to respect it."

"You mean that if you could get twice as many good calves by artificial insemination as by natural mating you'd still stick to natural mating?"

"I would," the Dunkard said. "The money the calves'd bring ain't everything. A man has got to live according to Nature—if he lives right."

Hess gave a low whistle and glanced at Claiborne. "Mr. Claiborne, you got one of the finest Red Poll bulls in the county. What do you think of that?"

Claiborne, while the two were talking, had sat silent, his eyes fixed on the ground. When Hess called his name he started to his feet and spoke in a voice so loud that George Crenfew, on a nearby chair, raised his head to stare at him:

"Think! If that fellow ever sets his foot on my place again I'll shoot him." And he strode off toward the house.

FOUR

George ran and caught up with him. "Where you going, Tom?"

"To Aunt Virginia's room," Claiborne said curtly.

George suddenly slackened his pace. "I already paid my respects once today."

"Good for you!"

"I believe I'll just hang around out here awhile."

"I would if I were you," Claiborne said, and walked on toward the house.

A servant appeared for a moment in the dusky recesses of the long hall, then when he made no sign to her vanished. He mounted the stairs until he came to a landing and paused.

A window was set high in the wall. The casement shutter was ajar. Through the branches of a maple he could look down on the west lawn. The big marquee, where they were still dancing, was visible from here, and the tents which housed the bull and the cow and calf, a few black-clad figures still clustered about them. In the immediate foreground were the long tables which an hour ago had held the luncheon dishes. He had not looked at his watch since he arrived but it was evidently teatime. Servants moved about the tables carrying trays filled with delicate china and silver vessels.

A bough moved. Sunlight, striking on silver, sent forth a ray of light so blinding that involuntarily he put his hand up to shield his eyes even while he continued to gaze at the people gathered about the tables. He did not see Vera anywhere. She was probably waiting for him in Aunt Virginia's room.

A servant was placing a tea service on a small table under the copper beech tree. Molly Archer came walking through the flickering light and sat down at the table and began pouring tea. Her husband and Max Shull stood beside her. As Claiborne watched, Cynthia, accompanied by a young man, came up and sat down on a bench. She was evidently heated from dancing; with one hand she took a cup of tea from Molly while with the other, for a few seconds, she fanned the air in front of her face. Max had turned so that he was facing the house. Claiborne fancied that he was looking toward the window at which he was standing. His hand had been resting on the window sill. He let it fall, then checked it in mid-air. All those people (for strangers, he thought cynically, usually found their way back to his house once they had been brought there), all of them, he thought, were bound to the house in which he stood by ties as intangible, as gossamer as the shaft of light that, leaping through the quiet air, had just struck against his eyeball. And no more to be denied. The figures themselves, to his narrowed eyes, seemed insubstantial, as if, even while they stood or moved about in the flickering, gold-colored light, they had moved on somewhere else. That woman, Cynthia, there on the bench. Something black swayed at her feet. Was it the shadow of a tree trunk or the wavering walls of a chasm? It crept on across the grass and she set her cup down and leaned farther backward, her hands clasped in her lap, her eyes staring straight ahead. Did she know that her bench stood on the lip of a chasm? And Molly Archer, in the blue-green dress that so set off her gilt hair, and Ed Archer and Max, they were all poised on the chasm's edge. A tilt of the hand could send them hurtling over. It would be easy, he thought. As easy as that, and watched the brown hairs on his lean right hand turn dark as the hand plunged downward to hang limp at his side.

There were steps in the hall below. He left the window, mounted the stairs, and after a perfunctory knock entered his aunt's room.

Vera was not there. Marcia Crenfew was poised on the

68

wide seat below the window, beside a huge basket filled with melons, squashes, gourds, grapes, and other fruits. A smaller basket which contained balls of orange-colored and scarlet wool lay at her feet. Her knitting needles flashed on for a moment after Claiborne entered. She was evidently at work on what Max called a "Mugwumboo sweater."

A large, black-clad woman whose head was wound about with braids of coarse gray hair sat in the low chair that was drawn up beside his aunt's bed. She did not change her position when he came in, but his aunt, propped high on her pillows, under the four-poster's broad canopy, withdrew her attention from her visitor long enough to turn her ravaged visage toward her nephew.

Miss Virginia Claiborne was sixty-six years old. Her hair, which Tom Claiborne could remember as a lustrous brown, was now pure white, and, gathered into a great coil on top of her head, was as heavy as it had been when she was young. This pallid crown had the effect of making the wastage of her body more apparent. One of her hands lay on the gaily colored quilt. It looked as if it had been modeled in wax. In the chalk-white oval of her face only her eyes showed alive. Brown Claiborne eyes, set under wide, arched brows and still luminous, they had in them at times an expression that made her nephew turn his own eyes quickly aside.

He felt the familiar griping in his entrails now as he approached the bed. Aunt Virginia put a feeble arm about his neck as he bent to press a kiss on her cold forehead. Marcia Crenfew came over from the window seat. "Tom, you know who this is?"

The big woman, still seated, her face upturned, was surrendering a large, warm hand to his clasp. "You haven't changed much," she said.

Claiborne looked down at her a moment, then said: "I don't think I'd have known *you*."

The woman still kept her face upturned to his. "I'd have known *you* anywhere," she said.

69

He looked away from her at his aunt. "How do you feel today?"

She made the little mouth which at once signified that she did not feel any better now than she had felt the day before but that the state of her health was of no importance. The frail hand moved again, this time to fall a little short of Catherine Pollard's knee. "She has been telling me such interesting things about John Wesley, Tom," she said in her reedy voice.

Catherine Pollard turned to face him. "Your aunt tells me that she used to belong to the Methodist church," she said.

"She was a big Methodist—till she lost her faith," Claiborne said.

Aunt Virginia smiled, dryly, but widely enough to reveal her shrunken gums. To his relief she was not looking at him. Her enormous brown eyes were fixed on the visitor. A slight curving of her pale lips indicated that she would have smiled outright if she had had the strength. At the same time he observed her finely cut nostrils flutter a little. She probably did not relish hearing about John Wesley. Methodism for her had been only a youthful vagary and one long since given up. The Claibornes had never "gone in" for religion. He had heard his father say once that anybody in the South who "took any real interest in religion" had turned Baptist or Methodist or Campbellite in the 'seventies or 'eighties (that was the kind of statement his father often made) but that the Claibornes had been "too mean to get religion." His father had called himself an "agnostic." His grandfather Claiborne had been an indifferent member of the Episcopal church, but he had given the Methodists the land to build their church on, and the timber too. The church still stood at the foot of the lane that had led up to Eupedon. He could remember dashing into the lane once on his pony and scattering a group of small Epworth Leaguers leaving the church under Aunt Virginia's guidance. He himself had never been a member of the League, though many of his playmates were. That was doubtless because of an unconscious fear of his father's ridicule. His father's face always wore the same expression when Aunt Virginia set off for church. "Virginia and Tom Fayerlee turned Methodist so they could hear themselves talk," he had said once. He usually sat on the porch reading Tom Paine or Robert G. Ingersoll on Sunday mornings. He said that the shortest verse in the Bible was "Jesus wept because Peter and Paul went fishing on Sunday." One of the stories that people liked to tell about him was of the time he had stumbled into the church, drunk, when they were taking up contributions for foreign missions and, hearing sums of money named, had thought that he was in a poker game and had proceeded to raise.

That might have been one of the reasons why his aunt had left home. She had gone in for Methodism on a wider scale after she left. He could remember her visiting them one Christmas, wearing a queer bonnet and a black, nunlike dress that his mother said was a deaconess's habit. She was working in a hospital in Atlanta then, a Negro hospital, at that. It was as if she wanted to get as far away from Eupedon and its ways as she could. He had heard his mother comment with asperity on "Virginia's goings on" and yet, he thought, they were no more unreasonable than the antics parents expected their girls to go through nowadays if they didn't get married their first or second season. There was the Kennedy girl, who was thought by the family psychiatrist to incline toward nymphomania, going off to a different camp each summer to counsel younger girls. And the Larrabee girl was working with abnormal children, he had heard her mother say proudly, and the two Porter girls, Vera had told him, did volunteer work two days a week at the state mental hospital.

But poor Aunt Virginia, stuck off at the end of that muddy lane, hadn't had much choice. Religion first, and when that didn't work, the law. That had been all she could think of. In the end, she was back where she started, at Eupedon, or as much of it as she could lay hold on, for the posts of the bed she was lying on had been carved by her great-grandfather's cabinetmaker out of cherry grown at Eupedon, and

71

the little feather mattress which was sometimes slipped under her when the modern mattress grew too hard held inside its ticking the feathers plucked from geese that were dead before she was born, even if she had to content herself with the attendance of a white, registered nurse instead of the tender ministrations of her colored foster sister, Polly, for whom she sometimes sighed. She had, doubtless, as much as she could expect, the world being what it is and she having taken the course she had taken. Then why did she sometimes, lying propped on her pillows or even flat on her back, open her blue-veined lids to give him out of brown Claiborne eyes— so like his own, people said—the stare of a person who, suddenly roused from sleep and told to save himself, finds that the house is already ringed with flames?

The big woman was looking at him. She was trying to calculate how long it had been since they had met.

"God knows," he said. "Have you seen Max?"

She replied that she had seen Max earlier in the day and had had a talk with him. "I always liked Max," she said.

"Who doesn't?" Claiborne asked, thinking that she had an agreeable voice, low-pitched but full, a voice that could easily have made itself heard at a greater distance—the result, probably, of experience in public speaking. Marcia had told him that she addressed religious groups all over the country, had said, even, that she was learned in theology. Cat Pollard!

Twenty years ago her voice had not struck so agreeably on his ear. When he heard it at a party, he suddenly recalled, he would sometimes move to another quarter of the room. What was it she was always talking about in those days? Vasilov, the bushy-bearded exponent of some esoteric doctrine that in those days was attracting intellectuals. What form of yoga had the fellow advocated? Fuller consciousness. That was it. His followers were supposed to pause often during the day and "turn their ears inward." That had been a favorite phrase of Horne's. A group of Vasilov's followers lived communally in an old house in the environs of Paris. Cat Pollard used to disappear for weeks at a time, and it was understood that she was at Fontainebleau then, developing her "extrasensory perceptions." Horne had maintained that she came back once with her extrasensory perceptions tuned to such a pitch that he himself could not repair to "the Roman baths" in peace; Cat knew what he was doing, day and night.

He moved his chair nearer hers. "Do you remember the time you and Horne Watts and Joe Paster tried to make the world?" he asked, laughing.

She suddenly threw her head back and laughed. He saw the red, arched roof of her mouth, the rows of still-sound, white teeth. She was laughing harder than he had laughed. She brought a not-too-clean handkerchief out and wiped her eyes and looked over at his aunt.

"We were trying to practice alchemy," she said.

"Indeed?" Aunt Virginnia said. "How did you go about it?"

"They put ten quarts of water in a big glass jar," Claiborne said, "and let it stay there awhile and then they poured some wine in and then they would squat down beside the jar to see what they could see. . . ."

"And could you see anything?" Aunt Virginia asked.

Catherine shook her head.

"They were supposed to see the Dawn of Creation," Claiborne said. "Horne always maintained that if they had changed the formula and put a little more wine in they would really have seen something. . . . Where did he get the formula, by the way?"

"From an old book that was supposed to be translated from Ethiopian into Latin. A friend of mine was showing me a copy the other day."

"An alchemist friend?" he asked.

"Why, no. She's a nun."

Marcia was getting restless. "Tom, you ought to go down to Catherine's place some time," she said. "George says she's like a medieval abbess, with her own chapel and her own priest and her own butcher and baker."

73

Catherine Pollard laughed. "We don't have our own butcher. I wish we did! But we have our own baker."

"A hundred loaves a day!" Marcia said. "It's the longest bread line in New York."

"Vera'll love that," Claiborne said. "I suppose you raise your own wheat and grind your own flour?"

She shook her head. "We don't have enough land for that . . . or enough labor. There's very little work left in our people when they come to us."

"Who comes to you?"

"Anybody."

"Anybody?"

She looked at him steadily. "Broken-down day laborers," she said, "bums off the Bowery, ex-prostitutes."

"In short, any human offal that turns up."

"They are not offal," she said. "They are Christ. We must be Christ to them."

There was a silence, then Marcia said: "The Tatawesh, the people who live in the hills above the Mugwumboo, have a legend to the effect that *no* guest ever appears in his proper person, but is always somebody else. . . ."

"I wouldn't doubt it for a second," Claiborne said. He was looking at the other woman. She had an Irish face, as Irish as his wife's, but of a different kind, and the tall, abundant figure that in certain racial stocks one finds in chambermaid and lady alike. Everything about her was on the same scale, from her mobile mouth and her wide-spaced eyes, of a very clear gray set a little slantingly in her head, to the feet planted solidly beneath her unfashionably long skirt. He tried again to remember the last time he had seen her. It had been at some party. Christmas or New Year's? He saw George, in evening dress, in a doorway, bowing and calling out punctilious good-byes before setting out for somewhere with someone who was much drunker than he was beside him. The girl's magnificent body had been wrapped in some sort of gold cloth. Her head, ornamented then with bright curls, had drooped sidewise against George's shoulder. Her lips were swollen.

74

Her eyes fixed the floor glassily. Bets had been made as to whether George would succeed in getting her home. Horne had said that it was like having one of Walt Disney's oak trees step out and wrap itself around you.

She was talking about Horne now. She felt that his had been a peculiarly untimely death. When he took his own life he had fulfilled only a small part of his promise. "Yes . . . ," he said. "Yes . . . yes." They all said that about Horne. But what was the poor devil to do? In two years he had written one short lyric and it was not much. Horne had thrust it at him over the table the last time they met, in that *bistro* on the corner of Vaugirard and Monsieur le Prince, and he had told him—what he had to tell him—that it was not worth keeping. . . . This woman probably thought that he ought to have kept on writing, no matter what the stuff was like. She had tried to write too in those days.

She was entertaining his aunt and Marcia by describing Horne's appearance the first time she met him. At a Fourth of July party at Vence. An empty nail keg fixed on his head for a crown, his face painted red, yellow, and green in what he called a "mystic design." (Everything was mystic with poor Horne!) He had kept pouring salt into a Victrola while he made it grind out the same tune over and over. That was the way he composed. First he got boiled, then, while playing a record over and over he laid hold of some line or image for the poem which he would start writing as soon as he recovered from his hangover. Claiborne had sometimes thought, watching Horne's antics, that it was almost as if the poem had a palpable body that floated in the air above Horne's head and that it was only when Horne was intoxicated that he became agile enough to reach up and grasp one of its members. That day, he recalled, Horne had been chanting a line which he afterward used in "Pontifex": "Where the last leaf invades the sky."

His aunt asked in her reedy voice if Horne Watts were not the literary friend that he had corresponded with when they lived in "Brother Robert's house on Oak Street."

75

"Yes . . . ," he said. "Yes . . . yes."

He had not really been listening to what that woman was saying; he had been too conscious of the sound of her voice—*A voice that to itself all night/Hummeth a quiet tune,/Like unto a hidden brook/In the merry month of June.* I'll be making an album of favorite quotations next! he told himself, and all at once had a feeling of ease, of relaxation such as he had never known before in all his life. The impression was so strong that it made him a little dizzy, and yet he felt extraordinarily gay.

He leaned forward, speaking with an undertone of merriment, as if they two had been alone in the room: "Do you know, I don't believe I ever saw you before when you weren't tight."

She laughed, glancing at Miss Claiborne as if to share the joke with her. "I've paid for every drink *I* ever took!" she said.

"How?"

"Nursing friends through *delirium tremens* is one way."

"The hospitals won't take them?"

"Not unless they have to." She smiled at him as if out of overflowing friendliness, then suddenly rose. "I have to go now," she said to the invalid, "but I will come again—if I can." She turned to Claiborne. "Your wife said you would show me the statue of St. Ciannic."

"Oh, I will!" he said. His curious lightness of heart had increased. He knew that he was only going to walk beside this woman along garden paths that he had traversed every day for years, but as he stood, waiting while she gathered up her gloves and purse and said her good-byes, he could not rid himself of the impression that they had agreed to travel together to some other goal, a goal so splendid that he had glimpsed it only in dreams and that not often. This feeling was still so strong upon him that when they had emerged from the invalid chamber and stood in the dim hallway he half turned to her as if to ask "Which way?" but she was already making the somewhat old-fashioned gesture of laying her hand upon

76

his arm and unconsciously he squared his shoulders and accompanied her down the wide stairs and into the garden.

They walked in silence a while, then he said: "Where did you go when you left George?"

"To the Daughters of Charity."

"How did you happen to go there?"

"I was passing by one day and rang the bell and asked if they had any work. The portress had just died, so they let me answer the bell, and later they let me tend the altar candles."

"How long did you stay there?"

"Three months."

"And you didn't send George any word?"

"I didn't know what word to send him," she said.

He laughed. "Poor Horne! He took a great interest in your 'elopement,' as he called it. He maintained that you were in Baluchistan or some improbable place, spreading the gospel of Vasilov!"

They had arrived at the garden gate. He unlatched it and held it open for her. She did not enter immediately but turned around and looked back over the lawn. He stood beside her, gazing too. The stands that held the exhibits had been arranged so that they radiated from a central point. Everywhere the eye fell on fruits or flowers or men and women in bright clothes, all of it a garland wreathing itself about the saffron-colored tent that held the bull.

It struck him that Max really had an extraordinary sense of design. But the scene was too rich. There were too many fruits and flowers, too many bright-colored sweaters and slacks. He said: "It's like something by Benozzo Gozzoli, isn't it?"

"I don't know. . . . What breed are the cattle?"

"Red Poll. It's an old breed that's only recently become fashionable. In Tennessee we call them muley cows."

"Dual purpose?"

"Yes. We never drank the milk, but Yankees seem to like it."

77

Her eyes still roved over the lawn. A smile came on her lips and lingered there after she had closed them firmly.

"What are you smiling at?"

"I was thinking that this is the Feast of St. Eustace."

"What happened to St. Eustace after the stag turned at bay and he saw Christ crucified between its horns?"

"He refused to sacrifice to the pagan gods so they threw him and his family to the lions."

". . . who lay down and licked their feet?"

She nodded.

"What did they do after that?"

"They made a bull out of brass and shut them all up in it and burned them to death."

"That certainly made it nice!" he said, and after a moment: "When Vera is in Rome she goes to his church. She's fascinated by the antlers on top of it."

She passed before him through the gate into the garden. They walked a little way down the main path, then went down an alley between rows of Lombardy poplars. A golden retriever dashed out from behind one of the trees, almost colliding with them. "Down, Bob!" Claiborne said, and would have caught the dog's collar but he eluded him and ran on. "After woodchucks," Claiborne said.

"Have you got many?"

"That old orchard over there is full of them."

"I wish we had some of them!" she said.

"What an odd wish!" he said, but she had stopped and was contemplating the bronze statue planted at the end of the alley: a woman, a little larger than life, who seemed to be marching toward them, hands outstretched. "But that isn't St. Ciannic," she said.

"No. It's Pleyol's 'France.' Do you like it?"

"I don't know," she said.

He looked about the enclosure, remembering the day he had first caught sight of the statue, in the tiny garden of the aged sculptor's Mediterranean villa. It was only after they had left France that they had decided they must own it and had

78

cabled Joe Altieri, their dealer. Pleyol did not answer letters or telegrams. Joe had had to fly down to Cannes. The suspense seemed intolerable, and after the statue arrived there had ensued a period that was almost as painful. It had taken them weeks to decide where it would appear to the best advantage. They had had it over there against the south wall at first until he waked up one morning realizing that that would never do. It had taken ten men and a Mack truck equipped with a special hoist to move it to its present position. And after it was settled there he hadn't been certain that that was the place for it. But that had been a long time ago. He hadn't given the statue a conscious thought in months, years, in fact. She was asking him whether he liked it. "I don't know," he said vaguely. "I used to think about Pleyol a lot, but now . . . Here's something you *will* like—if you're like Vera."

He led her past the bronze statue into a smaller walk bordered by box. A wooden statue sat under a wooden arch in a vine-hung recess. If it had ever been painted all traces of paint had long since worn away. The wood from which the figure was carved was uniformly brown, crumbled away in places and everywhere riddled with wormholes. The saint, in a ragged gown, sat with his head inclined forward and one leg crossed over the other. The pedestal on which he sat was covered with ivy and one or two tendrils clambering up over his crossed leg hung waving from the hand—or part of a hand—that he stretched out to an object that rested against his knee.

"See what's left of the deer," Claiborne said, and bent and brushed the vines aside so that a round of wood that might have been a stag's curving antler revealed itself.

She bent and ran her hand over the worm-eaten round. "It *is* St. Ciannic!" she said. "Every time he sat down to read, a stag came and held his book in its antlers. Where did you find him?"

"Outside a church near Quimper," Claiborne said. "You could see pieces of the book when we first put him out here, but they've dropped off. Do you think he'd be better in-doors?"

"No," she said.

"We bought him for the deer. Vera is very fond of them. Of all animals. That is quite revealing, isn't it? Don't the psychologists say that when we have an excessive love for animals we are worshiping the animal in our own nature?"

"I don't know," she said. "There's an Italian proverb that says that the man who isn't kind to beasts will not be kind to Christians either."

Her eyes, fixed on his, had the same look that they had had a moment ago, only brighter. Their gaze seemed limitless. He felt as if he had been suddenly plunged into an element hitherto unknown. A voice said: *"Save me! You can!"* He spoke to cover the sound, saying the first thing that came into his head: "Tell me, is a Mass valid when celebrated by a drunken priest?"

She said: "The efficacy of the blood is so great that no imperfection on the part of the celebrant can affect it."

He heard himself laugh on a thin, high note. "Marcia says you have your own chapel. I suppose you have your own priest too. Do you get him off the Bowery?"

"They land there sometimes. Usually from drink."

"And would such a priest be allowed to say mass in your chapel?"

"That is a matter of discipline, not dogma. Father Emmett did not say mass for us until his health was restored."

She was turning away as if to go back the way they had come. He made a gesture indicating that they would reach the others faster if they went on the way they were going. She moved beside him in silence for several seconds, then said: "I have always wanted to thank you for what you did for me."

"I did something for *you?"* he said in surprise.

"Do you remember when I gave you the manuscript of my novel to read and you told me I had no talent for writing and I asked you what I should do? You said, 'Anything! Get drunk. Join the Church. . . .'" She laughed. "You said, *'Join the Church!'* "

"I spoke metaphorically, using the first words that came into my head."

"I know it," she said, and laughed again. "But that was the first time it had ever occurred to me that *I* could join the Church."

"The first time?"

"Oh, I had been reading the Church Fathers all that fall," she said. "We were so broke that we couldn't even buy Penguin books and George had *The Moralia* and St. Cyril of Jerusalem and St. Basil in a set of little green books. . . ."

"But you had never thought of joining the Church—until I uttered my *Tolle, lege!*"

"I had never realized that what they said applied to *me*—until that day."

"I remember now!" he said. "I met you at the Deux Magots. It was in the fall. But it was before the braziers had been lighted. Horne Watts came along and then I had to go on somewhere else and left you there with Horne. As I recall, you tried to fulfill the injunction to get drunk first. I came back past there two hours later and crossed over to the other side of the street for fear you and Horne would see me. You were both quite plastered. Had you been talking about the Church?"

"No. But I started instruction the next day. With a terrible hangover."

He shook his head. "There's something about you Catholics that beats me. . . . Always will, I suppose. . . . How did you happen to ask *my* advice about your novel?"

"Horne told me to."

"Horne!" he said. "I was a pretty bright boy in those days, but Horne—he had no mind. Just genius. Yes, I think you could say that he had genius. . . . As I remember, we spent a good deal of time sitting around deciding who had it and who didn't. Horne was everybody's candidate."

"I liked to read his poems even then," she said, "but I

81

didn't understand them. I have a friend who makes them plainer to me now."

"Who is it?"

"A nun. Sister Immaculata."

He stopped to stare at her. "I didn't know that nuns read Horne's poems."

"She'd like to meet you. She's writing a book about him and there are some questions she'd like to ask you about his life."

"I'd be delighted to meet her," he said, and laughed. "But tell me—after all, you've been around—how in the devil could one go about discussing Horne's life with a nun? Particularly one named Immaculata."

She laughed too. "We talk about him often," she said. "But she wants to talk to you too."

"Correspondence would be better," he said. "I don't think I could keep a straight face in her presence. Is her book critical or biographical?"

"She's making a comparison of the images in 'Pontifex' and the images in St. Catherine of Siena's *'Divino Dialogo.'* Do you suppose Horne had ever read the *'Divino Dialogo'?"*

He threw back his head, laughing again. "I know damn well he never did. I wish Horne could hear that he is being annotated by nuns. What do you suppose they see in him? Don't they know that he committed suicide? Suicide is a crime against Nature. So is homosexuality. Two major counts against him, according to your categories."

She was silent a moment, then she said: "He had love."

"Of what?"

"Of love."

"Love of love? I would have said that it was love of art. And love of liquor. Toward the last the love of liquor got the better of his love of art. He wouldn't have killed himself if he hadn't rotted his brain with liquor."

"He was trying to find God."

"By getting drunk every night."

"It was for love."

He shook his head. "You Catholics beat me," he said again. "Tell me, what did you do about George when you entered the Church?"

"I tried to get him to take me back. But he was already engaged to marry Marcia."

"But it was *you* who left him," he said. "If you hadn't left him he never would have married Marcia. It was *you* who catapulted him into 'adultry,' as our man here in the village names it. Doesn't your conscience ever hurt you? Or does your religion provide some way out of that?"

"I pray all the time," she said. "I have been praying to St. Ciannic this afternoon."

"To an old man who lived in the depths of a Celtic forest seven hundred years ago."

She turned her head to look at him and again that feeling of being immersed, of being slowly lifted and borne forward on a powerful, smoothly rolling tide came over him.

"He is more alive today than I am," she said.

He never knew what he would have answered, for she stepped back with a cry. The dog had leaped through a gap in the hedge, a grayish, coarsely furred object dangling from its mouth.

Claiborne started forward, calling out sharply to the dog. The dog jumped away but not before he had given his head a savage shake to one side. The woodchuck dropped from his grinning jaws to the ground. "He always breaks their necks," Claiborne said.

The dog stood, panting and looking from one to the other. The woman laid her hand on his head a second then knelt on the ground. The woodchuck's eyes were glazing. His rubbery lips, stretched wide, exposed his white, pointed teeth, his lolling tongue.

"Yes, he's dead," she said.

The dog pressed against her, still panting. She pushed him away with one hand and rose. "May I have it?" she asked.

"That woodchuck?"

"Yes."

He made her a little bow. "Certainly, if you will tell me what you propose to do with it."

"One of our old men makes a stew of them," she said, "and there are so few out on the Island."

"It must taste a little like possum," he said. "My colored friends in the South used to tell me how good possums were. Is your friend colored?"

"No," she said. "He's Norwegian. A Norwegian seaman. He's our carpenter. . . ."

"And eats what he can get?"

She laughed. "And lives in an old root cellar. He's very clever. He's raised the roof and put a window in. . . . We have half a dozen old buildings like that that we are going to make into hermitages."

"When you get the money?"

"For the lumber," she said. "Nils can do the work."

"I'll send you a check. . . . How many of these hermits have you got?"

"There's Nils and the baker and old Mr. Raumpfeld. He lives in the old goat house."

"And I suppose you go to market and buy leftover fish and horse meat and all that sort of thing?"

"Sometimes they give it to us. If we go when they are ready to close up."

"I bet the stuff stinks sometimes."

"Yes. . . . You will send the check, won't you?"

"Oh, yes," he said absently, eying the long shadows that the poplars were already casting across the sward. Before him had risen a vision of an interior he had once seen in Connecticut, one summer when he and Vera were visiting the Richardsons. Taking a path across the fields they had come upon a dilapidated barn standing at a little distance from one of those abandoned, crumbling foundations that are so common in New England. "The old Parcher house," Edith Richardson had said. "This must have been the front step. See! There's an old lilac bush growing beside it," and then led them past the ruined stones to the rotting, vine-covered stable. "Old

84

Jim Abbott lived here till three years ago," she said. "He was a hermit. You know, you often get a hermit along with any place you buy around here. . . . I suppose people have come and taken off anything that was worth having."

They entered the runway of the old stable. The hermit's horse had evidently occupied this antechamber. Chickweed had sprung up luxuriantly around a mound of his droppings. His collar and crupper still hung from a nail on the wall but the place where a wagon or a cart might have stood was empty. A woolen carriage robe that still showed a pattern of raw reds and greens lay in the dirt where it must have been flung three years ago. In the hermit's bedroom there was a rusted iron bed, which had no mattress, a deal table, two straight chairs, an old-fashioned Victrola cabinet, an old poker, and a broken shovel. A patchwork quilt that must once have covered the bed lay on the floor beside it. On top of the quilt lay a picture, a "crayon enlargement": a young woman with black hair, in a tight-fitting striped dress. Edith said that they must have a souvenir and took from the wall a chromo that simulated a sampler, with the legend GOD BLESS OUR HOME, in Old English lettering. As they were going back through the runway Vera gave a little cry. The hermit's hen house had been divided from his bedroom by only a wall. The rough, homemade ladder by which the hens had ascended to their roost was still in its place and on the ground, which was littered with the tiny, fluffy down that grows on the underparts of hens, lay an egg with its shell still unbroken.

Claiborne, as soon as he entered the stable, had sustained a shock of recognition. It had seemed to him a place he had been in before or a place toward which he had been traveling for a long time. The feeling of recognition was so strong that he had felt an ache in the pit of his stomach. He had moved restlessly about the room, eying the stained, rotting objects with passionate curiosity. He had felt himself impelled to lay his hand on some of the objects. They held, he felt, some secret that he was on the point of discovering. At the door he had turned back for one last look, asking himself: What is it? What was here? What is still here? and he had wished that he could send the others on about their business and stay here, in this falling shed, with the rusted bed and the feathers fallen from long-dead chickens and the picture of a forgotten woman and the crumbling horse dung.

Later, as he walked back across the fields with the others, a voice—the voice that spoke to him so often that, at times, his life seemed to him no more than a despairing dialogue with a companion, an opponent who would not, who could not, who could never even be imagined as ceasing to speak—that relentless voice had said: *"That is the way you'd like to live. That is the way you want to live!"* He had acknowledged the desire, telling himself, however, that it was only a passing fancy. It's the bugger in me, he had said to himself, walking in the twilight across the fields where no crops were ever planted, none harvested. This is the way I'd like to have it. This is the way we'd all like to have it if we could only find it.

His companion did not seem to notice that he had not spoken for several minutes. She had moved a little away and stood staring out at the wooded rim of the valley, visible here through a gap in the poplar branches.

"I'll go get you something to wrap the woodchuck in," he said, and went past the privet hedge and through the drying yard to the back of the house. A flagstone walk led from the kitchen door to the driveway. The station wagon that the servants used stood there with its motor running. There was no one in sight. He went slowly up the walk to the back door. He was seldom in this part of the grounds but he never came here without thinking how pleasant they were. A trellis of grapevines shielded the drying yard from sight. The huge beech tree that shaded the walk reminded him of the beech trees that grew on those sunken roads along which he used to cycle in Brittany.

The kitchen was empty. He stood in the middle of the red-tile floor, gazing first at shining metal sinks, then at rows

86

of white cupboard doors. He must have something to wrap the body in but he did not know where to find it. There was a light step on the other side of a closed door. A voice said: "Gelatin . . . and pepper corns. . . . What was that other thing?" and Freda, the waitress, pushed open the swinging door of the pantry, saw him and gave a little cry. "Mr. Claiborne! I didn't know it was you."

Claiborne said: "I want something—to wrap something up in."

She came closer, smiling. A pretty girl, with the same Irish coloring that Vera had. "What was it you wanted to wrap up, Mr. Claiborne?" she asked in her ordinary voice.

"A woodchuck," Claiborne said. "He's dead," he added.

She looked about her uncertainly, then raised her voice: "Have you got something to wrap a dead woodchuck in?"

"Dead woodchuck!" The answering voice was fuller, richer, more Irish. "What would you be wrapping it up for? Rodney'll take it off," and Alice, the cook, waddled in.

She made a gesture that sent Freda off on her errand and faced Claiborne, her hands on her hips. "And now, Mr. Claiborne, what is it you'll be wanting?"

"A newspaper or a paper sack—anything," Claiborne said.

Alice stepped heavily past him and pulling the gleaming handle of one of the drawers, disclosed a stack of brown oiled paper bags. "Would one of them do ye?"

"They're not big enough," Claiborne said.

She compressed her lips while her eyes roved over the shelves. "Mr. Claiborne, why don't you let Rodney take it off? He scoops them up on a shovel."

"It's for one of the ladies," Claiborne said. "She wants to take it home with her."

A gleam came into her little piggish eyes. She said: "The ladies! Is there anything they won't do these days?"

"It's for a friend of hers," Claiborne said. "He eats them."

She stood shaking her head to and fro a second, her eyes still gleaming, then disappeared into the pantry. She came back with a voluminous coarse white cotton sack. "I'll have to give ye one of my laundry bags. Will that do ye?"

"Nicely," Claiborne said. "Thank you, Alice." And he turned away but not before he heard her murmur: "Some kind of diet, do ye think?"

"Yes," he said, "some kind of diet," and hurried out of the room.

She was not in the place he had left her. He went past the Pleyol statue and back into the box-bordered walk. The big, gray-haired woman was kneeling on the matted ivy that surrounded St. Ciannic's wooden statue. Her eyes were fixed on the saint's down-bent head. Her lips formed inaudible words. Claiborne remembered that he had heard somebody say that Protestants prayed with their eyes shut but that Catholics prayed with their eyes open. On the heels of that came another thought: *It has been a long time since I have seen anybody pray.*

She did not turn around as he went toward her. Her lips did not cease to move. He thought that perhaps she had not heard him approaching and walked with a heavier tread. She continued to address the statue.

He came to a halt immediately behind her, gazed over her shoulder at the objects at which she was gazing: a bony forehead, sunken cheeks, a nose whose tip had been eaten off by worms, eye sockets that a child might have hacked out with a dull knife. He thought: *I would give anything to pray!*

She was rising from her knee, smiling. "I was praying for my daughter," she said.

He was silent. Then she said: "I never saw a statue of St. Ciannic before. I thought that I would like to pray to him."

"I don't blame you," Claiborne said. "When you think . . . what fools . . ." The sound of his own words made him realize the incoherence of his thoughts. "You must excuse me," he said, and taking his handkerchief out wiped the sweat from his brow. "You must excuse me," he said. "I am not well. . . . I don't sleep. . . . I mean . . ."

A long shadow was suddenly projected across the smooth

88

turf. Marcia Crenfew was coming toward them. "We are ready to start, Catherine," she called, and stopped, staring at Catherine, who had stooped and was sliding the dead woodchuck's body into the white sack. "What in the world have you got?"

Claiborne took the sack from Catherine and walked beside her to where Marcia stood. "It's a dead woodchuck," he said. "Catherine's taking it home to a friend of hers. He's on a peculiar diet."

FIVE

Claiborne met his wife on his way back to the tents. They spent the next hour exchanging good-byes with guests. Miranda and Tim Proctor, who had driven over from Long Island for the day, were the last to leave. Tom and Vera walked with them to the gate, where they were still talking when Vera was called to the house to answer the telephone. She had not returned by the time the Proctors left. Claiborne strolled back to the tents and had a last drink with the musicians while they packed their instruments and then spent another half-hour directing the servants in the removal of litter before he ascended the stairs and entered his wife's room.

There was no answer to his knock. He pushed the door open. He could hear water running. The next moment she called to him from the bathroom: "Are they all gone?"

"Every last one."

"Jack the Bear too?"

"Jack the Bear too," he said, and walked into the bathroom. She was lying on her back in a tub so full of water that her narrow body, brown except for a girdle of white at breasts and loins, swayed to and fro on a miniature tide. She grinned

89

when she saw him. "I *was* coming back, and then I looked out of the window and they were already in the car and I thought I'd just grab a bath. You didn't mind, did you, darling?"

"No," he said, and stooped to kiss her mouth while she put a dripping hand up to touch his cheek. They were in the habit of caressing each other many times a day, whenever they met, it occurred to him now as he turned to the bowl and, while he let water run over his hands, gave his reflection the same earnest gaze he always gave it when he encountered it in a mirror.

The upper part of her body also was reflected in the mirror. He became aware that her eyes, too, were fixed on his face. She had actually turned a little on one side, as if the better to observe him. The last rays of the sun coming in through the window fell on her bronzed shoulders glistening with water. Her eyes glistened too. He had sometimes thought of her eyes as shedding a soft light—but it seemed to him now that they held a steely glint. It was doubtless the reflections from the water that made them glisten like that. The brownness of the face was, as it were, cleft by that line of steely blue —as if a slave stood, holding a sword in his upraised hands. Her eyes are *too* blue! he thought.

She was opening her lips to speak. He said hastily: "Sorry they stole your show like that."

Her brows contracted a little. "My show?" she asked.

"That heifer of Marengo's."

"Did you think she was better than Bud's Best Girl?"

"Lord, no. . . . But her being there at all rather put Bud in the shade."

She looked away. "I didn't mind that," she said.

"I'm glad you didn't mind," he said, and waited a moment and when she did not say anything else finished drying his hands and went back into the bedroom. It occurred to him that he might bathe and change into fresh clothes, but he felt a disinclination for effort of any kind. He looked vaguely about the room. An armchair was pulled up near his wife's dressing table. He sat down in it. The white linen dress she

90

had been wearing had been thrown over the back of the chair. The ornaments she had worn with it—heavy silver bracelets and a necklace that matched them—were tumbled in a heap on the dressing table. Something brown, glinting under one of the bracelets, caught his eye. He reached over and picked up a small, bronze medal, not much bigger than a ten-cent piece. The medal was not on a chain. Vera pinned it somewhere to her dress. She had worn the medal, night and day, for twenty years. It had been sent to her by her old nurse, Léontine, who was convinced that she had been cured of cancer by a pilgrimage made to the Black Virgin of Notre-Dame du Port at Clermont, a pilgrimage that he and Vera had made—for he had made the pilgrimage too, though reluctantly.

Vera was calling to him from the bathroom. She wanted to know if he had had any talk with "that inseminator man."

"No," he said.

"Well, I did. I told him that I thoroughly disapproved of his program and that I was going to see Mr. Laird personally and remonstrate with him. Tom, they do terrible things to bulls."

"What things?"

"Keep them penned up all the time and give them things."

"To stimulate them sexually?"

"Yes, and they never *see* a cow! I'm going to try to get the S.P.C.A. to do something about it. Don't you think that something ought to be done?"

"Yes," he said absently. "Bulls have it tough. We must all rally around." He got up and walked over to Vera's desk where a picture of old Léontine stood, a snapshot that Vera had taken when she was fourteen years old and the old woman around seventy: a lean, old peasant woman with high cheekbones and deep accusing eyes, backed up against the south wall of an ancient farmhouse in the Auvergne. Léontine Dedonne, at seventy, stood straighter than many a thirty-year-old woman of that savage region. That was because she had lived a third of her life away from it. She might have stayed in the Vincents' service all her life if her brother had not died and left her heir to what is still riches in the Auvergne: an acre of land, a farmhouse, a barn, a cow, six goats. The place was called La Tuilerie, the roof being made of tiles rather than of slate as is customary in that region. The road that ran past the door took its name from the farm: Le Chemin de la Tuilerie.

There was a smaller photograph beside old Léontine's: the south portal of the ancient church of Notre-Dame du Port at Clermont. He and Vera had had their first quarrel on the steps of that church. He corrected himself. That was the second quarrel they had had. They were regarded by their friends—by people, damn it, who knew them only by name —as an unusually devoted couple. The truth was that they had started quarreling almost immediately after their marriage, as soon, that is, as they had recovered the amount of consciousness necessary to stage a quarrel. Everybody at the wedding had been blind, of course, but he had carried with him throughout the afternoon the conviction that he was no blinder than the rest, if anything a little less blind. The conviction had not been shared by the family chauffeur. One of his last impressions of the wedding was of himself, with Vera seated beside him, looking out from their dark shelter at seamed cheeks, staring blue eyes, a pendulous moving lip: old Denis was begging permission to drive them. They must have driven off and left him still talking.

The drive had doubtless been as wild a one as either of them had ever had. Instead of driving along the Corniche they had headed for the mountains. During the night—he could never remember when or where—he had realized that the woman beside him had for some time been saying the same thing over and over: that she did not want to go to Antibes. He had pulled off to the side of the road to have his hands free, so to speak, for the quarrel that was impending. "What you mean is that you don't want to go with me?" But she would only weep and say that she didn't want to go on the cruise. "Why didn't you say so before?" Whereat she only wept more. That was the worst of Vera: she could never tell you what was in her mind, could only show you—often by a dumb show of resistance against something that had been proposed—what she really wanted. They had had to sit talking God knows how long on a lonely country road, in a darkness broken only by the fitful illumination each face received when a cigarette was lighted, before he found out what was troubling her: she had been informed only a few days before that old Léontine was stricken with cancer.

"Why didn't you say so?" he demanded again, and headed for the mountains. They had lost their way a dozen times in the dark, of course, and they had finally put up for the night —their wedding night!—in a small roadside inn. It was afternoon the next day when they struck the old, rutted road that led to La Tuilerie. The sick woman was alone in the house when they arrived. Marie, the old-maid daughter who tended her, had walked to the village to see if she could find a neighbor who would care for her mother while she went to take charge of her sister's household—the sister, who had four small children, had that morning gone to a hospital in Clermont for an emergency operation for appendicitis. Vera offered to stay overnight with her old nurse. It had been his task to drive Marie to her sister's house in Pradelles.

It was dusk when he got back. A gnarled old apple tree grew at the north end of the house. He had sat on a bench beside a stone table while Vera made the old woman ready for the night. Along the garden wall the chestnuts that grow to such prodigious size in that volcanic soil stood like gigantic fans, bronze colored against a rosy sky. The sun dropped out of sight. The chestnut trees turned black. He fetched a bottle of wine from the car. They ate soup, rye bread, salad, and cheese off the stone table. The moon came up before they had finished eating. The garden, which had lain in plumey shadow, glittered with light. But along the wall, under the chestnut boughs, the shadows were still black. They had walked past beds of lilies to lie there in the shadow of the wall with the black plumes of shadow hiding them.

Later that night they had gone into the house, to the small bedroom Marie had made ready for them. But the house was so permeated by the odors of the sick woman's rotting body that they had not been able to stay inside and had taken the mattress from the huge old bed and had laid it down under one of the trees. When the sun rose they carried it back into the house on tiptoe (Vera said that Léontine and, for that matter, Marie, would not have understood how they could have risked such a valuable possession in the night damps) and had gone to bathe in the little river that ran through the meadow. A few willows had been allowed to grow up along its banks. There was one pool up to his waist. When they came out and sat down on the bank to dry, a goose hissed at them. A little way off a boy, tending the rest of the flock, gazed at them curiously. He was one of the twenty-four children of the next neighbor, Pierre Tardieu, Vera said. The people in that region have names ending in "donne" or "dieu" when they are not derived from some portion of the anatomy of a cow, hog, or sheep. There was one neighbor, who was named "Bladder."

He knew himself for a true provincial, country bred for many generations. For him the measure of a mile would always be the distance between Eupedon and Sycamore, spring began when the redbud bloomed, a river was always larger or smaller than West Fork. He had been amused and a little touched to find that Vera had the same feeling for this ancient, crumbling farmhouse in the Auvergne. Léontine Dedonne had evidently gained an ascendancy over Margot soon after she entered her service. One year when there was an epidemic of fever on the Riviera, Léontine had persuaded Margot that *l'air des montagnes lui ferait du bien,* and every summer after that the young Vincents had repaired to the old farmhouse, much as children from New York slums may return year after year to the farm on which they encountered their first cow.

He had not been so much amused when he learned how Vera proposed that they should spend what was, after all, just the second day of their married life: in a visit to the cathedral town of Clermont.

The old woman was too ill to receive him but Vera had gone in to see her immediately after breakfast and had come out wearing on her face that hunted—no, *haunted*—look that he was to come to know so well. Old Léontine was convinced that she would recover if she could be sprinkled with water from the shrine of the Black Virgin at Clermont.

"Well, tell the Father to get some and sprinkle her," he said, but she only looked at him.

He had heard Margot and the others laughing about the piety that Vera had manifested as a child under old Léontine's influence and had liked to think that traces of it still lingered in her. But he *had* been looking forward to the cruise. It was eight o'clock and they had a hard day's driving before them if they were to join the Mortons at the time appointed. He had inquired sensibly and, it seemed to him, sympathetically enough, why everybody's wishes couldn't be gratified: a messenger could be dispatched to Clermont for the holy water and Vera could pray as earnestly for her old nurse at the first church they came to on the road.

She said that he might go on to join the Mortons if he wished. As for her, she was going to Clermont. There had been nothing for him to do but accompany her. They had driven the twenty miles in silence. He had been so angry, at first, that he did not trust himself to speak. Later he had become absorbed in watching the countryside unfold. It was no day, and he was in no mood, certainly, for *tourisme,* but he thought that he had never seen such a country, so tumultuous in outline that the mountains and valleys seemed to have been cast down by angels—or devils—in some tremendous play, the horizon itself a chain of extinct craters, the very meadows springing out of lava, and shadowed everywhere by the rocky mounds which seemed to have emerged from the earth to provide bases for the churches that crowned them.

They separated in the Place de Jaude. He saw her walking toward the cathedral and took it for granted that it was her destination, drove on to view Pascal's birthplace, spent a half-hour there and spent another half-hour conscientiously lounging along the Rue de Gras before he mounted the steps of the cathedral, and paced up and down the nave God knows how long—long enough, anyhow, to come to feel himself one of the motes revolving in the great wheels of color that the east windows cast on the harsh stone. Then an asthmatic little sacristan sidled up to him to whisper: *"La dame serait p't'être à l'autre Notre-Dame."*

He had a hard time finding the "other Notre Dame," in a hollow below the cathedral and so shut in by ancient, brownish-black houses and crooked side streets that you would think that Clermont wished to conceal its existence. He went in through the south portal, the same door through which prince and prelate, knight, priest, and monk crowded after Godefroi de Bouillon to confirm at the shrine of the Black Virgin the vow to free Christ's sepulcher while Peter the Hermit's cry of *"Dieu le veut!"* still rang in the *place* outside. A little nun was coming out of the crypt, duster in hand. He descended the winding stairs and found Vera kneeling before the image whose black wooden face can easily be thought of as on occasion wetting itself with tears, in a gloom made luminous only by tapers that, flickering before the altar, struck light off the marble tablets lettered in gilt that express thanks for heavenly favors and the gold and silver hearts that hang in neat rows on Romanesque columns painted to resemble the imitation marble of cheap restaurants.

She was so absorbed in her prayers that she did not know he was there. He had to kneel beside her before she acknowledged his presence by turning and dimly smiling at him. It seemed to him that she smiled at him only because he was kneeling beside her, and he was angered; she should have known that he was ready to bend the knee at any shrine that man had ever set up: Christian, Buddhist, Hindu, Mohammedan. He found some good in all of them—but he did not care to spend the whole day on his knees. They exchanged some sharp words as soon as they had emerged from the gloom of the church into the sunlight, and doubtless would have exchanged more if they had not had to hurry on to the hotel to telephone the Mortons. But the big modern hotel had provided them with a perfect omelet and an excellent *galantine de veau*. They were drinking *vin blanc mousseux* on the terrace when Vera looked off toward the Puy de Dome and said dreamily that she would like to live there, always, and he looked off too, and at one o'clock post meridiem, Baedeker in hand, saw flames spill over the lip of the old crater until the whole horizon was one fiery ring in which gigantic shapes moved among heaving mounds, rocky crags, columns of granite or black basalt tossed in air, and knew that the fires that had shaped that whole country were still raging underground and thought of the man whose birthplace he had just quitted, the man who, for many years, carried on his person the secret message—addressed to himself?— beginning: *"Feu . . . Feu . . ."* and knew that he could not stay in that place any longer and getting to his feet, so suddenly that his wine spilled over the table's edge onto the floor, told her that he was driving to Antibes immediately and that she could go along if she liked.

Neither of them had realized it at the time, but it was probably on that drive to Antibes that the idea of returning to his native land to live had first entered his head. It had been a long time, though, before he said anything to Vera about it. When he announced to her that he wanted to return to the United States to live, she had made no objection. . . . Well, here they were.

There was a flowery fragrance in the air. Vera had come out of the bathroom and was moving about behind him. She said: "Don't you think Cynthia has changed?"

"You know, I can't remember what she was like before."

"She's more—open, somehow. . . . I suppose it's because she's more sure of herself."

"Has some psychiatrist been making her over?"

"No. I think it's success. This is the first success she's had in her life, really."

"What with?"

She laughed. "Heavens! It's your doing. Don't you remember those poems I showed you last spring and the translations from Ausonius? You said you thought they were good."

"There was something about the poems I didn't like," he said, "but they were well written and certainly worth printing. And the translation from Ausonius was first-rate. I sent them to Bob Waite for *Spectra*. As I recall, he took several of them."

"He's taken three others. Poems, I mean, not translations. She's going to have lunch with him one day soon."

"Soon? How long is she going to stay with us?"

"Not any longer than we want her," she said in a hurt tone. "She's got an apartment rented in New York."

"But her husband's got a job in Wisconsin."

She did not answer. He looked at her sharply. "Look here, have you been encouraging her to leave her husband?"

She shook her head.

"Is she going to leave him?"

"She wrote me a month ago that she couldn't stand it any longer and was coming to New York."

"On the strength of publishing a few poems in *Spectra!* That's rather risky, Vera. You know what Bob can afford to pay."

"*Spectra's* not the only magazine."

"And she's a smart girl. Got some talent too. Oh, I suppose she'll make out—particularly if you stake her."

Tears had come into her eyes. "Why *shouldn't* I stake her? She hasn't got anybody else to help her. I think it's mean of you. Really, I do." She bent and childishly wiped her eyes on the sleeve of her dressing gown.

"It's your money," he said, and got up and went toward her. "I'm sorry, darling."

She flung her arms about his neck. "It's all right. I know you didn't mean it."

"Lord, no. I don't care what the girl does."

"But, darling, I *want* you to care. She's got some things she wants you to read. You will read them, won't you?"

"Sure," he said.

Her arms tightened about his neck. "Take your bath in here. I'll turn the water on now."

He shook his head. "I'm too tired."

"Too tired to *bathe?*"

He laughed. "I wish I had your faith in the restorative powers of water!"

She laughed too. Vera's fondness for bathing was a household joke. She believed that immersing one's body in water stimulated the brain's workings. He had once come upon her lying in the tub, holding her farm ledger in her hands.

She dropped down on the arm of his chair and put her arms about his neck again. "But, darling, it will rest you. Really, it will."

"I'm bushed, I tell you," he said, half angry again. "My God! You've been up here soaking yourself while I was wrestling with that mob. No wonder you're not tired."

Her arms fell from about his neck. Her body drew a little away from his. She clasped her hands in her lap. But she stayed poised on the arm of the chair. "I was up in Aunt Virginia's room for a while," she said, "and then the Rogers wanted to see the cow barn and I took them there and after that Mrs. Andrews wanted to see Max's herb garden but I couldn't find him so I had to show it to her. . . . I suppose I should have sent somebody else with them. But there were so many people."

He laughed on a kinder note. "There were so many people it didn't make any difference what anybody did."

She was silent, staring at her clasped hands. "Were there too many people?" she asked finally in a subdued voice.

"Hell, no!" he said. "If I'm going to have 'em I'd rather

have a lot of 'em than a few. Then you don't have to pay any attention to them."

She stood up and moved to the dressing table and began brushing her short, black hair. "I wish you'd told me," she said, still in the same subdued voice.

"Told you what?"

"That you didn't want me to have the party."

He stood up too. "You know perfectly well," he said, "that that kind of party bores me stiff. But that's not any reason for you not to have 'em. My God . . ."

He stopped speaking, his attention arrested by a small sound. He could see her eyes in the mirror. They had been fixed on his face but now she was looking away as if she had just heard somebody else call to her. The sound he had heard was the brush being laid down on the dresser, slowly and carefully, and as noiselessly as possible. She was leaning forward, staring straight before her, frowning a little as if in an effort to hear better. But there had been no sound in the room except his own voice and the minute sound of the brush striking against the glass top of the dressing table. What other voice was she listening to? What could it be telling her?

He felt his lips stiffly framing a smile. "Hell, darling! You don't have to give up all your pleasures just because I hate my fellow men."

As he spoke he took a few steps toward the door. He had not reached it before she came to him, so swiftly that the white robe she was wearing was slipping from her shoulders as she put her arms about his neck and pressed her body against his. "You *don't!*" she whispered.

"Don't what?" he asked, automatically tightening his arms about her.

"Hate your fellow men."

"No," he said wearily, "but I get damn tired of 'em."

Again he felt her body grow tense and draw a little away from his before she tightened her arms about his neck. "Is anything the matter?" she whispered.

He was silent a moment then he said: "I'm not able to work. But that's been going on for a long time."

The tenseness left her body. She pressed herself closer against him. "I mean really the matter," she said, still in a whisper.

He laughed. "That's enough to make me hard to live with."

She threw her head back so that her face was turned up to his. Her eyes looked into his mournfully. "I wish I could help you."

He laughed again. "You can't. Nobody can."

"But I want you to be happy!"

"I'm not of a happy temperament, like you," he said, and bent and set his lips hard against hers. But she still clung to him, pressing her face now against his shoulder. "You could be!" she whispered. "I *know* you could be!"

"All right, I *will* be!" he said, and caught her to him in one more swift embrace before he hurried from the room.

SIX

Molly and Ed Archer had come back for dinner. Cynthia sat on Claiborne's right; Max was across the table from her. There was a vacant place beside Vera. Robin Vincent, who would occupy it, had not yet arrived.

The mulatto butler, Gershon, stepped quietly about the table, proffering broiled chickens on a bed of wild rice, *tomates provençales,* the last lettuce from the garden, and poured Chablis into crystal glasses. Claiborne, as soon as they settled at Blencker's Brook, had imported an old playmate from Tennessee to fill the post of butler. Molly Archer had predicted that they would have trouble with him. A friend of hers, a woman farmer, had had to get rid of her Viennese

101

butler. Two years on the farm had made him feel that his calling was unmanly. He was always out at the stables instead of attending to his duties in the house. Claiborne had assured her they need have no worry on that score: Gershon had no desire to get out "to the field"; he had been born and bred a house servant. "My own third cousin, damn it!" he had exclaimed in a moment of irritation. As for getting along with the women servants, he had maintained that he had never seen the woman, black or white, that Gershon couldn't get along with.

Claiborne looked at his wife. She had put on a fresh white dress, but she had not put on any make-up and she had not taken time to brush her hair. She said that that was the advantage of having it naturally curly. But she was forever washing it, often under a tap in the stable lot. "Oh, my God," she would say, "I must wash my hair this minute," and off she would go and hold her head under that tap till all the lather was washed away, when she would rise up and, shaking herself like a dog coming out of water, start in helping Rodney do something he could do better by himself, lazy and inefficient as he was.

They were talking about Catherine Pollard. "I *like* her," Vera said. "She thought Bud was wonderful. But you know, I don't think I'd have recognized her. She isn't a bit the way she used to be."

"The torso's not the same," Max said, "but she's still got that look in the eye."

"What kind of look has she got in her eye, Max?" Vera asked.

"Oh, a bit *pazza,* but awfully *beanina.* She's just as full of beans as she ever was. . . . You know, I may give her my 'Vision of St. Eustace.' She remembered it from the old days. You know, she really likes that picture!"

"I always go to San Eustachio's church when I'm in Rome," Vera said. "It's got antlers on top of it. . . . Why do you suppose I'm so crazy about deer?"

"Marce'll get you off by yourself some time and tell you

all about *that*," Max said. "Vera, what did you think of the Lathrop boy's gourds?"

"I thought they were simply divine, Max. All those fruits and flowers."

"I got the idea from Marcia's collection," Max said modestly. "Garlands that the Pambas—I mean the *Upper* Pambas —tattoo on their enemy skulls in the long tropic evenings."

Cynthia laughed a little and said, "Pambas . . ."

She would have liked to join in the conversation—you could tell that by the taut yet eager way in which she held her body, the smile she kept on her face. But how could she? She didn't speak the language. It was a "little" language that they had been building up, now in one country, now in another, over a period of years. Half French, half Italian, or English words with French endings, or mispronunciations that time had endeared to them—people were never gauche but gauché; some friend of Max's had made that slip years ago and it had gone into the language. George Crenfew's colloquialisms were embedded in it too, and his wife's psychological jargon. A favorite sport was to "talk Marcian" with Marcia herself. Max never tired of that. He said it helped the vector of his reality stress to adjust. He had an odd, self-flagellating sense of humor. This summer he had discovered a new diversion: planting in his conversation from time to time references to the supposed homosexuality of some great man. Confucius, Isaac Newton, Thomas Babington Macaulay, Commodore Perry, Marco Polo—every man who had ever lived was grist for that mill, provided he was famous enough. Up to date Max regarded John Donne as his greatest triumph. As a result of his allusions, Marcia had read all of Donne's sonnets on sacred love as well as the elegies on profane love. He said that he expected to get her started on the sermons before snow fell.

Cynthia was asking if the Pambas were head-hunters.

"Only the heads of their hereditary enemies," Max said. "A Mugwumboo may paddle his canoe right past their huts. But let a Dunaboo show his head!"

"Do they always tattoo the heads after they have taken them?"

"They will try to tattoo any portion of the body, though there are some spots that so far have baffled them. Nipples . . ."

He emitted the word "nipples" with a little clucking sound. In a few minutes he would be describing the difficulties the Pambas confronted when they attempted to tattoo genital organs; Max could not talk five minutes without making some reference to sex. Had he always been like that?

He could not remember, but he did remember distinctly the first time he had ever seen Max Shull: slim, not more than twenty years old, walking past the Café Select in a dark cape that reached to his heels, his hands clasped in front of him in a modest, almost maidenly gesture. Horne Watts had walked beside him. Horne's hand had lain heavily on Max's shoulder, his round, lowering, rubicund face bent over Max. He had been talking earnestly. What about? Claiborne wondered. Horne's gestures had been those of one trying to persuade; Max's bearing that of one who might be won. But Max was already won. He and Horne were living together in that studio on Deux Anges when he himself came on the scene. In those days Max had taken himself seriously as a painter. A Cubist when he first knew him, later on he became a Vorticist, fond of quoting Ezra Pound's dictum to the effect that the directions which forces take in time and space "are more important than light falling on a haystack." I wonder if they are, Claiborne thought wearily. If he had not started up from his café table and hurried over to greet Horne, whom he recognized from a photograph Horne had sent him, Max might not be sitting here now, talking about the Pambas.

Or would he? Max and Vera would probably have got together somehow. They had liked each other from the start and now it was hard to imagine one without the other. If they were separated from each other as much as two days they rushed together like children to tell what had happened. He had not even known that Bud was ready to stand until Max mentioned it one day. "But darling, I never *dreamed* you'd be interested!" Vera said. I wouldn't, either, he thought. I wouldn't give a damn if he'd never been born, much less stood. . . . Was it because he was the kind of man he was that his wife had to have a fellow like Max around? Once, at a party, he had come near knocking down a fellow who had referred to Max as the "Claiborne clown" and had been prevented only by realizing, drunk as he was, what a fool that would have made him look. . . . Was it he, not Max, who was the "Claiborne clown"?

Max had been living in a squalid flat on Barrow Street for two months that year that everybody, even die-hard ex-patriates like Polly and Barry Craig, came back from France (Polly's new husband and Barry's new wife, and Polly's and Barry's children and Barry's children by his first wife, and even a small baby that Polly had contrived to have by her new husband, all on the same plane). He had driven out with the Claibornes to look at this place.

Max had an eye for places. For ten or fifteen minutes he paced about the house without saying a word, then stopped in the square front hall to say succinctly: "This is it, children. You're fools if you don't snap it up."

They had gone through the front door into the garden: grown wild but it was still a sight to behold that first spring, the grass all littered white with petals from the cherry trees and the wistaria in bloom everywhere.

They had followed the path to the little brick house at the end of the garden. Both doors were off their hinges and most of the window lights were broken, but the walls were in line, the beautiful, rose-colored handmade brick crumbling in only a few places. There was a big square room, a floor of oak planks at least a foot wide, and two smaller rooms behind that. He had known what Vera was going to say while her hand was still describing the rectangle in the air. "You could have a north light there."

He had hardly dared to look at Max's face. The poor fellow had stood there—not as plump as he was now, but already thickening about the middle so that he no longer cut the figure he once cut in evening dress. He had stood there, his hands hanging at his sides and, slowly, as if the very air might turn hostile if disturbed by too sudden a movement, had raised his head, saying in a low voice: "A north light . . ."

"Yes," she said. "It would make a fine studio, wouldn't it, Tom?" and she had given him that look that she gave him so often in those days, that she still sometimes gave him.

Max had given him a look too. There was no pleading in it. It was more the look that a bird, disturbed on its nest, or an animal come upon suddenly in its lair, might give you. The fellow had a kind of manliness: you had to hand it to him. He had kept his face impassive and yet he must have been taking into account all the objections to his occupying the little house which at that moment were running through Claiborne's head. He had taken them into account and refused to minimize them by word or look. There was only his glance, that intent watchfulness of the bird or beast waiting to know whether you would deal it life or death.

He had heard himself saying heartily: "Sure. Make a fine studio for you, Max. Better grab it before somebody else gets it."

Max had replied that the prospect was, indeed, attractive, and that he would think it over. Claiborne had realized then that Max was not going to take advantage of Vera's innocence. He was going to give him, Claiborne, time to warn her. He would have to be convinced that both of them really wanted him there before he would take over the house.

The next day Claiborne had told Vera that he thought it might, after all, be inadvisable to have Max living in the little house in the garden. "There's a side to his life that you don't know much about."

"Oh, but I do," she said. "I've always known." Then she

laughed. "I don't, though, really. I've always wondered what they *do*."

"Damn it!" he said finally. "The fellow goes to parties— 'drags' they call them—done up in white satin."

"Poor thing!" she said. "He's too fat to wear white satin."

A few days later she told him that she had had a long "frank" talk with Max and that Max had given her his word of honor that if he became the occupant of the little house in the garden he would never have any "drags" there. "And he says he doesn't wear evening gowns any more," she added.

He could only stare at her. "You win!" he said.

Well, she had won—on the whole. When Max came to live in the cottage he apparently severed connections with his "gay" friends, or, if he continued to see them, saw them only in town. It was true that he was sometimes absent for days, even weeks, at a time. But as far as Claiborne knew with any certainty, he had "slipped" only once since he had come to live at Blencker's Brook. A few years ago a mysterious telephone call had come after Max had been absent for several days. Claiborne, suspecting that he was in trouble, had hurried to the address given him by the unidentified voice and had found Max in a cheap hotel off Times Square, considerably bruised and shaken as the aftermath of an evening given over to his old pursuits. He had insisted on staying on at the Hotel Hibiscus till his injuries had had time to heal, and he was very desirous that Vera should not know of his "slip." Claiborne had promised that she should never know it from him and had kept his word.

Robin Vincent had now come in and sat down beside Vera. Cynthia was trying to talk to him across the table. Robin smiled politely and went on eating chicken. Claiborne caught Gershon's eye and beckoned to him to refill his glass. It seemed important that he should have more wine quickly. He knew now how Robin had looked when he parachuted to the earth. His hands would have been moving, slipping the silk this way and that, but his knees would have been drawn

107

up under him, and the face out of which his eyes stared straight ahead would have been so expressionless that it might have served for a burial mask. Like those mummies they bury with their knees drawn up under them, Claiborne thought, only he's still up and walking around, and he leaned a little farther forward, staring. Robin evidently felt himself observed. He looked up, eyed Claiborne, then, without any change of expression, looked down at his plate.

Claiborne glanced at his wife. Her face was deeply flushed, her eyes moist and mutinous. Ed Archer, sitting beside her, stopped talking and looked about the table, a little smile tugging at the corners of his lips, before he turned back to Vera. Claiborne listened and distinguished phrases. Ed had stopped by the Hesses' on his way over here and had found both brother and sister excited over another new "process" which the inseminator had revealed to them. Hogs this time. A method by which pigs were taken away from the sows as soon as they were born and brought up on cow's milk.

"But if you do that the pigs won't get any colostrum," Vera said. "They get colostrum in mother's milk. Every newborn creature has to have it."

"Joe's thinking that maybe we've been overemphasizing the virtues of mother's milk," Ed said.

"Oh, *no!*" Vera said earnestly. "And you say they breed the sows immediately after farrowing. That *can't* be good for a sow, Ed."

"Oh, it makes an old lady out of a sow in no time," Ed said.

"It's wicked!" Vera cried. "I'm going to talk to Joe."

"You'll find Joe a hard nut to crack," Ed said. "Joe's all for science. Joe's the farmer of the future, all right."

I wouldn't mind his kidding her, Claiborne thought, if she didn't fall for it every damn time! You'd think she was born yesterday. He said aloud: "Joe Hess isn't a farmer. He's an alchemist."

Ed looked up at this.

He always wants to know what I think. Makes him nervous if he doesn't know what I think about something. "An alchemist," he said in the same loud voice. "Hell, he makes no bones about it! What's that hex sign he's got on his barn but an alchemical symbol? *Prima materia,* in the form of a globe, weighed down by the crescent moon. Joe's in league with the Powers of Darkness. His farm isn't a farm. It's a chemical retort."

"Minta's the one I feel sorry for," Molly said. "She does just as much work in the dairy as he does, and the housework too. And they *could* afford help."

"She's his *soror mystica,*" Claiborne said. "He couldn't bear to turn loose all that free labor, so he hexed her on her wedding night—she was back home the next day."

"It's a fact," Max said, his eyes sparkling. "She stayed with Elmer Carfax just one night. I've often heard Joe say she was home in time to milk the next morning. Joe says he sometimes wonders what Elmer done to her."

Ed laughed. "What sort of mixture is Joe trying to shake up in his retort, Tom?"

"The same thing the achemist is always after," Claiborne said. "Something for nothing. Joe's bad enough, but he's got a pal that's an even bigger rascal. 'My Pen Pal,' Joe calls him. Lives out west. Up in our attic at Eupedon there were a lot of old letters from Thomas Jefferson. He and my great-uncle Jeems used to write back and forth about a fertilizer formula Uncle Jeems worked on all his life. They were for putting fertility back into the soil. Uncle Jeems drove all over Tennessee and Kentucky, buying up the carcasses of animals and treating 'em with sulphuric acid. But these bastards are set to rob the very earth! Joe's Pen Pal has been planting corn in the same field for five years and getting forty bushels to the acre. He claims he can keep on doing it if he only turns under enough each year."

"And can't he?" Ed asked.

"No, he can't."

"How do you know, Tom?"

"It's one of those things I was born knowing," Claiborne

said, "and if you weren't born knowing it you'll never know it."

"Eupedon science," Ed said. "Straight from the Eupedon lab."

"That's right," Claiborne said. *Some of these days I'm going to take Ed Archer out and beat the living daylights out of him. I could do it. I'm bigger than he is—even if he does keep in better condition.*

"Suppose you did," the Voice said. "What then?"

"I'd have the pleasure of socking him, that's what."

"Where would you sock him?"

"In the kidney. Or the groin."

"You're that kind of fighter?"

"Sure. Every man is."

"And after you'd socked him?"

"I'd put him on his back, and I'd say, 'Take that, Ed Archer, you . . .'"

"Hit him when he was down? After punching him in the groin?"

"Sure, and if he put that look on his face and opened his mouth . . ."

"You'd hit him again? But you couldn't spend the rest of your life hitting him. What would he say when you stopped?"

"He'd say I punched him because he was kidding my wife."

"Is that the reason?"

"It's one of the reasons. I'd punch him because he's Ed Archer, that's why."

"Who is Ed Archer?"

"You know that better than I do."

The Voice fell silent. He could silence it sometimes, with a remark like that. He looked about the table cautiously. They were all madder than he—he had no doubt of that—but it was hardly likely that they heard as many voices, or rather, that they heard one voice so often. It was always one voice. *I wouldn't mind it so much if there were more than one voice,* he thought—*or would I?* Vera was looking at him meaningfully. There was something she wanted him to do. He turned to the girl beside him.

"Vera tells me you've made more translations from Ausonius?"

Her eyelids fluttered and went shut. Her head jerked a little to one side, while the muscles of her mouth drew slightly downward. She said, "Yes, the one everybody tries . . . the one about the roses."

"I tried the nineteenth epistle once," he said.

A brightness came over her face. "Oh, may I see it?"

He shook his head. "I don't know where it is," but even as he spoke he had the feeling of entering a familiar, a secret place which he had not visited in a long time. . . . A house full of dark wood, a spring wind blowing in through the tall windows. . . . Old Pauncefort always held his seminars in his study in the spring term. He would still be in his dressing gown when you got there, but his beard would shine like silver. He gave you a glass of port while he drank his coffee. That day he had a heap of translations before him when his eye glanced down and fixed the paper that lay beside the heap. He put the paper he held in his hand down and picked mine up and read it through slowly twice before he read it to the class. I can't even recite the Latin now and all of my translations have gone out of my head, except lines he liked:

> Receive this prayer, this cry,
> Divine Boeotian Muse,
> Call the bard back with Latin song. . . .

"Felicitous, Gentlemen, I think we may say that this is truly felicitous. . . ." When you are young you think you have a lot coming to you. To be middle aged is to look back and realize that a moment like that—when some old codger puts his head on one side and seems to see you for the first time —is one of the best you'll get. Old Pauncefort had a fellowship fixed up for me at the American School in Athens, but the war ruined that and then Uncle Robert died and I came into that bit of money and went to Paris instead. . . .

His wife was calling to him. "You don't think so, either, do you, Tom?"

But he could not answer her for the spate of words that was suddenly in the air. If you listened closely enough you could hear Max's voice, follow what he was saying: the Laird and Laird people might have thought that they were stealing the show from Bud when they sent that heifer of Marengo's out here, but they hadn't taken into consideration the fact that Marengo was, after all, dead. There was a limit to the number of heifers he could sire, whereas Bud was just starting. Vera should not be discouraged. The Laird and Laird people had merely opened up vistas of future triumphs for Bud.

Claiborne fixed his eyes on Max's face with an effort. When Max stopped speaking Claiborne raised his glass. "Vistas!" he said. "For all of us."

Nobody paid any attention to him. Vera said, frowning a little: "I don't care! I don't *approve* of artificial insemination and I'm not going to let Bud have anything to do with it."

Claiborne set his glass down, spilling some of the wine on the table. "Time marches on," he said. "Can't let one good custom c'rupt the world. Bud'll have to face it."

She looked at him, smiling, then her face clouded. She thought that he was drunk. He averted his gaze from her shining eyes. He shook his head. "Who is Bud to be standing with reluctant feet where the brook and river meet? Only a muley cow bull. That's all he is.'

The girl beside him laughed suddenly. "He'll have to stabilize on a higher level," she said.

He turned to her, nodding emphatically. "That's it. All just matter of details."

"Details . . . ?" she repeated.

"This vista's been opened up," he said, watching her face waver before him in the candlelight. Her face and hair and bare shoulders were all the same color. Did she know that her eyes were as green as grass? She had told him that she was

112

thirty-four years old but she looked a hell of a lot younger than that, as women do when nothing that they want to have happen has happened to them. He frowned in the effort to fix her features more clearly, then fixed a heavy hand on her shoulder. "Take *you*. . . . Suppose you wanted to have a baby . . . by Winston Churchill."

He felt her shoulder give a little under his palm, then stiffen. Her laughter rang out, sounding fresh but faraway, like a waterfall gushing down a remote mountainside. "But I don't."

He let his hand fall from her shoulder. "You can't tell," he said. "Say you don't want to have a baby by Winston Churchill right this minute, but might change your mind. Remember that. You might change your mind and want to have a baby by him later on . . . or by John L. Lewis . . . or Joe Louis. . . ."

"You'd still have to get Winston Churchill's consent," Max said. "Or John L. Lewis's . . . or Joe Louis's . . ."

"Not necessarily. Might be just a matter of routine. Few complications to iron out, naturally. . . . *Could* be such a thing as too much Winston Churchill . . . or John L. Lewis . . . or Joe Louis. . . . Depend, of course, on how prepotent the sire was. . . ."

Vera said, *"Tom!"* in a low voice.

"Oh, all *right!"* he said, and lifted the glass Gershon had just refilled and drank from it. "But you can't say it doesn't open up vistas," he muttered.

Vera did not answer, only eyed him mournfully. He withdrew his gaze from hers and stared at the wine stain on the tablecloth. It was spreading. The last two times he had drunk from his glass he had spilled some of the wine. Gershon always filled glasses too full, but that did not excuse his spilling his wine on the cloth. They all thought he was drunk, but he did not see how he could be. He had had only two drinks before dinner and not more than five or six glasses of wine. How could a man get drunk on that amount of alcohol? It's just that I'm so damned tired, he told himself, and he thought of the young bull standing in his stall, slowly ruminating and gazing incuriously ahead of him, and of his daughter, the red heifer, in the stall across the runway, bedded down, no doubt, on sweet-smelling straw, with her daughter curled up beside her; and it seemed to him that he ought to be standing in the darkness beside them, listening to their gentle breathing and laying his hand first on one and then another warm, hairy head, instead of sitting here at this table, this table which at any moment might be caught up and transported at the rate of God only knew how many million miles an hour to be set down inside a great, brazen mechanism, shaped, perhaps, like a bull, in which he and his wife and their guests and everybody else they had ever known would be reduced to ashes—or some other utilizable product.

SEVEN

After the Archers had left and Robin had silently disappeared up the stairs they went into the library. Max went over to the record player. He asked them what they wanted to hear and when nobody answered said that he would play what he wanted to hear and put on the Beethoven *"Pathétique."* Vera and Cynthia had sat down side by side on a sofa. Claiborne took a chair facing the women. They had not stopped talking because of the music but they talked in such low tones that he could not hear what they said. Vera kept her eyes fixed on her cousin's face and seemed to be listening intently to what Cynthia said but it was plain that she was tired; she allowed her head to rest against the back of the sofa and her hands lay limp on each side of her. Cynthia's hands were clasped in her lap. She sat poised lightly on the edge of the seat, almost as if she were riding sidesaddle. . . . His mother had ridden sidesaddle all her life, but Molly

Archer was the only woman he knew who rode sidesaddle and she had stopped it after her first husband's death. "I don't know why, but I'm afraid. I never was afraid till after Jim died. . . ." She would tell you all about it if she got enough liquor in her.

Neither of them would look at him because they thought that he was drunk. But he was not drunk, just elevated enough to notice things that might have escaped him ordinarily: the two women's heads, for instance, floating against the crimson sofa back as if placed there for display. You would not think that they were related if you did not know their history. Vera's features were all short, upturned, high-colored, ardent. Cynthia's nose was long, her lips pale, her hair the color of a dead leaf. She had a habit of turning her head a little to one side immediately after she made a remark. When she did that the muscles at the outer corners of her mouth drew slightly downward and the mouth itself took on a bitter and at the same time avid look.

"Meraude!" Vera said. "Oh, by all means, Meraude!"

Meraude was the name of a sewing woman she had discovered a year or so ago on the East Side and who, under her patronage, was being encouraged to give herself the airs of a *grande couturière*. Vera always called her by the name Max had thought up for her and made Molly and Marcia and all the other women go to her. The thought of her protégée animated her now. She sat up straighter and for a moment lost her air of fatigue as she turned her brilliant eyes on her cousin. The eyes are the mirror of the soul. He had seen— or had he only fancied that he had seen?—strangers in the act of being introduced to Vera involuntarily take a step backward as if to avoid some impact. Cynthia was not listening very hard to what her cousin was saying. She turned her head aside again in that odd gesture. Was it the gesture of a person who, because of some secret necessity, suddenly finds the company of others intolerable? And what was the necessity?

Max had been tinkering with the volume and had finally got it to suit him. The sonata swelled softly, filled the room.

115

The *"Pathétique."* Beethoven was twenty-nine when he wrote that. At thirty-three he was almost completely deaf. . . . As for me, I am dumb. Have been for a long time.

> Silence destroyed the Amyclae. They were dumb.
> Silent, I lost the Muse. Return, Apollo!

Cras amet qui numquam amavit quique amavit cras amet . . . Allen Tate's "Tomorrow may loveless, may lover tomorrow make love" is better than Symons' version of the refrain. Wish I'd beat him to that. Haven't seen him in a long time. Don't know that I'd care to see him again.

He opened his eyes. Max still sat in his corner, in the attitude he was accustomed to take when he listened to music, leaning forward, his knees spread, his head supported on his hands while he stared at the floor. Vera was sound asleep, her head turned sidewise against the back of the sofa, her arms brought up and folded across her breast. He thought at first that Cynthia had left the room, then caught sight of her standing at a window, looking out into the garden. He went over and stood beside her.

She smiled at him faintly, then turned back to the window. The moon was up. The gravel of the walks showed between the flower beds. The brick wall that enclosed the garden was splashed with the black, swaying shadows of leaves.

She said in a low voice: "I'm going out and walk around a little."

"Yes," he said, and moved beside her toward the door. They were halfway across the room when he heard a heavy tread behind them. "Believe I'll take a turn too," Max said. They were opposite the sofa where Vera lay asleep. Max paused and looked down at her fondly. "Maud Muller on a summer's day," he said, and suppressed a laugh.

They went through the hall and across the stone-cold terrace to set foot on gravel almost as cold. "We'll go over and take a look at the Oratory," Max told Cynthia.

He called his little house "St. Cyprian's Oratory," in memory of the studio on L'Impasse des Deux Anges—a hangover from his Joe Paster days. Joe called whatever hall bedroom he inhabited, in whatever run-down rooming house, "St. Benedict's Oratory"—not the great St. Benedict but an obscure, eighteenth-century saint, Benedict Joseph Labre, who, unsuccessful in his attempts to become a monk, had turned tramp instead, and had been canonized in the year Joe was born. Max, who had been a good figure painter before he turned Vorticist, had presented Joe with a picture of "St. Benedict's Cell"—a hole in a crumbling Roman wall. Joe carried the roll of canvas about with him in all his wanderings. Max, and Horne too, had been delighted with the idea of having a patron saint. Max had taken Cyprian, the exmagician, as his patron. Horne, after much cogitation, had adopted St. Polycarp. Polycarp, Claiborne mused. The name signifies "much fruit." He had once looked St. Polycarp up in the encyclopedia and found that he had been burned in the amphitheater in the time of Commodus at the age of eighty-six. Horne had been thirty-two when he leaped into the sea. . . .

Cynthia had stopped to look back at the house. "It looks like Mio Sogno from here," she said. "That vine there on the terrace. And that black tree going up beside it."

"That tree's a Lombardy poplar, not a cypress," he said, "and there aren't any steps going down there at the side of the house, and no fountain."

Max said: "Oh, come on!"

But she still stood gazing and after a minute Max walked over and stood beside her and pointed out over the lawn. "Like something Claude might have dreamed," he said.

Claiborne had been holding the gate open for them to pass through but now he withdrew his hand from the cold iron and let the gate swing to. The landscape seemed to him, too, like something seen in a dream, with its long stretches of blond, glimmering sward, broken at intervals by the leafy trees, each of which had the crescent of its own black shadow resting at its foot, like a garment half slipped off at the end of some play. A few hours ago he had stood here at this same gate with another woman. People in bright-colored clothes had moved about over the lawn while they stood here, talking—about what? He could not remember. It seemed a long time ago and the place he stood in did not seem the same place. Even the trees did not seem the same.

He stared at the nearest tree, the copper beech. Its trunk was gray but the branches above were massed in shadow. One of the boughs swayed gently forward. A shaft of moonlight raced up the gray trunk to disappear among the plumey boughs, like a creature surprised and seeking shelter.

Max sighed. "Night like this I wish I wasn't so old!"

Claiborne did not answer. The breeze still played among the boughs. Something live ran, glittering, from leaf to leaf. They have been here all along! he thought.

"Well, let's take that turn in the garden," Max said.

He and Cynthia moved toward the gate. Claiborne let them pass through before him, then followed them down the box walk to the cottage at the end of the garden. Hollyhocks grew all about it, but the low-growing hedges that radiated out from it were of tansy and rue and Lad's Love—Lad's Love, God love us!—Max had a passion for growing herbs. Cynthia, walking a little ahead of the two men, stooped and thrust her hand down into a mass of silvery leaves. "Lavender," she said. "It grows wild around Hyères. Remember?" and she held a leaf out to him. He lifted it to his nose and inhaled the clean, pungent odor, then thrust the leaf down into his pocket. Cynthia, still holding in her hand the branch she had broken off, walked across the little brick terrace and through the open door into Max's cottage.

It had been the cobbler's shop in the old days. A large, square, beautifully proportioned room, whose four small windows when Max took it over had still contained what remained of the original panes of whorled, greenish glass. The two east windows were still there, but the north window and the low ceiling had had to go when Max turned the place into a studio. The cavernous fireplace was still surmounted by its long, low pine mantel, and over in the corner was a relic that Max prized highly, a big square block of oak on which the cobbler laid the hides from which he cut the soles and uppers of his shoes. Max used it to hold paints.

He had switched on an overhead light. Cynthia stood in the middle of the floor looking up at the square of *mille fleurs* tapestry over the mantel: blond rabbits and birds with reddish feathers gleaming in their long tails hopping about a darkish background, among plants that looked as if they might have been drawn by Dürer, every one of them with a blue or yellow or rose-colored blossom set among its olive-colored leaves.

"*Max!* Do you deserve this?"

Max went over and stood beside her. He had started in on the story of how he got it, week-ending with old Sophy Douglass, year after year, just for the pleasure of looking at it, till old Sophy died and Dick Fenshaw happened to mention that all the stuff was going to Hall, Crashan. So he took the bull by the horns and went straight to Jessica Douglass. . . . "Look here, Jessica, do you think Sophy would want you to sell the rabbits?" "But Max, I love it dearly, of course, but can you *see* it in my house?" "I certainly can't," Max had said, and got on a chair and detached it from the wall and rolled it up and stuck it under his arm and walked out of the room. . . . Later she had written him that she remembered now that her mother once said that she wanted Joe Steiner to have the rabbits. . . . "Joe was in Europe. It was just a dodge to get it into her clutches. I wrote her that we must remember that Sophy knew things now that she didn't know when she was with us and that I was positive that she would loathe the idea of Joe Steiner having the rabbits. . . . She would, too. The old girl could look at a thing and tell whether it was good, but Jessica and Dick have to pay Woodcock to tell them what to like."

He disappeared into the back room where they could hear him still laughing while he cracked ice. Cynthia walked over and sat down on a sofa. Claiborne did not move. She put her hand out and lifted a magazine from the table beside her then suddenly laid it down and looked up at him and smiled a little. A moment later her features were impassive again but her eyes still sparkled, as if at some thought which was secret and which she yet wanted to share with him. But Max was coming through the door, bearing a loaded tray. She looked down at her hands folded in her lap.

As Max walked past Claiborne to set the tray down on the table next to the sofa he gave Claiborne a quick look out of his black eyes. Claiborne stood where he was a second, watching the plump, deft hands hovering over the bottles and the glasses and the silver bowl filled with cracked ice, before he walked to the door and stood with his back turned, looking out over the garden.

In the long bed immediately in front of the terrace the herbs were planted in rows that slanted like the spokes of a wheel. There were three wheels, each one interlacing with another, as neat as a pin, the whole enclosed by a low border of some plant with silvery leaves. That was the lavender into which Cynthia had just stooped to thrust her hand. Lavender grew all over those slopes back of Mio Sogno. . . . What had Cynthia meant by that look she gave him a minute ago? The smile which accompanied it seemed to refer to some experience they had shared. Was it possible that when they had stood looking at that tree she had seen the same thing that he saw? The look, the smile had seemed to say so. The ordinary person did not think that things happened that way, but he knew that they did. Once his days had been filled with such happenings, but not for a long time. . . .

Max said: "Tom, here's your drink."

Claiborne shook his head and walked back and sat down in the chair drawn up before the sofa.

Max laughed as he set the highball back on the tray. "You *were* flying pretty high there for a while!"

"I was doing well to get off the ground at all," Claiborne said. "Do you realize that we've been at this since eight o'clock this morning?"

"Yes," Max said, "by then I was deep in the Overbecks'

120

squashes." He stretched his legs, yawning, then reached over and patted Cynthia's knee. "Think of having little Cynthia here!" he said. "You like it?"

"I love it," she said.

"We have a good time," Max said. "Don't we, Tom? But we don't have this good a time every day."

"God forbid!" Claiborne said, and wished he had not spoken, feeling the quick black eyes on his face again, but Max said only: "Tom doesn't relish the pastoral the way Vee and I do."

Cynthia's eyes met Claiborne's. The same smile trembled on her lips. "Are you sure it's pastoral?" she asked.

"It's the best we can do," Max said, "me and Vee and Bud —but poor Bud, he's going to be mechanized."

"Caligula made his horse consul," Claiborne said. "That bull will move in on us before we're through."

Max shook his head. "Bud won't move in on you. He's got it too soft as it is."

And so have you . . . and so have I. . . .

Some men are born eunuchs, some men are made eunuchs by men, some men become eunuchs for the sake of the King- dom of God. The words were Jesus Christ's, but they came to him in Horne's voice. When he was drunk enough Horne spoke of himself as a "holocaust." The artist must sacrifice everything—including love of women—for the sake of his art, must burn himself up on the Muse's altar. But it was the sea that got Horne in the end, and sharks, not flames, that picked his bones.

She was not looking at him now but at Max, a glance that was bright and at the same time speculative. She was trying to reconcile Max's suave, portly presence with the wild tales she had heard of his goings-on in Paris. "The Black Widow," Joe Paster used to call Max in the first days of his bereave- ment. The trouble was that Max had been bereaved so often, for Horne would not even pretend to be faithful to him. He would even go after women. That time he took off for Majorca with Deedy Maslow, and Deedy, when they got back, told everybody in boring detail how, night after night, duly fortified by resinous wine, they got into bed and nothing happened. "Simply nothing. I can't *understand* it!" . . . Why had Horne kept trying? That was the thing that in those days ran Max crazy, that Horne, every now and then, would go after some woman. Had Max suspected—feared—that Horne was not like him, that he was a man who ought to have been able to love women? He had made Horne terrible scenes whenever Horne showed any interest in a woman but he was calm enough when Horne went on the prowl. In fact those were Max's happiest times, the mornings when Horne came home with a shiner or a wrenched back or beaten black and blue. . . . He remembered the first morning he had come on them like that: Horne, in bed in the little room back of the big curtain, his round jowls so congested with blood that they looked as if they might burst, a compress made of two towels wrapped about his neck, holding a slab of *biftek* to his eye—Max was a great one for old-fashioned remedies, usually ones that had been used by his grandmother. He had explained that the compress made of one wet towel encased in one dry towel had practically magical properties for the cure of almost any ailment. When he got up to go over to the stove to wring the inside towel out in boiling water Claiborne had observed the sidewise roll of his hips; his old granny's gait, which had grown on him with the years, had been apparent, though he was still slim then. Horne had been a bit subdued and at the same time a little complacent. It had been too much for *him*. He had got away from the lovebirds as soon as he could, to walk up and down the Boulevard St. Germain in the October sunshine.

Horne had made his first—and last—pass at Tom Claiborne two days after he arrived in Paris. They were strolling down Monsieur le Prince late at night and Horne had stopped and, pointing to a light that burned dimly over the entrance to a cheap hotel, had suggested that they go in and take a room. When Claiborne said no, that he wasn't that way, Horne had given an odd, defiant laugh and they had walked on, talking about *Bateau Ivre*. But the laugh had been followed by a sort of lowering of the bullet head, a hunching of the shoulders. He had had the impression of a man trudging beside him buffeted by a storm invisible to mortal eyes.

He had learned later that Horne was used to such rebuffs. Most of his friends, as he said once when he was drunk, he had "weighed in the balance and found wanting." Joe Tyrone, Bob Waite, Jim Wragge, and their wives, all testified that Horne "never let it make the least difference," but he could still remember the sick feeling that had swept over that young man (he seemed to himself somebody he had known long ago) standing there on Monsieur le Prince at two o'clock in the morning. It wasn't hurt vanity (he could still read that young man's mind) or even moral indignation. It was that Horne had had to laugh like that! . . .

Cynthia set her glass down with a little click and leaned forward. "Do you see what I see?" she said.

Max sat back in his chair with an odd, sidewise motion, like a fat pigeon that in the act of dusting itself suddenly realizes that it is being admired. "Vera gave it to me on my birthday two years ago," he said. "It was *too* sweet of her! I *told* her it was too sweet of her. But Lord, I'm only human!"

She was on her feet and moving toward the opposite wall where the picture hung. Max went over and stood beside her.

Claiborne did not even need to raise his eyes to see that picture. All circles, one within another until you came to the last circle that was smaller than a bull's eye and black as night. A technical feat, certainly. But there was something about Carlo's pictures that he had never been able to stomach. Was it the color or the movement?

"It's the rhythm of life," Vera once said.

"I doubt that. The trouble with you is that you were raised on a bunch of baloney."

"My father was considered a fine painter. But now he's dead, so of course you can say anything you want to about him."

"If he was ever any good as a painter he'd be just as alive today as he ever was, but I don't believe he was ever any good. I've thought so for years."

"If that is so, it must be painful to you to have 'The Fountain' hanging in the library."

"I don't have to look at it. I've got so I can look straight through it and never see it."

"You'll never see it again!" she had cried, and caught up a pair of nail scissors and would have rushed downstairs in the middle of the night to slash the picture if he hadn't caught her wrist and held it.

"You touch that picture—now or any other time—and I'll give you a beating you'll never forget."

She had finally cried herself to sleep in his arms. It had been a tremendous relief to both of them when she remembered the next day that Max's birthday was only a week off. . . . "No, I *want* him to have it! After all, *he* likes it." Her lip had trembled. They would have been off on the old merry-go-round if he hadn't taken himself off for a walk. . . .

He stood up. "Cynthia, I'm going to bed. You coming?"

"She hasn't finished her drink," Max said.

"She can stay here and finish it if she wants to," Claiborne said. But she was already on her feet. Max went with them halfway, then turned back, walking slowly, whistling a song Claiborne had not heard in years:

> *Adieu ma mie, adieu mon coeur,*
> *Adieu, mon espérance. . . .*

They had taken a different path from the one they had followed a while ago and now they came into the great circle of box that had been planted to set off the marble fountain, the only piece of sculpture that Carlo had ever executed. It was of dark green marble, the kind that would show yellow veined in the daylight but here in the moonlight looked almost black. The water that lay in its depths was motionless and dark too, except for a faint shimmer where it spilled over the curved edge of the great round to fall into a larger, shallower round below.

He would have passed it unseeing but Cynthia stopped to stare. "It is the same fountain, isn't it?" she asked.

He said: "Oh yes. Vera had it brought over when they sold Mio Sogno."

She went nearer and bent and dipped her hand in the water. "It looks so strange here," she said.

"Carlo designed it for Provence, not for Bucks County."

She bent lower, plunging her hand deep into the water, then looked up at him sidewise. "You don't like it, do you?" she asked suddenly.

"I'm old-fashioned," he said. "Like to see water spilling out of something. This water doesn't seem to move till it hits the rim."

She straightened up. "It's like his pictures," she said.

He was silent. "Are you tired?" she asked suddenly.

"Yes. Aren't you?"

She shook her head in negation then stood on tiptoe, stretching her arms high over her head. "I don't think I'll ever be tired again!"

"That must be a nice feeling."

She laughed. "All evening I've been thinking about Mrs. Salisbury Hawks. . . ."

"Of Rapulgee, Wizconzin?"

"The dean's wife. She was at home every Sunday afternoon. . . ."

"And you?"

"I had to be at home on Saturdays. Every Saturday. For seven years."

"And now you don't?"

"Oh no. Never again."

"It's not all beer and skittles in these parts," he said.

"I know. But it's *different*."

"Maybe," he said.

"Oh yes," she said, and stooped to plunge her hand again in the darkly shining water, then turning to him impulsively, laid it, still wet from the fountain, on his arm. "You're tired. We ought to go in."

"I suppose we ought," he said, and started up the gravel path. She walked beside him. Her hand still lay lightly on his arm. He could feel its chill through his thin coat sleeve. A drop of water fell on the gravel between them. He put his own hand up and laid it for a second over her cold hand, then looked up to see where the moon had gone. When they had come this way a half-hour ago it had been almost directly over their heads, but it must be traveling west now; ahead of each of them his own black shadow wavered. The façade of the house looked white with the moonlight beating full on it.

In the library Vera lay curled in a corner of the sofa. She heard their footsteps and opened her eyes and smiled.

"Come on," he said, "let's go to bed."

She stood up—then, as if her legs had given way, sank back on the sofa and, still smiling, held out her arms. He stooped and she clasped her arms around his neck and he carried her from the room and up the stairs. The odor of her body, indescribable but as familiar to him as the rhythm of his own breath, came to him, mingled with the fragrance of flowers and the smell of cow dung. He felt his lips shaping a grin as he strode up the stairs with his burden. Cynthia had stayed behind to turn off the lights but he could hear her now mounting lightly behind him. As she came abreast of them Vera lifted her head languidly. "Have you got everything?" "Everything," Cynthia said, and opened the door of Vera's bedroom for him, then, smiling back over her shoulder, slipped down the hall to her own room while he carried Vera in and laid her down on her bed.

She lay for a second in the same position in which he had put her down, then, giving a long sigh, turned over on her face. Her husband stood looking down at her. "You're done in, aren't you?" he said.

She murmured something. He laughed and sitting down on the bed beside her, laid his hand on the small of her back.

"Come on, Vee! It's all over now. Don't you want to get in bed?"

There was no answer except her long, sighing breaths. He unfastened her dress and drawing her to a sitting position, slipped it over her head. She fell sidewise like a rag doll, her eyes still closed. He pulled her up off the bed long enough to draw the covers down, then stripped her of her underwear and pushed her gently in between the sheets. When he bent to kiss her she murmured, "Darling," and, curving her arm about his neck, held his cheek against hers, laughing a little. He said, "Wait a minute!" and turning off the light, stripped off his clothes, and getting naked into bed, pulled the warm, pliant body up against his own.

Later he woke with a start. The illuminated hands of his watch told him that it was four o'clock. Another hour till daylight and another two or three hours before anybody would be stirring in the house. Vera lay on her back, breathing lightly. As if unconsciously registering the movement he had just made, she suddenly flung one arm out so that it lay athwart his chest. The arm was warm and heavier than you would have thought such a slight arm could be. He endured the warmth, the light pressure for several minutes before he turned over and lying with his back to her stared before him into the dark.

That bunch of clothes there on the floor looked like a body, sodden and fallen in some dark encounter. Something curled like a worm lay at a little distance from one limp sleeve. The spray of lavender Cynthia had handed him a while ago, saying that lavender grew all over the hills around Mio Sogno. . . . Who knew that better than he?

He looked at his watch again. Seven minutes past four. Those objects on the floor were all in shadow now. Was the moon quite gone from the garden?

He got up and went on bare feet out onto the balcony. There was no glitter left on leaf or bough but between the dark shapes of the trees the sky showed a faint salmon color. The moon must just have gone down. Or was that color reflected from the eastern sky? *Was that dawn?* He brought his clenched fist down on the cold iron of the balustrade. "They think I'm through," he said half aloud. "But I'm not. They'll see. I'm not through yet!" and went back into the house, pausing a second to look down at the sleeping figure he had just left, before he passed into his own room.

PART
TWO

EIGHT

Claiborne entered his study, turned, and as was his custom, locked the door behind him. He had been locking the door ever since one of the maids, coming in with a message after her repeated taps had been ignored, had found him asleep on the sofa.

The room faced east and was flooded with morning light. He and Vera had taken great trouble with its furnishings when they moved here twelve years ago. They had both been very much pleased when Claiborne acquired a plantation desk that had belonged to one of his great uncles, but he had soon found that it slanted too much to hold a typewriter and was an inconvenient height when he wanted to write by hand, and he had abandoned it for a small pine table which he kept pushed up in front of one of the windows.

The rest of the furnishings were early American, to match the desk: four small "chicken coop" Hitchcock chairs, and on each side of the fireplace two big Pennsylvania Dutch settles. Over the mantel hung a family portrait, his great-granduncle Danvers Claiborne at the age of five or six, in buff-colored pantaloons and a frilled shirt, feeding his game chickens. The boy's hair was the color of butter, the cock's body bright orange, its feathers a bluish-green where they were not crimson. The picture had hung in the parlor at Eupedon. Tom Claiborne had liked having it here over the mantel and had often glanced up at it when he first took possession of this room. But that had been in the days when he was still able to work. It struck him as odd that when he was working he was more acutely aware of his surroundings than when he was not working. It had been a long time now since he had actually observed any object in this room—except one, the old-fashioned sofa, covered with black leather, that stood in a far corner. He had bought it at a country auction because it reminded him of the sofa his father used to take naps on at Eupedon.

He stood in the middle of the room now, and looked with aversion at the table which held his typewriter. There was a pile of typewritten sheets lying beside the typewriter and the machine held a sheet of paper half covered with typing. He had begun an essay on Keats several months ago for *Spectra* but the essay was long overdue—so long overdue that Bob Waite had stopped telephoning or telegraphing him about it. He had had some ideas about Keats when he started the essay, but they did not seem important now, and as he stood in the middle of the sunlit room he thought of his fellow poet with cold envy; Keats had been dead by the time he was twenty-six.

He adjusted one of the blinds so that the sunlight was a little tempered, then went over and lay down on the sofa. His blank gaze suddenly fixed upon his own books, two of poetry and four of critical essays, that Vera had had bound in expensive vellum—all six of them ranged in a solemn row at the end of the top shelf opposite him. . . . "Erudition and wit expressed in a prose of classical *ordonnance,* at once powerful and subtle." . . . He shifted his eyes to the window. The view from this corner was always the same: a patch of blue sky, with, thrusting up into it, the tops of two tall Lombardy poplars. Vera liked them because they had the same shape as the cypresses she had loved in the country around Hyères. No matter how hard he looked at the trees and the sky there was always something else in his field of vision: the row of drawers that formed the lower part of the old desk. The manuscript of the long poem he had begun when he first came here to live lay in one of them. Eight sheets of paper, meticulously typed (oh, he could always type something up once he got it written!), fastened together with a rusted paper clip and themselves already faintly yellowed. The other sheets of paper, on which he had written phrases, lines, sometimes even a stanza, had all gone into the wastebasket, to be hauled off by old Dan, the garbage collector, and burned on some dump, or, more likely, sold to the ragman to be made into paper on which some other fool could say what he thought he had to say.

As for him, he had, besides a few critical articles, only these eight already yellowing sheets of paper to show for almost twelve years' work. Twelve years? Forty-seven years! For every time you wrote a poem you put all you had and every year you had lived into it. Well, they could not say (who was it he was always expecting to say something?) that he had not tried. He had sat there, day after day, hour after hour, or walked about the room, or stood looking out of the window, or had lain here on this sofa, with his eyes closed as now, sweating, sweating, until it seemed that all the sweat and all the blood had gone out of him and there was left only this dry manikin of skin and bone. There was something—he did not know what it was—that tied him to the creature, and so he paced the room when it paced the room or stood beside it at the window or sat at his desk while it fumbled among his papers and then one day it had turned its head and he saw that it was grinning, and he took the eight pages and put them in one of the lower drawers of the desk and closed it. That was six months ago. He had not opened the drawer since then. But there would have to be a reckoning eventually. Vera thought that he was still working on his poem. If you told her that you had sweated blood all morning and had not been able to write a damn word she would look at you as if the world had come to an end. He had not been able to bear that look and so he had fallen into the habit of deceiving her. Nowadays his most strenuous mental effort was a simulation of the process of creation. Five lines? No, it was day before yesterday I told her I wrote five lines. Safer to make it three. Or maybe this is one of those days when I didn't get anything done but feel like I might be able to write something tomorrow. . . . Into each life some rain must fall. So don't you worry about me, little girl. Just get on with your farm work. . . .

He raised his hand and laid it on his forehead so that his eyes were covered. "I am in a bad way," he whispered to someone who seemed to stand always a little behind him. "Can't you see that I am in a very bad way?"

There was no answer. When could there ever be any answer? After a few minutes he moved his hand and opened his eyes. Some of the poplar leaves were showing yellow, but the patch of sky visible through the window was as blue as any summer sky. It was strange that there was never any sky in his dream, only water.

He had had the dream again last night, for the first time in months. But he had had it at irregularly recurring intervals for as long as he could remember. A man and a river. A river broader than the Amazon, which he had read about as a child in his geography books, broader than any river that ever flowed. Sometimes the man stood on the bank, with another person—was it a woman?—beside him. But oftenest he moved with the current, riding sometimes in a boat, or plunged deep in the waves. Then the banks of the river would seem so far away or so wreathed in mist that he could not even make out what trees grew there. The current flowed smoothly. The man seemed one with its movement until a certain moment when another current flowing into the stream enveloped his moving limbs with waves so soft, so arresting, that he stayed his course and, looking off over the broad, rippling expanse, saw on the bank (in the dream it was always the left bank) the cavern yawning. The dream always ended with that moment. He had never seen anything more than the cavern's mouth, a wide, overhanging ledge which glowed as if illuminated from within, had known it only as a place that would welcome him, that yawned for him if he ever left the main stream and swam toward it.

There was a knock at the door. He got up off the couch and, running his hand over his rumpled hair, debated whether he should open it. One of the maids, no doubt, with a message from Vera. But their knocks of late had been timorous and sometimes they would knock only once and then, if there was no answer, go away. The knock came again, soft but firm, as if the person making it were determined to be admitted.

He opened the door. It was Vera. She was evidently on her way to the field; she wore blue denim and had her "carpenter's apron" tied about her waist.

He said: "Come in. . . . Well, what are *you* up to this morning?"

"We're going to cut the Ladino this morning," she said.

"Who's going to ride the binder?" he asked. She called the machine the tractor but he always gave the machine the name he had known it by as a boy.

She said: "Rodney," and then hesitantly, "would you like to—for a while?"

He shook his head. "I've got some things to do."

Her face lighted up, or rather, reflected, for a second, a radiance by which it might have been transformed if the radiance had not faded so quickly. She took an almost simple-minded pleasure in her own "day's work" and every morning went forth and solemnly slopped pigs or cleaned out stalls or performed any other of the chores ordinarily turned over to hired men. But there was a thorn in her flesh. She could not give herself over wholly to these rustic delights unless she was convinced that he was enjoying himself too. She had as much notion of the dangers—and delights—of writing lyric poetry as one of her own muley cows, but she got uneasy when he went through one of his long "dry" periods. Still, she was—at forty—one of the most gullible of God's creatures. He could make her happy, for the whole day, for weeks to come, by saying what he could so easily say—for he was good at such maneuvers—that he had got hold of the end of a line that he thought he would keep or had a notion that it would take him some time to work out or had found a book that he found stimulating. Any one of these dodges would send her out of the room, reeling with delight, to work in the hay field till the sweat ran off her like rain—there was nothing she liked more than getting up a good sweat. But he would be damned if he would do it, he told himself.

She had sat down on the sofa and was apparently absorbed in rearranging the contents of the pockets of the apron of undressed leather in which she carried the tools she thought she might need in her "day's work." She drew a diminutive pair of pliers out of one of the pockets and held it up, frowning. "Tom . . ." she said.

"Well?"

"I'm worried about Robin."

"What's he up to?"

"I don't think *he's* up to anything."

"Isn't that his usual condition?"

She stowed the pliers carefully away in one of the pockets. "I wish he did have something to occupy him," she said after a moment.

"It's a little late in the day for that, isn't it?"

"He's only thirty."

"Yes, but he's never hit a tap in his whole life. I can't see him starting now."

"I can. . . . I mean I could if . . ."

"If what?"

"If he were married, for instance."

Clairborne laughed. "Some woman will have to marry *him*. He'll never take the initiative."

"That's what I'm afraid of."

"Why, you've just intimated that you'd like to see him married."

She was silent, head bent, untying the strings of her apron and then retying them more firmly about her waist. When she looked up she said: "Do you think I'm getting fat?"

"No," he said. "Look here. Something's on your mind. Is Robin in the toils of some *femme fatale?*"

She nodded. "I think she might be."

136

"Might be what?"

"Fatal—for him."

"For God's sake, Vera, what are you talking about?"

"Why," she said as if bewildered, "I'm talking about Cynthia—and Robin. Haven't you noticed how much they're together lately?"

"As a matter of fact, I haven't. But then, as you know, I don't pay much attention to what goes on around here."

"No," she said.

"You think there really may be something going on between them?"

"I don't know."

"But you wouldn't approve if there were?"

She was silent.

Her silence made him uneasy. No, it was not the silence. It was that blue gaze of hers. He could remember a time when he had seemed to bask in its effulgence. But not now. Not for a long time. Sometimes he dreamed of walking across a field, or some vast expanse, whose every blade, every leaf was bathed in shining light. But the light, the radiance had seemed to him intolerable and he walked steadily, head down, toward the place he had glimpsed where there was no grass, no leaf, no light, only velvet dark. He said explosively: "Well, suppose there *is* something going on between them? It might be a good thing for Robin. Anything to put some life into him. He goes around here like a zombie."

She said with a sob: "He was nearly killed."

"He had a bad time in the war, Vera, but good God, so did a lot of other men. He's still got both legs, even if one is shorter than the other."

"I'm not talking about the war!" she cried. "I'm talking about when he was six years old and loved so to go to Cassis with Denis but he promised Léontine that he would never get out of the car and he never did—till *she* told him that Denis wouldn't know and then they saw Denis crossing the *place* just as they were coming out of the *patisserie* and Robin started running and the car knocked him down and would have run over him if the brakes hadn't held. . . . Oh!"

He said coldly: "These reminiscences are very interesting. You ought to write your memoirs."

She had been sitting, her hands twisted together in her lap, staring at the floor as if she still saw the ancient Mediterranean cobblestones and the shining engine of destruction, with the child fallen before its wheels. But at the sound of his voice she looked up at him, as intently, or so it seemed to his disturbed fancy, as if she had never seen him before. She laughed. "I don't *have* to write anything!" she cried.

"No," he said, "you have a resident writer."

Her wide, fixed gaze did not waver. Suddenly her body was convulsed by a long sob. "Oh," she cried, "what are we saying?"

"Nothing," he said, "nothing that matters. We are both tired."

"That's it," she said. "We're tired. Both of us . . . And there are too many people. . . . There's nothing wrong. Is there?"

"No," he said, "nothing but the human condition and we can't remedy that in one morning."

She laughed. "No, not this morning," she said, and murmured that she must be about her work.

"Yes," he said. "The sun is high."

"Good-bye, darling," she said.

"Good-bye, darling," he said, and kissed her and when she had left the room went back and lay down on the sofa and raised his hand and laid it across his forehead so that his eyes were covered, pondering the origins of his dreams, those dreams in which he confronted a vast expanse that must be traversed or stood beside a river whose banks were so wide he could not see across it. He could not remember the first time he had had the dream about the river but he did remember a moment—it must have been when he was about ten years old—when, standing with his mother at the edge of a wide, green field, he had seemed to stand beside a strange

138

woman on the shore of a sea that was now green, now some shade of purple, but always illimitable and cold. Some vagary of puberty, no doubt. George Crenfew could ticket it and drop it into its proper pigeonhole if he asked him about it. But I'll be damned if I will, he thought, even if I do spend most of my time on the couch!

There was a knock on the door, this time a sharp knock. It came again, brisker and louder. He grinned and went to the door and opened it.

Cynthia Vail stood there in a white dress, carrying a Manila folder under one arm. She said: "Would you look at these translations?"

She spoke in a low voice, as if indifferently, but her lips twitched as she uttered the words, so wryly that she seemed almost to grimace at him. And he, on the other side of the door, had grinned when he heard her knock!

He said hurriedly: "Lord, child, I haven't read any Latin for years," but as he spoke one hand went out to take the folder from her while the other motioned her to a chair, then, turning his back on her, he went over and sat down at his desk and spread the folder open before him. There were only six sheets of paper in the folder. A few lines were written on the first sheet in a clear small script. Below the text was her translation of the poem.

He read the poem and then read her translation. When he had finished he laid the sheet of paper down carefully and sat for a moment looking out of the open window. In the south meadow red cows moved slowly about, knee-deep in alfalfa. A man and a woman stood leaning on the fence, watching them: Vera and Tom Abel, the dairyman. Vera's figure looked dwarfish beside that of the lean dairyman. From time to time they turned their heads solemnly toward each other, then resumed their contemplation of the beasts. Brooding on their line breedings and their outcrosses, no doubt, or trying to decide whether to graze off that alfalfa or save it for hay. Vera no longer consulted him about these matters. But why should she? For him her actions had been so long divorced from reality that they had lost all significance. This sharp pain he felt was not because his wife was so self-sufficient but because this woman sitting here behind him had used the English language with a precision and power that he would not have thought her capable of.

His big hand moved slowly to reveal the second sheet of paper. She had copied her poem out in the same small, unwavering script. He read it through twice. His hand fell to his side. With an effort he kept his fingers from clenching on air. She was still sitting there behind him, in the same chair, doubtless in the same position. You have got to get used to seeing somebody else do it. It's not as if you were still in there, pitching. You're through. Can't you get it into your head that you're through?

He heard behind him a short soughing of breath. She realized that he had finished reading the poem. He turned around.

"How long have you been at this?" he asked.

She sat with her hands folded in her lap, her eyes downcast. She was not the same color as these women around here. That was what gave her that look of a being in whom animation was suspended, a marble woman.

The eyes opened suddenly, gleamed into his. She said: "Seven years. I started writing—or trying to write—soon after I married."

"But you'd had your Latin before then?"

She shook her head. "In college I majored in art appreciation. Nobody told me any better."

"They all ought to be taken out and strung up by their thumbs," he said absent-mindedly. "How did you get your classics, then?"

"Lester gave me what help I needed. . . . It was hard to realize how little I'd need."

He smiled. "When you love the stuff." He laid the translation aside and picked up the sheet of paper that held her poem. "I'll read the others later. I want to think about this one a while first."

She closed her eyes again. Her head, on its thin neck, turned suddenly to one side while her lips drew downward in that same odd gesture which, when he had observed it before, had reminded him of a person who, beset by an intolerable thirst, suddenly finds the company of his fellow men insupportable.

He said: "Good Lord! This isn't the court of last appeal, you know."

She looked up at him. "It is for me."

"That's very nice," he said. "Very nice, indeed! But you know there are other people who could advise you just as well as I can."

"Who?"

"Oh, Jim Wragge . . . or Bob Waite."

She shrugged.

"But Bob can't read poetry? No. As a matter of fact, he never could. . . . But he and Jim Wragge are both still in there, pitching."

"You feel you're not?"

"I haven't been able to write anything for a long time," he said, then added hastily, "But let's not talk about that. How many of these things have you got?"

She let out another soft breath, smiling a little. "But you've read only one of my poems!"

He smiled too. "I don't need to read any more—right now. Have you got enough to make a book?"

"Eighteen," she said. "Twelve poems. Six translations."

"You haven't spent your time translating Ausonius?"

"There are three from Tibullus. One from Callimachus."

He whistled. "As good as the one I've read?"

"I don't know. Sometimes I think so. How can you judge? When you work all alone. Nobody to tell you anything."

He said: "Strikes me you've had some pretty good people telling you things. . . . Well, it's a pretty sight!"

"A *pretty* sight?"

"To see the ship leave the harbor, so well loaded. Doesn't often happen these days. Most of 'em can't read English,

141

much less Latin or Greek. You must have worked very hard."

"I haven't done anything else . . . for seven years."

"Well, it's paid off."

"You think I'll be able to go on?"

"I think you'll be a fool if you don't."

"Then you think I'll have—a career in letters?" she asked in what he was already calling to himself her "dry" voice.

"Oh yes. There won't be any trouble about that."

"You mean I'm good?"

"Yes."

"And there are not very many people who are?"

"Exàctly."

She got up and took a few rapid steps about the room. Her hands, held tightly clasped in front of her, shook a little. If he touched them now they would be hot yet clammy; there was a light film of sweat on her upper lip. "You'll help me?" she said.

"Of course," he said, and added after a moment, "What else could I do?"

"Not help me," she said in the same low, dry voice.

He shook his head slowly. "No-o, I couldn't do that."

She took a few more steps about the room, then sat down and faced him. "What will you do first?"

He considered, his head on one side. "Let's see. Bob has already published three of the poems, hasn't he? Did he tell you he liked them?"

"Oh yes."

"He needs stirring up. Always has. We'll make him like them better. . . . I'll give him three or four of these new poems and a couple of the translations before you see him."

"And you'll tell him you like them?"

"I'll convey to him the notion that they have—arrested my attention."

"So that's the way it's worked," she said.

"Not necessarily. That's my way. Now if you'd fallen into Joe Solmes's hands . . . On second thought I doubt if he'd take you on. You aren't bizarre enough. If you were an old

maid, now, who wore her dresses down to her toes and had
never had a drink in her life, or a putative Lesbian . . . or
had spent your life in the North Woods . . . or . . . or in
domestic service . . . But a girl from the Middle West! . . .
From Massillon, Ohio! Were you really born in Massillon?"

She laughed. "Aunt Margot was born in Massillon, and
look where she got to!"

"All the way to Mio Sogno! . . . Yeah, I've often wondered. . . ."

She smiled, but her eyes went past him to rest on the
Manila folder where it lay on the desk. A moment ago she
had made an almost imperceptible movement as if to rise
again, then had sunk back in her chair; she was still enough
in awe of him not to make a move until she was dismissed.
But her thoughts were not of him now. She had what right
now she wanted more than anything: his pledge to help her.
He would not take it back if he could and he could not take
it back if he would. He was a godsend for her, all right. But
was she not a godsend for him too? . . . *What shalle we do
now, Enobarbus? Thinke and dye.* . . . But you have to
have something to think on, some cud not spewed from your
own entrails. . . . She had what she wanted. She'd like to
get off now and do a bit of gloating: "Tom Claiborne thinks
my stuff is good. Yes, he really likes it!" . . . If she went he
would be alone in this room! . . . In this room!

But she was not going. Her hands had folded themselves
again tranquilly in her lap, her eyes left the folder, came
back to his face and dwelt on it wonderingly. Like a long-
desired, cooling bath, the tranquillity, the attention, the
wonder! . . . I really am one hell of a fellow, a fact that
ought to be paid more attention to, a fact that has been well-
nigh lost sight of, a fact . . . The very shape of your sen-
tences reflects a disordered mind. . . . Never mind that.
. . . *"Wondered?"* Did she say she had wondered too? . . .
A pretty trick, to repeat the last word he had uttered. Made
conversation a pleasure. . . . "Yes. . . . What I mean is

143

. . . Well, Margot was pretty well dissolved in liquor when I came on the scene."

"She was pretty far gone when *I* came on the scene," she said thoughtfully.

"How old were you then?"

"Eleven, my first visit."

"A strange household for an eleven-year-old girl to tumble into—fresh from Ohio. . . . You know, it's odd. I can remember your being around, but I can't remember what you looked like."

She said composedly: "I was small for my age, and on the mousy side. It *was* a strange household—for a person of any age."

"People used to say it was all Carlo's fault, that Margot would have been different if he had paid more attention to her. Shut himself up in that belvedere and didn't see anybody for weeks on end. God! You'd have thought the fellow'd have been afraid of the joint. Alfred Henry Watson moldered there for twenty years."

She said: "It was a nunnery of Poor Clares before Alfred Henry Watson got it."

"Must have been a mighty feeble bunch of nuns. When I got there you could smell Alfred Henry Watson all over the place."

She shot him a level glance instinct with secret mirth. "You couldn't smell Uncle Carlo?"

"He was not your uncle."

"No, but I always called him that."

"I never saw the fellow in the flesh. Knew him only by his work. . . . And it never smelled right to me. . . . What's the matter with you?"

For she was laughing, so hard that she felt the need to bend over to hide her face. "I'm sorry," she said. "It's a private joke."

"Must be a good one."

"No . . . it was a coincidence. You said 'in the flesh' and I thought of the first time I ever saw Uncle Carlo."

"In Massillon or at Mio Sogno?"

"In Massillon," she said gravely. "On the Fourth of July. He hadn't been back for years and there was a picnic on the banks of the river. All the Clancys and the Vincenzi . . ."

"They were Vincenzi in Massillon and Vincents in Rome. How Fortune doth spin her wheel!"

"Old Mr. Vincenzi was still alive then," she said. "He was a marble-cutter. One of those men who could bend an iron bar with his bare hands."

"Did he?"

"Uncle Carlo asked him to do it and was most attentive during the performance and then Mr. Vincenzi sang a Neopolitan song and they all laughed a lot and the father and the two sons walked down and swam in the river."

"What's funny about that?"

Her lips trembled again. "I suppose I thought a great man, like Uncle Carlo, ought to be an Adonis too. Old Mr. Vincenzi was a giant, so he stayed lean all his life. So did Roberto and Giuseppe. But Uncle Carlo was beginning to sag here and there."

"What a cruel little minx you are! Won't allow the poor man to take on a little weight. . . . He must have been in his forties then."

Her lips still trembled in that secret smile. "It wasn't the *weight!*"

"Come on, now, give! You know how dull it is around here."

She said: "Haven't you ever seen any of his later work?"

"We've got the last thing he painted downstairs."

"I mean later than that. . . . The last few years."

He said slowly: "When they found him dead there in the studio—died all alone, like Alfred Henry Watson, by the way—the place was full of stuff. On the walls and piled up to the ceiling. Margot was off somewhere. Vera had to handle it. She burned the pictures. . . . She tells me that she had a talk with him a few days before he died and that he repudiated every one of them. I was always glad she had that talk.

Made it easier for her to burn the pictures, though God knows that was tough enough. . . . She doesn't like to talk about it to this day."

She said, "No," on an even note and rose.

"You aren't going? It's hours till lunch."

"Oh, I must."

"Without telling me what's so funny?"

"I told you."

"Oh, no, you didn't!"

"You've never looked at any of the later pictures?"

"I told you Vera burned them up. I don't see what else she could have done—if that was what he wanted. Still, some people would have thought twice before throwing all that money into the fire. . . . Poor old Max was wild! I was venal enough to wish that he might have had some of the canvasses."

She was moving toward the door. "Maybe he'll get them yet."

"You mean you think they might be tucked away somewhere? Oh, no. Vera made a thorough job of it. She would, once she'd set herself to it."

Her hand was on the knob, her eyes firmly downcast, her lips no longer smiling. But he knew that the minute the door was between them she would be smiling again. At him? Or at Vera? There was something she knew which made a fool out of one or the other or of both of them.

He said: "There is something about those pictures. . . . What is it?"

She said hesitatingly: "On my last visit I got to Mio Sogno a month before Uncle Carlo died."

"And you saw the pictures? You were allowed to enter the studio?"

"Not—while he was alive."

"You were in there when Vera burned the pictures?"

"I went into the studio with Vera the day she found him dead. . . . I was in it again on one other occasion."

"When was that?"

146

"Somebody—somebody in the family had to help her."

"You helped her burn the pictures?"

"No."

He said suddenly: "You don't believe that she burned the pictures."

"No."

"Why do you think she didn't burn the pictures?"

"Because I helped her wrap them up and pack them in a long box."

"To be sent where?"

"I don't think they were sent anywhere—then."

"But you think that they were dispatched somewhere later. Where?"

"I should imagine that they have been reposing in your attic for the last twelve years," she said. "Have you ever looked?"

"Why, no. There's a lot of stuff up there that came from Mio Sogno. But I never thought anything about it."

"Why should you think anything about it?" she asked lightly.

"There's no reason, except that you've excited my curiosity."

"About Uncle Carlo's later pictures? I don't think it matters much what they're like, do you? He's been dead twenty-two years."

"An artist is never dead—if he was ever alive."

"Do you think he was ever alive?"

"I don't know," he said slowly. "I've wondered. I think he got off to a good start. There's something very impressive about his early work. And then something happened. He took the wrong turn, somehow. . . . I've never quite figured it out. He must have had the same notion, or he wouldn't have left orders for those later pictures to be burned. I've always wished I'd seen those later pictures."

"Well, next time there's a rainy day you can go up in your attic and see them."

"Provided you're right about the pictures being there."

"Provided I'm right."

His hand suddenly closed over her thin hand that was turning the knob. "Let's go find out now."

She drew a little away from him. "I'm supposed to go swimming with Robin at eleven."

"To hell with swimming. And Robin. This is much more fun."

She looked up at him, laughing. "It *is* fun!" she said.

NINE

The attic was enormous, lighted only by small windows level with the floor, on the east and west. Sunlight lay in a quivering pool on the floor and illuminated the corners of the room, where articles of furniture, shrouded in dust cloths, stood, with smaller objects heaped around them.

Claiborne stopped at the head of the stairs to draw a long breath. "Don't you like the smell of attics?" he inquired. "So much detritus and all so various!" He stopped and lifted from the floor a square, formed by tubes made of cast iron arranged in a row. "Candlestick mold," he said. "Found it right here in this spot first time I ever came up here. . . . And there's the bench the former owner was laid out on. . . . Vera thinks it's too grim to have downstairs. . . . Great God! There's the White Powder Wonder!"

He crossed the floor at a bound to lift from where it leaned against a chair a long object cased in canvas. He held it in his hand a moment and looked down on it intently. She came up to stand beside him. He turned the case in his hand and showed her the initials "T.C." marked crudely in ink in the lower left-hand corner of the case. "The first shotgun I ever had. The White Powder Wonder. George Crenfew got his the same Christmas. His was called the Hammerless Choke."

148

"What did you shoot?"

"The first thing we had a chance to shoot—legitimately—was doves. The next August. We used to pop away at sparrows during the year. But we never let my father know that. He was a very correct man—in his way."

"You're not even going to look at it!" she said, for he was carefully replacing the shotgun, still in its canvas case, in the same position.

"My sporting days are over," he said, and moved forward slowly. She moved beside him. They stopped before an easel which held a picture framed in black: a fat yellow bird perched upon a sagging spray of lilac.

"My mother's sister, Lucy, executed that work while in a state of trance at the Convent of the Visitation in Washington," he said. "She died at the age of nineteen. Her works were therefore religiously preserved."

She bent over the picture. "It's not painted. It's embroidered. What miraculous stitches!"

He did not answer. He was staring at a black leather couch half visible between two boxes of old books. It swayed to one side: the leg that he and George Crenfew had broken when they were scuffling on it one day had never been properly repaired. The leather was torn in places but the metal buttons that tufted it glinted even in this light. Those buttons shone even on the dullest day. . . . It had been up here all this time and he had been fool enough to go out and buy one for himself.

She was raising the lid of an old trunk to lift from the top of a heap of garments a long black cloak. "Your father's?"

"No," he said curtly. "*His* father's. She heard me say once that he wore it at the Nashville Convention of 1850 and so she had to bring it up here." He raised his head sharply and drew in through distended nostrils the warm air which a moment ago he had found pleasing but which now seemed insupportably acrid. Why can't she leave them alone? Why can't she let them stay where they were!

"She has the money to send anything anywhere she wants to send it," a low voice said.

He stared at her. Surely he had not spoken his thought aloud! But she did not seem to think that anything extraordinary had happened. She was not even looking at him, but gazing about the vast, cluttered room, a faint smile on her lips. He gave an uneasy laugh. "We'll have to face it," he said. "Vera's a bit of a magpie. . . . None of this stuff is worth a damn to anybody."

"One wonders why she troubles to pay freight on it," she said in the same low voice, a voice in which she might almost have been talking to herself, so little did she seem aware of his presence.

"Well, as you say, she has the money, and then it's a kind of insurance. . . . Where's that stuff from Mio Sogno?"

She laughed and pointed to a marble statue in another corner of the room. "That's not the work of the great Essentist!" he said. "Why, hello, it's Flora!" He set his big hand on the garlanded head and turned the female figure so that it faced them. "Remember? Flora, from the garden. She used to stand opposite that big La Peyre. The one that was all hips. Vera sold the La Peyre, but nobody would want this baby."

"No," she said, "the flowers look as if they had been crocheted. . . . I used to wonder how they could bear to have those two statues in the same garden."

He looked about the room vaguely, overcome by conflicting emotions. He had had to make an effort to pull himself together there a moment ago. He could not discuss his wife with this woman or anybody else. But he did not want this woman to go away and leave him. It was as if he had escaped some danger and at the same time had missed an opportunity that might not come again. When he had been talking with her in his study he had felt himself alive all over—for the first time in many months. The same feeling had swept over him a moment ago. It had seemed that they were talking about something very important—until his sense of decorum made him change the subject.

She spoke again. "You said it was insurance . . . ?"

He was so relieved that his words came in a rush. "Against a kind of animism that besets her. She might wake up some night and not be able to sleep for thinking of poor old Flora out in the rain. What's simpler than to bring poor old Flora over here where she'll stay high and dry? . . . If Vera's fond of a person it's hard for her to discard his old glove. . . . That couch over there in the corner ought to be made into kindling wood, but my father spent the best years of his life on it, so Vera had it shipped up here."

"What was your father like?"

"Very handsome man. One of the best wing shots in Kentucky and Tennessee. Good high duck shot too. And successful with the ladies."

"How did your mother like that?"

"It made her life a hell on earth."

"And she took it out on you?"

"If she did she didn't know it," he said, then heard with surprise, his own hard voice. "Joe Ryan was the best tenant we ever had. Five acres of tobacco, year in, year out. But he had one girl that went wrong. I will say for the old man that he wasn't the first. He gave her a rubber check. She got sore and brought it up to the house. Early in the morning. Uncle Dod was just bringing in the milk. My mother had come to the kitchen door to let him in. He stood aside to let this girl go first. She held the check out and my mother took it from her, said, 'What is this, May?' May said, 'You tell him I got things to do with my money. This is the third one that's bounced.' "

"What did your mother do?"

"She looked at the girl, then looked past her, and she turned her head to one side and shrieked. I only heard that sound one other time in my life. When the creek was in flood and I was trying to cross on old Cato and we got swept downstream and he turned around and looked at me and screamed. They say a horse never screams like that unless he thinks he's going to die."

151

One would have thought she had not heard him. She had moved a little away and was regarding an Empire *fauteuil*, gravely, as if she were considering its purchase, and now she had stretched herself out on it. He took his handkerchief out and wiped his forehead. She was not looking at him. She had turned her head and was staring out of the low window. He walked over and stood beside her. "Why, Madame Recamier, do you think that will look good in your attic?"

She looked up then, smiling. "Do you?"

"No," he said curtly. "None of this stuff suits you. Now why is that?"

"Maybe it's because I've never had an attic."

"But you must have had a *salon* of sorts."

"I told you that I was at home to students every Saturday afternoon for seven years," she said indifferently.

"Saturday afternoon? Why weren't they off at football games?"

She shook her head. "Not Lester's students. It gets cold out there around November."

"You mean they weren't red-blooded types? Still, they were budding classicists and you're no mean classicist yourself. Wasn't there any young man in spectacles sitting on a footstool beside your sofa on Saturday afternoons?"

She shook her head again. "I suppose there might have been—if I had wanted one. . . . But I didn't."

"What did you want?"

She gave her shoulders a faint shrug and laid her hand down on the faded, flowered satin that covered the *fauteuil*. "Aunt Margot had this in her boudoir. I used to think it was wonderful. Now I wonder why she had it. Nothing else there was Empire."

"Oh, somebody told her it was a good piece. The woman had no sense, no taste. Lived from one moment to the next— like all the Vincents." He stared at her, frowning. "How did you really happen to come to Mio Sogno? Was your mother ambitious for you?"

"She wanted me out of the way so she could pursue an

affair she was having. With Albert Crawford—his father was president of the bank. *My* father kept books for the Ramsey-Dodson Bushing Company. She was tired of that."

"How did the affair with the banker's son work out?"

"Oh, she divorced my father and married him."

"And you've left your husband. Do you have any intention of going back to him?"

"I don't see why I should."

"You don't care anything about him?"

"We have very little in common."

"Did you know that when you married him?"

"Yes. . . . I didn't think it would make as much difference as it has made."

"How did you come to marry him?"

"I met him when I was visiting his sister—one spring vacation."

"Visits have played a considerable part in your life, haven't they?"

"They've had to."

"You mean . . ."

"I mean that there was nothing for me at home."

He was silent a moment, then he said: "You've staked everything on this trip east, haven't you?"

"Everything," she said.

He studied her face in the shimmering light. She realized that she was being appraised and raised her head on its slim neck. He caught the gleam of her eyes. He had had a vixen's eyes gleam at him coldly like that once, from the hollow of a tree that he and George Crenfew were trying to smoke her out of.

"You have the pride of Lucifer," he said. "On what is it founded?"

Still smiling, she laid her hand lightly on her breast.

"On yourself? And what do you intend to do with yourself?"

She rose from the sofa to stand facing him. "I want to write some more poems that you'll like."

"That's all you want?"

"That's all I want—right now."

He laughed. "You'll get your wish."

He heard her catch her breath. Her fingers pressed his arm with a curious urgency. *"How do you know?"*

He laughed. "Oh, by the way you walk . . . or turn your head . . . or turn a phrase. Don't worry. You'll get there. Uncle Tom can still pick a winner—even if he has been left at the post. . . . What's this about those pictures of Carlo's?" he ended, realizing all at once that his voice was tinged with self-pity.

"They were in a long aluminum box. The man recommended aluminum because it is so light."

"What man?"

"The man in the shop."

"Were you with Vera when she bought the box?"

"In that little shop behind the station. You remember that little shop?"

"Yes," he said. "What's the matter?" For she had put her hand up as if to shield her eyes from a ray of sunlight struck suddenly from metal.

"Isn't that the box?" she asked.

"It's made of aluminum and it's the size you said it was." He was conscious of a mounting excitement as he bent and attempted to unfasten the rope that was tied about the box. "We'll have him out of here in a minute. . . . Regular Dracula, isn't he? Only he's resting on canvas instead of a box of earth. . . ."

She had not answered. Instead, she was pressing closer to him, whispering his name.

He raised his head, confusedly aware that this was the first time she had ever called him by his Christian name, and saw his wife standing at the head of the stairs.

Vera stood still in the middle of the pool of quivering sunlight and looked from one to the other. "What are you doing?" she asked.

Her husband straightened up to his full height. "Nothing

154

much. Cynthia was telling me about some pictures of your father's I've never seen and we thought we'd come up and take a look. . . ."

Vera was not looking at him. She was staring at Cynthia. Her eyes slowly came back to his face. "There are no pictures of my father's in that box," she said.

"No? Cynthia said she helped you pack a bunch of them."

Vera silently shook her head, not looking at Cynthia.

He took a step toward her. "Look here, Vera," he said impatiently, "don't get yourself out on a limb. I know what a rough time you had, but that's all past. If there's any of Carlo's later stuff around it ought not to be stuck away in an attic. Think what it might mean to Max!"

"There's not any of his stuff around," she said in a low voice.

"You mean that those pictures in that box aren't his? Whose are they then?"

She clenched her hands at her sides. Her eyes darted about the room then came back to his face. "They are *mine!*" she cried. "*Mine!* Can't you understand how you might want to *write* something and not want anybody to see it?"

Claiborne crossed the room and put his arm about her shaking shoulders. "Forget it, darling. Of course we don't want to see them if you don't want us to."

She drew her breath in with a long sob. "I know it," she said.

A bell pealed below. "Come on," he said, "let's go to lunch," and caught an arm of each woman and walked down the stairs. In the dining room there was conversation and laughter; Max had paid a visit to the Hesses that morning and every visit he made them yielded at least one anecdote worth telling. Once or twice during the meal Claiborne glanced speculatively at his wife. Her color was higher than usual but she gave no other sign of disturbance as she turned from one to the other, smiling, as they discussed plans for an outing. And yet a few minutes ago, up in the attic, she had averted her eyes from his while she contrived the first lie she had ever told him. He wondered why she had felt obliged to tell it.

TEN

"It *is* a good place, isn't it?" Vera said, and laying her hand on her husband's arm, drew a little closer to him.

Claiborne looked down at the little river that wound its sluggish way through the ravine. Its banks were lined with sycamores. Their shade would have been pleasant on a day like this, but Vera had made them cross the river on stepping-stones to climb to the top of this high, grassy bluff. She thought that the cave—visible from here only as a ledge of whitish rock covered with woodbine and some other trailing stuff—was more "exciting" viewed from this vantage point.

He was forty-eight years old today, so they had driven five miles to these woods, to eat cold chicken and hothouse lettuce and hothouse tomatoes and hothouse grapes off a cloth spread on a rock and to drink Chablis or Soave out of paper cups. There had been a discussion about the kind of wine they would bring. It had ended in their bringing two kinds. The toasts were over. He could stand here on the edge of the bluff and eat his grapes and look down on the sluggish river. The rivers in this country aren't any good, he thought, not enough rock, and was aware that the soft pressure he had felt against his side was increasing; Vera had joined him a few minutes ago. Involuntarily, he tightened the arm he had slipped about her waist. She was trying to say something to him with her body that she couldn't say any other way. All day she had been trying to say it, by a pressure of the hand as he helped her over a slippery stone, by a look, a smile. What was it?

He had not gone to her room last night; she had not come

to his. He had been afraid that she was angry with him for an invasion of her privacy which for him was as yet undefined; surely there had been anger in that look she had turned on him there in the attic yesterday. But whatever extraordinary emotions she had harbored yesterday had disappeared —to make way for the emotions that must be harbored today. That was it. She and Max had chosen this spot—an open, grassy ring, surrounded by rocks and stunted oaks on top of a high bluff—as a place to be merry in on this day of Our Lord, nineteen hundred and forty-six, in the forty-eighth year of the earthly pilgrimage of Thomas Crenfew Claiborne, so merry we must be in the good green wood, heigh-ho! That was what that look meant, that smile that was at once secret and sharing, radiant and diffident. *Enjoy yourself, you son-of-a-bitch. Eat, drink and be merry—or I'll cry!*

"Doesn't it remind you of your cave?" Vera asked.

He did not answer, watching Max and Cynthia walking toward them. She had on a dress that was striped green and yellow—or were those stripes buff-colored? Indeed almost the same shade as the sage grass that she was treading under her feet. (If you read off and on, half the night, night after night, year after year, the muscles of your eyes will cease vibrating to certain colors, or will, at least, vibrate at a different rate of speed.) Max was carrying a thermos jug of wine. He let him fill his cup from it. Vera was waiting for him to say something. "Which cave?" he asked.

"The one you and George discovered."

George Crenfew used to go with him and his mother in the summers to the "springs" on the top of Long Mountain. The summer he was fourteen he and George had enjoyed considerable fame as the result of their discovery of a cave at the foot of the mountain. He would never forget how, swimming on his back in the river, he had suddenly looked up into a tangle of laurel on the bluff above him and saw behind it a blackness that was not rock. *I was the first one who saw it,* he thought, *but George was the first man inside. Now how did that happen?* Aloud he said: "George and I have discovered more than one cave in our time. This cave reminds me more of Buzzard's Cave than the one on Long Mountain."

"Where is Buzzard's Cave?"

"Under water," he said, "like everything else at Eupedon. . . . It was just a cave George and I found one afternoon."

He had taken his arm from about her waist to throw the stem from which he had stripped all the grapes down into the stream. There must have been something in his tone that offended her, or it might have been merely that he had removed his arm from about her waist—she was abnormally sensitive. At any rate, she had moved off without waiting to hear anything else he might have to say. But Cynthia Vail still stood beside him, looking down into the water. He could see only the curve of her cheek but he knew that her eyes were following the dark naked stem as it swirled slowly downstream. If they were alone he would ask her what she made of that business in the attic yesterday. He said in a voice loud enough to carry to Vera's ears if she were listening: "So called because full of buzzards. . . . George and I had quite a time with them. . . . Why is it that buzzards never come north of the Mason-Dixon Line?"

"Hell," Max said, "I've seen them flying over your house."

"Those aren't buzzards," Claiborne said. "Those are George Crenfew's patients flying home. . . . George has a buzzard fixation, so his patients take the form of buzzards. . . . Count Dracula's used to impersonate bats."

She turned her head at that to give him her cool, secret smile. "I suppose George got his buzzard fixation from his early reading of Uncle Remus?"

He shook his head. "From dissecting a buzzard we found lying up on a rock in Buzzard's Cave."

"Was it dead?" Max asked.

"*Rigor mortis* had not set in, which made it easier for me and George to transport it—a whole mile, in a tow sack, as I recall."

"What did you do with it when you got it home?"

"I abandoned science about that time, but George was

158

staunch. He put it in the bottom of the old icehouse—that was the only place nobody ever went—and used to climb down at intervals to see it—till my mother told him it was time for his visit to be over."

"God, you're morbid today!" Max said.

"It's the cave," Claiborne said. "Wakens primordial memories."

"If we're going to explore the cave we'd better get going," Max said. "Wait, Vera," he added, for she had begun to repack the picnic hamper.

Cynthia went to help them. Claiborne sat down on a rock and drank off another cup of wine. They had finished with the hamper. Cynthia, straightening up, gave him an enigmatic glance and sat down on a nearby rock. Vera went on stooping about the grove, gathering up debris. He watched her stuff a newspaper into the sack she was carrying and speculated on how long it would have had to be exposed to the elements to become that sodden. She was collecting not only the waste from their own meal but from the meal somebody they had never seen or heard of had consumed in this grove weeks before.

She had a proprietary feeling about this place. She and Max, rambling through these woods last January, had found the cave below and had chosen it for a picnic spot. They had even, on that day—under a sky that must have been dreary, if not lowering, surrounded by the wet, black trunks of these stunted oaks—marked the long, gray rock on which ten months later they would set forth today's viands: the cold carcass of the chicken not yet hatched, the eggs spiced but then not laid, the fruits whose seed at that time had not even been committed to the earth. . . . It had been a long time since anybody had said anything. His own voice still seemed to reverberate in the sunny air. "Primordial memories," he said again. "They are stronger in me than in the rest of you. I come of a race of spelunkers. In my neighborhood everybody has a cave to retire to when things get too much for him. Why, I had one cousin spent practically his whole life in a cave. Cousin Fillinger Fayerlee. Had his bed set up in the mouth of the cave and used to sit there all day long. . . ."

"Just couldn't tear himself out of the womb?" Max said, and took the bag that Vera had filled with waste and dropped it on some soot-blackened stones and bent to put a match to it. Claiborne watched the flame rise, blue and wavering and somehow liquid—as if a thin stream of water were being poured into the air. Somewhere there must be a place, a point at which all elements meet and fuse. Anaximenes held that the primary substance of the world was air, as did Diogenes of Apollonia after him. "The flame does not look the same way to the others that it does to you. That is because you are drunk," the Voice said. "That's why I get drunk—in order to see things like that." The Voice did not reply. Those were the really frightening times, when the Voice would suddenly not answer, would break off as if there were nothing more to be said. Better the interminable, the wearying colloquy, better anything than that! "These obsessions are very strong in the limestone regions of Kentucky," he said. "I had another cousin fell in love with a corpse. . . . Here, I'll have a swig of that wine."

"I carried it up here. You want to carry it down?" Max asked.

"Certainly. . . . Name was Hazel. She had shot seven men in Alabama and had become petrified by a process I never quite grasped."

"What else do you want to carry?" Max said.

"Anything . . . any little thing," he said, looking at his wife, who stood staring dreamily at some twigs that had taken fire from the wastepaper and now glowed fiery red. She looked up as if aware of his scrutiny, then looked back at the embers. Suddenly she smiled. "When I was a child I used to worry about how peculiar my family was," she said. "You know, people were always talking about the strange things my father did. . . ."

"And your mother, off with first one arty young man and then another," Claiborne said.

"Yes," she said steadily. "My father and mother were considered strange, but now I've heard Tom tell about his family I don't worry about *my* family's being strange."

"Back my family against anybody's family," Claiborne said. He got to his feet and was annoyed to find his legs unsteady under him. He must be drunker than he had thought. Odd how that was happening to him more and more frequently these days. . . . But they were not listening to him. They were staring at the overalled figure that was advancing toward them through the dappled shade of the sycamores.

"It's Tom Abel," Vera said. "Something must be wrong."

"Not necessarily," Max said.

But she was already off down the path and across the stream. Max had followed her. Cynthia was picking up some of the small objects they had left behind. He waited and gave her a hand across the steppingstones. Up on the bank he could hear his wife's excited voice and the dairyman's more measured tones.

"It's Bud, Mrs. Claiborne."

"Is he hurt?"

"No'm, *he* ain't hurt."

"Oh, *please!* Has he hurt anybody?"

Claiborne came up the path in time to see the slow grin on Tom Abel's face. "He's hurt Miss Minta Hess's feelings."

Claiborne went up to them. "What's he done?" he asked roughly.

Abel took the grin off his face. "He jumped the fence into the Hess pasture, Mr. Claiborne."

"Where those hot heifers are," Max said. "God, I knew it would happen!"

"*Did* it happen?" Vera asked

Abel nodded slowly. "Yes'm . . . She maintains that Dewberry and Blossie ain't no better'n beef cattle now. She maintains that they won't bring more'n one hundred and twenty dollars apiece now, whereas yesterday they was worth three hundred apiece. They was Holstein heifers, Mrs. Claiborne."

"What does she mean, talking like that?" Claiborne asked.

"She's got a lawyer," Abel said. "He's up at the house now, but I thought I'd come over here and tell Mrs. Claiborne. . . ."

"Vera, the Hesses have been waiting for something like this," Max said. "Ever since you started raising Red Polls."

"Oh, *no!*" Vera said. "They're *crazy* about Dewberry, and Blossie too." She was pale and actually trembling all over, but she had a look about her mouth that he had come to know, the look that meant that her mind was made up and that nothing you could say would change it. She would never recognize the maneuver as a scheme by which two poor people and a shyster lawyer could extract money from a simple-minded rich woman, but would dance to any tune they called, going about for the next few weeks asking herself and anybody who would listen to her what was *right* and what was *wrong.*

He gave a short laugh. "These paternity cases are always best settled out of court."

"The poor brute couldn't hep hisself," Abel said.

"I don't know," Claiborne said. "Bud's quite stubborn, as you'll find if you ever have occasion to cross him. I think he ought to see George Crenfew. I had a long talk with him the other day and pointed out to him that it was all up with natural mating. But he couldn't see it. I bet he was planning this *coup* then."

Vera gave him a swift glance. "You told us all about that the other night," she said in a strained, harsh voice. "Do you *have* to go over it all again?"

"No," he said, and felt a foolish smile arrange itself on his face, "I just thought . . ."

"Suppose you stop talking for a few minutes, old fellow," Max said quietly. He turned to Vera. "There's no use in breaking up the party. If you want me to I'll go on to the house and make a date with that lawyer fellow and you and Tom can see him tomorrow."

"Oh, *no!*" Vera said. "There isn't any party—now. I'm going with you, Max."

"What about it, Cynthia?" Max was asking. "You want to go with us or stay with Tom?"

Tom! They spoke of him in the third person, as one speaks of idiots or children. "Whatever you say," Cynthia had said. But a look had passed between her and Max. They wanted her to detain him here while they talked to the lawyer—about what? About a bull raping a heifer. . . . But what are bulls—and heifers—for?

They were moving off through the grove. Cynthia was walking off too, in the opposite direction, along a narrow, wavering path that somebody's feet had bitten into the packed, white soil of the riverbank. This stream must flood every spring; there was no vegetation on either bank for a dozen yards. Strange how a flood could beat earth down so hard that nothing ever grew in it again. Those stripes in her dress looked tawny in the light filtered through yellowing leaves. Sycamore leaves always turned early and were the first to fall. If she kept on going he would be alone in this grove, from which all but him had departed—on a fool's errand, but gone nevertheless.

"Where are you going?" he called.

She turned around, smiling. "To the cave. We were brought here to see the cave, weren't we?"

"Certainly," he said, "it was my birthday treat," and ran a few steps and caught up with her. He could see the cave ahead of them. It seemed larger than when he had looked down on it from the bluff. The entrance was wide but shallow. A great, black hole yawned back of it: the "room" Vera had talked about. He pushed a hanging mat of woodbine aside and stood with her under the rocky ledge.

The earth under their feet was shaly but dry and warm from the September sun. From behind the curtain of trailing vines, he stared out at the grove. Not as many leaves had fallen as he had thought. The look—and the feel—were still of summer.

There was a rustle among the drying ferns. She had gone

over to peer down into the black hole. She said that she could hear water dripping.

"These caves up here don't make good stalactites," he said without turning around.

There was a faint sound, as of a stone being dislodged. She had stepped down over the threshold and was standing in the dark "room." "It's quite dry," she called.

"I told you it wasn't a real cave."

"But there *is* another passage. . . . How far do you suppose it goes?"

"Not far. . . . Would you like to explore it?"

"That's what we came here for, isn't it?"

"Yes," he said, "but we've got all day. . . . Why don't you sit down?"

As if obedient to his command, she came and sat down on a rock opposite him.

"Why wouldn't Vera let us see those pictures the other day?" he asked.

"I don't think I ought to tell you that."

"Why?"

"Because . . ."

"Because I'm her husband—and you're her cousin?"

She was silent a moment, then she said, "I've never felt very close to Vera."

"No?" he said. "Well, I can see how that might be. What I want to know is, what are those pictures of Carlo's like?" He felt his brain clear itself of the fumes of wine as if suddenly affected by some more powerful potion.

She looked intently into his face and then, as if she too had had a moment of illumination or had, at least, come to some decision, she laughed. "They are self-portraits," she said. "In the nude, or mostly in the nude. Sometimes he wears chain armor, sometimes a plumed hat. . . . In one he's St. George fighting the dragon . . . naked."

He brought his fist down on his knee.

"Mad as a hatter! I've always known it. . . . How long did this go on?"

164

"From the time they went to live at Mio Sogno, I should think."

He laughed. "People thought he had retired from the world to do something that never had been done before—and all he was doing was looking in the mirror!"

"And painting what he saw. He worked."

He shook his head. "Poor devil! It must have been a pretty sight."

"The pictures were—dreadful."

"How?"

"The color was—ugly."

"And the form?"

"Sagging flesh," she said dryly.

"But well painted?"

"With *gusto*—now like Franz Hals, now like Tintoretto. I think—from something Vera said once—that he had a theory that he was recapitulating the history of painting."

"Poor Vera!" he said. "The wonder is that she wants to hang on to the things."

She was silent, so long that he looked at her questioningly. She said then: "Isn't that half the trouble?"

"The trouble?"

"Her trouble?"

"Well, what is her trouble?"

"Don't you think that her uncritical attachment to her family may be part of it?"

"I never thought of that," he said. "I always knew the whole setup was crazy, but I never thought of that. Yes," he repeated, and felt a pleasure in hearing the words emerge from some remote, unexplored recess to quiver between them in the sunny air, "I always knew they were crazy. . . . But *she* doesn't."

"No," she said, "she doesn't."

They were silent. She still sat on the rock on which she had dropped down at his bidding, her head a little bent, her hands in her lap. He had a feeling that she could sit there a long time without saying anything, without even looking up. He studied the bent head, the long, rather thin hands, wondering how he could ever have thought of her as a negligible person. "Is Robin Vincent in love with you?" he asked abruptly.

"Robin?"

"Yes. Isn't he smitten with you?"

Her hand moved in an indifferent gesture. "I really don't know."

"You haven't given it a thought?"

She slowly shook her head.

"He's not the most exciting company in the world, but he's rich."

She looked up then. She laughed. After a second he laughed too. Her lips were moving. She was asking him a question. He could not answer it; he could not take his eyes from her green eyes and her pale face, flecked with light and shade from the trailing vines. It was not her face. It was her voice! Surely that dry, metallic voice had echoed all his life in some dark crevice of his brain, a wind whirring dead leaves, dead branches of trees standing in rows on the banks of a river that ran far underground. . . . The man was not standing on the bank. He was plunged deep in the current. The mist that hung low over the river was lifting. He could see the cavern yawning. The waves that caressed his limbs ran before him like swallows as he swam for the wide, brightly lighted ledge. . . .

He had frightened the girl, cool customer that she was. She was on her feet. There was an expression on her face he had never seen before. She looked first to one side of her, then to the other, repeated words: "Isn't it time we went home?" He set his hand on her shoulder. "Not yet," he said, and drew her, stumbling, over the stone threshold, to lie beside him on the earthen floor where a moment ago she had stood alone.

ELEVEN

During the next few weeks Claiborne busied himself with editing a symposium on contemporary letters for *Spectra*. The project was one he had undertaken several years before and had subsequently abandoned. Bob Waite had been surprised and pleased when Claiborne told him of his desire to undertake the symposium again. They had lunched together several times in order to discuss it and it had been agreed that Claiborne would try to have the contributions ready for the spring issue of *Spectra*.

"I might make it, at that," Claiborne said to himself as he went swiftly down the stairs one morning in late October, relieved to have surmounted what he had come to think of as the hurdle set at the beginning of each of his days. He had somehow to account for the time that he was more and more spending away from home.

He had gone into Vera's room immediately after breakfast to tell her that he would lunch with Bob and go on to a cocktail party Bob wanted him to show up at. She was in her bathroom, with the door closed, and called to him that she would be with him in a few minutes. Standing there, staring at the white door from behind which came the sound of rushing water, he had felt so great a disinclination to confront her, to exchange the kiss with which they were accustomed to mark so much as an hour's parting, that he had shouted that he had not time to wait and had left the room hardly hearing what it was she had called out in answer.

He had expected that she would go to the stable or out into the fields, as she usually did at this time of day, and was disconcerted when he came out of the house on the way to the garage to find her crouching beside the walk, under the great beech tree that spread its branches over the whole back yard. Walnut hulls lay all about her on the grass. She was hulling the nuts in the old-fashioned way, laying each nut on a flat stone and beating the hull off with a hammer. As he passed close beside her, she suddenly held one of the walnuts up. "Smell!" she said.

Obediently, he bent his head, then straightened up, his nostrils stinging with the odor that in boyhood had been so familiar. In the fall, at Eupedon, the walnuts from the three great trees that stood beside the smokehouse were gathered as they fell and heaped up in the brick runway between the kitchen and the old outkitchen. His father liked to sit in a low, split-bottom chair beside the heap and hull the nuts with a hammer, just as Vera was doing now. He himself, when he passed that way, would sometimes stop and pick one of the nuts up and hold it to his nose and inhale the smell that the greenish-yellow rind gave off, marveling each time, to find it at once so fragrant and so bitter. His father, as if reading his mind, would look up, smiling. "Smells like fall," he would say. "I always think walnuts smell more like fall than anything." "Wa'nuts," he said, like a Virginian, though he had been born in Tennessee.

"Did you see Aunt Virginia?" Vera asked.

"God, no!" he said, annoyed to recall that she had asked him to go in to see his aunt before he left.

"I did tell you," she said in an even tone.

"I'll miss my train."

She threw the wet, black nut into the basket that stood beside her and took another one up from the heap. "The ten forty-five gets into New York at eleven-forty," she said.

"I was going to stop at Shulte's. They've found a copy of Flanders Dunbar's book on Dante for me."

She did not answer.

"Did Aunt Virginia want anything special?" he asked uneasily.

She looked up at that. "She wants to know who Cousin

Tom Crenfew's youngest son married. The one who went west."

"He married a chambermaid in St. Louis."

"She wants to know the name of the chambermaid."

"Do we have to have a family conference about that? Adele . . . Adele B. Bristow . . . B for Bertha."

She laid her hammer down and crossed her blunt, little yellow-stained fingers in her lap. "She's your aunt. . . . And it's your project."

"Have it your own way," he said, and left her and went into the house. As he went he recalled how pleased he and Vera had both been a year ago, when, in response to her repeated pleas, he had thought of a diversion for his aunt: a family history in the shape of a memoir, in which the writer would not attempt to give any form to her memories, but would merely set down every day anything she could remember, concerning herself or any other member of her family connection as far back as hearsay or memory could reach. George Crenfew, who admired the scheme for its ingenious use of free association, called it the "Old Folks Project" and maintained that the government ought to subsidize it. This time last year they sometimes used to gather in Aunt Virginia's room and one of them would read aloud a chapter she had just finished, a chapter to which after they went downstairs Max would add a sequel—if he got drunk enough.

She was expecting him, propped high on her pillows. He did not give her a chance to tell him what she wanted—sometimes it took her several minutes to tell you what you already knew she had it in mind to say. Standing just inside the door, he said: "MorningAuntVirginiaHowyoufeeling-thismorningOfftotownAnythingdoforyouVerasaysyouwantto-knownameofCousinJohnCrenfew'swife."

She bent a bewildered gaze on him. "Why, I know her name, Tom. Octavia. Cousin Octavia Meade Manigault. She was a lady from New Orleans."

"I don't mean Cousin Sycamore John," he said, "I mean Cousin Wild John—the one that married a chambermaid in

169

St. Louis. *Her* name was Anna . . . Anna . . . Brunhilda
. . . Brewer. . . ."

She wrote something on the pad she held on her knee, then
held her pencil suspended. "Brunhilda . . ." she said.
"Brewer . . ."

"German. Father worked in a brewery. That's funny, isn't
it? Named Brewer and worked in a brewery."

She looked out of the window where the rolling fields lay
fallow under the October sun. "It isn't funny," she said sadly.
"Mother had a letter from Cousin Rachel, telling of a visit
this poor Anna made to them after John's death. She told
Cousin Octavia that he was the finest gentleman she had ever
known."

"And all he ever did was drink and gamble. . . . Well, it
takes all kinds," he said, and would have been gone from the
room if she had not stayed him with a motion of her wasted
hand. "Tom," she said, "I've been lying here thinking about
your father."

"It isn't his birthday, is it? Doesn't that come in December?"

She gave him that smile that showed how pale her gums
were, how shrunken. "I was thinking about something that
happened in December. Two days after his birthday—he was
born on December twenty-second, you know. . . ."

"I know," he said hastily. "Made it hard for him. Presents
and all that."

"I never knew until this morning what really happened,"
she said. "I was lying here thinking about them all and all of
a sudden it all came together in my mind. I don't know why
I never realized it before."

"What was it, Aunt Virginia?" he said patiently.

"How I came to find out about Santa Claus. It was through
your father, Tom. He was thirteen that year and I was seven
and the creek flooded and nobody could get to town to buy
presents. I suppose they thought it was best to tell me, so I
wouldn't expect a doll or anything. Anyhow, I was crying.

All alone on the back stairs. . . . Do you remember those back stairs at Eupedon, Tom?"

"*God,* yes!"

"I wish you wouldn't be profane, Tom. . . . It's vulgar!"

"All right," he said. "He came by and found you crying. . . ."

"And he went away." She sat up straight against her pillows to give him a sudden brilliant smile. "I never knew until this morning where he went."

"Where did he go?"

"He got on his horse and rode through the storm, all the way to Sycamore, to get me a doll. . . . He must have got it there. Anyhow, that was how I found out about Santa Claus. The doll had on a dress that was made of the same stuff as a ball dress Cousin Virginia Crenfew had. . . . But wasn't that kind, Tom?"

"Yes," he said absently. "He was always very kind—to children and niggers. Specially kind to children and niggers."

"The servants adored him," she said.

"Yes . . . yes . . . they did that, all right." He glanced at his watch. "Aunt Virginia, I've got to go."

The brown eyes, which no matter how hard she tried to die, kept on glowing in her pallid face, glowed brighter, became luminous. It was the look he dreaded. There was only one way to put an end to that. He crossed the room and bent and set his lips on her forehead. "Good-bye, Aunt Virginia. Now you take care of yourself." But she had put her hand up. The thin, chill fingers were closing on his wrist. She had raised herself on her pillow to turn that burning glance on him again. "Tom," she said in her reedy voice, "do you ever think that we two are all that is left?"

He eased himself back on his heels. "Of the family? Why, Aunt Virginia, the woods down home are full of Claibornes."

Her hand fell away from his arm. She turned her head toward the window. "Not even the place!" she whispered. "I lie here and think how the place isn't even there any longer. The trees, Tom! The wa'nut trees and the big elm that came from a riding switch your grandfather stuck in the ground. Nobody can even see them now. . . . All under water . . . all under water . . ."

"I wish we hadn't sold the place," he said after a moment. "I wish now we hadn't sold the place."

"You couldn't help it," she said wearily. "None of us could help it."

"No," he said. "There was nothing else to do. . . . I couldn't live there, and you wouldn't want to live there alone."

"No," she whispered. "We couldn't live there. We couldn't any of us live there any more. But we *did* live there, Tom. After all, it's something to be a Claiborne. I hope you'll never forget that, Tom."

He laughed. "I'm not likely to forget it," he said, and before she could answer bent and kissed her again. "I've got to go. Now you take care of yourself, Aunt Virginia." He was at the door when a sound made him turn around. Her head was drooping sidewise against her pillow. The sound he had heard was a whimper that might have come from a child. Reluctantly he turned back to stand beside the bed. "What is it, Aunt Virginia?" he asked.

"You wouldn't leave me?" she whispered. "Tom, you wouldn't leave me here with strangers?"

"Strangers?" he said roughly. "Do you call Vera and Max strangers?"

Her head turned on its long neck. She opened her eyes and fixed them on his face. He stood for a second, taking full the gaze he had always known she would one day turn on him, before he went silently from the room.

TWELVE

Vera was still sitting on the ground under the beech tree, hulling walnuts. Max had come to sit on the marble bench above her. He asked Claiborne what train he intended to take home that evening. Claiborne replied that he hoped to make the nine forty-five. "Not if I know the Waites," Max said.

Claiborne gave him a straight look. "Why don't you come along?"

Max shook his head. "The country is too good to leave right now. Did you know there'd been a frost? Very light frost. Sparkling all over the field when I came back from Hesses' this morning."

"What were you doing at Hesses'?"

"Calling on the little mothers," Max said airily.

Vera and Max had been in conference with the Hesses and two lawyers yesterday afternoon. Vera's lawyers had proposed that she buy Dewberry and Blossie for the price they would have brought before they were bred, but Minta Hess had showed herself unexpectedly sentimental, refusing to part with Dewberry and Blossie at any price that the lawyer would allow Vera to offer. It had therefore been decided that the heifers should remain in the possession of the Hesses but that Vera should have the privilege of buying the calves if any were dropped.

"How *are* the little mothers?" Claiborne asked now.

"Rounding out nicely," Max said. "Looks to me like Dewberry may get there first."

"How much are you going to pay the Hesses?" Claiborne asked.

Vera did not answer. After a moment Max said, "Three hundred apiece."

173

Claiborne let out a whistle. "That ought to pay for a lot of rape," he said, staring at the nape of his wife's bent neck where a few white hairs glistened among the black hairs that curled there.

Abruptly he went over and planted a kiss on the crown of her head then started for the garage. Max got up and walked beside him. "You going to have lunch with Bob?" he asked.

"Likely to," Claiborne said.

"Then I guess you'll see Cynthia. . . . How's she getting along?"

Claiborne turned his head to give him a straight glance. "Do you mean with the job or in general?"

"With the job. I think you could trust her to take care of herself—in general. Pretty smart cookie, that girl, getting the *Spectra* job just like that!"

"I'll try to see her at lunchtime," Claiborne said, "to find out how she's getting along with the job. After all, I recommended her."

They were at the garage. He bent and sent the wide door sliding upward, then got into his car. Max was still standing in the middle of the doorway through which the car had to pass. He was staring at a clump of larkspur that thrust up through the gravel. At the sound of the motor he looked up. "You really coming home tonight?" he asked.

Claiborne leaned out. "I'm going to stay at the Hotel Hibiscus," he said. "You remember it, don't you?" He paused and looked straight into the shining black eyes. "You might give me a ring."

Max looked away, stepped off the drive. Claiborne did not look at him again as he backed the car out and turned around but the image of the black, shining glance which had been so abruptly veiled stayed with him till he reached the highway.

Home! he thought. *Home!* Home is where the heart is, but the heart, nowadays, is on the run. Reposing nine months in the womb (women still have wombs though there is a question whether they are functional), it has time to surround itself with flesh, provide itself with livers, lungs, and lights, but once out of the womb there is no opportunity to acquire those other fleshly integuments that were once so dear. And yet how stubborn the human heart! Eupedon had long been under water: the house, the outbuildings, the old orchard, the garden, the tall trees that stood about the house, were all fathoms deep under water, and she lay here, thinking about musty portieres in the back hall of a house that no longer existed and a boy who no longer had human shape riding along a road whose particles were no longer dust to fetch a doll for a child who would have been better off if she had died that Christmas Eve!

As the car went down the public road he wondered how the two he had left would spend the rest of the day. Hulling walnuts that would never be used and storing them in one of the old stone outhouses, or pounding some of Max's herbs to powder in a mortar? They had a whole outfit for such work, including an ingenious little threshing machine that Max had rigged up. Whatever it was they would go at it conscientiously, with childlike absorption. No pains were too great to achieve the inconsequential results which they duly reported each time the family gathered at a meal. . . . Family? Did a half-crazy man, a childish woman, and a forty-five-year-old sexual deviate constitute a family? And if so, whose was the leading role in the triumvirate? Was not Max actually the prop and stay of the house? That was the role he had more and more assumed during the last few weeks. It was Max, not he, who had advised Vera throughout the altercation with the Hesses over the heifers. She had hardly mentioned it to *him* and it was Max who had just briefly informed him of the decision that had been arrived at. She was not a woman who liked to make decisions by herself. This was the first time that she had made a decision—a major decision, she would have called it—without consulting him. He concluded that she must have been offended by the offhand attitude he had taken from the first toward the affair. God knows what he had said over there on the bluff, but she knew he was tight. She ought not to have been offended.

But she took offense easily. She was, in some ways, the most sensitive person he had ever known. It was as if all her daily activities, her intercourse with her husband, her family, her friends, were films that the flesh had grown over some deep wound. He and she, he supposed, had "fallen in love at first sight," meeting, in that *allée* of sycamores, like pilgrims bent on the same mad quest. The first words they had addressed to each other were the phrases that intimates might exchange on being reunited, not the greetings that pass between strangers. Three weeks after they met they had become lovers. He had been delighted by her ardor at the same time that he was frightened by her assumption that he had powers that he had never thought of himself as possessing. ("You're *not* crazy!" "No, not now. Not *now!*") She had come to him as to a physician—or magician. He was to give her everything she had ever wanted and never got. When she found that he could not do it (what man could?) she had turned away from him (for she could not deny that in the last few years she had turned away from him!) to lose herself in frenetic activity. Pales, Pomona, even the noble Ceres become the plaything of a woman and a half-man, for Max abetted her in all she did. . . . But the wound still bled! Often, in his arms, which she had once held a sovereign refuge, she would weep for no apparent reason, or on a moonlight night pace that balcony outside her window.

"I can't stand it. I can't stand it!"

"Stand what?"

"Our life."

"Our lives?"

"No, I mean our life."

"I thought that this was the way you wanted to live."

"I didn't know it would be like this. . . ." But she could

176

never tell you what "this" was, or what she wanted life to be like.

He arrived at the station just in time to park his car and swing aboard the train. The smoker was crowded, but he found a seat halfway up the aisle, beside a woman. He had been sitting beside her for several minutes before she leaned forward to look up into his face.

"Hello, Marcia!" he said, startled.

Marcia Crenfew laughed mischievously. "Did you get it figured out?" she asked.

"Get what figured out?"

"The problem you were working on. It must be difficult, from the way you were gritting your teeth."

"I'm doing a piece for *Spectra,* and I'm already over my deadline," he said after a moment.

"I didn't know you ever bothered with deadlines and that sort of thing."

"Oh, I toil not, neither do I spin, but I do occasionally take a little thought," he said in what he hoped was a cheerful tone.

"I took thought all night long," she said with a sigh, "and this morning I told George I was going in to town and have a talk with that woman. It seems to me the only thing to do."

"What woman?"

"Catherine Pollard. Didn't Vera tell you? Dessy's been at her place for three weeks now. They've put Dessy in charge of the clothes room."

"The clothes room?" he repeated vaguely.

"The room where they pile up all the old clothes that people give them. My God, I positively defrauded myself, and Katie and Désirée and George too, when Catherine spent that week end with us. Désirée is there now, sewing buttons on the things. It seems to me that if you *give* them the things they ought at least to sew the buttons on themselves."

"So Désirée sews the buttons on," he said vaguely, wondering whether Cynthia would be at her apartment on Bedford

177

Street when he got there. Last Saturday he had gone by the office to pick her up but she had told him that she did not think he ought to do that again. And she was right. Bob Waite was no fool. In fact, he was better than the next man at putting two and two—or one and one—together. And as the devil's luck would have it Alma had been there that day. . . . He remembered the blow it had been to her when he resigned from *Spectra,* perhaps because she was shrewder than Bob and knew Bob's limitations better than Bob, himself. Her face had actually gone white when she heard the news.

"Are you sure you're doing the right thing, Tom?" she had kept saying. "I don't mean just from Bob's standpoint. It'll be hard for him to carry on by himself, but it can be done. But what about you? What'll become of you?"

He had tried to carry it off lightly. "What's going to become of any of us, Alma? The Lord is the only one knows about that."

The remark had infuriated her. She had suddenly thrust her face up close to his. "Don't you worry about Bob," she had hissed. "Bob'll get along. But you'll rot out there, doing nothing all day long. Mark my words: you'll *rot!*"

There had been a coolness between him and Alma from that time forward. . . . But that was a long time ago. Twelve years ago. Why was he thinking of all that now when he had so much else to think of? It was because he had run into Alma at the *Spectra* office the other day. In a way, it was a good thing. The encounter had put him on his guard, making him realize that from now on he would have to concern himself more with appearance than he ever had before. From now on he would have to watch his step. For how long?

". . . a blue denim skirt and a scarf tied over their heads and *sneakers,*" Marcia said. "They don't even have a regular *habit!*"

"Who is it dresses like that?" he asked.

"*Dessy,* Tom. She wants to *live* at Catherine's place and go around dressed the way those people dress."

"What people?"

"Those Catholic Laborers of Catherine's. It's a kind of third order, Tom. Daughters of Charity or something like that—because that's where Catherine went when she left George."

"When she left George?" he echoed stupidly.

"Tom, you remember how she walked out on him. And nobody had any idea where she was—least of all, poor George! —and all the time she was in a convent in the Faubourg St. Antoine, washing dishes and scrubbing floors or something. . . . That strikes Désirée and the rest of those girls as the height of romance!"

"Is she corrupting many young girls?" he asked.

"There's a girl left Leonard soon after the term began. Her parents can't get her to go back to college. She says it's just too dull. . . . George thinks that we ought to leave Dessy alone, that she'll get tired of it eventually, but I don't know. Catherine has an extraordinary influence over her."

"So you're going down this morning to combat her dread influence?"

She nodded. "I'm going down to have a talk with Catherine. I want to see exactly what problems are involved. I told George we *can't* act intelligently unless we know exactly what problems are involved."

She settled herself a little more firmly on the plush-covered seat, as if she felt herself on more familiar ground with the very utterance of the word "problem." How promptly, he thought, she would set herself to solve his "problem" if she only knew of its existence! His "problem" and its "complications." A sigh escaped him. It was only three weeks since that picnic on the creek banks. In the last three weeks his life had undergone such a change that he was still dizzy with thinking of it. He had regarded what had happened that day as a regrettable incident and had been prepared to express his regret to Cynthia when they met the next day, and was somewhat taken aback by the frankness and promptness with which she faced the consequences of that act. She would have to cut her visit short, she said, and take possession of the apartment she had rented in New York sooner than she had intended. "Won't Vera's feelings be hurt if you cut your visit short?" he had asked. He would not soon forget the look she had given him. "I can't stay here now—any longer than is necessary. Can I?" "I suppose not," he had had to answer.

Three nights ago he had almost missed the last train back to the Valley, lingering with his mistress (he had a mistress now!) till eleven o'clock on the little terrace at the back of her apartment. There was a tree in the courtyard below whose branches pushed up against the terrace and shaded it from the glare of the neighbors' windows. An ailanthus, of course. If you have only one tree you think more of it than a hundred stately oaks. The apartment consisted of one large, square room, with a small bedroom off one side of it and the conveniences off the other.

He felt more at home there than in his own handsome, well-appointed house and he never left it without a pang. He had told her so the other night.

"It's envy," she said. "I'm leading the kind of life you'd like to lead, the kind of life you ought to be leading."

"How do you know the kind of life I ought to be leading?"

"Do you remember the day I brought those Ausonius translations to your study?" she asked.

He could see himself standing there, listening to the knock and grinning, only now it was as if she were standing there beside him. On the same side of the door. She *was* on the same side of the door now. She did not have to exert herself to read his thoughts. She knew his thoughts because they were her thoughts. "You have a diabolical intelligence," he said. "Is *that* the secret of your charm?" "I aim to please," she said, with her faint smile that was smothered when he caught her in his arms.

Later, still smiling—for he had just told her how much she pleased him—she had said that they must take thought about their situation. "I know," he said, and groaned and put his head down in his hands, but she took his hands away from his face and held them in her own while she told him that she could not see that there was anything to groan about. "I take it you're no longer in love with your wife," she said.

"No. I haven't been for a long time."

"But you don't want a divorce?"

"I hadn't thought that far," he said, startled.

"I don't see why you should—at present," she returned calmly.

When he said that he did not like to see her placed in a compromising position she had laughed. "How horse and buggy can you get, darling? Don't you realize that if we're seen together in public it's more of a help to me than a hindrance?"

"I have to consider Vera," he said.

She was silent at that; then: "We both have to consider Vera. Do you feel that we have taken anything away from her?"

"No," he said, and groaned again. "I haven't had anything to give her—for a long time. . . ."

"Then stay with me—while you can," she said. "That's all I ask. Come to me when you can and stay as long as you can."

Later, lying side by side on long garden chairs on the tiny terrace, they had talked about the days when they had first known each other. She was such a remarkable woman, so free from ordinary female vanity that he could confess to her that in the old days at Mio Sogno he had hardly remarked her presence. He could summon up only the impression of a small, slight young person slipping in and out of rooms.

She smiled dryly at that. "I tried to make myself useful. Isn't that what's expected of poor relations?"

"Did you feel yourself so much the poor relation?"

"No," she said slowly, "I hardly thought of myself at all

181

that summer. It was as if somebody had opened a window before me—a showcase window containing all sorts of wonderful objects. Some of them things I'd never seen before. I was trying to find out what they all were. . . . But I knew, too, that there was something wrong. . . ."

"You mean that you knew all along that Carlo Vincent was crazy?" he asked.

Cynthia said that the idea had occurred to her the summer she had first visited the Vincents. At that time Vincent's seclusion was not complete. He had come into the dining room straight from the studio one night, staring-eyed, unshaved, in a ragged old jacket, and had stood in the doorway long enough to intone some Latin phrases and then had gone away. "Margot said, 'He's drunk again,' but Vera said, 'He's *not* drunk, Mummy!' and got up and went after him. The next day we were walking in the garden near the belvedere and I asked Vera if Uncle Carlo would let me look at his pictures and Vera said no, that he did not like people to see his pictures. 'But why does he paint them then?' I asked, and she said she didn't know and began to cry. She cried a lot that summer."

"But she never told you why she was crying?"

"No. I think her relationship to her family was very—unusual, so unusual that she wouldn't dare discuss it with anybody else. At least, she didn't then. Perhaps she does now—with you."

He did not reveal to her how illuminating that remark had been. He had not realized until then that he and Vera had had for years a tacit agreement not to talk about her family. They might spend hours rehearsing the eccentricities of the Claiborne-Crenfew tribes. There was nothing he liked better than discussing the differences between the two branches of the Claiborne family, the "Kinky Heads" and the "Anyhows." The "Kinky Heads" had kinks in their brains. A good many of them had been abolitionists. Old Crenfew Claiborne, for instance, had abandoned the culture of tobacco and planted his land with mulberry trees to feed silkworms, after shipping all his slaves to Africa. Fauntleroy Claiborne, an "Anyhow," had never worn shoes after he got out of the Confederate army and slept with all the money he had in a roll under his pillow. Vera's great-grandfather Clancy—he later made money in steel—had landed in this country just in time for the Civil War. He had been a sutler for the Union army. That was about all she knew about his early life. In her family so few anecdotes had survived that you could not even tell which of her immediate ancestors she resembled. Had she perhaps got her stubbornness from her Irish forebears, her simplicity from the Italian side of her family? In the past few weeks he had known a peculiar pleasure in pondering and discussing certain aspects of Vera's character. Seeing a person through another person's eyes was a little like seeing him through the keyhole of a door of the room in which he had thought himself alone. The pleasure was doubtless perverse as well as peculiar. He had never before discussed his wife's character with any human being; they had been too close—perhaps they had been *too* close!—for that. But then he had never before met anybody who seemed to know her better than she knew herself, or than he knew her. It was as if a torch—or a searchlight—were suddenly playing on a path along which he had been stumbling in the dark. But not alone! Vera moved ahead of him on that same path. What could he do but follow?

It was not on Vera alone that the light played. It was the Vincent family as a whole that had engaged the attention of this remarkable girl for two whole summers, as she admitted, half laughing. She seemed never to have taken them for granted, but always, from the time of her first visit, to have walked about among them wide-eyed and questioning. But the questions she asked herself about them, the questions she asked of them, were not the questions that anybody else would have asked. People said negligently that Margot had had probably more than a touch of nymphomania, that Carlo, for all his genius, was doubtless a "true alcoholic, basically homosexual." Not for her such easy dismissals. It was as if she—and he too, for he had joined her on her strange quest—wandered in some vast cavern underground, their only light the torch which played now on this marmoreal figure, now on that, figures whose pose, whose features seemed at first glance familiar but which in the gleam of the torch held up in her frail hand, would suddenly lean forward in an attitude never assumed in life, emit from under shadowy brows looks never leveled on fellow mortals.

He had begun to dream about the place, which gave it more the aspect of reality, made it more like a place he had actually visited, or, perhaps, a museum of which he had recently become curator. Like any conscientious curator, he added to his collection from time to time. The acquisition of a figure was the occasion of one of those intervals in which, again like the conscientious collector of works of art, he stood before his statue, pleading with it to reveal itself to him in its essence. Carlo was the strangest of all his acquisitions. Carlo would not consent to that silent communion in which it was nearly always possible to engage the others. Carlo—and this was the strangest thing of all—Carlo was not always to be found on the same pedestal, or even in the vast hall. In a dream he had had recently, Carlo was running down a winding corridor that opened off the hall, the rags of his worn jacket fluttering in a wind that seemed to beat up from regions colder and more infernal than any the dreamer had ever envisioned.

There was somebody running beside Carlo. Who was it? He took a fine linen handkerchief out of his breast pocket and wiped the sweat off his forehead. *"Stay with me while you can,"* she said, and, then, like any other woman, began estimating the duration of that stay. The other night as he was going out into the street she had followed him down the stairs to say good-by again, "because you may not come back." "There is nobody who can keep me from coming back," he told her. "Not even Vera?" "Not even Vera." He had not hesitated when he said that, and indeed, he felt in him a power for decision, for action he had never felt before. He had spent his life in aimless walking to and fro on the earth's surface, but a man must know, in the end, what it is he stands on. Saul goes to the Witch of Endor, Odysseus descends to Orcus, and Tiresias at his request spills the bullock's blood and summons the shades. The past twelve years had gone over his head as unmarked as if he had slumbered them away in a hammock slung between two of the magnificent trees on his richly nourished lawn. But the time had come for the sleeper to rouse himself, to leave the light summer air, even if it meant descending into the vaporous and shadowy underground. He clenched his hand on his knees. "I was a poet once," he thought, "and by God I'll be one again!"

The woman sitting beside him on the train started. "You don't *have* to read it if you don't want to, but I thought that since it was you who suggested it . . ."

"*I* suggested it?" he repeated, trying to keep his voice even.

Marcia gave him a curious glance. "Tom, you *know* you told me to investigate Baudelaire. You said I might be surprised."

"And were you?"

"Oh, of course I read *Les Fleurs du Mal* in college. But reading it now is a very different experience. I had no idea there was so much material. I think *Le Rêve Parisien* is the most rewarding. I've decided to concentrate on that."

"Are you going to write something about it?" he asked.

She laughed excitedly. "Don't you think that the very *sound* of excretion may have evoked the feeling of loathing he had for the sexual act?"

"The sound of excretion . . . ?"

"It's obvious that he must have seen his mother and his stepfather in *coitus* at some time."

He said absently: "*In coitu.*"

185

"Oh, Tom! What I mean is he must have, or he wouldn't have such a horror of the sexual act. Listen," and she began quoting:

> *"Babel d'escaliers et d'arcades,*
> *C'était un palais infini,*
> *Plein de bassins et de cascades*
> *Tombant dans l'or mat ou bruni. . . .*

What do you make of that? The color alone ought to tell you."

"The color?"

"*Or* . . . gold. . . . Urine is yellow."

"Yes," he said, "urine *is* yellow—unless a person has some kidney disease."

She laughed merrily:

> *"Et des cataractes pesantes,*
> *Comme des rideaux de cristal,*
> *Se suspendaient, éblouissantes,*
> *A des murailles de métal. . . ."*

"What of it?" he said.

She said meaningfully:

> *"Non d'arbres, mais de colonnades*
> *Les étangs dormant s'entouraient,*
> *Où de gigantesques naïades,*
> *Comme des femmes, se miraient.*

Oh, Tom, can't you *see* the way the woman's legs would look like mighty columns to a child of three or four? And the fountains and cascades that fall in gold. . . . Of course it was probably china but a vitreous china would look like metal to a tiny boy, and of course every child loves . . ."

"To look into a chamberpot full of urine," he said. "The poem, then, is a vision of Baudelaire's mother sitting on a chamberpot."

"Well, I think he must have seen her like that some time and got quite a trauma from it. . . . But the little boy gets *his* innings later on in the poem. After all, *he* has a *penis,* and

186

his mother, even if she is a giantess, doesn't have a penis. . . ."

"PENNSYLVANIA STATION . . . PENNSYLVANIA Station," a voice said.

She rose. Claiborne got to his feet too, and stood looking down on her. "God, you are one lucky woman!" he said.

She colored. "Oh, I know how you feel about psychiatry, Tom. I didn't expect you to agree with me."

"It's not the way I feel about psychiatry," he said. "It's the way I feel about poetry. . . . I was thinking what I'd do with you if you were *my* wife."

She tilted her round chin. "Isn't it fortunate for both of us that I'm not?"

He continued to stare down at her. "If you were my wife I'd hang you up by your heels till all the crap drained out of you—if it took the rest of your life."

Her face was crimson now. "Since you can't do that maybe you'll let me pass. I've got a good deal to do today."

He started, lifted his brief case, and made for the door, so hastily and determinedly that he had not time to look back and so was not aware of the sudden sharp glance that she sent after him out of eyes bright with anger.

THIRTEEN

Vera always began her Christmas preparations in October. They were formidable. The legal firm which handled the Vincent estate contributed considerable sums to various charities at this season, but Vera never seemed to feel that the money came out of her own pocket. She referred to these disbursements as "that money of Mr. Elliott's." She herself bought Christmas presents the year around—whenever she came across or thought of the present she considered suitable

187

for any person on her list, which ranged from the members of her family to the youngest child of the village grocer. There was a whole room on the second floor of the house given over throughout the year to presents. But it seemed that more presents must be bought. One Saturday in October she announced that she would go in to town to do "some serious shopping." Max said that he would accompany her. Claiborne had already announced that he was going in to town that day. The three boarded the nine fifty-five train together.

Max wanted to buy some phonograph records. They decided to go first to a book and record shop on lower Fifth Avenue. "You'll have time to go with us, won't you, Tom?" Vera asked. Claiborne had told her that he was lunching with Bill Trowbridge at one o'clock but he had not mentioned any other engagement. It seemed to him that he had no other choice but to accompany them. Max could not make up his mind whether he wanted Frescobaldi or Mozart.

When he put the Frescobaldi on for the second time Claiborne left the room and wandered about in the shop outside.

The counters were heaped high with books. He opened one at random. An "art" book, reproductions of masterpieces: *Aphrodite through the Ages*. It fell open at the title page and he saw that it had been edited by one of his old drinking companions, Joe Bliss, and reflected on how sometimes in the world of the arts men were able to turn their weaknesses to material profit. Joe Bliss, at twenty-four, had been as big a drunkard as Horne Watts and his literary interests had been chiefly pornographic. Now he was an authority—on art and love? Claiborne turned a page idly and came on that body whose lovely limbs Giorgione portrays as clinging to the earth as if to its cradle. But Luini's Venus sits at right angles to the earth and holds a mirror in her hand. He turned another page. Cranach's Venus holds no mirror. High-breasted, flat-loined, she stares straight into the beholding eye. For how long has that cold, heavy-lidded gaze been turned on man? He wondered how he would get

188

through the day. He had drunk too much whisky last night and had a dull headache, which, he knew from experience, would increase rather than diminish until the cocktail hour came around and he started drinking again.

The dream he had had last night still haunted him. Traveling along a shadowy road, he had rounded a bend and come suddenly upon a house. It stood close to the road and yet high above it. A woman sat on the threshold, as if throned. Her figure almost blocked the doorway but he could see light beyond her shoulders and he heard the sound of stringed instruments and knew that there was music and dancing within. It seemed to him that the woman had been calling out something in a loud voice until he came, when she rose and silently stood aside so that he might pass down into the house. Standing on the threshold, looking down, he felt his whole being suffused with a wild, secret pleasure, but the stairway down into the house was steeper than he had thought, and darker. He reached the foot and found himself in a vast, lighted hall where many people moved to and fro. And then he was seated at a table with others and the wild music was playing all about them, though with a strange softness, and, as it were, secretly, so that he turned to a fellow guest, planning to ask some cunning question which would reveal whether the music was heard by all or only by him, but the figure that turned toward him was fleshless inside its shrouding robe and its hollow eye sockets were lighted by flames fiercer than burn in any mortal eye and he looked about him and saw that every man in the vast hall was in like case and knew that he was in the depths of hell.

He looked back at the glass cubicle. Vera was no longer visible, but Max still sat there, bent forward from the waist, his elbows resting on his knees, his chin sunk in his cupped hands. When he assumed that pose he was supposed to be so rapt by the Muse that he was hardly aware of his own existence. Years ago, when he was working in that old studio on L'Impasse des Deux Anges, he used to beg Horne to "turn

189

that damned phonograph off," but now he could sit like this for hours. The less work he did, the more he loved music! What did the fellow hear when he sat like that? The wheels going around in his head?

The same wheels that go around in mine? he asked himself, and started; a hand had been laid on his arm. Vera stood so close to him that her shoulder touched his.

She looked smaller than usual today, and somehow more unfashionable. It was that dark fur stole she had drawn about her shoulders. It had belonged to her mother and she got it out religiously every fall since Margot died, a few years after their marriage, and wore it a few times—presumably in memory of her mother. She was saying that she wanted to buy Cynthia some books.

"Why?" he asked before he could collect himself.

She looked at him earnestly. "To put on her shelves, Tom. Lester Vail kept all her books. He said they were part of his professional equipment."

When would she ever take her eyes—which he had always found too blue—off his face? His hatred was so great that he felt his whole body tempered by it, like a blade held in readiness and drawn from its scabbard for some fell intent. There is a hatred that is reserved for the innocent. What right have they got *not* to know? But they are more formidable, more dangerous when they forsake the bliss that is their inheritance and strike toward knowledge. If only she had been content to remain what she was when he found her, a bird fluttering on a terrace that a man might pick up and warm in his bosom, a bird that would nestle tamely, grateful for any warmth it might come by, and not be always turning its fierce, golden eye on yours, not always be beating its maimed wing against your breast!

He knew as well as if she had confided them to him the thoughts that had gone through her head during the past week. She *had* suspected that something was going on between him and Cynthia and then had succeeded in convincing herself that her suspicions were unjust. With her a

190

thought was no sooner entertained than it was translated into action. She might have hated Cynthia last night—for she was capable of hate, for all her kindness—but today she would shower her with gifts to make up for having suspected her. . . . He must say something quickly or she would never take those eyes off his face. He said: "It's even Stephen, isn't it? She walked out on him."

"She had to, Tom. Has she ever told you anything about what it was like, living with him?"

"A little," he said. "Well, I don't think she'd like that book. Joe Bliss's introduction is fatuous."

She nodded docilely and moved off down the aisle, the dark thing that she had about her shoulders falling backward. A faint fragrance was wafted from it. She claimed that if she buried her nose in the fur she could catch a whiff of the rose geranium perfume her mother had used. The stole caught on a protruding corner of a book and slipped from her shoulders to the floor. She put her hand out absently. He stood where he was and watched the hand close on air, then watched her stoop and retrieve the stole and lay it again about her shoulders and thought of the years he had trailed in the wake of Margot Vincent—Margot Vincent, born Pearl Clancy, in life an ignorant fool—but it had taken all the will power he could summon not to move forward to lift from the floor her garment discarded these twenty years!

She was studying the books ranged in cases along the wall, her lips moving as she recited titles. Without taking her eyes off the shelves she called out to ask him whether he thought that Cynthia would like "a good new translation of the *Timaeus?*"

"God, Vera, how should I know?" he asked, and added, "It's too hot in here."

"You could get them to open a window," she murmured.

"Vera, I can't stand here all day while Max moons over records."

She looked surprised, then said: "I'll tell him."

"No. I'm going on over to Fourth Avenue."

"Fourth Avenue?"

"Yes. Cooper's saving some books for me."

"Couldn't you telephone?"

"No," he said, "I want the air," and walked toward the street entrance. Behind shifting panes of glass a face spun toward him. He had to stand and wait until the door completed its revolution and discharged Marcia Crenfew almost into his arms. She said: "Why, Tom, what are you doing here?" "Nothing," he said, and stepped past her without any other greeting.

The early morning had been chill, but the day had turned fair. A few light clouds scudded across a high, intensely blue sky. A wind blew a salt smell up from the river. He left the avenue and walked west. On the way he passed the grimy old-fashioned office building in which *Spectra* had its offices. He looked at his watch. A quarter of twelve. Cynthia would not have gone out to lunch. He telephoned her from a booth in a cigar store.

She laughed when she heard his voice—he had told her that he really intended to lunch with Trowbridge that day. She seemed reluctant to meet him for lunch; she had work on hand that had to be finished by a certain date. He knew then that he must see her before the day was over. "May I come there, then, for a few minutes?" She asked him where he was and when he told her she replied, after a second's hesitation, that she would meet him at her apartment in a few minutes.

She was not there when he arrived. He opened the door with his latchkey. The tiny apartment was in its usual exquisite order. The glass doors that opened on the terrace were closed but morning sunlight poured through them onto the fawn-colored rug. He sat down on the sofa in a square patch of sunlight. The opposite wall seemed nearer than it ever had before. Too near. The whole place was too small for occupancy by more than one person. When she came he would tell her that they must go somewhere else. To the beach, perhaps. One could be snug there behind glass walls and yet have sunlight all about.

The door opened. She stood before him in a gray dress and a dark coat that she had not taken time to fasten. When he had telephoned her it had seemed to him imperative that he see her, and now she was in the same room with him but it was not the way he had thought it would be. There had been a moment, as she came into the room, when she did not seem to want to recognize his presence, when she actually looked past him for a second—as if there were somebody else in the room whom she must greet before she greeted him. He made an impatient movement. She came closer to him and asked him if anything had happened.

"What should happen?" he asked, and took her in his arms, but even as she submitted herself to his embrace, she drew back to look at him questioningly. "You came into town with Vera and Max. Nothing was said? Nothing happened?"

"Vera was trying to decide whether you'd like the *Timaeus* for Christmas and Max was trying to decide whether to present himself with Frescobaldi or Mozart," he said, "but nothing had happened when I left them—at Sloane's and Reynolds'."

She laughed then. "You couldn't take it?"

"No," he said, "I couldn't take it."

She had been moving away from him as they spoke, into the kitchen. She opened the door of the refrigerator. "Cold tongue," she said, "and there's always canned soup. And there's some lettuce. . . . But you can't have any dessert."

"I want a monumental dessert today," he said. "The kind the waiter brings in and bows over—flaming."

She frowned a little. "Tom, let's don't do anything reckless."

"Would a *Baba au rhum* be reckless?"

"It depends on where we got it. After all, Vera *is* in town today."

"Then let's go *out* of town!" he said.

"Where?"

"Jones Beach," he said. "Atlantic City . . . Far Rockaway . . . the Canary Islands . . ."

She let the refrigerator door swing to and gave him a quick look, but her face remained composed, her eyes suffered no appreciable change as they received his own gaze. She walked back into the living room and sat down on the little sofa.

"You *are* in a state, aren't you?" she said.

Standing before her, his suddenly shaking hands clasped behind him, he said: "I am not going back there."

He had not known that those were the words he was going to utter and he heard them with wonder. Her expression did not change but she suddenly shifted her position on the sofa. "You mean to Blencker's Brook?" she said.

He said: "To Blencker's Brook," thinking how hard the syllables came, like something—a head?—cut off and falling on the frozen ground. But he must pay attention to what she was saying: "Do you think it's wise to break things off as suddenly as this?"

"It isn't a matter of what's wise or unwise," he said, "as you'd realize if you cared anything about me."

She was on her feet then. Her arms were about his neck. She murmured endearments. He let his arms come up about her slight figure and held it to him so tightly that he could feel his own slow-churning heart quicken its beat to keep time with hers. Her face was pressed so tight against his breast that he could not hear what she was saying. *It is better that way. Oh, my love, the hard winter sunshine is all about us, but there is a place if we could win to it, where no grass grows, no bird sings, no eye looks into any other eye, no word is spoken. . . .*

She freed herself from his arms with a quick twisting movement. At the same time he heard feet on the stairs. She was whispering: "They rang downstairs, but we didn't hear them. And now they are coming up."

"*They?*" he said. "*Who?* Who's coming up?"

She was no longer at his side. She was standing before the bookshelves. Her hand went out, took a book from the shelf. She whirled about, book in hand. Somebody had been knocking on a door for some time. "I'll get out," he said heavily, and would have gone into the kitchen but she shook her head. "No!" she said. "The place is too small." She went to the door and opened it.

Vera entered, followed by Marcia Crenfew. They were followed by Max, who lingered behind them to close the door carefully. Vera started at the sound and her eyes darted about the room before they came to rest on her husband's face. She said: "Marcia thought we'd find you here."

"You did," he said.

Cynthia moved forward quickly, the book still in her hand. She said: "Tom just told me you were thinking of giving me a copy of the *Timaeus*. But I bought one for myself the other day. . . ."

Vera turned her head and looked at her, then looked back at her husband. She said: "I know something's the matter. . . . I've known it for weeks. . . ." And then, though he had not spoken, she said: "It's all *right,* darling!"

Red burned in her cheeks but she held her head high. She held her head too high. She always had. He could not bear the way that head took color from the surrounding air. She took a step toward him. He stayed her with his hand upraised. *Somewhere an arrow cleaved the air and found its mark. But she was a stubborn quarry. Even while she flinched, she pressed on.* "It's all right, darling," she said again.

"No, it's not all right," he said.

"Marcia, let's get out of here," Max said. "Vera, why don't you and Tom go somewhere and talk this over."

"It seems to have been already talked over. By all of you," Claiborne said.

Vera made a quick, passionate gesture toward Max without taking her eyes off her husband's face. He gave her back her look. "We can't go on like this," he said, "as you would have seen long ago—if you hadn't been so blinded by concern for yourself."

"Myself!" she cried. Oh, the dart had lodged, all right! That head, with its crisp, springing curls was bent now over her own side from which all along the blood had been flow-

ing. She raised her head to utter the words he had known she would utter: "I see. . . . You never loved me."

"We are not talking about the past," he said. "It's a question of the present. We can't entertain the same emotions at forty-eight that we did at twenty-eight."

"You never loved me!" she cried despairingly. "I always knew it. . . . I don't see why you married me."

Claiborne remained erect, staring at her, but he felt as if he crouched in some vast, windy place beside a body that had just toppled to the floor. The body had been sentient a moment ago, but it was still now and no sound came from it. . . . There was something that had to be done before he could lie down beside it.

He said: "I should think that would be obvious."

Never had her eyes been fixed so intently on his face! "You mean for my money?" she said in a low, wondering tone and then, as if repeating words she had heard uttered by some other voice than her own, she said again, *"For my money!"* and said something in the same low tone to Cynthia and, followed by the two others, went from the room.

Neither of the two in the room stirred until the heels quit striking on the stairs, then Cynthia gave a low sigh. There were tears in her eyes, but a brightness on her lips. She was coming toward him. He moved toward her, but not without a moment's hesitation. It seemed to him that the man and the woman still lay dead on the floor. He had to step over their bodies before he could take her in his arms.

PART

THREE

FOURTEEN

"Well, Billy, I guess the next thing is to get these letters out," Ed Archer said.

The nervous, dark-haired young man said, "Right, Boss!" As he gathered up his papers he looked over at Claiborne, his eyes shining. "Then you'll be in Monday?"

"Monday?" Claiborne said.

"The sooner the better," Ed said, "but make it later in the week if you'd rather, Tom."

"Oh, I can make it all right," Claiborne said as he stood up to shake hands for the second time with the nervous young man. His name was William Pettigrew. Several years ago Claiborne had recommended a volume of his critical essays to a publisher, but that was before he joined the staff of *Parade,* where he was popularly considered Ed's right-hand man, as Ed, in turn, was thought to be the one of *Parade's* many executives whose advice and counsel were oftenest sought and taken by its millionaire owner. The sheet of paper that Pettigrew was carefully stowing in a folder was a list of the names of authors who were to be invited to write for the new literary magazine *Parade* was launching, a magazine whose editorship Claiborne would assume next Monday morning.

When the door had closed behind Pettigrew, Ed said indulgently, "This is a great day for Billy."

"For Billy?" Claiborne said.

"He's so excited over the prospect of working with you he

doesn't know what he's doing. It's a great day for me too, Tom. . . . The Old Man's had this notion of a literary magazine for two years now. I've had a hard time holding him back. But I knew there was no use in launching it unless we could get the right line-up. You've got to get some regular contributors to start with, I told him, and they've got to be good. Now this list we've made up—in your judgment, every one of those writers is a topnotcher, isn't he?"

"Topnotcher?" Claiborne said.

"I mean a literary man who, as a literary man, is of the same caliber as—oh, say Addison Skate." He laughed. "It never rains but it pours. We signed him up today too."

"Who's Addison Skate?"

"Why, I'd say that he occupies the same position among foreign correspondents that you do among editors, Tom. Always a step ahead of the rest. First man to get into Russia after the first Five-Year Plan just as you—you did publish Halloway's first stuff in *Spectra*, didn't you?"

Damn the fellow! Claiborne thought. He's trying to make me tell him how good I am so he can feel smart for hiring me! Aloud he said: "He sent us the manuscript. We'd have been fools if we hadn't published it. . . . As for your topnotchers, Ed, I don't believe you can classify writers."

"Oh, of course. Still, these men are all first class, or you wouldn't have them on your list?"

"They have some things in common—a certain amount of skill in writing, for instance—but I wouldn't attempt to classify them," Claiborne said stubbornly, and would have risen to end the interview, but Ed, almost as if forgetful of his presence, had swiveled his chair about so that he could look out of the window behind his desk. The window, an expanse of plate glass as wide as the wall of a small house, commanded a panoramic view of mid-town Manhattan. Ed's desk, fashioned of some kind of wood that nobody had ever heard of before, was as big as a boxcar. Everything of the largest and the best, Claiborne reflected, and he was now, or would be, come next Monday, a not inconsiderable part of it.

It had happened with bewildering rapidity, once he realized that he must look about for a job. His separation from Vera had considerably straitened his means; his inheritance from his uncle had been spent on *Spectra,* and he earned little. He had reminded himself that one can't get a job without letting it be known that one is looking for one and was casting about in his mind as to which of his friends to approach first when Cynthia suggested that he go to see Ed Archer before he saw anybody else. "He might have something that would be just the thing," she said. When he asked her how in the world she knew Ed Archer's plans she would only smile mysteriously. It was astonishing, he reflected, how quickly Cynthia had come to know her way about in literary New York. Three months ago she knew nobody except by correspondence, or next to nobody. Now she appeared to know everybody. She was like the goldfish that one moment is gasping for air on the living-room rug and the next glides sinuously about the tank over whose rim it has just slipped. That young man who had just left the room was doubtless the source of her information about Ed's plans for the literary editorship at *Parade.* He remembered now her telling him of meeting young Pettigrew at a party a few nights before.

Ed Archer was one of his oldest friends but he was somehow not one he would have thought of turning to in a difficulty (it was being borne in on him that his present situation was not without difficulties), but Ed's response when he telephoned him had been spontaneous and warm: "Of course we can find you a job, Tom—if you want one," and then, hesitantly, as if it were he, not Claiborne, who was asking a favor: "You couldn't run down here a few minutes? There's something I'd like to talk over with you."

The "something" was the editorship of a new literary magazine, to appear under *Parade's* aegis. It appeared that Ed had been planning it for some time. Young Pettigrew had said all along that there was only one man for the job. He was beside himself with joy at the prospect of working with Claiborne, for whom he had an unbounded admiration. It had all been settled—except for the contract which would be signed on Monday morning—within ten minutes of the time Claiborne had walked into the room. Ed did not seem to feel that he had acted with extraordinary dispatch. He was probably in the habit of making important decisions all day long: he was, after all, an influential man and as executive editor of *Parade* played his part in world affairs. Yet he sat there now, gazing out of the window as dreamily as if his work were over for the day. His stillness, his abstraction had a quality that struck Claiborne as unusual. *I never saw him sit like that before. What is he thinking about?*

He got up. Ed rose too, and walked with him toward the door. Halfway across the vast expanse of carpet he stopped before a group of framed photographs and pointed to one of the photographs. "Remember that evening?" he asked. Claiborne looked and saw his eighteen-year-old self standing with a sandwich in one hand and a bottle of beer in the other beside a table that was stacked high with newspapers. Ed stood at the other end of the table. "First issue we got out at school," Ed said. "Remember Bugs Graham came in and snapped us just as we got 'em all folded?"

"I remember we folded every damn paper by hand and it took us till two o'clock in the morning," Claiborne said, "but I don't remember Bugs taking that picture. And I never saw it before."

"Is that so?" Ed said. "I thought he sent you a print. . . . Poor Bugs! He's sports editor of some paper up in West Virginia but he gets to town every now and then and he and I and Charley Sloane have dinner together."

"I haven't seen Bugs Graham, or Charley Sloane either, for twenty years," Claiborne said. "How do you keep up with them all, Ed?"

Ed smiled. "Well, I've been here at *Parade* for ten years. They all know where to find me."

Claiborne laughed. "That's one advantage of staying put —or disadvantage."

"It's an advantage, on the whole," Ed said mildly. "I like to keep up with the boys. And you never know what a connection will turn up—in my business." He let his hand rest for a second on Claiborne's arm. "If I hadn't kept in touch with you all these years *Parade* wouldn't be getting you for a literary editor. . . ."

"That's mighty nice," Claiborne said.

They shook hands.

Ed's secretary appeared and piloted Claiborne through the outer office to the elevator. The elevator began its lightning-like descent from the thirty-eighth to the main floor. Claiborne, frowning, wished that he had not taken leave of Ed Archer so hurriedly. There had been a second there at the door—the second when Ed put one hand out for a handclasp while the other hand lay lightly on Claiborne's arm—when he had been aware of Ed's eyes seeking his face in a glance that was more intent, more prolonged than any glance Ed had given him during the past half-hour. The nature of that glance eluded him but he had an impression that it was out of the ordinary. There had been something in Ed's look that had never been there before—or was it that something that had always been there before was not there now? Or am I imagining the whole business? he asked himself, and heard somewhere a dry chuckle. *"Keep on like that,"* the Voice said, *"keep on and you'll end in some nice booby hatch."* The Voice, he noted absently, had become less discursive in the last few weeks. The few remarks it had made were ironic and it never engaged in argument. That was rather a relief, on the whole.

The operator was turning on her saddle-like seat to give him a reproachful glance. "Main floor, sir?"

"Right you are," he said, and left the elevator and joined the crowd that surged through the entrance out to the street.

✦

The restaurant where he was to meet Cynthia was three blocks away. As he walked, he looked at his watch. It was already one o'clock. He ought to have left the office half an hour ago but just as he was on the point of leaving young Pettigrew had come in with a batch of letters, letters written in response to the letters he himself had sent out two weeks ago. Not everyone whom he had addressed could accede to his request. Herman Blaine wrote that he hardly expected to live long enough to finish the work for which he already had commitments. At the same time he warmly applauded Claiborne's editorship of the new magazine. "It is," he wrote, "the kind of thing one has always thought ought to happen but which hardly ever does happen." Young Pettigrew had been delighted, and Claiborne himself, standing in the handsome, sun-lit office, had felt a lift of his spirit. It occurred to him that he had spent half his life avoiding offices. He wondered whether it had not been a mistake. The light routine of his new job provided an agreeable framework for his days and left him as much leisure as he could use; one always worked better when one had a deadline. He had finished his piece on Keats. There was no reason why he should not go on to write something else. In the last few days he had actually felt stirrings of his imagination.

He walked on faster. Cynthia was doubtless already at the restaurant; she had had time enough to finish her errand. It was an errand on which he should have accompanied her, since it was of interest to both of them.

It was almost as if his and Vera's separation were a fruit budding underground on some great swollen vine, apprehended by all, awaited by all, and hailed when it thrust forth into the light of day. Two nights ago Marianne Brodo had telephoned him to convey more or less delicately veiled sympathy and to offer him the use of the Brodos' apartment while they were abroad during the coming year.

His club, where he had been staying ever since he left Blencker's Brook, had relayed the call to him at Cynthia's apartment. When he told her of Marianne's offer, adding indifferently that he had no intention of accepting it, she had been silent a little, then had pointed out something he had not thought of: the present housing shortage made it next to impossible to find a desirable vacant apartment at any price. "Do you *want* to go on living at your club?" she had asked. "God, no!" he had said. "I hate the place." They had agreed that under the circumstances Marianne's offer was perhaps providential, and Cynthia had gone this morning to look at the apartment. Marianne and Edmund Brodo had already departed but Marianne had left instructions with the superintendent of the building "in case you change your mind."

He told himself now that he didn't much want to take over the Brodos' possessions, desirable as they were. On the other hand, one must live somewhere, and it was true that he was tired of living at the club. One of his classmates, Hock Andrews, lately divorced from a meat-packing heiress, always seemed to choose to eat alone in the dining room on the same nights that he himself did. They had shared the same table twice, and that, Claiborne thought, was worse than eating alone and looking up every few minutes to find Hock in the act of looking the other way. But he had had very few dinners at the club. Almost everybody he knew was asking him to dinner. And most of them wanted him to bring Cynthia.

They had dined with the Waites last night. Willy Stokes had been there. It had been fifteen years—twelve, anyhow—since he had seen Willy Stokes. He had seen a good deal of him that spring they came back from Paris when he and Bob Waite were editing *Spectra* in New York. Willy had hung around a lot then. He had been out of Harvard long enough to realize that even when you have as much money as he had it is hard to know what to do with yourself. A handsome fellow, with large, dark eyes and an engaging manner. Bob had a notion that Willy would have liked to play the role of Maecenas to *Spectra,* and used to go on about how bright Willy was. Tom had maintained that Willy was not bright enough to make a Maecenas. "Takes a hell of a fellow for that. All he's got in those Brooks Brothers pockets—besides his money—is some bad poems. If we let him put money into *Spectra* he'll be wanting us to publish them."

It had looked last night as if Bob were going to get his wish at last. Cynthia had a project to follow the symposium Tom was editing: a series of short books—long essays, really—on major British poets by half a dozen contemporary critics. She said that she had got the idea from his essay on Keats, and she and Bob both thought that the series ought to be under his editorship. Bob liked the idea and talked confidently of putting it into execution. He must be going to get the money from Willy; several times during the evening Willy had spoken up, quite as if he were in on the thing. He had more assurance now than he had had in the old days. But that was only natural. The fellow was a good deal older. It had seemed to him that it was no skin off his nose, anyhow, since he was no longer an editor of *Spectra,* merely a contributor. And it had been good to have for a whole evening the kind of talk they had had. They had stayed till after midnight and then he and Cynthia had walked back across Washington Square to her apartment on Bedford Street. They had stood in the Square, at two o'clock in the morning, under the dim light of a street lamp, talking so earnestly that they had not heard the cop approaching until he inquired deferentially if anything were wrong, whereupon they both burst out laughing. It was the kind of thing you do when you are young. The exhilaration of that moment still persisted.

Or was it the weather? The air that lapped his cheek felt as soft as honey. Spring was on its way. For some days now he had had a feeling of moving toward a goal, of being involved in some significant action. *"A new life,"* the Voice said. *"You are beginning a new life."*

Was he not beginning a new life? A writer of any stature, he reminded himself, becomes two or three different men during his lifetime. The early Yeats seems to have had only a bowing acquaintance with the later Yeats. It is hard to realize that *Richard III* and *The Tempest* were written by the same man. These inner changes have their outer manifestations, which is why so many people marry for the second—or third or fourth—time in their forties. He, after all, was still in his forties!

He had arrived at the restaurant. Cynthia was not in the first dining room. He walked through it and down a narrow hall back into the garden, still glassed in for winter, and saw her sitting at a table under an arbor at the far end.

She was wearing a light wool dress and a broad-brimmed hat. Shadows cast by the vines overhead swayed over her light dress. She sat motionless, her head a little bent, as if in deep thought. He sat down opposite her. She started, lifting a face that, even shaded by the broad hat brim, gave off something more like radiance than he had ever seen on it before. He said: "You look as if you had good news."

She leaned toward him. "You didn't tell me it was such a fabulous place!" she said. "And you didn't tell me that there were two apartments!"

"That's right," he said. "They took over that whole floor after Ned got sick."

Edmund Brodo had had a stroke a year ago and as a result had been paralyzed in one side of his body. Marianne, exhibiting a resourcefulness that all her women friends found commendable, had rented the apartment across the hall and had turned it into a miniature hospital. Edmund Brodo had spent the last year there, between wheel chair and bed, attended by day and night nurses, but some new treatment had lately improved his condition and Marianne was flying him to Majorca for a change.

He remembered the first time he and Vera had gone to see the Brodos after Ned was stricken. Marianne had given them tea in the lofty drawing room, the blues and pinks and roses of whose walls seemed to spring like flowers from the great fawn-colored carpet under their feet. When they had finished their tea they were taken across the hall to have drinks with Ned. The room Ned was confined to was as spacious as the one they had just left. He lay in a bed whose framework was

207

all crimson and gold, a miracle of painted wood carving that Marianne had brought back from Norway. The bed, for all its medieval splendor, was a hospital bed and had a crank by which it could be raised and lowered so that Ned, who was paralyzed on his right side, could assume several different positions. A fourteenth-century *mille fleurs* tapestry portraying a hunting scene covered the wall beside his bed. On the wall opposite hung the big Matisse, one of those that, as Max said, you could "get inside and run around in." The Brodos had been among the first people to rent pictures from museums. The bed faced the window. Ned had lain there for a year, looking out on the river. They had all gathered around Ned's bed to drink a great many Old Fashioneds. "The doctor says that liquor is *good* for Ned. Isn't that *divine?*" Marianne said. There was a girl, demure in dark dress and white collar and cuffs, who came in every now and then and stood with her back turned to them looking out on the river. Vera had laughed when he asked afterward who she was. "The *nurse,* darling! Marianne doesn't like them to wear uniforms."

"I can see that we need a place to live in," he said to Cynthia, "but do we need a setup as grand as the Brodos'?"

"But if it's simply handed over to us . . . ? I stayed there a full hour, just walking around. . . . It's a marvelous setting!"

"For what?"

"For you and me!"

"I'm a diamond in the rough," he said, "I don't want to be set."

She laughed. "It isn't so much the splendor of the place—though it is splendid—as what we could do with it."

"We couldn't change it," he said in alarm. "We couldn't do anything but live in it—temporarily."

Her smile deepened. "We could do things with it the Brodos couldn't do, wouldn't have the imagination to do."

"Their parties *are* pretty stuffy," he said. "That way before Ned took sick. Marianne thinks that two celebrities make a party. Sometimes she gets people who haven't spoken to each other for years."

"*Our* parties won't be stuffy," she said.

Claiborne was silent, overcome by an embarrassment that of late he sometimes felt in her presence. She was more forthright—more honest, he told himself—in going about their new life than he was. He told himself, too, that he must not forget that she was thirteen years younger than he and had lived most of her life in the provinces, in the company of dullards. Marianne Brodo was one of the worst lion-hunters he had ever known (he could hear her now: "Tom Claiborne? Why, at the moment he's living in my apartment in New York.") but to this girl she must appear like the fairy godmother and the Brodos' apartment the palace that the princess has always felt is waiting for her. Who was he to keep her golden coach waiting? He was asking a good deal of her now. It was in deference to what she called his "horse and buggy" prejudices that they had agreed not to set up a common ménage until both their divorces were granted. He wanted to sleep with her every night but he did not want to live in the same house with her as long as she was married to another man. She had burst out laughing when he told her that. She hardly remembered her husband's existence, she said, unless he reminded her of it. Neither of them had mentioned Vera. It would be some time, he thought, with wry relish, before his divorce went through. It took time to get a divorce, even if you had money. Robert Elliott, the Vincents' lawyer, had called him into conference soon after his and Vera's separation to announce that Mrs. Claiborne wanted a divorce. Mr. Elliott had mentioned other matters: income taxes, the division of certain properties that had been held in common, joint signatures that had to be attached to various instruments. As he was on his way out a younger member of the firm had appeared and had said that he had a message for him from Mrs. Claiborne. He had followed the young lawyer into a smaller office, whereupon the scoundrel, having taken the precaution to barricade himself behind his desk, had relayed the message from Mrs. Claiborne: His aunt, Miss Virginia Claiborne, had that morning arrived safely at Rest-haven, Tennessee. He did not hit the fellow, but he did say, "Do you think I give a damn?" before he walked out. Since then he had refused all invitations to conferences. His own lawyer, Joe Grant, had to handle everything as best he could. Joe had telephoned him two days ago to say that there might be further postponement; Mrs. Claiborne had not yet decided where she would establish her residence.

He watched the intricate tracery of leaf and stem waver over the white cloth, dissolve and wreathe itself again about the stem of the glass the waiter had just set before him. His own life, shattered four months ago (it was only four months since that morning in Cynthia's apartment), shattered, it seemed, as irrevocably as if some one of them had seized some precious, irreplaceable object and had raised it high to dash it into a thousand pieces on the floor, was reforming, taking on new proportions, dimensions, and if the vine, the leaf that shaped themselves before him appeared at times as tenuous, as insubstantial as those shadows wavering there on the table-cloth, they were nevertheless the only forms that presented themselves. It behooved him to lay hold of them.

"I suppose we *will* have to do some entertaining," he said.

"*We* can't entertain—in our present situation—but *you* certainly will have to do a certain amount of entertaining in connection with this job. I should think that it might be helpful—as well as agreeable—to have a female neighbor across the hall. . . ."

"Who will come in and put the flowers and things around and then run back across the hall and powder her nose and come back and make an entrance?" he said with a laugh.

"Exactly," she said. "Oh, you'll see! We'll have wonderful parties."

He looked at her curiously. "It's extraordinary," he said, "how you think things out ahead."

"And it's extraordinary to me, how you never think even

one step ahead. . . . But never mind. That's not your métier."

Claiborne did not answer. As she was speaking, he had looked up to find himself gazing straight into Robin Vincent's eyes.

Halting in the doorway, as if he had been on the point of entering the garden until something arrested his attention, Robin let his eyes travel slowly from Claiborne's face to that of his companion. It was the same look that Hock Andrews had given Claiborne once or twice in the club dining room, only Robin did not look away as Hock did when his eyes caught Claiborne's.

Claiborne felt his face flush. He looked straight at Robin and nodded curtly but unmistakably.

There was an appreciable instant during which Robin, not altering his stance by a hairsbreadth, stared back. Then his ordinarily impassive face seemed to undergo a further process of congealment. His eyes left his brother-in-law's face and rested briefly on the vine-clad trellis behind Claiborne, before he turned away.

Claiborne smothered an exclamation and got up.

"What is it?" Cynthia said quickly.

"A call," he said, "I forgot a call I've got to make," and started for the door.

"But you haven't ordered!" she cried.

"You order for me," he said, and without looking back, walked rapidly toward the door.

The little hall was empty. He passed through it swiftly and stood on the threshold of the dining room which he had quitted only a few minutes before. There had not been many people in the dining room, but now almost every table was filled. He stood in the doorway and looked from table to table, but he could not see Robin anywhere. A waiter, seeking to carry a loaded tray through the double doors, brushed against him with a reproachful murmur. Claiborne stepped aside and, flattening his back against the wall, stood there long enough to rake every table again with his eye. Robin was not at any of them. The waiter was on his way back with his empty tray. Claiborne shook his head in response to the questioning glance. "He's not here," he said, and turned into the hall.

It was narrow, paved with dark red octagonal-shaped tiles that had running through each one of them a long wavy line, with a shorter line reproducing the same wave on each side of it.

He had not been back to Blencker's Brook. He had not had to go back. His personal possessions had been packed up and deposited in a storage house where, a suitably junior member of the firm of Elliott, Bronson and Lathrop had informed him, he might go and select whatever he needed at his convenience. Astonishing how quickly and smoothly these things can be handled if one has enough money! Apparently he had all along been only a cog in the powerful, smoothly running machine that was the Vincent estate—a cog that once it showed an imperfection, a flaw, would naturally be got rid of. "I wouldn't, Tom," Max had said, "I wouldn't even try to talk to her. It would only make things worse. . . ."

The door at the end of the little hall was of glass and you could see the garden through it. Was there some imperfection in the glass of the door? Seen from the dark, oblong box that was the hall, the light out there was too bright, almost lurid. The shadows were everywhere too black, everywhere except on Cynthia's face, shaded by the broad hat. She was looking around as if to find out whether there was anybody there she knew and now she put her hand out and slowly lifted the Martini glass to her lips. But even when she threw her head a little back to sip from the glass the brim of her hat laid a band of shadow across her eyes and forehead. . . . He had seen her face once before in the shadow of a broad hat. Where was it? There is something about the sun being a light by day and the moon by night. Could it be the other way around? A man seeking to travel by day by the light of the moon? *What a fool you are! Because a woman's name is Cynthia. Be all right if she was named Betsy?*

The tiles under his feet suddenly blazed pink. A door had opened. A man emerged from the little room on his right, stared at him and went on down the hall into the garden.

Claiborne entered the little room. There was nothing in it except two telephone booths and under an open window a stand which held telephone directories. He glanced into the garden. A woman in black, with pearls about her neck, looked into his eyes, then looked away indifferently as she put a morsel of lobster into her mouth. "I don't think that that is exactly what she meant," she said as soon as she could speak. Claiborne pulled the window down and stood with his back to it, his arms folded. *What was the matter with Robin Vincent—* beside the fact that he had cut him "direct," as they said? To be "cut direct" is to have another human being deny that you exist and you cannot imagine what that feels like until it has happened to you. *But there is something else that has to be thought about now. It was the way he looked. Even if Cynthia and I had not been here he would not have stayed in the garden, he would have gone on somewhere else. He came here because he has to go somewhere and he has gone on to another place and from that place he will go on somewhere else . . . because he does not dare stop anywhere. . . . Why is it that he cannot stop anywhere?*

He stepped into the telephone booth and pulled the door to behind him and dialed the long-distance operator. The call went through quickly. He heard Gershon's muted voice: "Miz Claiborne's resid*ence.*"

He said: "Gershon . . ."

"*Tom!*"

"Yes," he said, "yes. It's Tom, Gershon. I want to speak to Miss Vera."

There was silence. A Catholic friend of his had told him that once in a confessional booth there had been, after he had recited his sins, a silence so long that he had had time to feel quite certain that he was damned. He heard with relief the sound that told him that Gershon was laying the receiver down on its little table. Gershon was too tactful to summon

Vera by the house telephone. He would go upstairs and knock softly on her door and utter the name of the person who wanted to speak to her. It might be several minutes before she came. She might not, at first, want to come. . . . But Gershon had not gone away. He was speaking: "Mister Tom, Miz Claiborne ain't here. . . . Not right now, she ain't. . . . Mister Max will be here in a minute."

He sat upright as if suddenly transfixed by an electric charge. Gershon had said *"Tom!"* at first. It had been twenty years since Gershon had called him Tom. . . . And he had not said "Miss Vera" as he usually did. . . . He had called her "Mrs. Claiborne." . . .

He cried out loud. "What is it? What's going on out there?" When he got no answer he flung the receiver down and would have rushed from the room but he heard inside the instrument a faint clicking and picked it up again.

Max said: "Tom?"

"Yes. Yes. I'm here."

"She's all right," Max said. "That is, Dr. Reynolds feels pretty sure she's going to be all right. Weak, of course, but she's conscious, and there's been no relapse."

"You are talking about Vera?"

"Last night," Max said. "She'd have been dead if Robin hadn't turned back. Started for the Browns and forgot his lighter and went back. . . ."

"Where? Where?"

"In her own room. In her bed. The door was shut but you could hear her breathing all over the house. Robin thought that it might be one of the dogs, but he couldn't find a dog anywhere in the house and he went out and got in his car and then he thought no dog ever sounded like that and he went back into the house and called and called but she didn't answer and all he could hear was that breathing and he went up and opened the door. . . ."

"I am asking you where she is *now*."

"In the hospital in Bethsaida," Max said. "Had to take her in an ambulance. In the middle of the night."

"I'll drive. Be faster than any train I can get." He was about to put the receiver up when he heard Max's voice, raised a note: *"Tom!* Hang on there. Tom!"

"What is it?"

"Tom, you can't go to that hospital."

"Why can't I?" he asked wildly. "Why can't I go there?"

"She's conscious," Max said. "I told you she was conscious, didn't I? She said not to let you in. As soon as she came to she told the doctor not to let you in and he's given orders. If you go there they won't let you in."

Claiborne sat silent.

"Hello!" Max's voice said. "Tom, can you hear me all right?"

"Yes," Claiborne said, "I hear you all right."

"I just wanted to be sure. God, I'm half crazy, myself. But don't worry about me. Tom, I'm coming into town. Can I get you at your office?"

Claiborne took the instrument away from his ear and let it fall on his knee. It went on babbling for several minutes. He could distinguish words: ". . . meet you . . . reach you . . . got to see you . . . know it's terrible but worst over . . . everything be all right . . . *Damn it, why don't you answer me?"*

It fell silent after that. He continued to sit where he was, staring straight before him. The door opened. A face protruded itself into his field of vision. A voice said: "The young lady wants to know is anything wrong, sir?"

Claiborne shook his head. "No," he said, "I was just sitting here, talking to a friend." The face disappeared. He got up and laid the receiver carefully on its hook and went through the narrow passageway out into the garden.

Cynthia was sitting with her eyes fixed on the door. When she saw him she got up and came toward him.

"Vera tried to commit suicide last night," he said. "Sleeping pills. They've got her in the hospital at Bethsaida."

"Is she all right now?" she asked quickly.

"Max said she'd been conscious for some hours and there's been no relapse."

"Was she alone in the house?" she asked after a moment.

"Robin found her." He gave a short laugh. "He thought it was a dog and then he came back and pushed her door open and found her. . . ."

She said: "Let's don't talk about it now, Tom. You mustn't talk about it now."

He looked about him, bewildered. "What must we do?"

She said, "I've already paid. And here's your hat. Let's go."

They went through the hall and the almost empty dining room. Out on the street Claiborne turned automatically to the left. They came to Madison Avenue and walked down it a few blocks. Suddenly she stopped. "Do you think you ought to go to your office now?" she asked.

"I suppose not," he said.

"Would you like to go down to my apartment?"

"It's too far."

She caught her breath. "I *can't* leave you like this here in the street!" she said, then added in a quieter tone: "I have an errand to do. Would you like to go with me—in a cab? It's too far to walk."

"As you like," he said politely, and stepping to the curb hailed a cab.

They went to the East River Drive. There they dismissed the cab and walked under trees that seemed vaguely familiar until they came to a green bench that sat on a bluff overlooking the river. She asked if he would rest there while she did her errand.

"I'm not tired," he said.

"I know," she said, "but if you keep on walking how will I find you when I come back?"

She went away and he sat down on the bench and stared at the river. The water was dull green but laced with yellowish foam; there was a great deal of traffic. He watched a tugboat nosing along in the wake of a South American freighter. What was that boat doing this far upstream? But he had not listened when Cynthia gave the driver the address. He did not know how far uptown he was. He turned around and looking at the street sign knew why the place seemed familiar. The Brodos' apartment was right around the corner. She must be there now. He wondered what her errand was there.

He heard light steps behind him and turned around. Cynthia was crossing the street. As she took her seat beside him, she held up a book. "I thought we'd be going up to look at the apartments after lunch and I left this there. Silly of me. I thought I'd better go and get it."

They sat without speaking for several minutes, then she said: "There's something I might have told you before. . . . I don't know whether I ought to tell you now."

"Tell me now," he said.

"Did you know that Carlo committed suicide?"

"How did he do it?"

"The same way. Sleeping pills. Only he kept walking around after he took them—until he fell over. The doctor thought at first that it was heart, but they had an autopsy."

He did not answer. She said in a low voice: "I know how you must feel, but these things—follow patterns."

"Yes," he said, "they follow patterns."

They sat and watched the river flowing past. A breeze had sprung up and it was full of whitecaps now. The tug had given up its pursuit of the freighter and had disappeared under the bluff. The Brodos' place must be just back of him. Both those apartments had magnificent windows framing wide views of the river, a sluggish river, whose waters were so stained, so polluted by the works that went on on its banks that it presented to the very clouds that hovered above it a surface of the same color and impermeability as a sheet of gun metal. Ned Brodo had lain there for a year, on a bed made of the intertwined gilded bodies of swans, looking out on this same river.

FIFTEEN

Claiborne looked over at the pretty, red-haired young woman who, for the past hour, had been sitting beside his desk, taking down in a shorthand which she said she had invented for herself, the letters he was dictating. "That about does it, doesn't it?" he asked.

She shook her head and indicated a folder that lay on the desk between them. "There are two more that seem fairly urgent."

"It all depends on what you call urgent," Claiborne said, frowning, as he opened the first letter. "Here's Jim Wragge wants me to write something about Joe Solmes's new book. Doesn't he know I'm a wage slave? I haven't got time to read that baloney of Joe Solmes, much less write about it. . . . Tell him I haven't read the book and I'm not going to. It's the same old baloney, only sliced thicker." Then, hurriedly, as he saw a tremor on her soft lips (she had once taken a course in creative writing with Joe Solmes at the advanced women's college she had attended): "No, don't tell him anything. That can go into TWAT."

Miss Golightly silently opened a drawer and drew from it a folder which had printed on it in large capitals: LTWATILALE. Claiborne, soon after assuming the editorship, had made two major divisions of his correspondence: LETTERS THAT WILL ANSWER THEMSELVES IF LEFT ALONE LONG ENOUGH and LETTERS MUST.

"I bet those other letters can go into TWAT too," he said now.

A faint color showed in Miss Golightly's cheek. "One's from Mr. Elton. He says he *was* editor of his college magazine."

"Then he's out, as far as I'm concerned," Claiborne said. "Tell him I'm sorry but I can't recommend anybody for a Rhodes scholarship who's ever been editor of a student publication. If he spent his time in college editing he won't have had time to learn anything. No use sending him to Oxford. He'd only clutter up the place."

There was a moment's silence as each of them recalled that one of the reasons Miss Golightly had been chosen as his secretary was that she had been editor of her college literary magazine.

"Make it a nice letter, Miss Golightly," he said uneasily.

"Oh, I will!" she said. "The other one is from a Miss Pollard."

"Miss *Pollard!* What does *she* want?"

"She wants an interview—for a nun who is writing a critical biography of Horne Watts."

He stretched out his hand for the letter:

Dear Tom Claiborne [Catherine Pollard wrote]:
Do you remember when I saw you that I told you about my friend Sister Immaculata, who is writing about Horne Watts? Sister Immaculata is on leave this year from St. Mary on the Mount, where she is head of the English Department, and has a grant from the Collier Foundation for this work. She has been staying at a convent near us in order to be able to talk with me about my memories of Horne. The illness of one of her colleagues has cut her time short, but she is anxious to talk with you before she leaves. It would be a great convenience to her if she could see you within the next few days. Could you possibly come to our place on Mott Street at four o'clock on Friday? Or if that time is not convenient for you will you set a time that is convenient?
Yours sincerely in Christ,
Catherine

She called him "Tom Claiborne" but signed herself "Catherine" as if she were a queen. "Friday!" he said. "Why, that's today."

Miss Golightly nodded.

"I can't get down there," he said. "Why, I wouldn't have *time* to get down there by four o'clock."

She glanced at her watch. "It's quarter of four now."

He handed her the letter. "Tell her I'm sorry I couldn't make it . . . and tell her I'll be glad to try to get together with Sister Immaculata some other time if she'll arrange the rendezvous."

A little laugh escaped her. "Mr. Claiborne, what sort of biography do you suppose a nun would write about Horne Watts?"

"A God-awful one," he said abstractedly.

"Oh, I love his poems so. . . . You knew him, of course. Did you know him well?"

He looked up and saw in her bright hazel eyes a gleam he had come to know and dread. "Like a book," he said. "Now you run along. . . . You might get that letter to Miss Pollard off this afternoon."

When she had left, giving him an only faintly reproachful glance as she gathered up her notebook and papers, he got up and walked over to the window and stood looking down on the street. He made it a point of honor to stay in the office until four o'clock every afternoon but it was getting harder to do every day. During the last few days the office had seemed almost unendurable. Was that because he was not, after all, very good at the job? Or, at least, not good at the details that make up such a large part of such a job. A note to Jim Wragge, written in the wrong tone, could very well offend a man for whom he had a real respect, and God knew what effect his refusal to recommend him for a Rhodes scholarship might have on the Elton boy. And yet he could not answer personally every letter that came to him. He wondered if the work would go better if he had another secretary. He had looked over some letters that were going out the other day and had found himself assuring an eminent British author that he was grateful for his "copperation." Miss Golightly could not be depended upon to spell any word of more than one syllable properly, could not punctuate a simple declarative sentence, and knew the works of Aeschylus (she spelled it Escylus), Sophocles, Euripides, Homer, Vergil, Tibullus, Catullus, Pliny, and Aristophanes only by hearsay, but she had a passion for trisyllables of Latin or Greek derivation. Was she, perhaps, taking desperate measures to remedy her lack of a classical education, as Southern poor whites sometimes supplement an insufficient diet by eating clay from some riverbank? But if she did not know her Latin and Greek she knew the names and the titles of the chief works of every well-known contemporary American and British poet, novelist, and critic and called some of them by their first names; the advanced women's college from which she had been graduated—with the degree of Bachelor of Arts!—had apparently kept a procession of famous men and women passing through its student lounges. He sometimes fancied that he himself was only cooling his heels in an anteroom dedicated to some postgraduate course in which Miss Golightly was enrolled, so persistently did she quiz him about his literary acquaintance. What she was after, of course, was what women like her were always after: the artist *en pantoufles,* only nowadays they weren't satisfied to have him served up *en pantoufles.* They wanted him in the buff. "Bough" she would probably spell it. Sometimes, at night, when he could not sleep, he found himself writing expository prose, using Miss Golightly's spelling and locutions. She had confided to him on the first day that she came to work that she was an "individualist." She was too lazy to study any of the established methods and too vain to acknowledge that she lacked the professional equipment for her job. He had told Bill Pettigrew that she was too ignorant to discharge the duties of a secretary satisfactorily. Bill had expressed surprise. She had been a classmate of his sister's at Gertrude Newman's, he said, and had graduated *summa cum laude.* He had advised Claiborne to keep her. "You *might* get a girl from Leonard," he had said. "So I might! God save me!" Claiborne had returned.

It must already be past the hour. During the last few minutes the throng of people pouring out onto the street had swelled perceptibly. This building occupied almost half of a city block and thrust the blunt tower in which his office was located God knew how many feet into the sky. High enough to dwarf the figures he was looking down on. Almost every figure hesitated a second as it reached the threshold of the building, as if reluctant to join the dark tide that was flowing so fast now that it filled the whole sidewalk. . . . *And boomerang on the dark tide to amber islands in the wave* . . . The bow of the boat from which Horne had dived would have been about the same height as this tower in which he himself now stood, and Horne, when he jumped, might have thought of himself as a missile, which would return to the hand that launched it—there had been an interval, they said, during which he threshed about in the water, calling for help. But there had been no return, and no amber island . . . unless you call the belly of a shark an island—the captain had seen two of them closing in on him. . . . He had tried to talk Horne out of "boomerang" in that poem; having no formal education, Horne never scrupled to use a noun for a verb any time it suited him, having that much, at least, in common with Miss Golightly, who loved his poems so. *Whose gory visage down the stream was sent,/Down the swift Hebrus to the Lesbian shore.* Keep that Gertrude Newman stuff up long enough and they'll make Lesbians out of the lot of them. . . . But it was nuns who were rending the gory visage now! The doings, doubtless, of that strange, large woman that George Crenfew's flighty young wife had turned into. Odd to think of her associating with nuns, or not so odd, perhaps. In the old days she had always been off on some mystic quest. Once she and Horne and Joe Paster had kept a jarful of rainwater sitting around the studio for days while they added this or that to it according to some formula of black magic they had got out of an old book. . . .

He looked at his watch. It was only ten minutes past four. If he left the office now he still had time to go down to Mott

Street and talk to that nun before Cynthia would expect him —long enough to knock some of the pious platitudes out of her.

SIXTEEN

"This is it," the driver said.

Claiborne saw a three-story house that many years ago had been painted white. Between the house and the curb a gray, unwieldy serpent crawled: unshaved men in ragged, grimy clothes were forming a line around the corner and marching up to the old mansion. It had a stoop a little elevated above the street. The soup kitchen was evidently located in the basement beneath the stoop; the serpentine line flowed steadily until it came abreast of the stoop when it wavered and coiled back upon itself before it slid out of sight down the steps.

Ever since Claiborne's cab had pulled up at the curb a few minutes ago, the men had been shuffling up to the house, three and four abreast. They came in silence, for the most part, and most of them looked straight ahead as they walked, though now and then some younger man, whose eyes kept roving over the faces of his companions as if he were surprised to find himself among them, would turn to the older man beside him and, emitting a short laugh, say something in a low voice to which the older man did not always respond. There was one man who had attracted Claiborne's attention when he first came in sight at the corner—a tall man who carried himself with a kind of jauntiness—or was it only that he moved with exaggerated lightness, as if he had a fearful care for his very bones? He was neatly dressed in a dark, worn suit. The battered gray hat that rode high on the back of his head might have been the hat a man in comfortable circumstances clings to because he likes the way it feels on his head, if its inner rim had not been so darkly stained with sweat.

The driver turned around. "Well, Mac . . . ?" he said.

"Wait a minute," Claiborne told him.

He had lost sight of the tall man as the line undulated back and forth and had just caught sight of him again, poised at the head of the stairs, waiting for the man ahead of him to take the first step down into the soup kitchen. He was older than Claiborne had thought; the black hair under the battered hat was rimed with silver, the stubble on the chin white. The man realized that he was being observed and turned his head. A pair of bleak gray eyes rested on Claiborne's face, the man's mouth stretched in a grin wide enough to reveal discolored stubs of teeth before he lounged with his dreadful lightness down the stairs and out of sight.

"Ma . . . ac!" the driver said.

"You want me to break through that line?" Claiborne asked roughly.

"It's the only way you'll ever get through it. . . . But it's all right with me, you want to sit here and run the meter up."

A short man in a dirty plaid cap, who, for some minutes, had been standing opposite the cab, staring at its occupants out of a pair of protruding pale blue eyes, started and jerked his thumb back toward the house. "Go right through, mister. It ain't going to cost us nothing," he said, and began ostentatiously making a gap in the ranks.

Claiborne got out of the cab after tossing the driver a bill, ascended the short flight of steps. The front door of the house was ajar. He pushed it open and found himself in a narrow, ill-lit hall. There was a long stairway at the rear of it and several doors opening off each side of it.

The clicking of a typewriter came from behind a door on the left side of the hall. Behind a door on the right a woman's voice soared in sharp syllables above a child's wailing. Claiborne slowly set his foot on the match with which he had just lighted his cigarette. . . . *There was no real resemblance. That man's eyes were gray. My father's eyes were*

224

brown. Darker than mine. . . . The dirty hall seemed to echo with the laughter that of late he heard wherever he went. *"Light is dark, and dark is light,"* the Voice said. *"But you are right. It was not his eyes, it was the way he moved. . . . The way your father used to move. . . . Was it for the same reason?"*

Standing alone in the narrow hall, the tall man shook his lowered head from side to side, like a beast beset by hornets. *"I didn't come here to listen to you. . . . God knows I can talk to you anywhere. At the office. At home."* *"At home?"* the Voice said. *"Where is your home?"* *"I mean where I hang my hat,"* he said savagely, *"that's home to me."* *"Hat!"* the Voice cried. *"Hat! He has a hat, too!"* And the laughter rose so loud and shrill that Claiborne looked about him uneasily, fearing that somebody might come into the hall and discover his plight.

The child's cry came again, to be smothered by the woman's reprimand. He knocked on the door on the left. When no answer came he pushed the door open and entered a room which was evidently a newspaper editorial office; two or three old-fashioned roll-top desks stood in a litter of discarded copy paper and a long rack at the far end of the room was heaped with newspapers. A young man who wore a green eye shade sat at a desk facing the door. In the far end of the room a shabby old man was bent over the rack which held newspapers. The young man looked up as Claiborne entered, fixing on him the blank gaze of a person who acknowledges an interruption but whose attention is elsewhere. Claiborne did not speak immediately. The young man gazed at him and said: "How do you spell 'eschatological'?"

"With an h," Claiborne said.

The young man smiled happily. "Good thing you came in. I was going to leave out the h. We had a dictionary around here but Tom Bedford keeps taking it up to his room. I don't mind—except when I'm working on an encyclical. . . . What did you say you wanted?"

"I have an appointment with Miss Pollard."

"You'll have a hard time catching *her*. She might be over at the chapel. . . . They've all gone wild over the chapel. Anybody else do?"

"I was to meet a nun here named Sister Immaculata."

"Is she a Little Sister?"

"I don't know her order."

"Those Little Sisters are in and out of here all day. . . . Say, why don't you go across the hall and ask Eileen? She keeps up with those people."

"I will," Claiborne said, and was turning toward the door when a sound from the other end of the room made him pause. The old man was standing up, holding a newspaper in his hand and shaking his head from side to side, and muttering while he read something from it.

"What's the matter with him?" Claiborne asked curiously.

"That's Joseph Tardieu," the young man said, not without a note of pride in his voice. He added in a lower tone, "Sometimes I wish it'd been his eyes that gave out instead of his brain. Every time he reads a newspaper he sees something that sets him off."

The old man growled and, flinging the newspaper down into the rack, lurched toward them, pulling a greasy notebook and a stub of pencil out of his pocket as he came.

The young man groaned. "He's on his way," he said.

"Where's he going?" Claiborne asked.

"He's not going anywhere," the young man said grimly, "but he *thinks* he's going up to Union Square."

"What for?"

"To talk to the men. Give 'em the true doctrine. That's what he's been doing for thirty years—till his brain gave out. He's had one stroke and the doctor says he may have another one any time now. Catherine doesn't think he ought to go out on the street by himself. . . . Say, brother, you couldn't keep him a few minutes? I've *got* to get this copy in." He laid his hand on the old man's arm. "Listen, Père, here's a fellow wants to talk to you."

The old man stood looking from one to the other, breathing heavily. "What does he want to talk to me about?" he asked in a foreign accent.

The young man was already seated at his desk. "About Chesterton and Belloc," he said, and gave Claiborne a mischievous glance.

"Chesterton and Belloc is fine," the old man said, "bud it dakes more than dose two. It dakes Christ."

He walked back to his seat beside the newspaper rack and sat down and, resting his hands on his spread knees, leaned toward Claiborne. "Now," he said, "what droubles you?"

"The world," Claiborne said, "and the flesh—and the Devil."

Joseph Tardieu nodded, staring at Claiborne out of red-rimmed blue eyes. "He will trouble you more before he's through," he said.

"Who?"

"The Devil. . . . You read St. Augustine?"

"Off and on . . . for years."

"Who told you to read St. Augustine?"

"I started reading him in college and kept it up."

"I read him in college too. L'Université de Grenoble. . . ." He looked away from Claiborne, shaking his head. "I was at Grenoble. I know that. Now I'm here." He leaned still farther forward. "You know how I got here?"

"Probably worked your way over on a cattle boat," Claiborne said.

The old man laughed delightedly. "The Holland What You Call Him Line. Fifty cows and one hundred sheep. And we had to sleep in the stalls. Some boys couldn't sleep, but Joseph Tardieu, he don't mind a little cow manure. Good for the land, cow manure. . . ." He looked back at Claiborne. "You on that boat?"

Claiborne shook his head. "I was in college at the time. Reading St. Augustine."

The old man laughed. "You sit up all night," he said, "and you read St. Augustine. . . . Maybe you read St. Thomas too . . . St. Bonaventura . . . but you don't listen." He

227

held a dirty, stubby forefinger up. "You listen more, you read better."

"What should I listen for?" Claiborne asked.

The smile widened on the old man's face. "Dat little child. De one St. Augustine heard. You remember what dat little child say?"

"He said: '*Tolle, lege,*' " Claiborne said slowly.

The old man nodded, his red-rimmed blue eyes twinkling. "You take and read," he said. "You do dat now!"

The young man was coming toward them. "I do thank you, brother," he said. "You've sure got the touch. He's quiet as a lamb."

Claiborne got to his feet, put out his hand. "Thank you for a most interesting conversation, Mr. Tardieu," he said.

Tardieu nodded again. "You come back?"

"The first chance I get," Claiborne said, and to the young man: "Who did you say might know where Sister Immaculata is?"

"Eileen," the young man said. "She knows who's coming and going."

"Where is she?"

"In the clothes room. Across the hall."

"Thanks," Claiborne said, then lingered a second with his hand on the doorknob. "What are you writing?" he asked.

"I'm just working on one of the Pope's locutions today. But I had to wind it up fast. We're making the paper up tonight. I have to do it by myself. Tom's helping with the chapel. Takes a whole crew to get those panels up." He sat down at his desk and began rapidly typing away with two fingers.

Claiborne crossed the hall and knocked on the door opposite. It opened immediately. A fat, dark woman stood behind a long table which was heaped high with garments. Children of various ages and sizes were ranged on a long bench fixed against the wall. A little girl in a bright red dress was parading up and down in the space between the table and the door.

The woman stared at him out of beady black eyes, then looked away and said indifferently, "Zhee crezzy for it. But too shot. Too shot for Lila. Zhee grow vast, I tell you."

The little girl clutched the bright fabric with each hand. "No, Mama, no!" she cried.

"Yess," the woman said stolidly. "Too shot. No use, too shot."

There was a small sound and a slim, black-haired girl stepped out from behind the door, gesturing toward an inner room. "The men's room is in there," she said. "Would you mind waiting a minute—till Mrs. Costa's finished picking out the clothes for the children?"

"I don't want the men's room," Claiborne said, "I'm looking for a nun named Immaculata."

The girl blushed. "Oh! . . . Sister Immaculata? She's in the library. Two doors down. On this side of the hall."

Claiborne was silent a moment, then he said, "Would you mind showing me the way?- There are so many doors in this hall."

She hesitated and looked at the Puerto Rican woman. "Iss oll right," Mrs. Costa said gloomily, "but oll of them too shot."

The girl emitted a sigh as they started down the hall. "They're all like that," she said, "every last one."

"Do you get many Puerto Ricans?"

"I should say we do. They come here to be outfitted from top to toe, complaining every minute, of course."

"All the clothes too shot?"

She laughed. "When they're not too lung. But that's not what's *really* annoying. What's really annoying is that they haven't the least idea that we're Catholics too. All the time they're taking the clothes they're looking down on us for being pagans!"

"That must be hard to take!"

They had arrived before another door. She put her hand on the knob. She was a pretty girl, with Irish coloring, wearing a round-collared white blouse and a blue skirt. It was strange how different the hall seemed when she stood there, with her hand on the doorknob. He said quickly: "I have a young friend who works here. In your clothes room, I believe."

"Désirée?" she said. "Oh, we all love Désirée! She's in *charge* of the clothes room. I'm just substituting for her—that's why I made the mistake about you." She laughed and he laughed too.

"Where is Désirée?" he asked.

"Over at the chapel. It's *her* friend who's doing the mural, so of course she's over there a lot. And I'm glad to have a chance to learn the ropes in the clothes room. We all change jobs, anyhow, every so often, you know—all except Ed Bülow. Nobody can do *his* work."

"Why is that?"

"Nobody knows as much as he does—except Joseph Tardieu, of course. And he couldn't write anything—now."

"What is this work of Ed Bülow's?"

"Theology," she said gravely. "He writes on the Pope's encyclicals. At least that's what he mostly writes about."

"The old party," he said, "Joseph Tardieu—he's a little bit ga-ga, isn't he?"

She nodded. "He's been that way for over a year. The doctor says it's arteriosclerosis. It's settled in his brain. Catherine says we should expect that."

"You mean he's always been a little touched?"

"*Oh, no!*" she said earnestly. "He was very brilliant, and taught Catherine and Ed Bülow all they know. But he stripped himself to put on Christ till his brain was all he had left. Catherine says that naturally he has to offer that to God too before he dies." She opened the door, calling out cheerfully: "Sister Immaculata, here's someone to see you."

An old nun was seated at one end of a long table, with many papers spread out before her. A sharp-featured little man in ragged clothes sat at the other end, reading a copy of *Pic.* The nun raised her head and stared at Claiborne over the rims of her spectacles. Suddenly her frosty blue eyes sparkled. "Is it Mister Thomas Cleboorne?" she cried. "I've been crazy to meet you—ever since I read some of your letters to our boy. It was good of ye to come today."

"Not at all," Claiborne said politely. "I was anxious to see you too—as soon as I found out that you were writing a book about my friend."

The girl had disappeared. Sister Immaculata gestured toward the window where a much smaller nun sat in a rocking chair reading a breviary "Me parrtner, Sister Perpetua," she said, "and this"—she indicated the sharp-featured man, then paused. "What did ye say your name was, me man?" "Joe Fagan," the bum said in a hoarse voice. Sister Immaculata compressed her lips and shook her head slightly. "So now ye know all of us. Sit down."

Sister Perpetua, who had acknowledged Claiborne's presence only by a silent bow, had returned to her reading. "Are you and Sister Perpetua collaborating on this book?" he asked as he took a chair opposite Sister Immaculata.

The old nun (she had three stiff, white hairs growing out of a big mole on the left side of her nostril) leaned across the table, wheezing with suppressed laughter. "She's not me collaborator, she's me chaperone. We go about in pairs—it's better in case of trouble." She cast a glance at the oblivious Joe Fagan.

Claiborne eyed with apprehension the leathern cincture about her waist, as wide and as stout as a horse's girth. A memory from his childhood came to him: there had been at Eupedon a certain gray mare, Bessie, who made a practice of swelling up when her "belly-band" was cinched, so that one could never ride her as much as a quarter of a mile without having to dismount and recinch it, an arduous procedure when one was a small boy and was only just learning to mount from the ground. He dismissed as irreverent the fancy that Sister Immaculata might have swelled up when her superiors cinched her girth, and said: "It isn't too hot in here for you, Sister?" for she was fanning herself rapidly with her left hand.

"No, no," she wheezed. "It's me bronchial tubes. . . . Delightful in here, isn't it?" and she gave a rapid glance at the walls which were lined with books. "But we mustn't waste time. I've many questions to ask ye, and maybe some things to tell ye too, for I flatter meself I've found out some things about our boy not known to everybody." She shook her large head, frowning. "Ah, there's me pride rearing itself up! An ugly sight now, isn't it . . . ? But why write a book if ye can't say something that's not been said before?"

"We'd be spared a lot of suffering if every critic subscribed to that," Claiborne said. "What do you intend to call your book?"

"Companions in the Blood," she said.

"Companions in the Blood," he repeated.

"I see ye don't get the point. Have ye never read the *Divino Dialogo* of St. Catherine of Siena?"

He shook his head. She lowered her head and regarded him over the rims of her spectacles again, but abstractedly, as if he had not as yet engaged her full attention. He found himself glad that this was the case; she had an eye rather like a gamecock's, fierce yet clouded, as it were, by an inner light.

She nodded suddenly, as if she had received an answer to her question. "I thought as much," she said, and swept all of the folders except three off the table and into a brief case. The three folders were conspicuously labeled: MAGIC, BLOOD, and BRIDGE. She was opening the one labeled MAGIC. "Will ye read that now?" she asked.

He read:

Jurain, Hyle and Coahyl: *aus dem Aethiopischen ins Lateinische,* and *aus dem Lateinischen in das Teusche translatiret und ubergesetzt durch D. Johann Elia Muller.* (Hamburg 1732).

The most recent account comes from a treatise alleged to have been translated from Ethiopian into Latin and from Latin into German, of which Ch. VIII, "The Creation," reads:

The Creation

Take common rain water a good quantity, at least ten quarts, preserve it well sealed in glass vessel for at least ten days, then it will deposit matter and feces on the bottom. Pour off the clear liquid and place it in a wooden vessel that is fashioned round like a ball, cut it in the middle and fill the vessel a third full, and set it in the sun about midday in a secret or secluded spot.

When this has been done, take a drop of consecrated red wine and let it fall into the water, and you will instantly perceive a fog and thick darkness on top of the water, such as also was at the first creation. Then put in two drops, and you will see the light coming forth from the darkness; whereupon little by little put in every half of each quarter hour first three, then four, then five, then six drops, and then no more, and you will see with your own eyes one thing after another appearing by and by on top of the water, how God created all things in six days, and how it all came to pass, and such secrets as are not to be spoken aloud and I also have not power to reveal. Fall on your knees before you undertake this operation. Let your eyes judge of it; for thus was the world created. Let all stand as it is, and in half an hour after it began it will disappear.

By this you will see clearly the secrets of God, that are at present hidden from you as from a child. You will understand what Moses has written concerning the creation; you will see what manner of body Adam and Eve had before and after the Fall, what the serpent was, what the tree, and what manner of fruits they ate: where and what Paradise is, and in what bodies the righteous shall be resurrected; not in this body that we have received from Adam, but in that which we attain through the Holy Ghost, namely in such a body as our Saviour brought from Heaven.

He looked up into her sparkling eyes. He said: "I'm *damned!* . . . I mean, why, that must be the very formula they were using!"

She had crossed herself at the profane word but her brilliant gaze did not waver. "The secrets of God," she said. "It's what we're all after. . . . Catherine says she doesn't know whether the wine was consecrated or not. Would ye be knowing that now?"

"I'll bet it was," he said after a moment's hesitation. "Horne would have insisted on that. He was very particular —in his strange way. . . . Joe Paster!" he added excitedly. "Joe Paster was the one started them on that black magic stuff. He could have got the wine for Horne. He was friends with a lot of priests around there. You know, I remember that fellow sitting by the stove, carving something with a jackknife: the 'wooden vessel, round like a ball' I'll bet my hat! . . . Horne and Joe were having an affair that winter and they wouldn't let Max Shull in on their magic. I came by the studio once and he was standing outside, crying. We both set our shoulders to the door and broke it in and found 'em all on their knees. Horne gave me the devil. Said I'd ruined everything. . . ." He paused in confusion. "Excuse me, Sister. I got carried away on this flood of reminiscence."

"Ye're probably in a state of invincible ignorance," she said mildly, "but ye ought not to take the Lord's—or the Devil's—name in vain. Have ye prayed about it?"

"No," he said, "I'm not much on prayer. . . . What does Catherine Pollard think about all this?"

"She was a wild young girl in those days and had no notion of what it was they were after."

"And what do you think they were after?"

"I told you: the secrets of God."

"They took a roundabout way of getting at 'em."

"Ah, magic is always roundabout!"

"It wasn't the black magic alone," he said. "It was the company they kept. Some rather unsavory characters went in and out of that studio, Sister . . . this Joe Paster, for instance— I ought not to mention that fellow's name in your presence."

"Catherine says he was a Catholic."

"Why, yes, of sorts. Used to fall on his knees in the middle of the street. Had to acknowledge the visitation whenever it came, he said."

234

She looked at him sternly. "Do ye deny that he had the visitation?"

"I doubt very much that the Holy Ghost ever visited that fellow, Sister. He was a notorious homosexual. Used to go out with the boys every night and then get up and go to confession every morning."

She shook her head sadly. "A hard struggle he must have had. . . . Catherine thinks the Lord made a mighty use of him—in showing Horne the wonders of the Blood."

"The blood!" he exclaimed. "Horne had an affair with this fellow and they used to nick each other with knives—if that's what you mean by the blood!"

She nodded calmly and picked up the folder marked BLOOD. "It's that I wanted to talk with ye about. Catherine thinks that in the last years of his life Horne was drawing near to the Blood."

He said slowly: "Sister, as you know, Horne spent his last days in France. I saw him frequently and he evidently underwent a period of moral degeneration which may have been connected with his homosexuality. An erotic craving for blood was one of his symptoms. Miranda Proctor wrote me that when he visited her she had to ask her gardener to keep his fourteen-year-old boy out of the way; Horne attacked him once, with a knife. I've got a letter somewhere in which he says that he suspects that his powers are failing but that he feels that they would come back—if only he could see blood. Enough blood was the way he put it."

She sighed deeply. "Ah, yes. Enough to inebriate him. That's all he asked for. That's all any of us ask for. Enough of the Blood of Christ to inebriate us."

"Horne asked for about a quart of whisky a day too," he said.

"I come from the Old Country," she said. "The men of me family are all drunkards. It takes a power of whisky to still a man's longing for the Blood of Christ."

"Maybe it takes more of the blood of Christ to inebriate homosexuals than it does ordinary men," he said with a laugh.

"They've an extraordinary longing for it," she said, "and a place in the Kingdom. Our Lord Himself said the last word on that: Some men are born eunuchs, some men are made eunuchs by men and some become eunuchs for the sake of the Kingdom of God."

Even while the words stirred echoes in his memory they swelled the rising tide of his impatience. With an effort, he controlled it, saying: "Sister, it's immensely interesting to talk with you, but you must understand that there are certain aspects of these men's lives . . ."

"That ye can't talk about with a nun?" she said with a laugh. "I've not had the experience of the flesh that ye'll doubtless have had, but you must remember that a nun is a woman too. . . . I left the world when I was twenty-one. The first flush of youth they call it. I was no beauty but I had a few lads after me. There was one—I won't tell ye how far we went, but many's the morning—and, mind ye, after I took me simple vows—many's the morning I've waked up and the feeling that he'd been lying beside me the night would be so strong that I'd put this hand"—she extended toward him her large, work-roughened finger on which she wore a plain gold ring—"this hand, with its bridal ring, I'd lay down on the pillow where his head would have lain the night. . . ."

"After you went into the convent you realized what you were missing?" he said with a laugh.

She sighed. "Every human soul is different from every other human soul. But all human hearts are the same. Desperately wicked the prophet Jeremias calls the human heart and St. Augustine tells us we are not responsible for the 'first movements' of the heart. It is only when we yield to them that there is sin."

"Armed with the sayings of these worthies, you doubtless had no trouble in lying down and sleeping," he said in a voice which he allowed to become tinged with irony.

"Till I was around thirty," she said simply. "The temptations of me flesh became really terrible then. . . . But I had

the grace of a good confessor. 'Not a wink of sleep, Sister?'
he'd say, 'God must love ye, indeed, to grant you so much
concupiscence!' . . . Catherine tells me that these gels she
has working with her here are much the same. The twenty-
year-old gels have no trouble with the custody of their eyes.
It's the gel who has turned thirty who plays the devil among
the men with her sidewise looks. . . ."

"How long did these temptations of the flesh assail you,
Sister?" he asked curiously.

"Till I was well past fifty. But praise be, that's over! I'll be
sixty-five come the Feast of St. Agnes."

He said: "I'm much interested in all you say, Sister, but we
are talking, after all, about the temptations that beset normal
men and women. Horne Watts and his intimates are a different matter. I don't think you realize what these men's lives
were like. They were not tempted carnally by women but
by their fellow men. The relations between Horne and this
Joe Paster were a travesty of the relationship between a man
and a woman which I, for one, couldn't stomach. . . ."

She said with something like his own impatience: "And
what makes you think that you—or I—are so much better than
they were? When it comes to love, we're all like eunuchs in
the presence of the Bridegroom. Husbands and wives, priests,
monks, nuns . . . It's the Blood that matters. Read this, will
ye?" and she pushed toward him the folder marked BLOOD.

He opened it and read:

Drown yourself in the blood of Christ crucified, and bathe
yourself in the blood; inebriate yourself with the blood, and
clothe yourself with the blood. If you have been unfaithful, bap-
tize yourself again in the blood; if the demon has darkened the
eye of your understanding, wash it in the blood. . . . Dissolve
your tepidity in the heat of the blood, and cast off your darkness
in the light of the blood. . . . I wish to strip myself of every
raiment which I have worn up to now. I crave for blood; in the
blood have I satisfied and shall satisfy my soul. I was deceived
when I sought her among creatures; so am I fain, in time of
solicitude, to meet companions in the blood. Thus shall I find

the blood and creatures, and I shall drink their affection and love in the blood.

He sat staring at the page after he had finished.

"Ye see," she said, "she craved blood too!"

"Who is she?" he asked wonderingly, "and who is she writing to?"

"Saint Catherine of Siena, to Blessed Raimondo. Her Son and Father she called him."

He looked down at the page again. "From the *Divino Dialogo*," he read.

She compressed her lips. "They call ye a great writer and ye've never read the *Divino Dialogo!*"

"I write very little," he said, "and what I write is not great."

"Ah, it's hard to tell whether that's pride or humility speaking there—but thank God, it's not for me to judge."

Joe Fagan, who for some minutes had been observing them with mournful attentiveness, now laid his magazine down and walked slowly from the room. When the door had closed behind him, Sister Immaculata leaned across the table. "Did ye see anything in his coat pocket?" she asked in a whisper.

"A pint bottle of whisky," Claiborne said.

She heaved a sigh and crossed herself, then pointed to the bookshelves. "I wouldn't want temptation put in the poor soul's way, but it's hard for me not to be glad he's got his whisky for the day. I've an undue attachment to good books, God forgive me, and many's the time I've begged her not to put her fine books out on those shelves. Do you think she'll listen? 'Sister,' she'll say, 'suppose one of the men wanted to read Blessed Angela of Foligno or Brother John the Evangelist's *Kingdom of God in the Soul?*' 'Not likely,' I tell her, 'as long as they've got *Pic* and *Look*.' She had her way and Blessed Angela of Foligno went last Thursday. . . ." She drew the corners of her large, mobile mouth down and made the gesture of whipping a book off a shelf and into a coat pocket. *"The Kingdom of God in the Soul* is still there if ye'd care to take a look at it."

"I'd rather talk to you," he said.

She flashed him her brilliant smile. "Ah, we've so much to talk about!" she said, and drew another of her folders toward her. " 'Pontifex,' now. Catherine tells me ye argued against his taking that title."

He said: "It seemed to me that no man-made mechanism could stand up under the weight of the imagery he hung on that bridge. And who, after all, is his 'Pontifex'?"

"It's that I wanted to talk with ye about. Do ye suppose *he'd* ever read the *Divino Dialogo* of St. Catherine?"

"I'm sure he hadn't. He had no formal education, and was ill read. Not as well read as I am, as a matter of fact."

"It's easy to see ye're a man of parts. How ye'll shine once your true worth is revealed!"

"Do you mean after I'm dead?" he asked with an embarrassed laugh.

"Ah, it may happen any moment! Ye're a staunch member of the mystical body now, invisible as ye are. How ye'll shine when ye become visible!"

"Do you mean that if I should join the Church I'd become visible?" he asked curiously.

"What else could I mean? Where's your theology, man?"

"I haven't got any theology," he said.

"It's a bad time—a time of Occam, not Aquinas. . . . Did ye ever read Marsiglio of Padua?"

He shook his head.

"He writes about the same thing they write about today: the self-sufficiency of the natural man and the exaltation of the state that always goes along with it. Existentialism we call it today. He was much read in Siena in the fourteenth century. . . . Now here's a thought for ye. Siena was a great city and produced many saints—saints were the glories of cities in those days. But along with the saints it produced more homosexuals than other cities."

"That's extremely interesting," he said.

239

"Ah, the more ye study his life, the more ye are reminded of hers. Both of them born into a bad time, and with no education. Catherine tells me that he didn't even graduate from the high school."

"No," he said. "He was almost completely self-taught."

"Taught the same way *she* was taught! Do ye know how she learned to read?"

He shook his head.

"It was God Himself Who taught her, so her heart that He had filled with love might not burst. Ah, was Blessed Raimondo surprised when he got her first letter!"

"Who was Blessed Raimondo?"

"He was a man, maybe like our Horne. . . ."

"You mean that he was homosexual?"

"No. He had other failings. God had given him a great heart by nature but it all turned into pride and anger on the natural level. He had to be lifted above himself—like Horne. St. Catherine was often picking him up and carrying him a way in her arms." She gazed at him earnestly. "Does it make any difference what gifts or burdens a man has as long as he lays them all at the feet that were nailed to the cross?"

Her gaze was too bright. He felt as if he had been out in blazing sunshine too long. He left her question unanswered and stared out of the window. They must have stopped serving soup and bread downstairs. In the dingy square across the street a few men—men who had probably been standing in line only a few minutes ago—were sitting on benches. One of them was reading a newspaper that he must have salvaged from a gutter; it had a great brown splotch zigzagging across it. A long time ago, in a wood a long way from here, Vera had picked up off the ground just such a sodden newspaper. As Claiborne watched, a man on the other end of the bench leaned forward and picking a cigarette butt out of the dust stuck it into his mouth. He could not remember when he had been in this part of the city before, but Horne would have come here often. "Those fellows in Times Square are too natty," he had told Claiborne once, adding that sometimes after a party he liked to go down to a place like Mott Street "to see what was going on." Homosexuality had not been as fashionable in literary circles when he was alive as it is today, and he had despised "pansies." His intimates were all those whom he had "weighed in the balance and found wanting." Toward the last most of them stopped inviting him to parties; he invariably arrived drunk and the gaiety that had once been so spontaneous and hence contagious had turned febrile. He was preoccupied with sex and would look about a room, muttering obscenities, speculating in a hoarse and audible undertone on the sexual ties and habits of the other guests, and often as midnight approached would reel off in a drunken frenzy to find in some squalid quarter like this one the outcast who would be his bedfellow for the night. A creature must go to earth somewhere, or had he been roving all this time and only now gone to earth—in the cracked brain of an old nun?

"Ye say he never read the *Divino Dialogo*—and I don't doubt ye—but tell me then, where did he get his notion of the bridge? The same notion she had."

"Why can't you leave him alone?" he cried. "The poor devil's dead! And he hated women all his life. Why can't you women leave him alone. . . . *What are you laughing at?*" —for her old face was suddenly crinkled all over with laughter.

She had got her handkerchief out and was wiping the tears from her eyes. "It's the mercy of God," she said. "It takes me that way sometimes. . . . Ye aren't angry with me?"

"No," he said sulkily, "but the man's dead. You ought to quit picking his bones."

"It's the bridge," she said. "It's because he wrote about the bridge. Catherine says he could never live far from it. . . ."

"Because there are hangouts for sailors in that neighborhood and he could pick the sailors up as they came off the boats."

"It was the Humanity of the Word kept him there," she said. "It's the Humanity of the Word is the bridge between earth and heaven. And it has three steps: the feet that were

241

nailed to the cross, the side that was pierced to reveal the ineffable love of the heart, and the mouth in which gall and vinegar were turned to sweetness. Horne ran to and fro among creatures like a madman, but he ran along the bridge too, else how could he have brought back the stones of virtue that he planted in his garden?"

"He took his own life," he said. "Isn't that a sin?"

"He wrote about the sea all his life and he cast himself into it in the end. We all have our own ways of abandoning ourselves to God's mercy."

"You think, then, that because he was a gifted poet God will forgive him for taking his own life?"

She did not seem to consider his question worth answering. The interview was evidently at an end; she had set her brief case on the table between them and was stowing her folders away in it. All at once she raised her head. The smile on her old, wise, kind face was like a lantern set out on a dark night. "Who can tell what God will do?" she asked. "All we know is that He is mad with love for His creature and drunk with desire for her salvation. When we flee Him fastest may be when He seeks us most."

She came out from behind the table and settling her voluminous skirts picked up her brief case. "Sister Perpetua," she called, "let's be going to the chapel."

Sister Perpetua came forward and the three of them went silently down the hall. As Claiborne held the outer door open, Sister Immaculata turned to him: "Ye'll be coming to the chapel with me to say a prayer for our boy."

"I'm afraid not, Sister. I'm due uptown now."

"Ye won't find a better time to pray for him than now," she said calmly.

But he could not answer her for staring at the man who was coming up the street.

SEVENTEEN

Max saw him and stopped dead. "Tom!" he called. "What are you doing here?"

"What are *you* doing here?" Claiborne countered.

Sister Immaculata descended the steps and, followed by her smaller companion, moved majestically off down the street. As they passed him, Max bowed low and said, "Be seeing you, Sister," and then came and stood at the foot of the steps, looking up at Claiborne. "I get it," he said. "You came down here to have a talk with Sister Immaculata."

"I was summoned," Claiborne said, "by either St. Catherine of Siena or St. Catherine Pollard—I haven't figured out which." He looked after the retreating figure of Sister Immaculata. "I'm not sure I'd have come if I'd known what I was letting myself in for."

Max turned and looked down the street too. "You'd think she had one of those old-fashioned steamboat paddle wheels installed in her, wouldn't you . . . ? I don't blame you, boy! Was she very rough on you?"

"Not exactly rough," Claiborne said. "Formidable. As formidable a woman as I ever met."

"I had a session with her when I first came," Max said. "She turned *me* inside out in no time at all!"

"I thought nuns had to stay put," Claiborne said. "What's she doing roaming all over the country?"

"She's a Big Wheel," Max said. "D.Phil. of Louvain and all that. When you get to be that big a wheel you can pretty well do as you please, provided, of course, ye have the proper reverence for your superiors, and humility, which is the groundwork of all the virtues. She's hell on humility. Has she given you her talk on humility yet?"

"We talked mostly about what a saintly fellow Horne Watts was and how much he resembled Blessed Raimondo Somebody."

"That'd be one of the followers of St. Catherine of Siena. She's death on St. Catherine. . . . But she's got the whole Middle Ages at her finger tips. I wish I knew half as much as that woman."

His quick, black eyes had kept roving over Claiborne's face as he talked and now he smiled, as if this meeting, which was taking place after months of separation and domestic upheaval, were a casual affair. "What say we go get a glass of beer? There's a little joint in the next block."

The "little joint" consisted of four tables in the back half of a delicatessen. The proprietor came out from behind the counter, wiping his hands on his apron when he saw them enter. Max called him "John" and told him he wanted the biggest mug he had of the "dark." "Boy, am I thirsty!" he said when the mugs of beer were set before them.

John lingered behind Max's chair a moment after he had brought the beer. "Thirsty work," he said. "Look at painters! Drink hair tonic or anything else they can get. . . . You been up on the scaffold?"

Max shook his head. "I've been working at the lower level, but I've had to climb up every now and then to give 'em a hand. . . . It's no work for a fat man." He glanced down at his middle. "Tom, you think I've lost any weight?"

Claiborne eyed him curiously. Max certainly had not lost any weight but he had had the impression as they walked down the street together that he was moving more lightly than he had seen him move for years. There was an air of suppressed excitement about him too, an air of *haste* that he had never known him to have before. He said: "No, you haven't lost any weight that I can see, but you don't seem to be feeling any pain. . . . What are you up to, Max? What are you doing down here?"

"I've got a commission," Max said, "and such a commission! It's giving me a chance to fulfill a life's ambition. When it's finished I'll be known the length and breadth of Mott Street as the Master of the St. Eustace legend."

"That's what you were known as the length and breadth of the Riviera," Claiborne said.

Max shook his head. "More satisfaction in dazzling these birds somehow. This is a mural. And I've got as nice a little apse to put it on as you'd ask. The chapel was Greek Orthodox once, so it's round as a barrel. Then some youth movement took over but the president and treasurer of the society got involved in a holdup and went to the reformatory, so the board offered it to Catherine—on St. Eustace's day, boy!"

"That's the day she was at Blencker's Brook last year. Did she ask you to decorate the chapel then?"

"She didn't know she had the chapel when she was at Blencker's Brook but as soon as she got back here and heard the news she thought of me. . . . Where else could she find a master of the St. Eustace legend?"

"I remember your telling me that she admired the version of it you had on display that day. . . . She has a discerning eye."

"That's what you need in a patron."

"A patron ought to have a little something else," Claiborne said.

"She hasn't got any money—can't be bothered with the stuff. But she knows where it grows."

"She's paying you for this job?"

"I'm making enough out of it to carry me for the next few months."

"Then you aren't living at Blencker's Brook any more?" Claiborne asked after a brief pause.

Max shook his head. "There's nobody at Blencker's Brook —except Tom Abel and one of his men."

"Alice and Freda and all of 'em packed off?"

"On board wages."

There was another longer pause, then Claiborne asked bluntly: "Where is Vera?"

"I'm not allowed to tell you," Max said soberly.

"You mean she told you not to tell me?"

Max nodded. "She doesn't want you to know where she is. But I don't see why I can't tell you something else."

"What is that?"

"She's all right, Tom! I know you've been worrying about her."

"How could I help it?"

"Of course. But you don't need to worry about her any more. She's all right. Better than she's ever been, as a matter of fact. . . . *Happier*. . . . How's Cynthia?"

"Her health is excellent. . . . I suppose you wouldn't feel like coming to see us?"

Max shook his head. "When two of my friends separate I make it a rule to take one side or the other. That way you don't get caught in the cross fire."

"Very clever of you," Claiborne said.

There was a silence, then Max said, "Would you like to see the chapel?"

Claiborne said, "Sure," and they set off down the street. The chapel, a round, squat structure built of ugly red brick, stood on a narrow lot between two tall tenement houses. The houses, swaying a little toward each other, from age and decrepitude, took on, for Claiborne's fancy, the look of a couple of harridans engaging in conversation over the head of the stunted youth or dwarf whom they had taken in charge.

It was dark inside except for a pinpoint of light far at the back and the light which came from several large electric bulbs, which, encased in wire cages, were laid along the edges of a canvas sheet that covered most of the floor. A scaffolding had been fixed beside one wall. Claiborne saw figures perched on its top plank. Three or four other figures moved about below the scaffolding or stood with their backs to him grouped around a stand that held a big tub.

Max called, "Dessy, here's Cousin Tom!" and one of the figures detached itself from the group and came forward. There was something dedicated, almost nunlike in Désirée's manner if not in her dress, Claiborne thought. She greeted

246

him quietly but made no inquiries of him and volunteered no explanation of her own presence there, merely stood beside him for a few minutes, staring at what was visible of the mural, then suddenly, with a wordless smile, went back to the group around the stand.

"She stands there all day and stirs the stuff," Max said. "We're putting it on with rollers, so it has to be pretty thick."

"What are you using?"

"Oh, part Venice Turpentine, part white lead. It holds fine."

In the dim light several young men went to and fro, filling buckets from the tub and handing them to men who stood on the lower rungs of the platform, who, in turn, handed them to the men above them. As one of these men leaned down to receive a bucket from his helper, his face was clearly visible in the circle of light.

Claiborne turned to Max. "What's Robin Vincent doing up there?"

"Why, he bosses the roller crew. I couldn't get along without Robin. Got a natural knack. . . . You know, his painting's coming along like nobody's business. I'll show you something he's just finished. . . ."

"I thought it was sculpture he excelled in," Claiborne said.

"That was months ago," Max said. "He paints now. Time flies fast in St. Cyprian's Oratory."

"Where is the Oratory located these days?"

"Robin and I've got a loft up the street. Had to clean up the place before we could move in. Pretty good light, but the stairs are narrow. It works all right, though. We break the panel up into blocks three by four and they can just get 'em down the stairs. . . . You know, Tom, it's awfully handy having all these 'unemployables' hanging around. Soon as we get a panel finished we put the word out and three or four of 'em come and whip her down the street."

"You're quite the medievalist these days, aren't you? With your 'prentice painters and your patron—and even the poor, whom you seem to have always with you."

"It's a fact," Max said. "You know, these bums love lending a hand. No good on the long haul but they *like* to do little jobs. Several men from the line have come in and asked if there was anything they could do. They'll take even more interest in the chapel when that old wind blows up from the river."

"Are you going to have the chapel heated in the winter?"

"We hope to get hold of a furnace, somehow," Max said cheerily, "but Rome was not built in a day. Neither was St. Eustace's. . . . If you'll come and stand over here I think you can get a pretty good light on the altarpiece."

He was moving over to stand beside one of the round concrete pillars that supported the vault. Claiborne followed him. Now that his eyes were growing accustomed to the half-light he could make out the designs that filled the entire wall of the apse. Figures, apparently of men and women, the men distinguished from the women chiefly by the relative scantiness of the one garment that covered them, but all short and square-barreled, with the squareness of the bodies oddly echoed in a slight flatness of the heads, all moving from each end of a semicircle toward a small eminence which was crowned with a larger, squarer mass. The bull's body, composed of metallic scales which overlapped each other and gleamed even in this dim light, rested on four stocky pillars. Its head was lowered, its jaws closed. The elongated apertures which perhaps represented its eyes seemed to brood over the four figures that confronted it. Something that was no doubt the plume of a helmet depended down St. Eustace's back. The figure beside him, a woman's, seemed to sway a little toward his. The movement was arrested by the determined uprightness of the small figure on her right, to be set in motion again by the smaller figure on the left.

Claiborne slowly put his hand out and sketched in the air the movement of the four standing figures. "I don't see how you ever brought *that* off," he said.

"Took doing," Max said modestly, "but after all, I haven't hung around Hieronymus Bosch all these years for nothing."

248

"Well, I want to congratulate you. It's the damnedest thing *I've* seen in many a year."

"Can't have that kind of talk around here," Max whispered, and pointed down the nave. Claiborne saw what he had not noticed before, a large black and white mass, with a smaller black and white mass beside it: the two nuns, praying at the altar rail. Another, darker mass motionless beside one of the pillars midway down the nave, was probably somebody else praying. After all, that was what people came into churches for: to kneel at an altar and pray. *An altar is a raised structure, or any structure or place, on which sacrifices are offered or incense burned in worship of a deity, ancestor, etc. (I have what is known as a "photographic memory" and am, besides, possessed of a little learning.) . . . Jacob was journeying from Beersheba to Haran when he came, about this time of day, "into a certain place." And he took of the stones of that place and put them for his pillows and lay down to sleep and dreamed and behold a ladder set up on the earth, and the top of it reached to heaven: and behold the angels of God ascending and descending upon it, which caused Jacob to wake, trembling, and saying: "Surely the Lord is in this place. . . ."*

"And sooner or later we're going to have a *parclose*," Max said. "There's no reason in the world why we shouldn't."

"None that I can see," Claiborne said.

"And the other side will show St. Benedict on his way to the Sacro Speco, with the old shepherd, Montanus, walking on the cliffs above him. After all, the place where Eustace saw the stag must have been on that mountain that rises up opposite the Sacro Speco. . . . But we won't get to that for a while. . . ."

"No . . . I mean yes," Claiborne said. "Well, I've got to get uptown."

"Don't you want to wait and see Catherine?" Max said. "There she is now."

The two nuns were still at the altar rail but the other dark mass was detaching itself from the pillar and moving slowly forward. Claiborne looked up at the altarpiece. Even in this light those strange hooded eyes glowed crimson. *And he was afraid and said, How dreadful is this place. This is none other but the house of God, the gate to Heaven. . . .*

The woman had emerged into the aisle and was moving toward them. "There she comes now," Max said. "Wait a minute."

"I *can't*," Claiborne said, "I *told* you I had to get uptown!" And hearing his voice high-pitched and almost unrecognizable in his own ears, he turned abruptly and started for the door. Max followed him, but Claiborne did not slacken his pace until he had crossed the threshold and the little vestibule and felt the evening air cool on his face. He waited there till Max came out and stood beside him. Max did not speak. In a minute I'll be gone from here and on my way uptown, Claiborne thought. He turned to Max. "Is Vera here in the city? You can at least tell me that."

Max slowly shook his head. "She's on a farm."

"Another farm?" Claiborne cried. "What does she need with another farm?"

"It's not her farm."

"Well, what's she doing there?"

"Tending to some pigs," Max said. "I believe there's a cow too, and some chickens."

"Hell on husbandry, isn't she?" Claiborne said. "What breed is it now?"

"Scrub," Max said.

Rocking to and fro on his heels, his hands thrust deep into his pockets, his face a little lifted, as if to greet the evening air, he spoke politely but abstractedly; it was apparent that he had affairs on hand that he would be glad to get back to, once his guest had departed.

Claiborne's rage was so great that he could not contain it. Before he knew what he was doing he had raised his stick. "*You!*" he shouted. "You and Vera . . . and your games!"

Max slowly turned his head to look at him but he made no other move. The stick, which fortunately was not long enough to reach him, sank in Claiborne's hands and struck on the concrete. Max still did not speak or move. Claiborne left him and walked rapidly toward the square where he hoped to find a cab which would carry him uptown.

EIGHTEEN

Half a dozen people were coming in after dinner: the Waites, the Crenfews, who happened to be spending the week in town, and the Proctors. Tom had asked the Archers too, but Molly had been evasive. They might be able to make it, she had said, but they had to go somewhere else first.

There had been some discussion as to which apartment they would receive the guests in. It had been settled that Cynthia was to appear under the wing of the Waites, who would come early so as to give the impression that they had brought her. It had been decided too that the guests should be received in the larger of the two apartments, the one Cynthia was occupying, since it was, after all, designed for entertaining.

Cynthia had bought in a shop off Lexington Avenue some orchids that were brown and yellow and pink-spotted and had set them in a wide bowl on the shelf below the great Florentine mirror. She was standing in front of the mirror now, with a sharp-featured young man who wore his hair in a bang and stood with his head thrown far back, studying the thirteenth-century triptych that covered the west wall. He was, no doubt, attached to some museum; a few minutes ago he had given Ned Brodo's collection of clocks the same smiling, detached consideration. . . . Why is it that people who have no formal occupation so often collect clocks? *Sous le règne de Louis XIV, tous les arts furent perfectionnés, l'horlogerie seule en fut exceptée.* . . . Was it because he was *le Roi Soleil* that Louis XIV took so little interest in the mechanical marking of time? He was passionately interested in architecture, above all in the arch. "I am a martyr to symmetry," Madame de Maintenon wrote a friend. And to *courants d'air,* she might have added: The king insisted that most of the windows at Versailles be kept open, even in the dead of winter, having suffered overmuch in his youth from the overheated air, which, no matter how richly perfumed, could not conceal the odor emanating from the cancer that gnawed at his mother's breast. . . . A girl came into my arms once, on warm earth, beside a wall. Dark cypress boughs waved over us. There was a woman standing in the shadows who had a cancer gnawing at *her* breast. . . . But I was thinking of Louis XIV and Madame de Maintenon. My memory, you see, is still serviceable. . . . *"An indifferent servant,"* the Voice said, *"preserving the worthless with as much pains as the precious and not always obedient; it even refuses to furnish you the name of that young man."*

That request is unreasonable; I have never seen him before. There is a question in my mind as to whether he ought to be here. I don't believe in having people in your house whom you have never seen before. *This isn't your house. It's the Brodos' apartment, or rather, it is Marianne Brodo's apartment. Edmund Brodo's apartment is across the hall. He is an invalid and cannot stir from his bed, so he is kept across the hall, where any untoward action which his illness should lead him to commit will have no unsympathetic witnesses, and where, also, carefully tended and made as presentable as a person in his unseemly condition can be made, he is exhibited at intervals for a certain length of time, to certain visitors. . . ."* But tonight, he thought, we are reversing the usual procedure; we are exhibiting him in Marianne's apartment. No, he corrected himself, Ned is in Majorca, so he cannot be exhibited here. *I* am taking his place. It is *I* who am being exhibited tonight—in Marianne's apartment. She would be pleased if she knew it. She was always trying to get me here.

". . . It's the word 'carrot' that puts you off," Marcia said. "You'd lap it up if it were called *'Elixir d'or'* or something like that." She wanted him to take carrot juice for the twitching of his left eyelid which she had noticed and remarked upon as soon as she entered the room. She had also asked him several times in a low voice if she could not make an appointment for him with Rudolf Scharp, a Freudian analyst whom she much admired. "He's horribly busy, of course, but I know he'd take *you.*"

"Yeah," he said, "but I can't take *him!*" And under the pretense of fetching more ice for the highballs he got up from the sofa where he had been sitting beside her and went through the narrow hall that, running the length of the apartment, formed a sort of gallery for the display of pictures, back into the vast butler's pantry. He heard steps behind him. George Crenfew entered and stood looking around him.

"This isn't the kitchen," Claiborne said. "It's just the pantry."

"Make a good operating theater," George said.

"Damned aseptic, ain't it?" Claiborne said. "I remember when they were doing this place up. Seth Owens wanted it French Provincial and Marianne was tempted but she decided that all that wood that didn't have to be scrubbed might make the maids slack." He laughed. "George, you ever notice how sanitary rich Yankee women are? It's a wonder Marianne is willing to have *me* here."

"You ain't so sanitary," George said, "but you're famous."

"Yes," Claiborne said, "I'm famous. Here, let me have that."

He was about to take the bowl of ice from George but George said, "No, I'll carry it," and then, "You tied up for lunch tomorrow?"

"No," Claiborne said.

"What say we lunch together?"

"All right. What time?"

"I can make it by one," George said. "Want me to come by for you?"

253

"No. I'll come by for you."

They walked back up the hall. George stopped to look at one of the pictures. Claiborne stopped too. Marianne Brodo had so many pictures that her walls would not accommodate them all at one time and she had had for years a regular schedule for their showing. Max kept a copy of it and timed his visits to the Brodos by it: "Next Tuesday'll be the first of February. Time for the Manetta." And he would call Marianne and propose himself for dinner on that date. . . . The picture George had stopped to look at was a Manetta, a small canvas, evidently a rehearsal for the great meeting of St. Anthony and St. Paul of Thebes. The hermit was seen emerging from his cave at the left of the canvas to set forth on a woodland path along which another figure was advancing toward him. It was not, on the whole, a successful composition; the middle ground was cluttered with Manetta's black, curiously undersized tree trunks, each trunk crowned with bronze-colored leaves, arranged in symmetrical layers.

George laid his finger on one of the tree trunks. "Looks like the woods around Ware's," he said.

"It does, at that," Claiborne said with a laugh.

The preparatory school they had attended had been located on the edge of a famous Civil War battlefield. Most of the battlefield was covered with a forest of third-growth oaks. The boys used it for recreation. A forest of stunted oaks, whose leaves, in autumn, showed a somber brown, the kind of growth that one might expect to find on that bloody field —or on the edge of one of Manetta's deserts. . . . How real Manetta's trees were! Once, in the waning light of a December day, he had been walking along a path, past just such trees, and hearing footfalls, had turned to see George Crenfew coming toward him. He had been beeched by old Rufus that afternoon and had flung off into the woods to be alone with his hurt. Beeching was one of the high traditions at Ware's and to be beeched by old Rufus himself instead of "Son Joe" was rather an honor. But old Rufus made a point of laying it on thoroughly and one's legs and backside stung for hours after an encounter, which was one of the reasons he had wanted to get off into the woods by himself.

He had stopped, though, to let George catch up with him. George had something shining in his hand. "Here," he said, and thrust his hand out, with much the same look on his face and much the same intonation of voice with which he had kept hold of the bowl of ice a moment ago. "Here," he had said, and when his cousin, seeing George's best Barlow knife, the one with which George had made himself mumble-the-peg champion of the school, would have protested, he had uttered what both of them knew was a lie: "I like the one Uncle Jim sent me better than this one. You want it?"

"If you don't," Tom had said.

"I *told* you I like the one Uncle Jim sent me better than this one! You don't think I want two knives, do you?"

"No," Tom said, and thrust the knife deep down into his pocket while they walked side by side, up the path, back to the dormitory. . . .

There had been a rearrangement of the company during his and George's absence. They had emigrated to the far end of the room and were now grouped in front of the great window. Alma Waite and Miranda Proctor sat together on a sofa. Cynthia and the young man with the bang had concluded their tour of the room and stood vis-à-vis beside the window, talking animatedly. Willy Stokes, who had been talking with Bob Waite, suddenly got up and strolled over to them. Claiborne thought resignedly that he was likely to have to see a good deal of Willy Stokes. Cynthia had been talking with him on the telephone when he came in this evening and at the conclusion of the conversation had invited him over, because, she said, he seemed at loose ends.

Willy had just been divorced from his second wife and might be expected to be somewhat at loose ends, but on the whole, Claiborne thought, looking over at him now, he seemed surer of himself than he had been twelve years ago. Perhaps he had come to realize that after all he had something to offer besides his money. He was, certainly, a handsome, well set-up fellow, by any standards, and there was something attractive about the dark animated glance with which while he talked he continually searched his interlocutor's face. He was turning it on Cynthia now as they stood before the wide window which was framed in some ancient hangings, straw-colored silken stuff, dimly shot with gold. The stuff had been chosen, he fancied, with an eye to the way it would show against the tapestries, the *boiseries,* the gold and silver and jeweled surfaces with which this apartment abounded.

Cynthia had given him a smile as he re-entered the room. He reflected as he filled Marcia's and Alma's glasses that nobody except himself was likely to recognize it for what it was: the bright, veiled look a hostess gives a host during the course of an evening, particularly if the evening promises to turn out well, as this one did. Everything had gone according to schedule. The Waites had come early, as they had been requested. Cynthia could have been supposed, by anybody who gave the matter a thought, to have come with them. Her coat and purse lay on the bed in one of the guest rooms, alongside Alma's. Her personal possessions had all been put in her bedroom and the door securely locked. If anybody wanted to know why that particular door was locked (and old friends would ask you anything!) he was prepared to say that Marianne had a few treasures that she was not willing to entrust to his keeping. He fancied that some of the same thoughts he was thinking had passed through Cynthia's mind; she held her slender figure a shade tauter after that exchange of looks; there was, perhaps, an added brightness in the smile she turned on her companion.

In the labyrinths of illicit love women pursue their tortuous courses more evenly, more gracefully than men. He had had a bad moment at the beginning of the evening when, at the spectacled young man's request, she had set off with him on a tour of the pictures and *bibelots.* On the surface she was here tonight only as a guest. Did the fact that the young man had asked her and not one of the other women to show him the sights indicate that he had divined their true relation? Claiborne had been so disquieted by this thought that he had watched their progress about the room in some alarm. But his fears had been quickly allayed. She had called out some question to him and he had thereupon joined them long enough to observe and admire the grace and serenity with which she steered her middle course, alternately rapt in admiration of the beauty of some of the objects they were viewing and prettily deferential toward him for having—if only temporarily and by proxy—these marvels in his keeping.

He himself, he thought gloomily, cut a more awkward figure. At noon today, for instance. He had slept late and a messenger sent by Pettigrew with a note that required an immediate answer had found him in her apartment when by rights he should have been in his own apartment across the hall. The messenger had got past the doorman and had rung so persistently that he had had to appear at the door of this apartment in pajamas and dressing gown. The incident was of little consequence but it had left an unpleasant impression. The messenger, an elderly, gnome-like creature, had stared hard at him before a knowing look came over his wrinkled face and he mutely surrendered the letter. The vulgar mind always finds something ludicrous in the manifestations of illicit love: *"You* are amazed, my dear; *we* are surprised." Still, the Scriptures say that it is not good for man to live alone. A notion picked up in the Babylonian exile, no doubt; the Shabbath says that it is indiscreet for one to sleep in a house as its sole occupant, for fear Lilith may seize hold of him. The word Lilith is popularly derived from *"layil,"* night, but Baudussin believes that the idea of Lilith seeking her prey by night is a Semitic conception, pointing out that the Accado-Sumerian root, *"lil,"* which has no gender, means a "dust storm" or "cloud of dust," from which comes the Sumerian *"lila,"* wind. The darkness these demons loved was that of the dust storms which rage in the desert, a conclusion which is confirmed by the incantation against madness in the Magical Texts addressed to Mero-dach. . . . *The incantation is against madness.*

The disease of the head coils in the desert, in the wind it blows
This man it strikes, and the man like one who is faint at heart
staggers. . . .
With its life it devours the man, to death it binds him. . . .
The madness is as a heavy storm whose path there is none that
knoweth. . . .

The three had left the window to join the larger group. The young man with the bang, as if realizing that he might command a wider audience, had turned to the company and was recounting an incident that had taken place last night at a dinner party that Molly and Ed Archer had given for a visiting British publisher. A young composer, after regarding the great man in a long, brooding, alcoholic silence, had challenged him toward the shank of the evening: "Why don't you take that mask off your face? Why don't you show what you really are? You're not fooling us. You're not fooling anybody except yourself. Why don't you take that mask off your face?" "But I'm not so bad," the great man had protested. "I've got a soul. I've got fully as much soul as you. But this is a dinnah pahty? Have I got to carry my soul around on my sleeve to all the dinnah pahties?"

They were all laughing, as much at the skillful rendition of Sir Owen Albert's accent as at what was being said. The young man drew a long breath and let his features subside into their usual prim expression.

His name is legion, Claiborne thought. I have been meeting him off and on for years. One of the first times was on the French Riviera. He was wearing his hair in a bang then and talking on and on about François and Francis, anecdotes designed to show that he was just as intimate with François Guillemin as he was with Francis Pereira. In Paris he was often at Gertrude Stein's. And in Rome he once stuck his behind in my face, in his hurry to lift to his lips, and not quite kiss, the hand of a countess. . . . In a few minutes he will tell an anecdote about a ballerina. . . .

But it was Willy Stokes who was talking: about William and Dorothy. He had been reading the agonized entries in Dorothy's journal before William's marriage. What were people to make of a mature woman's reclining in her brother's lap—except incest? Coulter was right.

"He may be," Claiborne said. "Even if he is, what's that got to do with literary criticism? Times change, so do customs. Dorothy put her head in her brother's lap a hundred and thirty years ago. You talk as if it was something that happened last night—in the literary demi-monde which you frequent."

The gesture with which he accompanied his words was so violent that he knocked his glass off the arm of his chair onto the floor. Fortunately, it was empty, even of ice. There was nothing to clean up. He straightened up and set the empty glass down on the little table before him. But he was aware that during the interval in which he had been bending over—an interval of mere seconds—the atmosphere of the room had insensibly altered. Something had gone wrong. In the last few seconds something had happened, momentous enough, untoward enough, to change, to chill the air of the whole room.

Willy Stokes seemed to feel the change too, and seemed to feel that he had to do something about it. He said good-humoredly: "Coulter's book is not a book I can imagine you liking, Tom. Still, I think there's something to it, besides scholarship."

"I'm tired of incest," Claiborne said.

"So am I," Miranda Proctor said. "I feel about it just the way Mrs. Hibben did at Princeton. She said it made her nervous."

Claiborne was looking at Cynthia. A moment ago she had turned a smiling face on the company but she sat now with her face averted, gazing through the great dark window.

There was something about her pose that arrested his

whole attention. He had never before seen her so motionless, as if her faculties were congealed and would have to be set in motion by some force outside herself. What could she have seen or heard that had so worked upon her?

He was about to go over to her when a bell pealed in the back of the apartment. Ed Archer's voice came through the speaking tube: "Party still going?" "Sure," Claiborne said. "Come on up."

As he moved toward the door, he glanced back into the room and saw that Cynthia had gone to sit beside Miranda Proctor. The expression on her face as she leaned toward Miranda was not out of the ordinary. Apparently whatever it was that had so disturbed her had passed.

The door opened and Ed and Molly entered. They had evidently come on from a dinner party. Molly's shoulders were bare and the fine network of reddish veins showed clearly in her sun-burned cheeks, as it always did when she had been drinking. She said in a loud voice: "Well, Tom, this is the last place I'd ever expect to find *you!*"

"Sh-h-h, honey!" Ed said. "These people here don't feel as good as we do."

Molly looked at the group in front of the window. "They do look kind of sour," she said in a penetrating voice.

People were rising to their feet, exchanging greetings, seeking other partners for conversation. Claiborne judged it wise to seat himself beside Molly. Ed refused a highball and made a slight negative inclination of his head when Claiborne asked Molly if she would have one. But Molly put her hand out for the proffered glass. She had evidently had a great deal to drink. Her handsome, bulky body was already as stripped as custom allowed, but she seemed to feel heated and put her hand up to her bared breast every now and then as if to tear off still another covering. Meanwhile her head turned slowly from side to side as her eyes, which had always reminded Claiborne of twin sapphires embedded in old Spanish leather, roamed over the room.

"Where's the Matisse?" she asked.

"It's in the other apartment," he said.

"Oh," she said, and turned and for the first time looked at him directly, "you have that apartment too?"

"I sleep and work over there and entertain over here," he said.

She gave him a long, deliberative glance. "Oh," she said again, "you *are* fancy!"

"I thought I might do myself as well as I could while I'm here," he said.

Her face was suddenly contorted with laughter. "You really have to see it to believe it!" she gasped.

"See what?"

"*You*—in this apartment! Several people told me about it, but I had to see it to believe it."

"Who told you?" Claiborne demanded.

"Oh, mutual friends . . . You know what they are like."

"I do," he said coldly. "Well, now, you've seen it—and me —are you satisfied?"

She laughed again. Her gaze had sharpened. "No," she said calmly, "I haven't seen the other apartment, since—oh, way back last winter."

"Would you like to see it now?" Claiborne asked in the same cold tone.

"I'd love to, Tom," she said, and rose and followed him out into the hall. He was aware that Ed Archer eyed them speculatively as they left the room, but he was so relieved to be away from the brightly lighted drawing room and the company it held that he told himself that it did not greatly matter what Ed Archer thought.

He had been living in the long room in which Edmund Brodo had lain practically immobile for a year. He had taken that room for his study. His desk sat in the embrasure of the great front window but he did not sit at his desk often; he already felt a strong disinclination for the view from that window, for the wide window itself, for the very desk that stood in it, and the other day had moved his typewriter and papers to a small table at the other end of the room. Prob-

261

ably be writing under the bed before I'm through, he thought.

There were no lights burning in the other apartment and he found himself delaying the turning on of a light under the pretense of showing Molly the view from the window. Standing there beside her, in the half-dark, looking down on the black river, he was acutely and uncomfortably aware of objects of furniture which would be revealed if a light went on; the great, carved and gilded bed, the enormous desk of Spanish oak. It was as if some poverty that he had been successfully concealing from the world at large would be revealed if these objects were exhibited to the eyes of his visitor or if the eyes of his visitor dwelt on these objects.

Suddenly the stout, jeweled woman was weeping and beating her hands up and down on the window sill. "Ed *made* me come! He said we *had* to come. . . . But now I'm here I can't stand it . . . I can't. . . . Why do I have to?"

He was appalled and could say only: "Molly, don't! . . . You're upset."

She turned on him a face furious and streaked with tears. "You think just because I'm fat and have a lot of money that I haven't got any feelings."

"On the contrary, Molly, I've always thought of you as having a superabundance of feeling."

"Oh," she cried, "you have a ten-dollar word for everything! But you don't fool anybody but yourself. Not even that nasty little Spencer with his bang that got himself invited up here tonight because he said he wanted to see the love nest. . . . I don't think you're really bright at all. If you had been, you wouldn't have fallen for that little bitch. I saw what she was up to from the start, and so did everybody else. I went to Vera . . ."

He felt that he must interrupt her at any cost. "Don't you think that if Vera wanted me to know what went on between you and her she would have told me herself?" he asked.

"She's not going to tell you anything. She's not going to see you again if she can help it. That's what she told me:

'I don't want ever to see him again. It was a mistake and I never want to see him again. . . .' "

"People our age often discover that their first marriages were a mistake," he said.

She was weeping wildly. "You don't know what it's *like!*" she cried. "You *will* know, but you don't know yet. . . . Jim's been dead nearly two years, but it's just like it happened yesterday. . . ."

"You didn't waste any time in remarrying," he said cruelly.

"I didn't know what it would be like without him. That was what I was afraid of. To find out what it would be like. I thought that if I married again I never would find out. . . ."

"But you found out?"

"Yes," she cried, *"you fool! . . .* I found out!"

A ray of light showed from an open doorway. "I hope you two are up to some good here in the dark," Ed Archer's voice said.

Claiborne said with deliberate slowness: "Well, you can't see the river if you have the lights on. . . ."

"Besides, it makes my head go round," Molly said, with a strangled sob.

Ed advanced into the room. "I didn't know you felt that bad, Molly."

"I feel terrible," Molly said.

"I'm afraid I haven't been much help," Claiborne said.

"Oh, yes, you have, Tom," Ed said. "You did just right. Come on, Molly. Let's go home. I've got your coat."

"And not tell anybody good-by?" she asked childishly.

"Tom'll tell 'em good-by," Ed said firmly. He threw the coat over her shoulders and together he and Claiborne escorted her to the elevator.

Claiborne stood for a while after it had descended, staring at the cage whose black iron grillwork was patterned in scrolls of cornucopias spilling into space an endless succession of fruits. He had never noticed before that each cornu-

263

copia appeared to be lined with brass and that the rounded edge of each fruit showed a glint of brass too.

The door behind him opened and the Crenfews and Proctors emerged, followed in a few minutes by the Trowbridges and young Spencer. Alma made a point of telling him that she and Bob were going to "let" him take Cynthia home. "If you still want to go on to the Hawleys," Cynthia called from the open doorway. "Maybe it's too late."

"No," Bob said, "no, it's not too late. . . . And we promised we'd come."

The leave-takings were finally accomplished. The cage plunged downward again. He entered the apartment.

She was standing at the window, as she had stood once before this evening, but when she heard his footsteps she turned around and began moving toward him down the long room. There was an expression on her face that he had never seen before, or was it, rather, he asked himself, that an expression, a disposition of features that he had become accustomed to was no longer discernible? Or did the strangeness reside only in the eyes? Her eyes, which he sometimes thought of as "green as grass," looked dark in this light—as if somebody you had never seen or heard of were suddenly standing at the window of a house that you had supposed unoccupied.

With an effort, he looked away from her, down at the low table, with its array of crystal and silver and ice. He could not remember when he had last had a drink. That was odd. As a rule, he had too many drinks in the course of an evening. Perhaps, he thought, it would have been better if he had followed his usual habit; he felt extraordinarily sober, and the unaccustomed sobriety was accompanied by a sharpening of all his senses: he literally felt as if he might see or hear anything.

She had come to stand beside the long low table. He had filled a glass with crushed ice and had doused the ice liberally with whisky and he now held the glass toward her in a silent gesture of invitation. She disregarded the gesture. He set

264

the glass down and said carefully as he filled another glass for himself: "Well, I think it was quite a success!"

"*Success!*" she said in a hoarse, reverberating whisper. "The Archers had a dinner party last night for Sir Owen Albert. Everybody in this room was there—except us."

He was silent a moment, then he said: "Do you mind if I sit down? I'm beastly tired."

She sat down opposite him.

"Did you mind very much not being invited?" he asked gently.

She said: "Did you know that Sir Owen Albert was coming to this country?"

He shook his head.

"Why didn't you?"

"I don't know. I have correspondence with him from time to time . . . but heavens, I don't know the man so well that he has to account to me for all his movements. . . ."

"But you are Ed's literary editor. It would seem natural that Ed should invite you to meet him."

He said slowly: "I don't imagine that Ed thought about it, one way or another. He's got a good many rings to his circus. He may not always realize when they overlap."

"He would have realized it if you had called his attention to the fact that Gower and Gower are publishing my poems."

"That is not the kind of fact I am going to call his attention to."

"No," she said bitterly, "you would never make an exertion of that kind. . . . You couldn't even refrain from mowing Willy Stokes down tonight."

"Good God!" he cried. "What does he expect when he sticks his neck out like that?"

"I thought he behaved very well," she said. "But I don't imagine he was surprised. He told me that you never liked him."

"I don't like or dislike him," he said. "I don't pay any attention to him—except when he meddles in matters that are not his concern."

265

"Would you call putting up the money for the new series meddling?" she asked coldly. "I don't know that he'll still be willing to back it after this evening. But he was very enthusiastic the last time Bob talked with him."

"That's Bob's funeral, not mine. I've got nothing to do with the editorship of *Spectra* now. If Bob can get money out of Willy more power to him."

There was a long silence. Her face was still averted from him. He could not see what expression her eyes held. He said more kindly: "I can see that this means a lot to you. And I'm sorry. But Willy has known me for a long time. He'll overlook it. . . . As for the other business, have you ever thought that there may be a reason for our not being invited last night?"

"You mean—our situation?" she asked without turning her head.

"Yes. Molly Archer is very fond of Vera. I don't imagine she wants either of us around. She came up here tonight only to please Ed."

"I suppose that's why you took her off into the other apartment. To talk about Vera!"

"I took her over there as a favor to Ed—because she was on the point of making a nuisance of herself."

"But you talked about Vera."

"Good God!" he said with a groan. "How do I know what we talked about? She was tight, I tell you. . . . Look here, Cynthia, have you ever thought that we may have made a mistake? You're on the way up. It's easy to see that. I've got a notion that I may be on the way out. . . ."

She turned her head quickly, and said, after a moment, with a wry smile, "You spoke of 'our' situation. What you really meant was *my* situation."

"Damn it, your situation *is* anomalous. You happen to be living with a man who is married to another woman. . . ."

"At your request. Do you deny that it was at your request?"

"I asked you to go away with me," he said.

"For a night . . . a week end!" she cried. "That was all

266

you wanted. You were never serious. And why? Because you're still in love with Vera."

He stood up. "I'm not in love with any woman," he said.

Her eyes held a gleam he had never seen in them before—as if the occupant of that unlighted house were all at once betraying his presence by paroxysms of glee.

"Do you think I don't know that?" she said. "Marcia Crenfew says that you have never been aware of the existence of any other human being. She says that you are a classical case of . . ."

"Marcia Crenfew is the fool of the world," he said, and walked from her to the window and stood looking down on the city. There were not as many lights as there had been an hour ago, but still a great many. He wondered what it would be like if every neon light were turned off and the city veiled in merciful darkness. Some words, whose source, for the moment, eluded him, came into his mind: *While all things were in quiet silence and night was in the midst of her course . . .*

Night, he thought, darkness. That is what I long for, what I have been searching for all my life, and he leaned over and laid his hands, palms downward, on the cold stone window ledge. It was so low that a tall man had to stoop to reach it. What would it be like if he crouched lower, lower and still lower until his body hurtled over the ledge and drawing to itself soft plumes of darkness, plunged into the very heart of silence? *That was what she wanted!* he thought. *That was why she did it. She wanted darkness. Night. Nothing. That was what she wanted: Nothing. I brought her to that. . . .* A cold sweat had broken out on his forehead. He took his handkerchief out and wiped his forehead.

There was a slight sound in the room behind him. He felt a prickling at the base of his scalp and turned around. The woman he had turned his back on was standing not a foot away, addressing him in a low voice.

She said that she was sorry if she had offended him. She was too brusque, too direct. It was a habit she had fought against all her life. He must help her overcome it. . . . But perhaps

267

she was not wholly to blame. He was right: their situation *was* anomalous. The fact that each of them had been married before must be taken into account. Her own first husband was certainly unlike him, while Vera . . .

Her voice was softer than he had ever heard it before and she spoke with an odd hesitation before each phrase. *That is because she makes it up as she goes along. She doesn't know how other people feel. She has to make it up. . . . She is a woman with movable ways!*

He felt again that prickling of the scalp. *I called her*—out of the night! She would not stand here if I had not called her out *of the night!*

He said: "Yes, you and Vera are different. She's got her faults, but she is a woman. . . ."

Her eyes glittered. Involuntarily, he took a step backward. As if recalled to herself, she veiled her gaze with downcast lids. But the words still hung in the air between them. "Well, what am I?" she asked finally in a hard voice.

"I don't know," he said. "God help us all! I don't know!"

She raised her still glittering eyes. "And you? What are *you?*" she asked in the same hard voice.

"A son of a bitch," he said. "That's what I am. A son of a bitch," and with the words left the room.

NINETEEN

As far back as he could remember, when he was wakeful at night, he put himself to sleep by roaming the woods of Long Mountain. The hotel stood back from the brow of the mountain, in an ill-kept garden, the village lying to the east of it, the woods pressing it hard on the western side. Judge Clendenning, who was so old he no longer knew who he was, sat on the veranda in the afternoons, Miss Eloise Perkins tending him while his daughter napped. He had been in Pickett's Charge and knew what you were going to do before you knew it yourself. *"What you going in them woods for, boy? Don't you know they're full of painters?"* And, indeed, wildcats often howled near the western gate at dusk. If Miss Eloise saw you she would make you go to the village and fetch the Judge some ice cream, so you slipped through one of the long parlor windows onto the path and then from boxbush to boxbush till you reached the western gate.

The main path led to a broad promontory called Sunset Rock, frequented by children and nursemaids during the day and by lovers after dark. But halfway between Sunset Rock and the hotel a path struck off down the side of the mountain. Not everybody knew the path was there; a big rock jutted out where it started. We felled an oak so it lay across the entrance to the path. The last time I walked along that path the tree trunk was still there but it had gone doty. You had to step over the trunk or push through thick brush to get at the path. You went straight down the side of the mountain through laurel higher than a man's head till you got to the hollow where the deer used to come to lick salt.

The pool is still there, with the rocks all around it, but the salt no longer outcrops. The water in the pool stays the same level, winter and summer, because it is fed by springs. The entrance to the cave is a hole in the side of the ravine and has laurel growing all about it. A creek runs through the cave, south, to join the river. I saw the cave first, but George Crenfew was the first man inside. You pushed through the laurel and crawled till you came to the banks of the creek. You had to be careful as you swam or your hand would strike the roof of the cave. But there was enough air. Inside the cave the creek goes to earth between two leaning rocks, in a room that is high enough to stand up in. You think when you come up out of the water that the room is full of people, but it is only the stalagmites. The stalagmites are thicker than a man's body and shine green in the light from the lamps fastened on our miners' caps. The floor is covered with dust except where it is pitted with the drops that fall from the stalactites. It is hard to know which way to go; the room has more passages opening off it than a man has fingers on both hands. . . . George Crenfew was with me a moment ago, but somebody must have called to him; he is not here now. . . . But there is somebody on ahead.

He walks a little way and waits for me to catch up with him. If I had stopped to consider I might not have taken this path; it may not lead to the river. . . . He is running now and turns to look over his shoulder to see if I am still following. . . . He says that we are running to the sea. . . . If he did not run so fast I could see the expression his face wears when he turns around. . . . Somebody else passed me then, so swiftly that I could not see his face either, only felt the wind fluttering the rags of that jacket he wears. . . .

It is a cold wind. They say it blows up from the sea. They say that the sound I hear is the sea wind roaring through these corridors. I think it is their footfalls and mine, following close behind. One of them runs head-on into the wind. The other keeps his head down and lets the wind make queer shapes out of his fluttering rags. . . . Who are they and why will they not let me see their faces? . . . *Is it because this corridor does not lead to the sea?*

They cried out at that. *"The sea, the sea, the wine-dark sea!"* they cried, and each one stooped and shielding his face with his hand, picked up a handful of dust with his other hand and threw it at me, but the dust did not fall on me, for I had turned and was running the other way. I ran a long way and there was nothing except the worn, smooth sides of the passage and the dust splattering my feet until I came to the path that wound along the side of the cliff. I knew that it was getting narrower all the time but I could not stop running—until I saw the man seated on the heap of rocks. The man heard my footsteps and rose and I had to take his hand and he led me to the edge of the precipice and I looked down and saw the two runners flung down far below, on a bed of bracken, their legs sprawled wide, each head, now only

270

a grinning skull, lying at a little distance from the neck from which it had just been severed and I turned to the man and he grinned too, and put up his hand to tear his own head off and fling it over the cliff, but I could not bear that and stayed him with a shriek, and he, still grinning, shrieked too, until the whole mountainside resounded with the dreadful clamor.

TWENTY

It seemed to him that he had been talking on the telephone a long time, but Miss Andrews' intonations continued smooth and inflexible: something unexpected had come up. Dr. Crenfew was forced to cancel today's engagement but he would be glad to lunch with Mr. Claiborne on Thursday.

Claiborne said, "Thursday hell! You tell him I'll be there in fifteen minutes," and slammed the receiver down and went into the bathroom. The telephone rang all the time he stood under the shower and again while he was shaving, so persistently that he cut his chin twice. But he was dressed and on his way to George's office before the fifteen minutes were up.

Miss Andrews half rose from her desk as he entered the outer office. He leveled his stick at her as if it had been a foil and she his opponent and when she fell back with a flicker of white eyeballs, pushed past her into George's office.

George was sitting at his desk, looking down at some papers, pulling at his long lower lip the way he did when he was trying to think something out. He said, "Oh . . . I thought Miss Andrews got you. . . ."

There was a narrow sofa upholstered in red pushed back against the wall. Claiborne sank down on it. "She tried," he said, and was suddenly aware that he was grinning and panting, like a dog that has run too far on a hot day. "She tried, all right, but I eluded her."

George shoved the papers in a drawer and snapped the drawer shut. "I'm glad you made it," he said, and laid his hand on Claiborne's shoulder for a second as he went past him to the door.

"Where are you going?" Claiborne asked. "You said you'd have lunch with me. Now where are you going?"

"I've got to speak to Miss Andrews," George said. "I thought we might have something sent up from downstairs. You want a hamburger? They have chicken sandwiches too, but they're no good. But you could have a hamburger, and some soup."

"I want both," Claiborne said. "I want both, George. . . . And George, why can't we have a drink?"

"It looks to me like you are already feeling no pain," George said.

Claiborne shook his head emphatically. "George, I haven't had a thing to drink since—oh, since around midnight."

George gave him a sharp look. "Is that so . . . ? That's a long time to go without a drink. . . ."

"Yes," Claiborne said. "Yes, it is, George."

"We'll fix that," George said, and went into a closet and came back with a bowl filled with ice and a bottle and two glasses which he set on a table near his desk. But before he mixed the drinks he gave Claiborne another glance and went over to the window and adjusted the blind so that the sunlight did not fall so strongly on Claiborne's face. Claiborne felt that he had never before received such exquisitely thoughtful attention. Tears came into his eyes. He said: "George . . . I have the *damnedest* dreams!"

George smiled as he handed him his glass. "I'd be surprised if you didn't."

"You mean because I'm a poet?"

"You're a poet," George said, "and you're a Claiborne. They aren't called 'Kinky Heads' for nothing."

"It's the worms!" Claiborne said eagerly. "That was what

272

was wrong with the top of his head, George. The skull showed right through the skin and had deep grooves in it—where the worms had been crawling."

He was aware that George's eyes were fixed more attentively on his face than they had been a moment ago. "Where did you see him?" George asked as he sat down at his desk.

Claiborne took a drink. "In the cave at the foot of Long Mountain, George. You remember the time we were in there and you took your cap off and the light struck that place and we saw what we would have fallen into if we'd taken one more step?"

George nodded slowly. "I was so weak I had to go and sit down awhile."

"I couldn't sleep that night for thinking about it," Claiborne said. "It was the same place, George. . . . My father was sitting there, waiting for me!"

"Waiting for you?"

"To keep me from going over the edge."

"Had he been there a long time?"

"All my life," Claiborne said with a sob. "George, he'd been there all my life!"

"How did you get into the cave?"

"The same way we went in the first time. Pushed the laurel aside and crawled till we got to the creek. It was just like it was when we used to go there. The earth was damp along the banks of the stream but dry as dust everywhere else. . . . You remember how *cold and dry* that dust used to be, George?"

George said, "Yes. . . . Were you alone?"

"You were with me, at first, but you went away."

"Was anybody else there?"

"Horne Watts!" Claiborne said. "He was running along ahead of me, and there was another fellow. . . ." He paused to stare at his cousin. "It was Carlo Vincent! The other fellow was Carlo Vincent, but I never knew that till this minute."

"What were they doing?"

273

"Running. . . ." Claiborne said. A sly smile came over his face. "They told me they were running to the sea, but I knew better."

"How did you happen to know better?"

The same smile reappeared on Claiborne's face. "I felt the wind on my cheek. They said it was a wind blew up from the sea. . . . But I could tell—by the feel on my cheek."

"Did Horne Watts and Carlo Vincent go over the cliff?"

"My father showed 'em to me—lying way below. They fell so hard their heads jolted off their necks. He showed 'em to me and then he gave me a look and he was about to tear his own head off, George, and throw it over the cliff . . . but I couldn't stand that. I woke up screaming."

There was a light knock on the door and a white-aproned, white-capped boy entered, bearing a tray. Balancing the tray on one hand, he crossed the room and opening a door, drew out a folding table which he placed between the two men, then set the tray upon it. He was about to leave the room when George called him back and drawing out a bill, pressed it into the boy's hand, saying: "Some more of the same, Bill," whereupon the boy pocketed the bill and scampered from the room.

"You're always playing games!" Claiborne said with a scowl.

"Yeah," George said, "helps to pass the time. . . . Here's your soup," and he handed Claiborne a cup of chilled consommé.

"Thought you said it was going to be hot," Claiborne protested.

"I did, but they said it was going to be cold."

The two men ate in silence. Crenfew did not remark on the fact that Claiborne left his sandwich half eaten. When he himself had finished his sandwich, he lighted his pipe, and, tilting his swivel chair back, extended his lean body its full length.

Claiborne watched him for several minutes, then said with a sneer: "Good, gray soothsayer pulls on pipe! . . . Well, what about it? Am I going nuts?"

"No, you're not going nuts," George said, "but I think you need help."

"Why don't you help me then? God, man, it's your business!"

George sat up and looked at his cousin gravely. "I'm not the man to help you, Tom. We know each other too well."

"You mean that if you took me on you'd always be thinking of the family angle?"

George smiled. "Something like that. It'd be like those history grades I made at Ware's. Old Rufus always gave me a C. Said none of the Crenfews could learn history."

"I don't suppose it'd take much of a specialist to figure out my case," Claiborne said bitterly. "Pretty run-of-the-mine, I imagine. Lack of a father pattern, don't they call it? I suppose I'm lucky I didn't turn out a pansy."

"The Freudians might look at it that way . . . but there's more than one way of interpreting dreams."

"Well, why don't you have a shot at it?"

George smiled again. "One way of looking at it might be that the dream is merely a dramatization of some ideas you have about art. You never could take that Essentist stuff of Carlo's and I've heard you say that the only logical end of Surrealism is madness. . . ."

"Andre Breton admits that himself, in his Manifesto," Claiborne said.

"That's right," George said, and then was silent.

"Is that what you think the dream means, George?" Claiborne asked.

George shook his head. "No. I think it's a warning."

"A warning! . . . From whom?"

"Your father. I take it he was waiting there to warn you not to take that particular road."

Claiborne laughed. "A hell of a fellow to be giving advice! I've got myself in a jam, all right, but it's nothing to the jams he was in all his life."

"Maybe that's why he's warning you. Knows what he's talking about."

275

Claiborne stared. "George, you didn't have to live with the Old Man! . . . A roisterer and a whoremonger and never did an honest day's work in his life. How could *he* give anybody any advice that was worth taking?"

George gestured with his pipe. "That's why I wouldn't be any good to you as an analyst. He doesn't seem to have worked out too well for you as a father, but he was all the father I ever had. . . . I don't believe I'd ever have amounted to a damn if it hadn't been for him."

"What did he ever do for you except teach you how to shoot?"

"He taught me about the heroes," George said. "One of the first things I remember in this life is sitting on his knee in front of a wood fire and him telling me about how Hercules captured the golden-horned stag of Cerynea. I can see those yellow flames now and hear him saying 'Kerynea' . . . and then Aunt Virginia came in and wanted him to read to us out of *Tanglewood Tales* and he said, 'Virginia, Hermes is not a Harvard man!' and he took the book and threw it into the fire. . . ."

"I remember!" Claiborne said. "Little old tan-colored book . . ."

"He told me about Perseus too," George said, as if dreamily. "Perseus and Andromeda and Bellerophon . . . and Amor and Psyche . . ."

"I'm glad you think so highly of the Old Man, George," Claiborne said. "I always hated him being such a bastard." Suddenly he was laughing wildly. "Amor and Psyche! George, there aren't any women in that dream. S'that mean what I think it means?"

"I wouldn't worry about that," George said. "Trouble with Freud he never got around to but one myth. . . ."

"Oedipus!" Claiborne cried. "Skewered through his Achilles tendon, so we all have to limp. I've got so I hate the fellow."

"Maybe that's what your father meant," George said.

"I don't get you, George. . . . God, you're a deep one!"

276

"I'm not deep," George said. "I'm just a fellow keeps on thinking about the heroes. . . . And there's more than one. . . . I don't believe Oedipus would be any help to you in this cave; he solved the riddle of the Sphinx by his *mother-wit*—as Sophocles has him boast. . . ."

"Sophocles was right, George!"

"The poet is always right."

"Even if people don't know it, George?"

"Even if people don't know it. But Oedipus wouldn't be much help here. He'd say use your mother-wit to get you out. It may be that a more masculine intelligence is needed here, so your Old Man . . ."

"I haven't thought about the bastard for years, George. What did *he* say?"

"It isn't what he said. It's what he was going to do. . . ."

"He was going to tear his head off and throw it over the cliff," Claiborne said.

"What do you suppose he'd have done next?"

"He was going to throw *my* head over right after it. That's what the bugger was up to. But I stopped him. Woke myself up screaming."

"I wonder why he was going to throw his head over the cliff?"

"It had worms in it, George! You could see where they'd been crawling."

George said: "Tear out the tight vermiculate crease where death crawls angrily at bay."

Claiborne shook his head. "That metaphor sounds wild to me."

"Still the poet is always right."

"Even if he don't know it!" Claiborne said. "George, how come you can get drunk like this here in the middle of the day?"

"I've got to take the nut off some time," George said. "And we don't get together often."

The white-aproned boy entered silently through a door in

the back of the room, laid something on George's desk and as silently withdrew.

"What's he sneak in like that for?" Claiborne asked.

"Too much traffic on the front elevator," George said absent-mindedly as he thrust the small package into his pocket. "You want another drink, Tom?"

"Well, it's been a long time," Claiborne said.

George went into the closet and came back in a few seconds with a fresh highball. Claiborne took the glass from him and raised it and waved it in the air. "You know what, George? I'm going to come up here every day about this time and we'll have us a talk."

"That's right," George said, and raised his own glass.

"You know one reason I'm going to come? It's because you're the only one there is to talk to. The rest of 'em are such fools, George! You know that, George, as well as I do. . . . God, you're a deep one!"

"I'm not so deep," George said. "It's like I told you. I'm just a fellow keeps on thinking about the heroes. . . . And there's more than one. . . . You always were a kind of hero to me, Tom. You know, when I was fifteen years old I realized that I never would be as smart as you are. I owe that to your father too. Remember that summer he took a notion we ought to do fifty lines of Vergil a day? And we were out under the big sugar tree and he came along and stopped to check up on us and of course neither of us had cracked the book but you gave a beaut of a sight-reading and I couldn't do a thing. . . ."

"You can't read at sight like I can, George," Claiborne said, "but you're a deep one for all that. . . ." He paused, scowling. "That wife of yours, though. She's one of the biggest fools I ever met. She wants me to go to see Rudie Scharp."

"You can't see him right now," George said. "He's up at Greggs, having a rest."

Claiborne laughed loud. "Strained his Achilles tendon, I expect."

"Those boys do seem to have to rest a lot," George said.

"It's their heels," Claiborne said, rocking with laughter. "You take and drive a sharp spike through your heels soon after you're born, George, you ain't going to get very far."

"They don't seem to cover much ground," George said.

Claiborne was scowling again. "That's the trouble with that wife of yours, George. Skewered through the heels. I told her the other day that if she was *my* wife I'd hang her up by the heels till all the crap drained out of her. But God, it'd take a long time, George, and I don't know that you'd have anything worth taking down when you got through. I believe she's just a natural-born fool."

George said: "In my father's house are several cellars. . . . That's what He's been telling us all along. Marcia ain't got down very deep yet, but she will, give her time. . . . She hasn't had our advantages, Tom. Ain't hardly anybody got any education these days unless they're over fifty years old. Marcia ain't but forty-four and got a scholarship to Leonard when she was seventeen. . . ."

"She hasn't had much chance," Claiborne agreed. "But that other one you had didn't turn out so good either, George. The wild one that went off and left you. . . ."

"It was the best turn anybody ever did me," George said.

"I always thought you were worth ten of her."

"I wouldn't have been worth picking up in the big road if I'd gone on the way I was going. And she knew it."

"Is that why she left you?"

George nodded. "You know how she was always hanging around Horne Watts and Joe Paster? She came in late one night—I'd been out too, but I got in first and was standing up to the easel, trying to look like I'd been there all along—and she walked up to me and said that Horne Watts and Joe Paster said I wasn't any good as a painter. You know how they were always sitting around, talking, about who had it and who didn't? I said, sure, I'd known that a long time. She wanted to know what I was going to do about it. I said I didn't see that there was anything I could do about it. She stood there and looked at me awhile and then she went up

279

on that mezzanine where we slept and when she came down she had a suitcase in one hand and the baby on the other arm. I thought she was going over to Jean Jarris's to spend the night and get over her mad, but she was gone for good. . . ."

"It was a dirty trick, George," Claiborne said. "We all thought it was a dirty trick."

"If she'd stayed we all three might have starved to death," George said. "Having her leave that way built a fire under me. . . . And I don't know how else she could have done it. I reckon she had to. Women don't like you to stand still. . . ."

"They like you to *lie* still, George. That's what they want—to keep you lying down, and they don't care how they do it."

"They'll keep you lying down if they can," George said, "but the minute you get up on your hind legs they want you to be going somewhere. They don't much care how slow you move as long as you're going somewhere."

"That's the trouble with me," Claiborne said sadly. "I haven't been going anywhere in a long time, and my wife knows it. That's why she left me. . . ."

"The general impression is that you left her," George said.

Claiborne shook his head. "I'm surprised at you, George, to be deceived by outward appearance, deep as you are! . . . She left me one evening in June. Nineteen hundred and thirty-four I think it was. Anyhow, we were all sitting around at the Deux Magots, talking about Empedocles. . . ."

"Who was doing the talking?"

"Oh, I was," Claiborne said wearily. "Anyhow, she gave me that look and she went away and didn't come back for a long time. . . . Then she left me again. In the winter that was. In the dead of winter, George. I can't remember what I was talking about that time. But you know, George, I can talk about almost anything. . . . She don't talk much, but she's a fool, just the same. A fool from way back."

"Maybe that's what your father meant," George said.

"My father? Why, George, he never even saw Vera."

"In the dream he knows her old man. . . . Doesn't seem to think much of him."

Claiborne laughed. "The Great Essentist! Got off by himself to show what he could do and all he did was look in the mirror. . . . Trouble with Vera, she believes all that stuff he handed out. 'Rhythm of life' she calls it. . . . But she's the best of that lot."

"It's like you always said, Tom. Those birds got off to the wrong start. Wandered into the chambers of the deaf unconscious and thought it was Plato's Cave. Thought that noise they heard was Plato's *Mousiké* and all it was was their own heels pounding the dust."

Claiborne gazed at him with admiration. "Did I say that, George? That's good now, isn't it. I may be a son of a bitch, but I'm bright. Always have been . . ."

"Maybe your father thinks you're *too* bright," George said. "Maybe that's why he wants you to throw your head over the cliff."

Claiborne shook his head. "Can't be too bright these days."

"Maybe he wants you to try a new tack. Maybe that's why he wants you to throw your head over the cliff."

Claiborne shook his head again. "I'd be in a hell of a fix then, George. Way things are these days . . . But I'm glad you think so highly of the Old Man—I always hated him being such a son of a bitch." He was silent for several minutes, then muttered: "Son of a bitch . . . But my wife's a *fool*. . . . You know what she's doing now, George? Tending pigs."

"Well, somebody's got to tend 'em—till they make a plastic pig," George said.

The sly smile came over Claiborne's face again. "Yeah, but it ought to be somebody that *has* to tend 'em. This phony farming is hard to take, George, when you know the real thing, like I do."

"But you don't do any farming yourself."

"God, no! I know better."

"Well, a woman has got to have something to do. And I

281

can't see a woman married to you getting all worked up over raising money for the symphony or being a Grey Lady. . . . Vera wants to do something creative."

"She don't need to tend pigs—or cows either."

"A woman has got to tend something. And she hasn't got any children."

"I never thought about her wanting a child," Claiborne said.

"No," George said, "no, I don't suppose you ever did."

"I couldn't stand Afghan hounds," Claiborne said. "Smack too much of the desert. . . . But she don't need to raise pigs."

"I knew a woman raised llamas once," George said. "Her son turned out a pansy. What's wrong with pigs? The pig is a mighty chthonic animal, Tom. Sacred to Demeter. Why, the boys tell me that in the navy they always called their girls 'Pigs.' "

Claiborne shook his head slowly. "You sure are a funny fellow. Religious too, aren't you?"

"Sure," George said. "If I'd lived a thousand years ago they'd have castrated me and put skirts on me, the way they did all the doctors. . . . As it is, I raise goats. . . ."

Claiborne had for some time been maintaining his balance on the little sofa with difficulty. He straightened up now, staring at his cousin. "George, you know where those pigs are?"

"Why, it's over a hundred miles from here," George said. "On that farm Catherine's gang has outside of Sleighton. 'Mary Farm' they call it. But I don't imagine she'll be there long. A girl raised like Vera . . . Why, man, they don't even have any bathrooms!"

Claiborne laughed. "That shows how much you know Vera!"

There was a rap on the door. Miss Andrews' face appeared. George went over and held a whispered colloquy with her. When he turned around the room was empty.

TWENTY-ONE

We went on like that for a long time. He didn't seem to have
a care in the world. When Miss Andrews would come to the
door he would say, "All right. In a minute." But the minutes
went by and after a while when she came he would just wave
his hand and she would go away. . . . The cave is right there
in the side of the mountain, but laurel grows all about the
entrance. You would not know it was there unless you looked
twice. I was the one who saw it first but George Crenfew was
the first one inside. . . . He's been down there all this time,
delving away . . . while I've been going to and fro on the
earth and walking up and down upon it. . . . My Old Man's
been down there in that cave with him. He says he learned
everything he ever knew from my Old Man, that it was my
Old Man first told him about the heroes. . . . I used to
think a lot about the heroes too. . . . Perseus had winged
sandals and a magic shield and cut off Medusa's head. Medusa,
even though she lay with Poseidon ἐν μαλακῷ λειμῶνι καὶ ἄνθεσιν
εἰαρινοῖσιν (I always liked that line), was born to a woeful fate,
being mortal, whereas her two sisters were immortal. Yet it
was from the blood that fell from her severed head onto the
ground that the winged horse, Pegasus, sprang. . . . Could
he have sprung from any other blood? . . . Theseus killed
the Minotaur but would never have found his way out of
the labyrinth but for the thread which Ariadne, whom he
quickly deserted, put in his hand. A great man for the underground, Theseus, going down into Hades just for the hell of
it, with Pirithous, who had a yen for Persephone. They came
near not getting back, being tempted to stick fast to the rocks
of the underworld. . . . It is difficult not to confuse Theseus
with Herakles, who even in his cradle showed more stuff,

strangling the two snakes Hera had sent to kill him, but he went mad just the same and when he came to found that he had killed his wife and children. The neighbors held that he was not to blame; the gods punish only those who kill willfully. But he could not accept this reasoning, and besides, he had to have something to occupy him, so he wandered through the mountains, seeking the proper punishment for himself until he found two-timing Mercury, who advised him that the way to get clean of the blood he had shed was to become the slave of the King of Argos for twelve months. . . . But after he had accomplished his Twelve Labors the gods sent him into slavery again, to Queen Omphale, who used to dress up in his lion skin and parade with his club while he sat spinning among her women. He was with her a year and got so he liked it. . . . George said that my Old Man told him about Amor, too, and Psyche, who, to appease Aphrodite had to put Demeter's temple in order. . . . A hell of an authority on Amor, my Old Man! . . . But *love is blind*. . . .

There is not one of them that you can trust. George said he wasn't the fellow to help me and all the time he was giving me a treatment. . . . A good thing, when you are drinking a lot, is to raise your head and look around the room, whatever room you happen to be in, as long and as hard as you can. I learned *that* at the University! . . . I didn't see him drop the pill in the glass but I saw him easing the bottle back into his pocket—when he came out from that closet he keeps his liquor in. . . . Love is blind! All the time I was thinking what fools they were—they all knew me for what I am. George, Max, Molly, Ed, even Marcia, all of them knew me for what I am. Everybody but Vera. *She* didn't even know what was wrong with her father. The poor fool! . . . The poor fool! Love *is* blind!

Yes, Officer, I *am* going to a funeral. . . . Whose funeral? . . . My father's. He's been dead a long time. . . . In no town you ever heard of, Officer. In a cavern underground. He's a miner. Forty-niner. I used to be a speleologist, my-

284

self, in youth, but I gave it up—for my health, which has always been precarious. . . . But my name is still Floyd Collins. . . . Ah, there we are. I knew we could find it! No, no, Officer, it is *not* too much. No indeed, not when one is speeding to the bedside of one's dying father, who has been a long time underground. . . . I *will* drive very, very carefully. In memory of you. It will be nice to have something to remember each other by. . . . *She was the only one who didn't know what I was like all the time!*

TWENTY-TWO

"I'm glad to see you," the old man said.

The other man turned a heavy, lowering face on him and pointed to the gas pump. The old man took the keys which he extended and unlocked the gas tank. When he had inserted the hose into the tank he went up to the side of the car and thrust his wizened face nearer to the other man's and peered at him out of childishly bright blue eyes.

"I'd just sat down on that bench when you came by. I said to myself, 'Take a good look at that fellow. We won't see him again. In one piece.'"

The other man passed his hand over his face. "I'm looking for a place called 'Mary Farm,'" he said in a hoarse voice. "They told me at the drugstore to take the first right turn on the Hidden Valley road . . . or maybe they said the first left. . . ."

The old man shook his head. "If you want Mary Farm that's it," he said, and pointed to where an old farmhouse stood on a low rise, in a grove of tall pines. "They got a sign down at the mailbox, but the morning-glories took the post, and the sign too. But that's Mary Farm, all right. I ought to know. I set here every morning and look at it. . . . You need any oil?"

"Better check it," the other man said absent-mindedly, staring at the old house. It was like the house on Mott Street in that it had not been painted for years, but instead of being three stories high it was long and low and clung to the hill as if it had been there a long time. Behind it was a larger building which had evidently once been a barn, surrounded by half a dozen dilapidated outbuildings. Between the house and the filling station was a long stretch of greensward. The sun, which half an hour ago had seemed to roll along beside the traveler, like a fiery ball, now hung stationary over the tallest pine in the grove. Its rays, spilling off the dark boughs onto the grass, edged every blade with light. In the middle of the greensward a large, dark almost square mass reared itself immobile.

"I'm sorry to say you can't take none," the old man said. Still holding in his hand the greasy instrument with which he had checked the oil supply, he followed the direction of his customer's gaze.

"Pretty now, ain't it? I sit here every morning and watch the sun shine on that grass. You know what makes that grass so pretty? Sheep."

The man in the car said, "That's not a sheep!"

The old man laughed. "You mean that bull? They got him some weeks back. But they keep sheep on that grass too, all summer. They ain't got any fences, so they have to stake all the animals out."

He thrust away the greasy rag with which he had wiped the oil stick and straightened up with a jerk. "My coffee's about to boil over."

The man in the car withdrew his gaze from the old house on the hill and stared about him, then passed his hand over his face. His skin felt hot and dry, and the hand moved, he thought, like a wind rustling through dry stubble. He could not remember how long it had been since he had shaved.

The old man put his head out from a doorway at the side

of the filling station. "I got a nice Gents here if you want to use it."

The other man descended from the car and walked stiff-legged to the doorway. The tiny room was clean and smelled strongly of some disinfectant. There was a little mirror above the bowl. When he had relieved himself he turned and looked into the mirror. He saw a man who wore no tie and whose shirt was open at the throat. The lower part of his face was dark with what he estimated as a two days' growth of beard. He could not remember how long he had been driving but he concluded that he must at some time have got out and investigated the mechanism of the car. There was a smear of grease on his forehead and another smaller smear on his chin.

He shivered and, filling the bowl with cold water, soaped his face and neck and plunged them deep into the water three times, then shaking himself like a dog, rubbed his face and neck dry on paper towels.

When he emerged the old man was sitting on a green bench in the sunshine, holding a cup of coffee in his hand. A coffeepot sat on an empty oil drum beside him.

"You want sugar?" he asked.

Claiborne shook his head. "Just coffee," he said, and took his seat on the green bench beside the old man.

The old man poured his coffee into his saucer and drank from the saucer slowly, pausing at intervals to blow on it. "I don't come from around here," he said. "I was born over in the next valley. I only been living here three years. My son got me to come." He glanced over his shoulder at an ell projecting from the back of the filling station. "Him and his wife, Eloise, are back in there now, asleep." He gave a dry chuckle. "That's why they like to have me here. Neither one of 'em don't like to get up in the morning. . . ." He tilted the coffeepot invitingly and when he had filled the customer's cup held up his hand. "Hear that now?"

"I hear singing," the other man said heavily.

The old man nodded. "They start praying and preaching

around seven o'clock every morning and keep at it till about this time. . . . As I was saying, we get along all right. But Eloise wasn't for having me come. Told Albert, 'Papa Edson'll never stand for those folks next door.' 'What's the matter with 'em?' I says. 'They're Roman Catholics.' 'I'm seventy-one years of age,' I says, 'and I'm not going to have the Pope of Rome telling me what to do. Not at my age.' 'They've got strange ways,' she says. 'That's all right with me,' I says, 'long as they don't expect me to join in their mummery.' 'Oh, they keep their mummery pretty much to themselves,' she says, 'but there's no telling who'll turn up over there.' "

He laughed and glanced at the other man out of bright blue eyes. "She was right," he said. "There ain't any telling who'll turn up over there. I don't know that I could have stood it when I was young, but now I ain't got anything to do but watch the pump I find it kind of entertaining. . . . Take that bull now. I was sitting here on this bench the day he drove up."

The other man turned a bloodshot gaze on him. "Drove up?"

"Come in his own car, like you did, only it was a truck. And he had somebody driving him."

"Who was driving him?"

"A colored fellow was driving. There was a lady sitting on the seat beside him and when he stopped she jumped out and they let the end gate down and she took aholt of the bull's halter and her and him walked up that path as cool as cucumbers. You don't see a sight like that every day."

The other man suddenly leaned forward. The bull had turned around and was moving slowly toward them. The links of his chain glittered as they slid over the grass. His red coat gleamed almost as bright in the rays of the morning sun. There was a figure moving beside the bull, as slowly as if it too were tethered to a stake driven deep into the ground —a man who wore black skirts that fluttered as he walked.

"It's Father Emmett," the old man said. "Comes out here every day and says his prayers, walking up and down by that

bull. Only he don't say them like we do. He reads them. . . .
He'll be over here in a minute. To get him a Coca-Cola. The
big lady, the one that runs the place, come over and talked to
me about that. Said it was all right to give him a Coca-Cola
any time we felt like it. Pepsi, too. Or an orange drink. Anything, long as it was soft. . . . Look at them bums now! You
can't tell *me* it's much of a religion! They come out every
morning, after all that preaching and praying, and take their
seat on that bench and sit there, warming their asses all
morning. Don't never do a stroke of work if they don't feel
like it. The big lady explained that to me too, when she come
about Father Emmett. Says they regard them bums that come
off the Bowery or stumble in here off the road as their hon-
ored guests. Says they look on each and every one of them
bums as Jesus Christ. I said, '*Lady!*' . . .''

But the man he had been addressing was almost out of ear-
shot, striding up the path toward the bull and the priest who
walked up and down beside him.

TWENTY-THREE

The priest had just made one of his turns and was striding
toward him—a burly Irishman, with fine gray eyes and heavy,
reddened jowls. The bull stood, as Claiborne had so often
seen him stand, knee-deep in grass, gazing straight ahead out
of amber-colored eyes while his jaws moved rhythmically
from side to side. Claiborne put his hand out and let it rest
for a second on the dark red rump. "You old son of a gun!"
he muttered.

The priest looked up from his moving page. "Don't do
that, man!" he cried irritably. "Haven't you ever been around
a bull before?"

"Sorry, Father," Claiborne said.

The priest stared at him. "You want service?" he asked. "It'll cost you five dollars—that is, if you can pay for it."

Claiborne shook his head. "I've gone out of the cattle business, Father. . . . I'm looking for my wife."

"What's her name?"

"Claiborne. Mrs. Thomas Claiborne."

The tall Irishman turned around and looked back at the old farmhouse. "That'll be Vera," he said. "She's up in the potato patch."

"Where is that?"

"It's up in the high bog—the one we just finished draining. If you try to go across the fields you'll mire down. Best take the Way of the Cross. . . . That lane there, between those old stone walls," he added when he saw that the other man did not understand him. "If you'll wait till I finish my office I'll show you. I'm going that way myself when I'm done." And without waiting for Claiborne to turn around, he opened his breviary and resumed his reading, striding up and down as he read.

Claiborne walked slowly along the path. When he came to an old barn, half stone, half timber, he stopped to look inside. A big stall at the right of the runway was full of baled hay, and bales of hay were scattered down it at intervals, but the rest of the building was evidently used as a dormitory. Flimsy doors, sagging ajar, disclosed cell-like rooms, furnished only with cots. The stone walls had been freshly whitewashed. A crucifix made of two pieces of cherry wood fastened together, the bark still on them, hung over one cot. On another wall a bright-colored chromo showed Jesus pointing a tapering finger at the rays that crackled about his bleeding heart. Rhythmical snores came from a figure that lay stretched at length, face down, on the cot beneath the picture. He sat down on a bale of hay and lit a cigarette.

Out on the lawn the black-clad figure strode up and down beside the tethered beast. Suddenly the priest executed a military right turn and was coming toward him. His hands were fumbling with the buttons of his cassock. "If you'd step up to the house," he called, "fetch me a bit of breakfast . . ." He passed Claiborne on the run and dove into one of the cells, whence his voice floated back, muffled: "Save time . . . getting into my work clothes. . . ."

Claiborne said, "I'd be delighted, Father," and started toward the house. It looked even longer from here than when viewed from the filling station and it sat solidly on the sloping mound of earth that had been thrown up long ago when its cellar was dug out. Sugar maples dotted the wide, ill-kept lawn, and scraggly lilac and mock-orange bushes grew at the corners of the house. A retaining wall made of stones ran along one side of the mound. A bench had been placed against the wall. Three men sat on the bench. One of them had a wooden leg. Two bushel baskets stood on the ground in front of the bench. The one-legged man had a knife in his hand and was cutting potatoes up for seed. The other two men were idle. One of them, leaning back against the bench, had sheltered his face from the spring sunshine by placing a folded newspaper over it, as Claiborne had seen homeless men do in city parks. The other man sat leaning forward, his elbows resting on his knees, his face supported by his cupped hands.

Claiborne asked to be directed to the kitchen. The one-legged man pointed to a rusty screen door on the left. Claiborne, approaching it, thought that he was about to enter a boiler room. Gusts of fierce heat rushed out through the holes in the screen. He applied his eye to one of these holes and saw through a haze of simmering heat stone walls whitewashed like those of the barn. The blasts of heat came from a huge old-fashioned cooking range of the kind that is still found in country restaurants. A young girl was bending over it. A young man in ragged blue jeans lounged against a wooden sink opposite, watching her as she stirred the bubbling contents of a black iron pot. "Sure, I'm going up there in a minute," he said, "but there's others that could go and won't. Why can't they help?"

The girl lifted a face rosy from the heat. "Oh, Joe, what

291

difference does it make who does the work as long as it gets done?" she said, and seeing the man outside put her spoon down and went to the door.

"I've come for the Father's breakfast," Claiborne said.

She laughed, and, taking an old army canteen down from the wall, filled it from a big coffeepot set on the back of the stove, then opened a vast breadbox and took four doughnuts out of it and put them into a paper sack. As she handed him the objects, she looked at him intently, opened her lips as if to say something to him, then closed them. He had thanked her and was turning away when he heard her voice behind him. "Would you like some breakfast yourself?"

He stared down at the gravelly path. It was laced with the shadows of leaves, and set among them were other star-shaped shadows; the scraggly mock-orange bough above his head must be carrying blossoms. He had not known that it was time for the mock orange to bloom. And he could not remember whether or not he had had breakfast. Indeed, he could not remember when he had last eaten. He turned around. "I'd be very glad for some breakfast," he said.

"Will you take it hot or cold?"

"Why, what is there?"

"There's some oatmeal on the back of the stove, but the Father . . ."

"Is in a rush. Have you got something I can take in my hands?"

She went quickly to the big refrigerator in the corner, then paused and looked at the red-haired youth. "That ham sandwich . . ."

"That I was too tired to eat when I come in from the field last night," the youth said, and flipped a lean hand toward Claiborne. "Take it, stranger, and welcome."

"Here's one more doughnut," the girl said as she gave him the sandwich. "Take that too, and then the Father can't say we're holding him up."

"Why is he in such a rush?" Claiborne asked.

The boy laughed. "It's the dark of the moon, man. We

have to plant the praties by the dark of the moon, in May and June, the way they did when I was a bhouy in County Kerrrry, Arreland."

"I come from Menominee, Wisconsin," the girl said, "and my dad always said to plant potatoes by the dark of the moon."

"So did my father," Claiborne said.

The youth stared at him truculently. "I come from Grand Street myself, but I used to go up to a farm in Dutchess County with the Fresh Air. Fellow name of Rogers. And I never heard *him* say nothing about the dark of the moon. . . . What did your old man raise?"

"Tobacco," Claiborne said.

The youth laughed. "I wish we had the—I wish we had him around here! I was over to the filling station a while ago and old Edson swore he'd run out of butts. *I* think he was holding out on me."

Claiborne said, "Here!" and hurriedly brought out his cigarette case and opened it. There were only two cigarettes in the case. The youth, who had slid off his perch and had taken two steps toward him, sank back when he saw that there were only two. "Much obliged, just the same," he said.

"*No!*" Claiborne said. "You take 'em."

The boy slowly shook his head. "You'll need 'em when you get up in that field with Father Emmett."

Claiborne went up to the boy, holding the case out in a shaking hand. "Take one. You've got to take one."

The boy slowly put his hand out and, lifting one of the cigarettes from the leather case, held it up to his nose, sniffing at it delicately. "Tailor-made," he said. "My wud!"

Claiborne was suddenly conscious of the figure he must cut, unshaved, his clothes torn and wrinkled, reeking, for all he knew, of whisky. But they would find nothing strange in that. *Anybody can go there. . . . Anybody can stumble in off the road.* It was because he had stumbled in off the road that the girl had offered him breakfast. The puzzled look in her eyes, the mocking note in the boy's voice were occasioned by the way he was dressed. He looked down at his trouser legs. When he had got out of bed to see George Crenfew he had seized the first clothes that lay at hand. They must have been the clothes that he had worn the night before. A dark suit that he wore in town when he was going out in the evening and not wanting to dress. The hat he held under his arm, crushed against his left side, was a black, soft hat that he wore also in town on occasions.

"It's a dirty habit, Joe, just the same, no matter what it costs," the girl said softly, and turned to the stove.

Claiborne started. "I'd better be taking the Father his breakfast," he said.

The boy laughed. "Tell him I'll be seeing him."

"I'll tell him," Claiborne said, and left the room.

The priest met him on the path. He had changed his cassock for a pair of army-issue khaki trousers and a torn blue work shirt and he wore heavy work shoes whose toes had been reinforced with copper. Claiborne handed him the canteen and the sack that contained the doughnuts. When the priest had had a long draught of coffee he wiped his mouth on the back of his hand and thrust the canteen at Claiborne. "Will you be staying the night?" he asked.

Claiborne shook his head.

"The dormitory's full up," the priest said, "but there's always the hen house. There's a cot there I could get Matt Rourke to shift to if you've a mind to stay the night. . . . You might *need* to stay the night."

"I don't think I'm likely to be spending the night, Father," Claiborne said as he handed him back the canteen.

The priest nodded thoughtfully. "Having a little trouble?"
"A little."

"She's a good girl. One of the best we've had here. But no doubt she has her ways. . . . Well, there's no other state that'll so fine and refine whatever gold is in a man. . . . PHIL CARRNEY!"

The last words were roared at the recumbent figure on the cot. It did not stir. The priest shook his head. "We'll not

waste time on that one," he said, and took another swig of
coffee, handed the canteen back to Claiborne, and strode off
down the path, followed by Claiborne. When he came opposite the men on the bench he stopped.

"It's an act of mercy," he said in a loud voice. "An act of
corporal mercy, I tell you!"

The man who had the newspaper over his face removed it,
sat up, and uttering a light groan pressed his hands against
his middle. "Ain't nothing I'd like better, Father, wasn't for
these cramps. Had me going all night. Must have been something wrong with them beans we had last night."

"I'm not talking to you, Bill Porter," Father Emmett said
sternly. "You can sit there on that bench as long as it'll hold
up under you. But Matt Rourke here is in different case and
it's my duty as his parish priest to advise him of his opportunity. . . ."

The man who had been sitting with his elbows on his
knees raised the wizened face he had been supporting between his cupped hands. "Did you get your faculties back
now, Father?" he asked in a soft, sympathetic voice.

The priest made his big fist into a ball and pounded his
left hand with it. "You know very well, Matt Rourke, that
I've had me faculties back now for three weeks—ever since
herself called on the theologian of the diocese. And it would
look better—you being in the shape you were in only last
week—not to twit me with my weakness. I'm doing all I can
to overcome it."

The man turned his wizened face slowly from side to side.
" 'Tis a peculiar parish. I wouldn't know what would be going on in it." His eyes gleamed green between reddened lids.
"Are you sure now, Father, that it's an act of corporal mercy
to plant them potatoes? Them potatoes ain't human. They
can't feel."

" 'Tis an act of corporal mercy to keep fellow creatures
from starvation," the priest said. "You'll be the one is feeling
pain next fall when there's no praties." His voice sank. "Come
on now, man," he said coaxingly. "Look on it as a penance.

Put in a good morning's work and it'll go far toward undoing all you did last time you went to New York. A whole week you stayed and we all saw the shape you came back in."

Claiborne reflected dreamily that they must spend whole mornings in talk like this. He bit into the ham sandwich. The bread was dry and had never known butter. The ham was dry too, and thin, but it had for him a delicious flavor. He ate the sandwich in three bites, then ate the doughnut. When he unscrewed the top of the canteen he found that there was at least a half-cup of coffee left. He lifted the canteen and let the pale brown, tepid liquid trickle down his throat.

Matt Rourke was saying, "Business before pleasure, Father. I'll have to be seeing you after the mail comes. I'm expecting an important letter. . . . Might be registered."

The one-legged man, who had silently kept on cutting up potatoes during this conversation, now dropped a last fragment on top of a basket that was already heaped high with other fragments and delicately wiped his hands on the sides of his pants legs. "There you are, Father. Wish I could carry them up for you."

The priest bent and, picking up one of the parings, nodded. "I see you left two eyes in, like I told you. Don't you worry, Johnny. Matt'll bring a basket up—after the mail comes in. And me friend here'll give me a hand. . . . What did you say your name was?"

"Tom," Claiborne said, and picked up one of the baskets. The priest lifted another. They went down a side path into a grove of young poplars. The priest went first, talking volubly. "You say you've given up the cattle—but you still keep the farm?"

"In a manner of speaking," Claiborne said.

"Hold on to it. A man's got to have ground under his feet. . . . I'm glad you came along today, Tom. I want you to see that high bog. Nothing like peaty ground to bring potatoes . . . There's another bog. Beyont that wall. We'll get to that next year."

They had come to a small house, painted dark green, set in the middle of the grove. "I'll just step inside," the priest said, "or maybe you've a call yourself?" When Claiborne declined the invitation he went into the privy and shut the door. Claiborne walked on a little way. They were at the head of the lane of which the priest had spoken. It lay between two old stone walls and, except for a single track in the middle, was grown up in grass and weeds. On the left the land sloped away in a wide field. The ground beyond the other wall was swampy and grown up in tall clumps of bracken: the low bog that the priest had not yet got around to draining. His head was beginning to clear but he felt curiously weak and he was glad to sit down for a bit. It would not be long. Inside the privy the priest was probably proceeding with the same dispatch he used outside of it. . . . The privy at Eupedon had had jasmine vines climbing up its walls and depending in long sprays from its roof, interspersed with some other vine that had a white flower—probably clematis. . . . Joe Solmes thought that the fact that the Mississippi River was no longer allowed to inundate its banks and fertilize the fields on each side of it was prophetic of the downfall of North American civilization, and he found in the water closet a symbol of the coming disaster: man bent not only on self-destruction but on removing from the earth all trace of his existence. Joe was writing a book about it. . . . A big burdock plant thrust up near his right foot. Strange how many plants make their way around the world, keeping always the same character. Growing beside the stone privy back of old Léontine's house outside of Pradelles there had been just such a sturdy dock plant. He remembered stopping and looking at it a long time, marveling that the leaves should spread themselves there, as broad, as richly green as in his own country. There had seemed to be a kind of omen about it, but he could not think now why he had fancied that. It was all so long ago. He wondered whether his and Vera's lives would have been different if they had stayed on in France, as she had wanted to do. . . . He had never thought of there being any particular sympathy or understanding between Vera and George, yet George, in a conversation he had had with him recently under circumstances which he could not clearly recall, had told him things about Vera he had never known before . . . and about himself. There was one question he had not asked George: Would she go back with him?

"*Back?*" the Voice asked. "*Back to what?*"

"*Back to whatever it is I have to go back to.*"

"*There isn't anything to go back to—except that circle that long ago you described and then of your own free will stepped inside, keeping it inviolate by flailing down any living thing that sprang up in it, so that there should be left in it nothing but yourself and the air that goes in and out of your rotting lungs. Would a woman want to step again inside that circle, breathe again that impoverished air?*"

He heard a rustle behind him. A black snake that had been sunning itself on a rock glided across the path and flowed through a crevice in the old stone wall. There was a litter of discarded tins and paper cartons next to the wall. Beyond it rose hummocks out of which the bracken grew. The soil between the hummocks glistened wet. The fronds of a tall fern swayed and dipped and swayed back into place as the snake coiled about its roots, then flowed on to the next hummock. Here one second and the next second out of sight, but you knew that he was gliding on into the heart of the swamp, over earth as black, as moist as his own skin.

A bird flew past him, so close that he felt the flutter of its wings. Off in the swamp another bird called, three rich, full notes. He turned his face up to the May sunshine, smiling secretly.

I drew the circle. I stooped down and drew it with my own finger. But I drew it, not in the air, but in the earth. There is, after all, no other place in which one can draw such a circle, whatever notions to the contrary may be entertained. I drew the circle and stepped inside it, but I drew it in the earth, the earth that everywhere, even in the most desert

*places, even when overlaid with brick and mortar, holds al-
ways infinitesimal particles of water, water of which we are
all prisoners, day by day, moment by moment. . . .*

A huge red face loomed opposite his face. Under bristling
brows fiery gray eyes stared into his. The priest was bending
over to lift his basket of potatoes. He got to his feet, took
up his own burden. They proceeded down the lane. The priest
talked as they went: "Herself thinks I'm too hard on them.
Says: 'Don't waste your breath, Father. There's no work left in
them time they get to us. Leave them in peace, Father,' but
it does a man no harm to be reminded of his duty even if he
doesn't get around to it, and besides, as I tell her, how are
we to get the land worked?" He stopped to genuflect and
cross himself before a pole which had affixed to it a cigar box
that held in its recess a small, roughly carved wooden plaque.
"Our Blessed Lord before Pilate. Matt Rourke carved all the
stations and made the shelters for 'em, too—out of cigar boxes
or whatever came to hand. Oh, he'll whittle the day long but
try to get him to hoe a row!" He sighed, then stopped to
genuflect and cross himself again: "Our Blessed Lord receives
His cross. . . . You can come back and make your stations
later, if you like, Tom. We turn off here."

They left the lane and followed a path that curved along
the edge of the low bog, through a strip of fallow ground on
which last year's weeds were brown and waist-high on a tall
man. The path was too narrow for two to walk abreast. The
priest went first, carrying his basket. Suddenly he stopped
short: "Look, man!"

The field stretched before them. Not more than a quarter
of an acre, but rich, dark earth, all of it, with a wide strip
at the western end laid off in neat hillocks. Two men were
wielding hoes, making hillocks. There was no one else in
sight.

He said: "Where is Vera?"

The priest said: "Eh? . . . Oh, Vera?" He turned to the
men. "Ed, where did Vera go?"

Ed pointed with his hoe toward the bog. "The old one got in the way, so she took him and the kid to the spring."

"Where is the spring?" Claiborne asked.

"Down in the ravine," the priest said. "Here, Ed, you can start with this basket. Albert can take the other one. Tom, you want to lend a hand?"

Claiborne shook his head. "Not right now, Father."

He walked along the edge of the field and took the path that opened before him. The ground fell away more sharply than you would have thought; he was walking on the edge of a bluff. The spring they spoke of probably came out from under this bluff and flowed south through the swamp. When he looked off through the woods his eye caught a serpentine glint of water—as if a shining hoop had been flung down among the trees.

He went down the last few steps of the little eminence. He was right. The spring came out at the foot of the bluff, in a pool walled in by ancient, moss-grown stones. The stream flowed easily for a few hundred feet, then striking a great boulder, divided into two branches which encircled a little island. It was grown up in willows, down to the water's edge. There was a gap in the willows. Patches of blue were visible through the blur of new leaves. A woman was kneeling on the bank. A small boy crouched beside her. They were trying to dam up the stream; rocks were piled in an irregular heap halfway across it. As Claiborne approached, a strange, piercing cry broke from the child. He staggered out into the water, dropped the stone he was carrying on top of the heap, staggered back to the bank and, once more emitting the strange cry, stood with his lips parted, his pale eyes fixed on the woman's face.

Vera laughed and set her hands on his shoulders, then suddenly laughed again and caught him to her in a quick embrace.

She was holding the child's body pressed against hers, her head was bent, her lips were brushing the sparse stubble that crowned his head when she heard the footsteps and looked up into the eyes that were regarding her from across the stream.

Very slowly she let her arms fall away from the child. One who has thought that the siege is lifted from the city might as slowly withdraw the hand he had just stretched out toward some long-coveted object, fruit, jewel, it might be a golden casket, when he hears the shout, not heard for a long time but once heard echoing always in the memory, which tells him that the enemy is within the gates. . . . But he did not think of that till long afterward.

She got to her feet. She was wearing blue work clothes, and the leather apron her husband had been accustomed to see her wear on the farm was tied about her waist. Her skirt was wet around the knees and splashed with mud. There was a streak of mud on her forehead. Her hand went up, passed over her forehead and clasped her throat. She said: "I'm sorry. . . ."

He said: "I came up here to tell *you* that."

She averted her eyes from his face. "I meant that I am sorry to have been so slow," she said.

"To have been so slow?" he repeated.

"In deciding what to do. . . . But I know now."

"What are you going to do?"

"I am not going to get a divorce."

He said, "Oh, *Vera!*" and started toward her but she stopped him with a gesture at once impatient and despairing. "So *you'll* have to get one," she whispered.

"But I don't want one."

"Has Cynthia . . ."

"I don't know," he said stupidly. "I'm not in her confidence."

She looked at him then and laughed. "I have never known anybody who was in her confidence."

He said: "Yes. I see that now. I see, too, how painful it must have been for you to watch her leading me up the garden path. Molly gave me quite a song and dance about that. Still, I asked for it. . . . You understand that I was quite off my chump," he added hastily. "I'd like you to know that —not that I expect it to make any difference."

Tears glittered in her eyes. She said: "Where is she?"

"You will be a fool to worry about *her*," he said roughly. "There are eight million people in New York. And no dearth of sick intellectuals. I believe that Willy Stokes is the next prospect."

She was silent. He looked down at his feet. It struck him as odd that they were so solidly planted on the path. For a second there—when he had taken that false step forward—he had had the illusion that his body was actually reeling to and fro in the still, bright air of this vernal glade where there was no sound to be heard except the controlled, furious voices of a man and a woman and the discordant cry of a maimed child.

The child, as if realizing that he had been the subject of speculation, uttered his strangled cry again and tugged at Vera's hand. "In a minute," she whispered, bending over him. *"Please,* Donny. In a minute."

In a minute, when I am gone, her husband thought. Aloud he said: "He makes strange sounds."

"He has no larynx," she said coldly.

"Was he born that way?"

She said in French: "Burned. In a tenement fire . . . His mother died. . . . They have made him a new larynx."

"They can do almost anything nowadays, can't they? . . . Except raise the dead . . . Are you going to adopt him?"

She set her teeth on her lower lip in that way he knew so well. "His mother is dead. He is going to be my child."

"Ah!" he said. "I see!"

He could still make her start. "See what?" she asked in a low voice.

"Why you have decided not to get a divorce. . . ."

"And why have I decided not to get a divorce?" she asked in the same low voice.

"Because of the child," he said, and felt his fury edge his words, like the glint of light along a knife's blade. "The authorities don't like broken homes, as we laughingly call them. . . . But don't you think you'd be better advised, on the whole, to go on and get a divorce? Then you could marry again in a few months. As it is, your lawyer is going to be hard put to it to contrive—shall we say—a simulacrum of me lifelike enough to deceive the adoption people. . . . Still, I suppose he can manage even that. I suggest something stuffed, or made, perhaps, of plastic. Naturally, of a super-quality."

She had put her hand up to dash the tears away from her eyes and now, her head a little on one side, continued to look at him intently, without answering, as if someone he had never heard of had asked her a question about him and she, taken aback that she could not answer it, was using this opportunity to study him in order to be able to report to her questioner. That—as God was his witness—was all there was in that look of hers.

His astonishment—and fear—were like a blow in the pit of the stomach. It is her eyes, he thought. I was always afraid of them, of that straight look that asked more than I could give. . . . I did not know what it would be like to have her look at me and ask nothing.

He threw his head up sharply. His thoughts hummed in his skull like angry bees. Nothing. That is all she asks of me now. No more than she would ask of any other bum who strayed into this ravine. To go away. That is all I can do for her now, all she asks of me. . . . *But where can I go?*

He gazed about the glade. Maple trees grew at the top of the bluff. He could see the sky through their branches. There was no sky down here, only the yellowish blur of the willows and the paler blur of those other leaves that were so newly opened that they looked wet. There were tears in his eyes. That was what made the whole glade swim in that unearthly light, as if some live thing quivered under every leaf. . . . No. The willows on the bank were actually in motion. A rabbit was slipping through them. Or a fox. Or even one of those hogs that Vera tends when she isn't tending mutilated children. . . . *The more fool I, to think that she would re-*

*main love's fool! . . . But what is she doing in this bog, with
no company except that of a deformed child?*

He saw the gray, writhen locks first, and then the counte-
nance, suspended among the reeds, like a mask fallen in some
ancient play. But shepherds, who whiled away their idle
hours with goat song in glades as sequestered as this, carved
their masks from stone or molded them from clay. These
eyeballs rolled dreadfully in their reddened sockets, the
mouth, taut, almost square, in the ageless grimace, was drawn
to one side, the tongue lolled to one side too. As the body
heaved itself slowly from the stream he saw that broken twigs
and leaves were matted in the gray hairs that covered the
chest.

The old man staggered as he came up the bank, clutched
at a willow bough and, regaining his balance, stood, swaying
a little, staring at the man and the woman out of bloodshot
blue eyes. He was bare-footed and wore nothing except a pair
of earth-stained trousers and a medal that hung from a chain
about his neck. He seemed unaware that his trouser fly was
open and his withered, sagging member protruding, but tore
at the waistband of his trousers and then, as the clasp eluded
him, bent forward, muttering. Vera cried out, "Oh, Joseph!"
in the same instant that Claiborne, seeing the bright drops
spatter on the leaves, went forward, saying: "Here, old son!
Can't have that. Ladies present!"

The old man lurched out from under the hand Claiborne
had set on his shoulders and looked at Vera. Saliva dribbled
down his chin. He uttered broken syllables.

She was beside him, murmuring the immemorial phrases
with which women assure children, even while chiding them,
that their offense is not unforgivable: *"Ne bouge pas. Sois
gentil et ne bouge pas! Véra en a pour une minute, attends."*

She was unfastening the metal buckle that clasped the
waistband. The cotton trousers slid down over the thin old
shanks. She gave him a little push. He stepped out of them.
She had taken a clean pair of trousers out of her leather
apron. The old man stood docilely while she invested him

304

with the clean garment. Suddenly he raised his domed head and staring at Claiborne again uttered incomprehensible words.

"What's he saying?" Claiborne asked.

"He wants to know who you are."

Claiborne said, "I'm Tom Claiborne. . . . I'm very glad to see you again, Mr. Tardieu. I enjoyed our little talk."

The old man continued to stare at him out of red-rimmed eyes and faltered something.

"Oh," she said, "speak French. His English is all gone."

"His English was pretty good last time I saw him. But it struck me that he was slipping even then."

"Where did you see him?" she asked quickly.

"At that joint of Catherine Pollard's on Mott Street. . . . You must realize that I too get around a bit. We had a nice talk about St. Augustine."

The child, who had all this time been tugging at Vera's hand, jostled the old man, and gave his harsh cry. The old man shook his head.

She said to the old man: *"Va donc. Il veut finir son gué. Va donc, l'aidez un peu."*

He shook his head again, growling.

"What does he say?" Claiborne asked.

"He says that Donny pinches him." She turned to the old man. *"Il ne te pincerait pas si tu ne le poussais pas. Allons, Joseph. Il faut finir le gué."*

He growled again but she gave him a light slap on the shoulder. The child ran up and seized his hand. They lurched off toward the stream.

"He thinks that Donny is his oldest brother," Vera said. "He doesn't remember anything now except the Chemin de la Tuilerie."

He said: "The Chemin de la Tuilerie?"

"Don't you remember the Tardieus? Next to Léontine's house. There were twenty-four of them. He is the *savant* Léontine was always talking about."

"So that's why you get the care of him?" he said slowly.

"Yes. Isn't it lucky? And it's coming back to me—the Auvergnat."

"I noticed that you spoke as if you had mush in your mouth. . . . Quite the happy family, aren't you? How long is he likely to be with you in this interesting condition?"

"Till he dies. It's hemiplegia. As a result of arteriosclerosis. He's had two strokes already. You can see that he's paralyzed on one side."

"Poor old devil. Nothing to do now but go on downhill."

She looked at him with that expression in her eyes, which, for all their quarrels, had never been there until this day. "I think he is a saint," she said.

"He may be. . . . Still, he's pretty incontinent and 'Back Ward.' . . . Vera, I don't want to be intrusive but I don't much like the idea of leaving you here alone in this ravine with this old Silenus. . . ."

She brought her shaking hands up and clasped them in front of her. "He's not going into any ward! I sleep in the same room with him every night and I'm going to go on doing it till he dies and I'm going to adopt the child too, and keep him—as long as he needs me. And now, will you go on back to wherever you came from?"

"Yes," he said, "I'll go. Not to where I came from. But I'll go—and leave you alone with your happy family. . . . But I want to tell you one thing. For your own peace of mind. You don't have to keep on defending yourself to me. In a minute now I'll be gone. Pouf! Like that." He snapped his fingers in the air. "You never have to see me again if you don't want to. So don't waste your breath, telling me what you're going to do or not do. You're rid of me! You can do any damn thing you want to do. Spend the rest of your life working in an orphan asylum . . . or an insane asylum if that suits you better. . . . Have a religious conversion! . . ."

The sound that broke from her was as harsh, as discordant as the cries that came from the child's mutilated throat or rolled off the old man's lolling tongue. "I think maybe I have had it!" she cried.

He left her and began the ascent of the little hill. It seemed steeper than when he had come down it a few minutes ago. Her voice still rang in his ears. He heard his own voice too. It seemed to him that he had addressed the same words he had just uttered to another woman, but it was in another country and a long time ago and he could not remember who the woman was.

TWENTY-FOUR

The priest saw him as he came up out of the glade and put his hoe down and came over to him.

"Did you find her?"

"Yes," Claiborne said, "I found her."

"And would she listen to reason?"

"She listened. I don't think I got anywhere."

"Did you remind her that wives should be subject to their husbands, even as the Church is subject to Christ?"

Claiborne shook his head. "I'm not in a position to make highfalutin statements like that, Father."

" 'Tis not you nor me making the statement. 'Tis the Apostle Paul. In the nuptial mass. She's a good girl, one of the best we've ever had here, but there's no woman living who won't say things she doesn't mean when her blood's up. We'll give her time to cool off and then I'll have a talk with her. . . . Would you like to lend a hand with the praties while we're waiting?"

"No," Claiborne said, "I'm not going to hang around here."

"You're making a mistake, man. I'm not speaking as your parish priest, but as your friend."

"I'm not a member of your flock, Father."

The priest nodded. "It's as Matt Rourke said. 'Tis a peculiar parish. It's hard to tell who's in the flock and who isn't."

Claiborne said abruptly: "Good-bye, Father. I thank you," and wrung the priest's calloused hand and turned away.

The men sitting on the bench eyed him curiously as he strode past them. The old man was not visible as he approached the filling station. Claiborne had got into his car and was about to drive off when he heard rapid footsteps on the path. The priest laid a hand on the door of the car, panting. "I forgot to tell you, Tom. There's always room in the men's dormitory. The old chicken house."

Claiborne controlled himself with an effort. "You are very good, Father, but I won't be coming back."

The priest's powerful hand still clasped the door of the car. His eyes dwelt intently on the other man's face. "Any time," he said, "day or night. There'll always be a bed for you."

Claiborne could keep his anger in no longer. "A hell of a lot of good that'll do me! And now, will you stand back?"

The priest slowly withdrew his work-roughened hand from the shining metal. His eyes had not left Claiborne's face. "Any time," he said, "day or night. Just remember that."

Claiborne menaced him with a clenched fist, then, as the other man did not stir, but merely kept his curiously shining eyes fixed on his face, drove off in a whirl of dust. He kept the same speed till he reached the highway, where his car came perilously close to overturning as he swung it far to the right to escape collision with a truck carrying gasoline. After his car had righted itself—miraculously, it seemed—he looked into the mirror. The red-capped youth who was driving the gasoline truck had pulled it off the road and was sitting with his head in his hand.

"*Feu . . . ,*" the Voice said. "*Feu . . .*" And as he drove on the whole horizon was ringed with flames and the flames crept up over the fields until they were licking at the edges of the strip of macadam in front of him and the macadam undulated as if it were a river of lava and the air was full

308

of heaving columns and gigantic shapes whose eyes shone through all the flames. . . .

"It's going on here too," he said, but the Voice did not answer and he halted his car in the shade of a tree and with trembling fingers lit a cigarette.

The red-capped youth drove up while he was sitting there. He stopped his engine and looked at Claiborne hard for several seconds; then he said: "I was married last Saturday."

Claiborne did not answer. The boy's face worked. He said in a harsh, breaking voice: "God damn it! Her name is Irene," and drove off.

It was late afternoon when Claiborne let himself into the apartment. A white envelope was lying on the rug, just inside the door. He picked it up, slipped the folded note out and held it in his hand for a moment, then thrust it back into its envelope and threw the envelope into the fireplace and then stooped and set it on fire with his cigarette lighter.

The air in the room was dry and still; the windows were all closed. He could not even hear the traffic outside, only an occasional shrill cry of a street vendor, some Italian hawking geraniums from a horse-drawn cart. I should like to go to Italy once more before I die, he thought; and then: No, it would not do any good. There is nowhere to go, and nothing to do, and he turned over and lay with his face pressed against the cool pillow, while scarlet and yellow flames that had tinier scarlet and yellow flames branching off from them ran up and down a somber curtain that somebody had hung there long ago.

The flames died. The curtain turned gray, billowed out and then backward and dissolved into cool darkness. He put his hand out and touched cool stone.

There was somebody in the cave beside him, somebody who was leaning over to lay a hand on his shoulder, to whisper in his ear. "Yes," he said, and got up and walked with his guide over the chill, dry dust to the bank of the stream and slipped into the current and, his guide still beside him, swam until they came in sight of the other cave, on the far bank.

It was larger than the cave they had quitted. The greenish light that pervaded it emanated from the writhen columns that supported the roof. They took strange shapes. A man and his wife, standing hand in hand. A boy riding on a donkey. A hunter, dog at heel. The large column in the middle of the cave was not a stalagmite in the form of a kneeling woman. It was a woman, who, still kneeling, turned her head to look at him. "What is it?" he said. "What is it, Horne? What does she want with me?" Horne only pressed his shoulder, smiling, and pointing to the woman.

But when he went up to her there was no woman, only a column dripping with green lichen in a cave far underground and when he turned to Horne he was not there either, and the cave itself faded and the air grew hot and dry all around him and he knew without raising his head from the pillow or opening his eyes that he was back in Ned Brodo's room, stretched out on Ned Brodo's bed.

But for all that he leaped to his feet. "Where?" he cried. "Where? Tell me! What does she want?"

There was no answer. He went over to the desk and sat down, staring vacantly at its lid, as if the dark and polished surface were a palimpsest which under prolonged scrutiny might reveal the message he sought. After a little he got up and raised the blind and opened the window. The geranium vendor had halted his wagon under one of the three trees which ornamented the block, and was smoking a cigarette. Hearing the noise of the upflung window he looked up and with a flash of white teeth smilingly indicated his wares.

Claiborne called, "All right," and checking the impulse to throw down a bill, left the room and descended to the street. The geraniums were in pots. Impatiently he asked the vendor if he did not have a knife. The young Italian whipped a knife out of his pocket and, severing the stems of half a dozen of the flowers, bound them into a bouquet, which Claiborne carried when he got into his car.

It was seven when he entered St. Eustace's chapel. Half a dozen shadowy figures were perched on the scaffolding which ran alongside of the mural. At first he thought that there was no one else in the church. Then he saw the dark mass beside one of the pillars of the nave. The large woman raised her head and got at once to her feet. "Shall we go outside where we can talk?" she asked, and started moving up the aisle.

He moved beside her.

"What is it you want with me?" he asked.

She stopped. They faced each other. "Horne Watts," he said. "He came to me in a dream and pointed to where you were kneeling and you turned your head and looked at me."

She reached out and took the flowers from his hand. "You brought these for the altar, didn't you? . . . That must have been because I was praying for you. I started praying for you soon after George called."

"George . . . ?" he said.

"He told me that he suspected you'd gone up to see Vera. I wish I could have seen you before you went."

"What would you have told me?"

"I would have reminded you that a wife is subject to her husband, as the Church is subject to Christ."

"Your whisky priest told me that. He gave me the works. I told him that since neither of us is a Catholic . . ."

"Surely you know that Vera is in the Church. She was baptized when she was a child."

He said: "Old Léontine . . ."

She nodded.

"I didn't know that," he said. "I didn't know anything." And he saw the crypt deep in the ancient earth of Auvergne and the woman, on her knees before the statue of another woman, a statue carved out of black wood, God knows how long ago or by whose hands, whose glittering eyes were said, on occasion, to exude tears, and thought again, No. I didn't even know what she was doing when she was praying in that church. A wife is subject to her husband? She had been subject even in her secret.

Catherine had started on again. He followed her. They were over the threshold and into the little vestibule where he had stood with Max. The light of the street lamps fell slanting through the doorway. The flowers that she carried in her hand blazed scarlet. He said: "Tell me, do you pray for Horne Watts?"

"Yes."

"How long have you?"

"From the day I heard he had committed suicide."

He put his arm about her shoulders and would have kissed her cheek but she turned her head so that his kiss fell warm on her mouth. She was still standing on the threshold when he got into the car. He waved to as he drove off, and in the same instant, pulled out his watch. Even with fast driving he could not get there before eleven o'clock. The bums would have turned in for the night. But drunk or sober, the old priest would hear him knock and would get up and let him in. He could sleep in the hay if there was no bed. He could be sitting there on the bench with the other bums when she came down in the morning.